D1454322

THOUGHTS
IN A
MAKESHIFT
MORTUARY

THOUGHTS IN A MAKESHIFT MORTUARY

Jenny Hobbs

MICHAEL JOSEPH
London

MICHAEL JOSEPH

Published by the Penguin Group
27 Wrights Lane, London W8 5TZ, England
Viking Penguin Inc., 40 West 23rd Street, New York, New York 10010, USA
Penguin Books Australia Ltd, Ringwood, Victoria, Australia
Penguin Books Canada Ltd, 2801 John Street, Markham, Ontario, Canada L3R 1B4
Penguin Books (NZ) Ltd, 182–190 Wairau Road, Auckland 10, New Zealand

Penguin Books Ltd, Registered Offices: Harmondsworth, Middlesex, England

First published 1989

Copyright © Jenny Hobbs 1989

All rights reserved. Without limiting the rights under copyright reserved above,
no part of this publication may be reproduced, stored in or introduced into
a retrieval system, or transmitted, in any form or by any means (electronic, mechanical,
photocopying, recording or otherwise), without the prior written permission
of both the copyright owner and the above publisher of this book

Typeset in 11/12pt Ehrhardt by Cambrian Typesetters, Frimley, Surrey
Printed and bound in Great Britain by Richard Clay, Bungay, Suffolk

A CIP catalogue record for this book is available
from the British Library.

ISBN 0 7181 3220 3

The impetus for this work of fiction came from the tragic photograph in the South African *Sunday Times* of Jackie Quin and her husband Leon Meyer lying side by side in a Lesotho mortuary, after they were murdered in December 1985 by unknown gunmen.

It is dedicated to Jackie, and to the many young South African women like her who follow their convictions and their hearts through the barricades that so artificially divide us.

Acknowledgements

In my research for this book, I acknowledge in particular the help of the Africana Library, Johannesburg, and that excellent and indispensable publication, the *Weekly Mail*. Reference books used include *Soweto* by Peter Magubane and Marshall Lee, *South Africa* by Graham Leach, *South Africa's Yesterdays* (Reader's Digest), *A Cradle of Rivers* by David Dodds, and *A Dictionary of South African English* by my old pellie blue Dr Jean Branford, who also kindly checked the definitions in the Glossary.

For their help, I thank Heidi Holland, Judith Garratt, Ray and Sheila Hasson, Winfried Bauer, Peter Laughton and my editors, Jenny Dereham and Alexander Stilwell. For massive encouragement and support, I thank my family and my indefatigable agent, Dinah Wiener.

The futility of violence as an attempted solution to political problems is all too apparent. It does not breed peace. It breeds revenge, bitterness, an upwelling of sorrow and anger. The anger is both pitiless and pitiful: it is tragically self-perpetuating in the way it offers continuing incentives to further rounds of revenge action. Somewhere, and sometime soon, the spiral of violence must be broken.

The Star, Johannesburg editorial, 18 March 1988

I must condemn a terrorism which strikes blindly in the streets . . . and which one day might strike my mother or my family. I believe in justice but I will defend my mother before justice.

Albert Camus, on Algeria

1

Her name is Rose. She lies on her back on a woven grass mat, head to one side, mouth open, teeth jutting under lips that seem to have drawn back into themselves like touched sea anemones. Her skin has the grey drained look of meat that has been standing in water. Under swollen lids her dead blue eyes stare at the mud wall of the makeshift mortuary, a thatched hut with a single small glass window through which an extension cord dangles. At the end of the cord is an electric fan which turns its whirring head from side to side, languidly redistributing the stifling air.

The blood that has been seeping from her mouth and nose and matting her long blonde hair has congealed and darkened in the heat. There is blood on her T-shirt too, caked in thick craters round the mess of flesh and shattered bone and beige locknit where the bullets hit, their harsh death-spits silencing the room that a minute before had been noisy with reggae and laughter. The T-shirt was wrenched out of her jeans during her death agony on the floor, in the dust and the blood, her choking cries unheard by the husband who now lies next to her with most of his belly shot away. The already fraying cotton thread that held the metal button of her jeans snapped with the violent jerking of her dying muscles; thread ends stir now every time the fan swivels in her direction.

The stained sheet loosely thrown over her legs and his yawning wound is not wide enough to cover her feet. They are dirty underneath, with the fissured heels of one who often went barefoot on concrete floors. Her mother, Sarah, who sits on a wooden chair by the door keeping vigil, remembers when those feet were small and pink and kicked happily in the sunlight under a pram net that kept the flies and the cat off.

Sarah grieves and remembers while Rose's father rages through the government office building down the track,

1

demanding the privacy of a coffin – 'Two coffins, for God's sake! You can't just *leave* them there. It's nearly midday, man!'

'We have telephoned twice for the undertaker, sir. Please understand, there are certain procedures to follow, arrangements to be –'

'What arrangements? They're dead! They've been dead for nine bloody hours already!' Gordon is stocky and red-faced, his checked cotton shirt stained under the arms and down the back with patches of sweat. He wears baggy khaki shorts and long khaki socks, and carries a green felt hat with a guinea fowl feather stuck in the band, to keep the sun off the already dangerously freckled dome of his head. Because of the specialist's warnings about skin cancer, he never goes into the sun now without his hat, and he snatches it off in a reflex action every time he enters one of the offices.

'We know they are dead, sir.' The dark brown face behind the desk is also sweating. 'We have telephoned for the undertaker.'

'Where is he, then?'

'There are certain arrangements to be made, sir.' The official hand-off, bland expression, clerical fist clutched round office-issue ballpoint pen poised over a form that is being filled out in block capitals.

'Don't you have any ice, then? Ice, man! Ice! That room is like a bloody inferno!'

'Here, sir?' The face moves to look out the window at a landscape worn down to the bone: bare rock, bare hard-baked earth, cattle paths, erosion gullies, thatched mud and stone huts that huddle close together into the ravaged soil like hibernating tortoises, with every orifice tightly shut.

'Anywhere!' Gordon shouts, banging his fist on the desk.

The man turning back from the window says through pink-lined lips that part sullenly, 'There is no ice. And we have already telephoned through to Maseru more than once.' His black eyes say, Don't try and throw your weight around with me, white man. This is my country.

Gordon rages out and goes back to the death hut where his daughter lies next to her husband with bluebottle flies already buzzing at the window. Where his wife grieves and remembers, rocking her heavy body in the terrible anguish of having an only child die by gross violence. 'Why her, Gordon? Why her? She was such a good person.'

Down the dusty road in another stifling hot room, a fretful

baby turns her head away from the hard plastic teat she is being offered, with its different-tasting, too-cold milk. Her mother's milk has run dry now, and her father will never hold her again in his tender, calloused hands, his stubble-rough cheek scratching her small soft one, his deep voice in her ear: 'Meisietjie, Meisietjie.'

In the heat, the last drops of her mother's milk have crystallised on the dead brown nipples. Gordon paces and curses and sweats. Sarah grieves and remembers.

2

Sarah remembers Lindiwe, the black woman who looked after Rose in her first year. Gordon was still at university and earning no money, so after their marriage they had stayed on at her home, one of the old Durban mansions skirted with verandas that crown the Berea like a row of supercilious dowagers looking down on the lesser suburbs. 'After all, there's plenty of room,' her mother had said.

Lindiwe had a round face with bright bird's eyes and teeth like two strings of well-worn pearls that showed shyly every time she smiled. She would bend down to the child's pram saying, 'Hawu, Missie Rose, but you wet, eh? Come, let Lindiwe change you.' The cloud of net would be lifted off, and the capable hands would scoop her up into a snug nest of plump arms and feather-pillow bosoms overlaid with a white apron crackling with starch.

Lindiwe would carry her like a princess in a chariot across the sunny lawn, up the steps next to the frangipani tree, along the creeper-heavy veranda and through a french door into a cool, cavernous bedroom with a mahogany bed and mirrored wardrobe. She would be laid on a blanket in the middle of the bed's green counterpane and her wet nappy taken off, leaving her fat little legs to wave about for a few minutes of airy freedom before being caught and powdered and trapped again in warm dry towelling.

Lindiwe would sing as she bent over her, a song like the golden syrup her mouth sometimes smelled of after she had been in the pantry. Stretching open the leg holes of the frilly plastic panties that went over Rose's nappy, she would guide the little pink feet through, singing, 'Come to Lindiwe, come to Lindiwe,' until the panties were pulled up and the dress smoothed down and the baby decorous and sweet-smelling again. During the trip down the passage to the kitchen for her

4

bottle of fresh orange juice and back to the pram, Lindiwe would sometimes have to run the gauntlet of Sarah's mother, who was very particular about the correct care of babies, never having had to lift a finger for her own.

'Keep the child clean and dry, Nanny,' she'd say, 'we don't want any nappy rash in this weather. And make sure she has plenty of liquids.'

Lindiwe found the last instruction, of the many she was given, by far the easiest to comply with. Sarah went out often. When she was late for feeds and Rose began to fret and whimper, Lindiwe would take her into the bathroom, lock the door, close the lid of the lavatory, sit down, slide her free hand under her apron to unbutton her uniform, and pull out her full brown breast. She had always had more than enough milk for her own babies, and was used to suckling little strangers whose mothers were late home, or running dry.

'You are a good cow, my child, like I was,' her own mother said. 'If I missed a feed, my breasts would leak down to *here*,' pointing with dramatic pride to a spot just below the waist of her faded overall that grew lower with each telling.

A doubt had crossed Lindiwe's mind the first time she gave Rose her breast, driven to it by the child's hungry sobbing on her shoulder, as to whether her milk would be of the same taste and quality as the white mother's. But Rose's little pink mouth had fastened on her dark nipple with the greedy alacrity of her own babies, tugging at it with snuffles of contentment, and kneading at her breast with hands like stars. Lindiwe had thought, quite surprised, It must be the same, white milk and black milk. Now I am a good Friesland cow! and laughed softly so the sound would not slip through the bathroom keyhole and alert the grandmother who would not, she was quite sure, approve of substitute cows, least of all black ones.

Lindiwe took what she considered to be her due payment in kind: talcum powder shaken into a twist of tissue for the year-old child being looked after by her mother in the township, dregs of baby oil, white sugar scooped into an empty cigarette box, occasional oranges from the red string bag in the kitchen. In the prodigal plenty of the big house they would not be missed. She and the cook and the housemaid and the gardener divided the leftovers from meals between them, with the cook getting the largest share. She took hers home to give her children a taste of other things than putu, the stiff mealiemeal porridge they ate twice a day, a bag of mealiemeal being part of her wages.

'You'll spoil them,' her mother had grumbled, 'giving them white people's food. Already they cry that my phuthu isn't as good as yours.'

The old woman was a chronic grumbler; Lindiwe's home-comings were vinegared by her complaints about her bad back and her neighbour's malice and the children's undisciplined ways. 'They raise their voices to me. Me, an elder!' she would mutter in the grating voice that Lindiwe had fled from at sixteen, and returned to out of necessity with three small children when their father had deserted her.

'I want them to know the taste of cake, even if it is hard and stale.' Lindiwe pushed her lower lip out in the stubborn way she had, that Sarah's mother called mulish.

'That girl has a mulish look to her,' she said. 'She'll cause trouble with my staff. She probably steals too.'

'Oh, Ma!' Sarah had flounced away from the window where she had been standing looking wistfully out at the swimming pool while she burped the newborn Rose against her shoulder, hoping she wouldn't bring up again and make her smell of baby sick. 'You're always so predictable. I like the girl. Isn't that enough? She smiles a lot and she's got three children of her own.'

'All from different fathers, no doubt. Are you sure she's not pregnant again? They breed like rabbits, these black girls. You never know where they've been sleeping. Make sure she washes properly with soap before she touches the child.'

Sarah's mother called Rose 'the child' because she could not forgive her for wrecking all her meticulous plans. After Durban Girls College and a good Matric, pretty, bright Sarah at eighteen had been in her first year at university, destined to graduate with a good BA and an upper-crust fiancé, followed by a lavish garden wedding attended by the cream of Durban society. But she had climbed into the back seat of Gordon Kimber's mother's Austin A 40 once too often, and his unskilled precautions had been inadequate.

'I'll ask Douglas to do an abortion,' her mother had said, white-lipped, after the worst of the shouting and tears had died down. 'He'll keep his mouth shut.'

'It's too late,' Sarah had sobbed.

'Douglas operates at the Ridge, I think, and he'll know a

discreet anaesthetist and theatre staff. Just as long as they're not Catholic. I'm told the Catholic ones make trouble.'

'But *Ma*, it's too late. I'm more than four months.'

Sarah had dreaded the anger and tears, but had expected afterwards the indulgent softening she had always been able to count on as an only child of well-off parents. Not the cold fury of thwarted ambition that carried her mother grimly through preparations for a severely curtailed cocktail reception with Sarah in loose-waisted palest pink, and Gordon Kimber's father brick-red and glowering. 'Don't you know what a bloody FL is for?' he had yelled. 'That spoilt little tart is going to ruin your career.'

The condition of the bride had not been lost on anyone. Rose had been born towards the end of 1956, when men who got together at parties argued about Suez and Hungary while their abandoned wives and girlfriends had to make do with the lingering romantic glow of Prince Rainier's wedding to Grace Kelly. It was also the year of the march by ten thousand women to Pretoria's Union Buildings to protest the new pass laws and, on the very day Rose was born, of the arrest of 156 people for treason, including Chief Albert Luthuli, future winner of the Nobel Peace Prize. But these two events were not discussed at parties, being greatly overshadowed as news items for Durban people by the prowess of Jackie McGlew's Natal cricket team in the Currie Cup.

Except for the baby's feeds, which limited outside excursions to four hours, Sarah's life was not much changed at first by her marriage. Gordon was away at varsity all day and she filled her time pleasantly with tennis and lunch parties, shopping, and weekend socials where she and Gordon perfected their rock'n' roll steps while Lindiwe sat in their darkened bedroom minding Rose and worrying about her own children being brought up by a crabby old woman who couldn't even make palatable phuthu.

Rose took her first few steps towards Lindiwe. She was a happy child with two mothers, a laughing young one who played games with her until they both tired, when she would hand her over to a comfortable older one who tended to her needs with experienced hands. Three other servants kept the big house running so efficiently that her grandmother seldom had cause to raise the gimlet voice. Her grandfather was a silent, grave presence in double-breasted navy suits and sombre ties whose

7

Jaguar slid in and out of the drive at regular intervals, symbol of his power as senior partner in an accounting firm.

Just before Rose's first birthday a tense Gordon wrote his final exams and Sarah, deprived of parties while he was swotting, had a furious argument with her mother. Hearing a note of finality in their angry voices, Lindiwe fetched her suitcase from home during her time off the next day and filled it with some of the surplus sheets and towels in the linen cupboard, several of Sarah's maternity dresses, the baby clothes that were now too small for Rose, and a dozen nappies, in preparation for the child she was expecting by the cook. Since he had a large family of his own to provide for in a distant reserve and no money to give her, he filled a cardboard box with hoarded groceries by way of a dowry for the coming child; she carried it on her head as she stumbled down the drive late that night with the heavy suitcase. Parked under the jacaranda in the street outside was a getaway cart pulled by two donkeys and driven by the township coal delivery man, a gentle muscled giant whom she had chosen (although he did not yet know it) to be her children's future father.

All the way home she thought about the child she would never see again, remembering the weight of the downy blonde head she had held in the crook of her arm even last night to stop her frantic sobbing as her mother and grandmother yelled through the big house, shattering its equanimity. There had been no milk left, but the child had fastened gratefully on her nipple and sucked herself to sleep in the bathroom with the door locked.

'Ai, Missie Rose, my baby,' Lindiwe mourned, rocking herself backwards and forwards on the coal cart's wooden seat as Sarah would do in the stifling hut nearly thirty years later. 'There's nobody now to look after you nice, like me. Shame, Missie Rose.' Her arms were folded under the feather-pillow bosoms that were to suckle many more questing little mouths. Their promise was not lost on the coal delivery man, who began to look sideways each time they passed under a street light on the road to the dim smoky township.

On her last night in the big house, Rose slept on.

3

My poor Rosie. In her short life she went from one extreme to the other, Sarah grieves, remembering that gracious many-roomed house as her eyes travel over mud walls and dusty thatch and the still, bloody bodies lying on the floor. She remembers too that last bitter fight with her mother. Remembers shouting, 'You think you can control everybody, Ma! But I'm tired of being told what to do. I'm going.'

'Suit yourself.' Her mother sat stiff-backed in the Sanderson's linen armchair in what she liked to call 'the drawing room'. With its glazed chintz curtains and Persian carpets, it would have blended effortlessly into English suburbia except for the brassy fanfare of bougainvillea at the window, and the sound of jacaranda blossoms popping under car tyres in the drive outside. 'Let's see how my sheltered hot-house flower copes with the big wide world and a howling baby and no money.'

'I'll cope,' Sarah boasted. 'I'm not stupid.'

'What do you call getting into a car with a boy and falling pregnant at eighteen, then? An act of genius?'

Sarah said, as she had so many times, 'It only happened once. Gordon and me were just unlucky.'

'I.' Her mother's vowels had always been precise. 'Gordon and *I*, you mean.'

'That's great.' Sarah dropped the hands she had been waving around and stuck them in the pockets of her jeans. 'That's just great, Ma. I'm trying to talk about our lives breaking apart, and you're correcting my grammar.'

'It's part of my job as your mother, to bring you up properly. Or so I thought. It seems I've failed.'

If Sarah had blinked away her tears of rage and self-pity, she would have seen her mother's hands clenched in her lap, and the tremor in the grey-blonde curls created once a week by Mr

9

Brian of Salon Musgrave. But she saw only the puppet-master who had pulled all the strings in her life for so long that she had no idea how to let go. She shouted, 'Ma, it's too late to talk about bringing me up properly, can't you see? I'm married. I have a child. I've already grown up.'

She would always remember the sound her mother made then, a gasping bray of betrayal and disappointment. 'You? Don't make me laugh, Sarah. You're a spoiled brat with a shotgun marriage and a feckless boy for a husband who'll never make anything of himself. And we had such high hopes for you. I can't think why.' The ugly words severed the last of the silk fetters that had bound her to her beautiful, comfortable home. 'Well, you've made your bed, my girl. Now go and lie on it. And don't come snivelling to me when that boy walks out on you. Don't try and dump the child on me either. One daughter was quite enough.'

'You really are a bitch,' Sarah whispered. 'I didn't realise until now. I thought there was something wrong with me.' The door slammed behind her.

Her mother did not appear next morning when she and Gordon left the house with Rose. After two tense months with Gordon's parents, during which they made their feelings about girls who deliberately trap unsuspecting young men into getting them pregnant abundantly clear, they found a one-roomed flat in a building near the beachfront that looked as if it had been finished off with grey oatmeal. Their view was a brick wall with globs of cement oozing out of the joints, but it was only five minutes from the beach where Gordon liked to surf, and on the bus route to his new job.

Sarah's father had called her into his study before she left and given her a cheque to put into her building society account and draw on if ever she needed money. He said, 'Try not to think too harshly of your mother. She had great plans for you, and the baby has embarrassed her terribly. She's always cared far too much about other people's opinions.'

'And you, Dad?' Sarah took the cheque but kept her distance. 'Are you embarrassed by my baby too?'

'No,' he said, 'but I've got to live with your mother. I loved her once, and I won't abandon her now that she's lost you. She's going to need me more than my secretary does.'

Sarah thought about her father's secretary, who had cow eyes and a vulnerable mouth and a girlish laugh that belied the stringy skin on her neck. 'You'd get a better deal from Miss Fairley, Dad.'

His smile was a glimmer in pale blue eyes that excelled at raking balance sheets for hidden misdemeanours. 'Maybe, but I wouldn't feel right about it. I'm known as a man who keeps his word, and I promised 'for better for worse, for richer for poorer, in sickness and in health . . . till death us do part'. So did you, Sarah. I expect you to stick to your word too. And while you do, I'll help you when I can. Just telephone Miss Fairley any time you need to speak to me, and leave your new address with her so I know where you are.' His bony old man's fingers were cold on her arm. 'I don't want to lose touch with you, or Rose. I'll miss her lovely little dimples.'

Sarah kissed him then, astonished at the unexpected tenderness in this remote man she hardly knew. And in the taxi to Gordon's home she wondered about love. Whether it still drifted in wisps about the big house, and whether the things she and Gordon did in bed with such relish would chill one day to the temperature of a kept promise long after the reason for keeping it had been eroded away.

The novelty of being able to make love whenever they wanted to (unlike their friends, who still had to make do with back seats and dark verandas) soon wore off. So did the sophisticated thrill of using a specially fitted diaphragm and KY Jelly, both prescribed by Sarah's mother's gynaecologist after the birth. 'I hate that damn thing!' Sarah yelled, throwing it across the room after it had wriggled out of her jelly-slippery hand once too often.

'But we've got to use it, babe, you know that.' He lay with his stiff cock jutting out purplish-white against the deep surfer's tan of his thigh. The sheets beneath would be gritty with the beach sand that stuck to his skin long after he got home from surfing.

'Why don't you? Why don't you wear something for a change? Why is it always girls who have to be careful?' Her face was mottled with angry pink splotches. She had been looking after a grumpy baby in the flat all afternoon while he rode his surfboard down glide after green glide with his friends.

Trying to conciliate, he said, 'I would, but you know they aren't really safe. Not completely. I mean, that's why Rose —'

'It was your fault! Not holding the rubber on when you pulled out, so that all your stuff went inside me. It was so dumb of me to trust you! I should've known better.' She slammed into the small dank bathroom where mould grew in the tile cracks, her bare buttocks under the white T-shirt noticeably larger than they had been before Rose had begun to grow in her belly.

He felt himself going flaccid and rolled on to his front. Beach sand prickled his skin like spilt grains of sugar. His body felt tired all over from the effort of paddling out through the waves and carrying the heavy surfboard home. 'Don't be like that, babe,' he said in a lazy voice. 'It turned out OK. We've got each other and the baby and our own place. We'll make it.'

'Our own place. One crummy room looking on to a brick wall.' Her bitterness had been growing for weeks. He was enjoying his new job as a management trainee with a shipping company and going to cricket practice and surfing in the early evenings, while she had to clean the flat and cook and look after Rose. With no one to baby-sit, there were no more parties.

'You shouldn't have fought with your Ma, then. We could have stayed on there until we had saved enough to put down on a house.' He had been furious when it happened. Having assumed responsibility like a gentleman and married her at an age when his friends were still playing around, he felt that the least she could have done was to put up with her mother for a few years, if it meant being able to live comfortably and saving most of his new salary. 'You asked for this, Sarah. Don't start moaning now.'

Her splotched face came round the door. 'I asked for it! Christ, Gordon, you didn't have to listen to her all day telling you what to do.'

'Every evening was enough.' He turned his head into the pillow, feeling sleep overwhelming him as it always did after a long afternoon's surfing.

'Listen to me! We couldn't have stayed on there. She would have tried to take us over completely.' Sarah came out of the bathroom with her prim white cotton panties on under the T-shirt. Like many other things she believed in and used, they were a legacy from her mother. 'Always wear cotton down *there*,' she would say. 'It's cool and doesn't harbour germs like nylon does.' Sarah often wondered how her mother, who had a horror of germs and what she called Loose Sex, had ever managed to conceive her.

Gordon had fallen asleep, his arms around the pillow and his

12

head thrust into it as though he were trying to shut her out. 'Wake up and listen to me!' she yelled, rushing over and hitting his bare tanned back. 'Listen to me, goddamn you!'

He came roaring out of his sleep with a clenched fist and a backhander that caught Sarah's nose and made it gush bright red blood. She screamed and began to cry, long shuddering wails that owed as much to her loneliness as to the blood dripping all over the sheets. Rose woke in her cot by the window with a howl of terror. The neighbour thumped on the wall with a broomstick.

This was the pattern of life in the flat.

Sarah, grieving and rocking her heavy body in the stifling hut, thinks of those first terrible months, and how rough she was sometimes with the baby who crawled and staggered round the room pulling pots and plates and shoes out of cupboards, tipping over the nappy bucket in the bathroom, spilling things all over the floor. She had a talent for finding containers with loose lids: Vim and soap powder and dry baby porridge and left-over stew from the bottom shelf in the fridge. She smeared herself with cigarette ash from the dirty ashtrays Gordon and his friends left lying around, and dabbled her fat little hands in their beer dregs. Once, waking with a soiled nappy and no frilly plastic panties to hold it in place, she spread its contents all round her cot and finger-painted a stinking mural on the nearby wall.

You always were a questing soul, Rosie, her mother thinks. So much more of an adult than I was at nineteen. Ma was right. I was a spoiled brat when I left home.

She had to grow up quickly. Gordon felt that, as he was nobly fulfilling his responsibilities as a premature family man, he deserved time off with his friends for cricket and surfing and drinks after work. When Sarah demanded her own time off, he suggested that she hire a nanny with some of her father's money in the building society account. 'That's what it's supposed to be for, isn't it? To make life easier for daddy's little girl.'

She turned away, blonde pony-tail swinging, so he wouldn't see the sudden tears in her eyes. His malice over her parents' parsimonious wealth was growing as he discovered how hard it was to support a family and stand rounds at the club and save more than a few pounds a months towards a home of their own on his starting salary.

'I wouldn't know how to find a good nanny,' she admitted, another deficiency revealed. 'And I couldn't leave Rose with just anyone.' It was futile asking him to look after the baby occasionally. He had never had to mind her for more than a few minutes at a stretch, and like most young men of his generation, he considered it women's work anyway.

'Ask around.' He picked up his beach towel and went towards the door. 'The old woman next door has a girl who comes in most days. They always know of somebody who wants a job.'

'But how will I be able to tell if a stranger is trustworthy with children?'

'Ask for references, of course.' Her continuing helplessness in household matters irritated him. 'And check her over when you interview her. My Ma always reckons you can tell if a girl is clean by looking at her fingernails, and if she's honest by looking her straight in the eye. The ones who look away have nearly always got something to hide. See you later.' He went out.

The old woman who lived in the next flat looked disagreeable, and there was the embarrassment of screamings and broomstick thumpings between them. Sarah waited for the click of her door closing next morning, and with a pounding heart went into the passage and called out, 'Excuse me –'

She was limping towards the lift with an Indian vegetable basket in one hand and a rubber-tipped walking cane in the other. One of the black lace-up shoes beneath her long grey skirt had a built-up sole which dragged on the floor as she swung round. 'What do you want, girlie?'

'Please, do you have a maid who comes in? I need someone to help me look after my baby once in a while.'

'You want to steal my girl away? No chance. She's worked for me for twenty years. She'll only work for me because I treat her nicely.' Close up, the old face looked like an antique leather goatskin Sarah had seen in a Spanish museum on a family trip overseas, its once supple beige darkened to a sere and wrinkled tan. The green olive eyes glaring up at her looked as though they still had preserving oil on them.

Sarah blurted, 'I don't want to steal anyone!' She was not used to asking for favours, or to expressions of distaste on the faces of people who looked at her. 'I just wanted to ask

14

if she knows someone who can look after my little girl sometimes.'

'You the screamer?' The olive eyes scanned her face as though trying to strip away all seven layers of skin.

'What?' For a moment she did not understand.

'The screamer. The one that's always waking me up at night. Does he hit you?'

'No!' The denial was out before she could stop it. She felt one of her sudden blushes bloom on her face. 'Not really. Not intentionally. I just get upset sometimes, and then I shout at him, and then he –'

'Hits you.' The goatskin nodded. 'You shouldn't let him do that, girlie.'

'I deserve it sometimes.' She was learning humility along with cooking and cleaning. 'But look, Mrs –'

'Miss. Miss Florence Hodgkiss, if you please. Never let a man lay a finger on me, and proud of it. Only virgin over twenty-five in Durban.' She cackled.

The passages in the grey oatmeal building were draughty, being near the sea. Wafting from Miss Hodgkiss came the musk of a seldom-washed body, a tingle of mothballs and – Sarah was almost sure, having been given some for Christmas once – a faint whiff of Chanel No 5. She said, gaining courage from the cackle, 'Miss Hodgkiss, please, I'm just asking you to ask your maid if she knows a woman who could look after my little girl. Someone with references, of course,' she added quickly.

'You want to steal my Gertrude, that's what! No go, girlie. Gertrude's mine. I trained her. I'm not letting her go to anybody else, least of all a screamer. What a waste.' Miss Hodgkiss shook her walking cane in a threatening way and turned to hobble off.

Sarah checked with a backward glance that the door latch was up so it couldn't slam shut, and went after her. 'Please couldn't you ask Gertrude? I don't want to steal her. I just need a nanny for a few afternoons a week so I can have a break sometimes. I'll pay well.'

Head forward like an old turtle, cane stabbing at the rubber floor, Miss Hodgkiss limped along muttering, 'A nanny, she wants. How should I know where to find one? Never been my problem. Thank God. Life sentence, brats. Never leave you with any time to yourself.'

'Exactly,' Sarah slipped in, hurrying next to her.

'At least the kid's not a screamer. Small mercies.' Miss

15

Hodgkiss thumped to a stop next to the lift doors and turned the goatskin up to Sarah. 'What's in it for Gertrude?'

'Well – a tip, I suppose,' Sarah said uncertainly, not having given any thought to Gertrude other than as a procurer of help.

'A pound?' Miss Hodgkiss demanded. 'She needs it. Too many brats of her own, usual thing. You promise a pound, and I'll ask her. Ask, mind. No guarantees. I'm not a labour bureau.' Again the cackle, followed by a shrewd upward flash of the green olives. 'Nor a lonely hearts club.'

The lift doors chuntered open, grey enamel with FUCK and POES scratched in several places. Sarah had been quite shocked when she first saw them; four-letter words were not common schoolgirl currency then. She wondered what the professed virgin limping into the lift thought, confronted by them every day. She said, 'I'm not really lonely, but I do need to get out sometimes.'

The old woman swung round in the lift with that disconcerting suddenness, giving off another whiff of Chanel No 5. 'Well don't let him hit you again, you hear? You've got to stand up for yourself in this life, girlie. You've got to be –' The lift doors closed on the rest of her advice. FUCK and POES, and a heart with 'EL loves SV' in it.

Gertrude, spilling generously out of her XXOS pink housemaid's uniform, came knocking at the door two days later with her cousin Doris. 'She's got number one top references, Nkosazaan, but there's too many kids for a full-time job. Maybe you like Doris, eh?'

Doris produced a tentative smile. She was a tall thin woman with cheekbones that stuck out like rock ledges from a pale ochre face pared to the bone, dressed in a blue print overall that hung off coat-hanger shoulders. The contrast with the plumply beaming, very dark brown Gertrude could not have been greater.

Sarah looked from one face to the other. 'You're cousins?'

'Mother's mother the same, s'true's bob.' Gertrude was looking straight back. (Her fingernails were clean too, Sarah noted with a quick downward glance.) 'Mix up Zulu and Xhosa, and you get some black coffee, some with cream. It's the way.'

Sarah flushed. 'Sorry.'

Gertrude chuckled. 'Ai, Nkosazaan, don't worry! Nobody

believes us, is true. Only the passbook.' She patted her bulging breast pocket where the passbook that had recently been issued to women had already been moulded to a parabola.

Mindful of the need to conduct a proper interview, Sarah asked them into the flat, and then to sit down at the cheap pine dining table. It seemed only polite to say, 'Would you like some tea?'

'Please, Nkosazaan.' Gertrude lowered her massive pink backside into one of the second-hand chairs. When Doris hovered, shy of sitting in a white woman's living room, she said in Zulu, 'Sit, cousin. This is a young madam, not like the old ones. We might even get our tea in proper cups instead of enamel mugs. Didn't I promise you a good job?'

Sarah did not have any mugs, only the OK Bazaars cups and saucers that she and Gordon used, which she set out on the tray with the stainless steel teapot and some biscuits, thinking, Ma would drop dead if she saw me fraternising with servant women. And insist on sterilising the cups afterwards, probably.

Her vociferously United Party mother considered herself a beacon of enlightenment, and made a point of being ultra polite to servants. She greeted her staff formally each morning and spoke to them in well-enunciated English rather than the kitchen Zulu most Durban madams used. She had never allowed Sarah to talk about 'the cookboy' or 'the washgirl'.

'They're fully-grown adults,' she instructed. 'Charlie is a cook, not a cookboy. Sipho is a gardener, not a garden boy. And I won't have you using any of those other awful words for blacks. "African" is what they prefer, I'm told.'

But the wages she paid were at the lower end of the scale, supplemented by the cast-off clothing employers of servants like to think makes up for their meannesses, and her staff mimicked the Madam behind her back, using her la-di-da voice and gracious gestures. Sarah had seen them laughing in the back yard as they crooked their little fingers above their mug handles and took dainty sips with pursed lips at their strong sweet bush tea, just as her mother did at her fine Ceylon. She shrank from the thought of these two cousins laughing in the same way about her, and wondered what Gertrude had said in Zulu. She poured the tea and passed the biscuits and sat down thinking, What am I going to talk to them about?

But Gertrude knew how to entertain; Miss Hodgkiss's training had included techniques for the relaying of information and gossip that could keep an old woman in touch with the world even in an isolated flat. Gertrude began to talk, as she stirred sugar into her tea with a vigorous clinking, about her children and her two-roomed tin-roofed house, moving on to a vivid description of township life and her everyday problems.

'Black womans like Doris and me, you understand, we got double trouble, Nkosazaan,' she said with a laugh that erupted like hot magma. 'One trouble by our madams in town, one trouble by the house when we get home late and the kids want supper and helping with the homework, and the man wants all our money for the shebeen. But it's OK, we got good strong blood. We can do all these things easy.'

'I wish I were as strong.' Sarah felt shamed by the revelation of hard lives so far removed from her relative ease. As they left, she pressed the promised pound into Gertrude's hand, tightly folded to keep the transaction discreet.

Gertrude took it cheerfully as her due, however, and showed it to Doris. 'My lucky day, eh? Thanks too much, Nkosazaan. This one is for the school books.' She pushed it into her straining breast pocket next to the passbook.

'Next week, then?' Sarah said to Doris, and watched them walk away down the passage like Jack Sprat and his wife.

Doris began to come on three, and later four afternoons a week, with a bird-peck at the door and the tentative smile on her gaunt face. After the first few afternoons when Sarah stayed sewing at the pine table while Doris played with Rose on a checked rug spread on the floor, both eyeing each other self-consciously across the room, Sarah felt confident enough to go out.

The hours of freedom from baby babble and household chores were like being released from a stagnant pool into a running stream oxygenated with bubbles of sunlight and space. She went to the beach and swam and lay face-down on her towel, feeling the sun warm her sea-cold body like a lover. Or she would go walking along the beach or window shopping, or spend a luxurious hour in the library choosing books to read, free to be herself again. Not Gordon's wife or Rose's mother or even the girl who used to live in the big house on the Berea, just Sarah.

It was like getting to know a new friend. Who am I really? she wondered, watching her reflection flickering along in shop windows. And realised that in the fullness of her privileged growing up, of private school and nice clothes and boyfriends and parties and the taken-for-granted university that was like an extension of all the good times she had known, she had never given more than a passing thought to her future. Ma planned and did so much for me, she thought, and I took it all as my due. But that's over now. The thing is, can I decide what I want to do now, or am I as trapped by my circumstances as black women are by theirs?

Her mother certainly thought so. She expected her to fail, to go running home begging for help. Or crawling, preferably. That's the opinion she has of me, Sarah thought with bitter accuracy, and I've never done anything to make her think otherwise.

It took her a month of free afternoons to reach that first painful rung of self-knowledge, fuelled by the memory of what Gertrude and Doris had told her. If they could rise above almost unsurmountable hardships to sit laughing over tea, surely she could make something of her infinitely easier life? She had, after all, her Doris-given free afternoons in which to explore the possibilities.

For a while she was too self-absorbed to be lonely or bored. Her resentment at Gordon's absences faded, and her loss of friends from her former life seemed to matter less. But the inevitable afternoon came when the introspection palled and the beach walk was too familiar, and window shopping a futile occupation when there was no money to buy the things she coveted. She wandered along to the corner café for a *Daily News* and a cooldrink, intending to take them down to her favourite spot near the fishing groyne which caught the afternoon sun. As she stood in the queue at the till to pay, her eye was held by a hand-lettered poster sticky-taped next to the tatty For Sale and To Let notices on the café door. AFTERNOON ART CLASSES, it said. The hours were almost exactly those during which she was free.

She came to believe that it was meant for her to see the notice at that moment in her life. All the events of the previous three years seemed to have led up to it: the furtive back seat initiation into sex, having Rose, the fight with her mother, moving to the flat. When she signed on with the elderly artist who gave the classes in a nearby church hall, she thought only, I need something to do, a focus. But within weeks Mr Sneddon was saying, 'You are a painter, my dear, no question.'

19

Her father added willingly to the building society account for tuition, paints and canvases, saying, 'If you've got the ability, I'll give you as much as you need. You missed out on the rest of your university education, and I believe quite strongly that women must have interests outside their families, or they get sucked into the maze of aimless middle age like your mother. I don't want that for you. Or for Rose.'

'Thank you, Dad.' When she kissed him, she noticed that the hands holding hers had a tremor in them. He had aged, his face fallen into austere folds, his eyes an even paler blue with a smoky brown age-ring round the irises. Miss Fairley had moved on that year to another job, finally giving up hope.

While Sarah was feeling her way into her newly-discovered talent, Rose was making a beloved friend in Doris. Shy with strangers and frequently beaten by a bad-tempered husband who drank, she felt at ease only with children. Her own seven were kept clean and well dressed to the point where her township neighbours whispered behind envious hands that she had pretensions: 'Stuck up, nè?' On Rose she lavished her special love for the babies she could no longer bear, having been kicked in the stomach and miscarried the last time she was pregnant.

For two years of regular afternoons she sang and played with Rose, took her for walks and to the paddling pond, taught her Xhosa songs and games, and with unwavering patience helped her to dress and undress and put to bed and wake up her family of dolls and teddy bears, washing and ironing their miniature clothes when they got sticky with the biscuit crumbs and orange juice Rose liked to share.

It was Doris who first recognised and fostered her impulsive generosity, who rescued the toys given away to other children and swept up the bread crusts and nibbled-off bits of cheese that Rose insisted on leaving under the sink for the mouse she had once seen whisking behind a saucepan. They were a two-woman rescue squad for drifting toy boats and crying kids and lost dogs, the small blonde girl and the tall ochre woman who hated to see people unhappy.

It was good, kind, loving Doris, Sarah thinks, who first set her feet on the path which brought her to this place of death.

4

The hut has become very hot. Sarah moves uneasily in the wooden chair, remembering another young woman lying too still in a mess of her own blood, and Doris bending over her with frantic dread, shaking and shaking.

The grey oatmeal flats kept their secrets well hidden. Sarah had been living there for months before she realised that there was another floor above the fifth, where the lift stopped. An unobtrusive green door round the corner from the lift opened on to a flight of narrow cement steps worn to half moons, leading upwards into dimness.

'You should hang your washing up there, girlie.' Miss Hodgkiss was limping next to her one morning as she wheeled Rose's push chair down the passage. 'It dries quicker on the lines than on that silly contraption you use over the bath.'

'I didn't know there were washing lines up there?'

'Now you do. And you should also know it's a waste of money to send washing out to the coolies. They'll wear your things out in six months, the way they slap them around. Always bring the washing back damp too. Gets mildew if you don't air it properly.'

Miss Hodgkiss unleashed one of her green olive glares, and Sarah blushed at being found out in another domestic dereliction. She had been sneaking the sheets and nappies and Gordon's shirts out to an Indian laundry in Greyville via the dhobi who called on Mondays, paying for them by skimping on the groceries. In the humid coastal climate they had taken days to dry in the bathroom, and Gordon was eloquent about having to fight his way through wet washing to get to the bath.

Is there anything Miss Hodgkiss doesn't know about us? she

wondered. Gertrude had told her of the old woman's incessant speculation about the other flat residents. 'That one! She never stops, Nkosazaan. I think she likes to know even what time the amagundane come out of they holes in the night.' She erupted into a massive chuckle. The aging wooden-floored flats were a hospitable home to battalions of mice and whole armies of the giant whiskered cockroaches for which Durban is famous.

Sarah had grown up in a home where there were never less than three servants, plus a washing and ironing woman who came on Mondays and Tuesdays. Patience had laboured since she could remember in the laundry behind the garage. It was a small dark damp room with twin stone troughs and a round speckled enamel washing machine old enough to have a mangle. Sarah had loved helping with the mangle when she was small. There was something vastly satisfying about feeding a corner of dripping wet washing into its churning black rollers ('Mind fingers!' Patience would warn) and watching them swallow it up, gobbling buttons and zips and squeezing out rivers of soapy water to disgorge the limply subdued garment ready to hang up.

Patience had her own way of doing things. She used a corrugated zinc scrubbing board and little squares of washing blue tied up in rags in the rinsing water to keep sheets white. Crackling-dry cotton from the line would be sprinkled with flicks of water off her brown and pink fingers before she ironed it. Nobody told her what to do, not even Sarah's mother, who glossed over her failure to command by telling everyone how reliable Patience was. '*Such* a gem, and so clean and respectable. She's already put her eldest daughter through training college. I don't know how she does it.'

She did it by working six long days a week for lazier women, smelling of soap and starch and April Violets talcum powder which collected in the creases of her neck as she sweated and sighed with back pain in the laundries her employers never went into, unless they absolutely had to. Why interfere with a system that produces weekly offerings of fresh, beautifully ironed laundry for a minimal outlay of cash?

Because of Patience, Sarah had never had to wash more than a pair of panties or press a dress she needed in a hurry. She loathed everything about the washing she had to do in the flat: scooping the sour-smelling clothes out of the wash basket, rubbing at the dirt rings on Gordon's collars and the foul stains on Rose's nappies, bending double over the bath heaving wet sheets around in the rinsing water. But the dhobi was expensive, and if there were lines on the roof where the heavy washing could be hung to dry in a day, she had no real excuse for not doing it herself.

The following Monday she piled all the wet washing into Rose's plastic baby bath while she slept and carried it along to the lift, up to the fifth floor, and up the dim flight of steps behind the green door. The stair light had long ago been smashed, and she had to feel her way with her feet. At the top, a second door grimed with finger marks led out on to a tarred rooftop where lines of other people's washing snapped and jitterbugged in the wind. Beyond them was a row of small brick rooms with dingy windows that Doris had told her was where the flat maintenance staff and live-in maids slept. The servants' quarters, Ma would have called it, she thought. (It was disconcerting how often her mother still cropped up in her thoughts.)

'Sometimes I also stay up there with my friend Lizzie when I'm working late,' Doris had gone on, lowering her eyes to show that it was a confidence. 'You tell nobody, Madam, OK? Only one person per room, the Superintendent she say, or else the police is coming.'

'Oh, please don't call me Madam, Doris.' Sarah had grown to depend on her, and being called 'Madam' seemed to create an uncomfortable vacuum between them.

'What must I call the Madam then?'

'Couldn't you call me Sarah?'

Doris giggled, then put her hand quickly over her mouth to stifle it. For someone who had had her servitude rubbed in her face by years of madams insisting on their traditional honorific, the idea of calling one by her first name was unthinkable. Despite the fact that the white girl who was looking at her with such earnest goodwill was almost young enough to be her daughter. 'Please, no, I can't do that, Madam.' She looked away in embarrassment.

'But Gertrude calls me Nkosazaan.' An imperious note had entered Sarah's voice. 'I really don't like being called Madam, Doris.'

'I will try,' Doris had said, but there wasn't anything to take its place. When a 'Madam' popped out unthinkingly she felt she had to apologise, which created even more of a vacuum between them. Sarah thought crossly, I can't seem to get it right with black people.

When she went up to the rooftop in the late afternoon to fetch her dry washing, it was no longer the bleak windy place it had been earlier, inhabited only by flapping sheets and shirts and bellying socks. The wind had dropped and off-duty staff were sitting outside their rooms looking very different from the ingratiating, neatly-uniformed maids and flat cleaners she met in the passages during working hours. With uniforms unbuttoned and shoes off and doeks unravelled to release unfamiliar frizzes of black hair round their heads, they sat with sprawled legs talking and laughing, their fingers dipping into greasy bags of hot chips that someone had fetched from the corner café. One woman sat in front of another on the step of her room, having her hair worked into a pattern of tight plaits. A group of men squatted in a circle playing a gambling game with cards and stones, punctuated with stabbing arms and staccato shouts. Another sat in his vest with a towel round his shoulders as a friend shaved him, making curving brown sweeps through snowy shaving foam.

None of them took the slightest notice of her; she could have been a ghost or a robot designed for unpegging and taking down washing off a line, present but unseen. It was a curious feeling being ignored by black people when it was usually the other way round. She thought, This is what it must feel like when we go on talking to each other in front of them as they serve tea or drinks or dinner. As though they are household appliances that can be switched on and off at will to do our bidding. She had a small surge of pride at being able to sympathise with the exploited, and at no longer being an exploiter herself, forgetting for the moment her free afternoons courtesy of Doris. She thought, Wouldn't Ma's eyes pop to see me doing my own washing and ironing? She wouldn't know where to start if she had to do hers.

Feeling smug and efficient, she turned discreetly away so as not to invade their after-hours privacy as she folded the washing into Rose's plastic bath, then carried it through the door to the stairs. There were heavy footsteps coming upwards, moving fast as though they were familiar with the worn places. With the plastic bath in front of her piled high with washing, feeling her way down in the gloom with her feet, she did not see who it was until he passed her. His head was turned away, but she recognised him by his beige safari suit and thick hairy legs as Mr Prinsloo from the second floor back. A pharmaceutical salesman, according to Miss Hodgkiss via Gertrude, with a sick wife and two pale cowed kids who wiped their noses on their sleeves in the lift. I wouldn't have expected him to have been the type to help with the washing, she thought. Just shows how you shouldn't judge people.

It could not have been more than a month later when an agitated knocking at the flat door interrupted the coffee and newspapers she and Gordon were sitting over one evening after supper.

He went to the door. 'Who the hell could it be at this time of night?'

It was Doris. 'Please, Master,' she gasped, 'I must see the Madam. Please.'

'What for?'

'Is trouble upstairs with my friend Lizzie. She's very sick, Master.'

'Who's Lizzie? She doesn't work for us, does she?'

Hearing Doris's distress, Sarah had got up from the table and was coming towards the door. 'Lizzie is Doris's friend. She works for someone on the second floor, I think.'

'Well, she's not our problem then, is she?' Gordon started to close the door, adding with some annoyance, 'Why did you come and worry us, Doris, hey? You should go to Lizzie's Madam. It's her problem.'

'But Master, she's very sick!' Doris pushed herself urgently between the closing door and its frame. 'And her Madam is not there. I try already.'

'Go to the Superintendent, then. She can call an ambulance if the girl's really bad.' Gordon jiggled the door, trying to get Doris to move backwards into the passage. 'Go on. It's nothing to do with us.'

'Master, please!' Doris's voice rose to a sobbing wail. 'I think Lizzie is maybe going to die!'

Reaching the door, Sarah was shocked by the terror and tears on her face. 'Gordon, let me –'

A door opened down the passage and someone called, 'What's the matter there?'

Gordon stuck his head and shoulders out. 'Some trouble upstairs. One of the girls is sick. Don't worry, I've told this woman to go down to the Super. It's her job to sort out these things.'

He turned back to Doris. 'Go on, scram! The faster you get down there, the faster she can get help.'

'Madam, *please!*' Doris appealed over his shoulder, anguish pulling her lips back to show the gaps in her teeth that she usually tried to hide behind her hand.

Sarah began to push past him. 'Let me talk to her. Doris wouldn't be so upset for nothing.'

He put his arm across the door frame to bar her way. 'It's not our indaba, babe. She should have gone straight to the Superintendent, who could have called an ambulance by now. But no, she'd rather stand here yelling her head off the way these coon girls always do when something goes wrong.'

Sarah was furious. 'Gordon, how can you? This is Doris who works for us, not just some – some woman off the street! I'm going upstairs with her to see what's wrong.' She ducked under his arm and put her hand out to the sobbing woman.

'No, you bloody aren't! It could be dangerous.' He made a grab for her, missing as she sidestepped.

'Yes, I bloody am! It's the least I can do for her. You stay with Rosie.' She touched Doris's arm. 'Come on. We'll run up the stairs. It's quicker than waiting for the lift.'

'I'm ordering you not to go!'

Sarah turned round. In the doorway stood an ugly, hectoring man she had never seen before, his face and neck and ears flushed red. She shouted, 'I don't take orders, Gordon!'

'You're my wife. You'll do as I say!'

She felt her throat swelling with rage. 'You don't bloody own me! So fuck off, OK?'

The look on his face was disbelieving. 'But I –'

Almost dragging Doris down the passage, she was too angry to answer. *What have I married?* was echoing like a sound chamber in her head. How can he be so nice one moment, and such a bastard the next? Nor did she notice the sharp gleam of Miss Hodgkiss's eye at her slightly open door. Trying to comfort the still-weeping Doris, she said, 'Never mind, I'll try and help Lizzie. What's wrong with her?'

'It's blood all over.' Doris's face was a livid yellow under the low-wattage lights in the passage, the gaunt cheek-bones sticking out like razors.

'But why?' Sarah insisted. They were at the door that led to the stairs, and she pushed it open.

Doris dropped her eyes. 'Shame, Lizzie. She's stop from

26

having a baby. That's why I can't say for the Master.'

'An abortion?'

Doris nodded. 'Come quick please, Madam! There's too much blood.'

Running up the stairs, Sarah remembered her mother's tight face saying, 'I'll ask Douglas to do an abortion. He'll keep his mouth shut.' It would have been performed under anaesthetic in a sterile operating theatre and passed off as a routine D & C. How had this abortion been done, to produce 'too much' blood? I'm so ignorant about things! she fumed.

On the last flight up to the rooftop they had to feel their way through pitch darkness, but it was lighter once they were outside in the open. Low clouds overhead reflected the glow of the city's street lights. Across the rooftop, its tarmac still radiating the warmth of the afternoon sun, the windows of the staff quarters glowed with the soft orange light of candles and paraffin lamps.

'Don't these rooms have electric light?' Sarah could hardly believe it, in the centre of a modern city.

'No, Madam. But the Superintendent, she says it's a good thing. "You people can't be trusted with electricity. The whole damn lot of you would be leaving your lights on all day," is what she says.'

Doris had caught the exact intonation of the Superintendent's vacuum-cleaner whine that could be heard all day in the passages, and Sarah nearly laughed. But they were getting near the rooms, and there were dark figures outside the dimly-lit doorway towards which Doris was leading her. She wondered what they would say when they saw her. How dangerous was this alien territory in the city sky where people still led their night lives by firelight?

Doris muttered something in Zulu, and a flickering from inside the room slid like glycerine across the faces that turned towards her. There was a musky smell of bodies and hot paraffin, threaded with pungent dagga smoke swiftly hidden in a cupped hand. Someone said, 'First floor? The Nkosazaan for Gertrude?'

Sarah nodded. 'Go in,' the same voice said, and she felt hands urging her towards the doorway through which Doris had already passed, throwing a huge shadow on the peeling door.

The room was just big enough to hold a bed and a grey tin trunk and some wooden shelves nailed to rough brick walls, jammed with clothing and cosmetics and bulging shoe-boxes. A candle stuck in a fish-paste bottle guttered next to a jug of wilted flowers. From a row of nails above the bed hung dresses and skirts and blouses on wire coat-hangers, two or three deep in places, their colours muted in the candlelight. Two women were standing by the foot of the bed, and as they turned to Sarah the movement set the hanging clothes shifting and stirring, giving her the disturbing feeling that there was a silent crowd of restless women up there looking down at her, waiting to see what she would do.

Doris's voice sobbed, 'See, Madam! She's not talking now.'

Lizzie, as pert and talkative as a canary in her yellow uniform, had come to the flat often to visit Doris. Now she lay very still on her back with her eyes closed and a cheap grey blanket drawn up to her chin, breathing slowly with long pauses in between. Uncertain what to do, Sarah said, 'Can I touch her?'

'Please, Madam.'

She went closer and put her hand gingerly on Lizzie's forehead. It was clammy with cold sweat. So was the wrist she lifted from under the blanket to feel its faint thready pulse. She pulled back the blanket last, and saw with a sick lurch in her stomach that there was dark red blood everywhere, drenching Lizzie's uniform and the striped coir mattress. In the hollow between Lizzie's legs, the blood had congealed into a viscid mass on whose glistening surface multiple reflections of the candle flame leapt and shivered in a deadly dance.

She had to bite her cheeks inside to stop the threatening need to vomit. If Lizzie was bleeding after an abortion, she reasoned, surely the best thing would be to try and stop the bleeding while an ambulance was sent for? They would have to find something to push up between her legs, something clean and thick and foldable.

'Doris?'

'Yes, Madam?'

Don't call me that here! I don't want to be a madam! I can't do what you're asking of me! Sarah wanted to shout into the blackness of this place and its veering shadows and its whispering figures waiting outside. But Lizzie's life was bubbling out, and she was responsible now. She said with a firmness she did not feel, 'We need clean cloths or towels to stop the bleeding. And someone must run down to the Superintendent and ask her to phone for an ambulance. We've got to get Lizzie to hospital quickly.'

28

'No, Madam!' Doris was vehement. 'This is a bad thing. If she goes to hospital, the police will catch her.' There were murmurs of assent from the other two women, and a shaking of heads.

'She'll die if she doesn't get to hospital. You know that, don't you?' Sarah looked at each candlelit face in turn.

'We know.' They looked at her like hanging judges, gravely accepting the burden of their decision.

'But you can't let her!'

'That's for why I call you, Madam. I tell these peoples you will know what to do. You are a good madam.'

The trust on Doris's face made Sarah cringe. This middle-aged, capable woman calls me a good madam, and hopes for a miracle because I'm white. She had never had to think about what it meant to be white rather than brown or black or yellow, privileged rather than poor. Now she saw that it was much more than having a light-coloured skin or more money or a better education. It was also having access to authority and knowledge, being able to tap into the treasure-house of information in the books and newspapers and magazines that had lain around her home in casual drifts, nothing special, just part of the background. She had taken for granted a richly endowed life that was as unattainable by these women as the South Pole. It was the first time she had felt the magnitude of the gap.

Agonised thinking would not help the woman bleeding to death on the bed, however. 'We must stop the blood first, then,' she said. 'Get some cloths, Doris. And you two, find something to put under the bed legs at the bottom so we can lift her feet up higher than her head. Bricks will do. Or bits of wood. Quick!'

They jostled out the door, sending the candle flame into a frenzy. She heard the feet outside shuffling aside to let them pass, and an urgent murmur of voices. Then it was quiet again, though she felt the press of people waiting in the dark. On her narrow iron bed Lizzie lay like an effigy on a tomb, her still face fallen into the look that Ethiopia made famous, the hollow grief of extreme starvation. Her eyes were sunk so deep in their sockets that they could have been drowning.

Sarah took her cold hand and held it, as much to comfort herself as Lizzie. In the shifting light the mean brick walls seemed to be closing in on her, just as they had in a terrifying story she had once read where the hero found himself in a room that grew smaller and smaller, the spiked walls and ceiling

29

clanking with hidden machinery as they advanced. She began to feel panicky. What if she couldn't do anything to help Lizzie – if she bled to death, and the people waiting outside in the dark blamed her, Sarah, the inept white madam? Up here on the whispering rooftop lit by fire was a different country to the trim grid of tarred streets below where the city totems, traffic lights and neon signs, continually flashed their mechanical defiance of darkness and disorder. Up here was the dark continent she lived on, and never saw.

She shivered and glanced round the room. The clothes hanging above the bed looked hardly worn. Hooked over the nails they hung from were several chic feathered felt hats of the kind Berea matrons wore to the races at Greyville and Clairwood. Looking down, she saw a row of neatly paired high-heeled shoes on the pocked cement floor. Lizzie was a snappy dresser in her off hours, apparently. Where does she get the money from? popped up in Sarah's mind like cash register numbers, followed hastily by, It's none of my business. I'd better check her again.

Her mother had said often that the best way you could tell a person's temperature without a thermometer was to press your lips against her forehead. Sarah remembered waking in the night when she was small and sick to feel her mother's cool lips on her feverish face, a loving reassurance that had soon sent her drifting back to sleep. That mother was a figment of the past now, but she herself was a mother. She could work the healing magic with her own lips.

She knelt down next to the bed and put her lips to Lizzie's cold sweaty forehead. Her eyelids did not even flicker at the touch. Close up, she saw that Lizzie had recently tried to straighten her hair, which stuck out from her head in dull frizzy hanks like wire wool, smelling faintly of chemicals. How futile our vanities seem when we're facing death, she thought, stroking it. And here but for the grace of a white skin go I.

'Madam.' Doris was hovering in the doorway holding a wrinkled bath towel. 'Is this OK? It's clean washing off the line, nice and dry.' Behind her, eyes shone like those of mesmerised animals trapped in a torch beam at night.

Sarah got up, brushing her dusty knees and wondering why she felt she should apologise. 'That'll do fine. We'll have to try and push it up – you know, where the bleeding is.' She did not know what word to use. 'Help me, Doris. You pull back the blanket and her skirt, and try to lift her hips a bit. I'll ease the towel under her and up through the front.'

As Doris lifted the blanket, the hot sweet stench of Lizzie's blood rose in a sickening belch and Sarah felt her stomach lurch again. But I can't! Not now, she thought, and clenched her teeth and closed the back of her throat as she had learned to do while changing Rose's dirty nappies, so she would not smell them. Doris peeled back the sodden skirt. Lizzie was naked underneath, with the swelling hips of a fertility goddess and a vigorous fuzz of pubic hair. Her skin was slippery with blood, and Doris struggled to lift her. As Sarah tried to force the folded towel under her buttocks, a sudden gush of fresh bright blood bloomed over her hands like a shocking scarlet hibiscus. 'Oh, Madam!' Doris's arms sagged.

'Don't let her drop down! I've almost got the towel under. Where are the others?'

'They look for bricks.'

'I need more help here. Call another woman.'

Doris turned her head and called out, and someone shuffled in and stood by the bed. Sarah recognised the trodden-down slippers of the Superintendent's maid, a fat surly woman whose passing always left a fishy wake. She let go of the towel with one blood-slick hand and gestured what she wanted done. 'Bend her legs up at the knees and hold them open a bit so I can get the towel through.' The woman did not move. 'Quickly. She's bleeding very fast.'

'I don't like,' the woman muttered.

'Do you want her to die?'

'I don't like. Is dirty things.'

'Do what I say, Goddammit! If I can, you can!' Sarah would have clouted her if she'd had a free hand.

The woman moved round behind her and put one reluctant hand on Lizzie's hip. 'I hold here.'

In the dim light, the fresh blood running out between Lizzie's legs looked like a live thing. And it was. Her life was draining away while the fat woman stood vacillating. 'Go away if you can't help!' Sarah yelled at her. 'Go on, bugger off! We'll do it ourselves.' She turned to Doris. 'You can let her down now. Just come and help me push the last bit under her, then hold her legs apart. I've got to pull the towel through here –'

She heard the slippers shuffling away and the fat woman's raised voice complaining to the watchers outside. Every

31

sentence seemed to contain a venomous 'i-Madam!' Doris leaned towards her and said, 'Never mind, Madam. That's rubbish, that one.'

'Lizzie's more important. She's bleeding badly now.' Sarah wrestled the end of the towel through, then wadded the thicker middle part up hard between Lizzie's spread legs with her fist to try and stem the bleeding. She moved the legs together again and crossed one over the other to hold it in place. 'Who did this, Doris?'

'I can't say, Madam.'

'How was it done, then? Tell me. Maybe we can save her if we know how.'

Doris gave her a long, considering look then put her hand up to hood her mouth and said, as though from under a stone, 'It was this afternoon, Madam. An old woman is coming. I don't know her name, but she is one who knows about these things. Lizzie, she ask me to stop from going home today, so I can please sit with her.

'Number one, she must pay the fifty pounds from her boyfriend. Number two, the old woman she takes out a cooldrink bottle with muti in, muti that is white like milk, and she's pushing a long red rubber thing up – ' She hesitated, as much at a loss as to what word to use as Sarah had been, '– up inside of Lizzie. First thing, Lizzie she feels nothing. Only the muti running in. She says to me, she says, "It's OK, Doris, it's nothing. You can go now."

' "Aikona!" says the old woman. "Wait. You must stay with this one all the night, Mama. She will have pains, and maybe she will also have plenty of blood, if the child is too big. You must not leave her." And then the pains, they come. Ai, Madam, such pains! I never see anybody cry so hard like Lizzie, not even with having a baby.'

They both looked down at her, free at last of pain but perilously close to death. Already blood was beginning to seep through the wadded towel.

Doris went on, 'The old woman, she stays until the baby comes. Is her job, she says. Lizzie, she's got so much pains, she's crying so hard, she doesn't even know when the baby comes out. "I must show her it is done good, then I can go," the old woman she says, and she's picking up the baby to show her. Here, Madam. Look.'

Tears spilled down her cheeks as she bent and reached under

the bed to drag out a chipped green enamel washbasin. The foetus was floating in a puddle of blood and mucus, a human comma curved round the dark red mass of its placenta, still joined to it by the whorled cord. Sarah took the basin in both her hands, as curious as she was appalled. Even in the candlelight she could see that the child was well formed, though too small to live. And that its skin was the colour of old ivory, intricately carved into tiny limbs and curled fists and feet, and a blunt sleeping face that would never see daylight.

'The father is white, then,' she said, understanding at last. It explained everything: the smart clothes, the fifty pounds, the need for secrecy – even, like a roulette ball dropping into an unexpected slot, passing Mr Prinsloo on the stairs a few weeks ago as she carried down the washing.

Doris went on as though she had not heard, in a voice like breaking glass. 'When she sees the baby – oh Madam, I think I will never forget her face. Lizzie, she's always laughing, you know? Nothing is trouble for Lizzie, she likes a good time, she likes nice things, she likes to dance and to sing. But when she sees this little baby – shame, Madam. It's like she's never sing again. She looks the other way and she doesn't talk nothing, not even cries any more for the pains. Then the old woman she goes away. I don't know where she stays. She comes from far, I think, by the bus.'

'When did Lizzie start to bleed like this?'

'One hour since, maybe. When I see it's coming out too much, I talk for these other peoples what I must do. They say, no ambulance, no hospital. They don't want any trouble up here, or else maybe they lose they jobs. That Superintendent, she's kwaai, hey? So I come to talk with the Madam. I tell them you will know to help Lizzie.'

They stood staring at each other over the bloody washbasin with its pathetic little burden that would have to be got rid of somehow. Buried? Thrown into the sea off the fishing groyne? But that could cast it up again on the morning tide to terrify some living child. She thought, Imagine a child's horror at finding a dead baby on the benevolent beach. Wrapped in plenty of newspaper and plastic bags and put deep into a municipal dustbin, then? Was it breaking the law, to dispose of an aborted foetus that you hadn't caused?

But Lizzie was the immediate problem, and thinking about children on the beach had given Sarah an idea. She passed the

33

washbasin carefully back to Doris. 'Hide it again, far under the bed. I know what we'll do for Lizzie. I'll run down to the tickey box and phone Dr Van Coller – you know, the young one I took Rosie to, that time she cut her foot on the beach? He lives quite close by. I'm sure he'll know what to do.'

'Sure-sure? This doctor, he won't make trouble for Lizzie and all the peoples here?' Doris's face looked as though someone had been grinding more hollows into it.

Sarah thought about Dr Van Coller with his tired young face and ginger eyelashes and thick-lensed glasses through which he had peered tenderly at Rose's little cut foot, stammering his explanations of how he would stitch it up using a local anaesthetic. 'He won't make trouble. I'd better go quickly. Don't leave Lizzie alone, Doris. If they find some bricks, put them under the legs at the bottom of the bed. She should be lying with her feet up and her head down. You under-stand?'

Doris nodded, drained of speech, and squatted down next to the bed with her hand on Lizzie's arm. Sarah glanced round the room again, thinking, I mustn't forget it. This is how they live. Candle. Tin trunk. Clothes hung from nails. Bare bricks, bare floor, no ceiling. And bleeding to death because they're afraid to cause trouble and lose their jobs.

In a surge of anger she pushed her way through the huddle of people outside saying, 'I'm going to get a private doctor for Lizzie.'

Hands clung to her arms as voices muttered in anxious Zulu. She felt rather than saw the fat woman move to stand in her path, a blackness against the radiant cloud above. The woman said, 'No ambulance. No police. Is too much trouble. The Madam, she hears what I say?'

Sarah felt her guilty anger blaze into fury. 'Oh no, you hear what I say! Lizzie's dying. She must have a doctor, or there'll be real trouble.'

She pushed past the fat woman and away from the clinging hands and ran under the empty washing lines towards the stairs and the rest of the nightmare. Telling Gordon what had happened, and slamming the door on his irritable, 'I told you not to go, but you wouldn't listen, as usual. Don't ask me to bail you out now.' Phoning the doctor from the public telephone in the entrance hall, telling the story in a low voice and waiting outside like a conspirator for him to come hurrying down the street. Up in the lift and into the rooftop darkness again, where Lizzie lay on her blood-soaked bed paying for her sins.

Paying in excess. She was dead by the time they reached her, with Doris frantically trying to shake her into breathing again. All the doctor could do was phone the mortuary and wait to make sure that the baby was laid next to her in the plastic bag they sealed her in before they took her away. Her anger numbed by exhaustion, Sarah asked him down to the flat afterwards for a cup of coffee and to pay him, both of which he refused. 'You've done plenty.' His ginger eyelashes blinked under the bright light at the entrance to the flats. 'Though it's never enough. Black women are at the bottom of the heap in every way.'

'I'm ashamed at what I saw.'

'Shame's a useless sentiment, Mrs Kimber. None of us can change what we're born into. But we can keep our eyes and hearts open.' He walked out with his shoulders stooped like an old man's.

Next morning when the police came, nobody knew anything about how Lizzie had died. 'We never hear her cry out, nothing, sir,' Sarah heard the fat woman say to the police sergeant as she wheeled Rose's push chair past the Superintendent's flat, which opened into the entrance hall. 'Lizzie, she thinks she's too good for everybody else. She's asking for trouble, sir.'

'They know damn well what happened, but they're not telling,' the sergeant confided to the Superintendent. 'It's always the same story. That's the trouble with these town Bantu: it's everybody for themselves, and bugger the rest. Not like it was in the old days when the chiefs called the shots and the tribe listened. Man, if we could only get some names out of them, we could hammer the back street abortionists.'

'I've been watching that girl Lizzie.' The Superintendent was chipping bright pink nail polish off a leprous fingernail. 'She had too many fancy clothes for what she was getting in wages. Quite the little madam on her off days.'

'Ag, that's normal where there's flats. These girls make a bleddy packet on the side. Your average boy who works in town leaves his wife behind in the kaya not just to look after his kids and his cows and his mealies, but because he doesn't need a wife here with the selection of girls he's got to choose from. I should be so lucky.' The sergeant guffawed. 'So long, then. You can clean the room up now, you hear? We've finished there.'

'I've had six girls already come to ask me for it.' The Superintendent patted the floral scarf tied over her curlers. She could charge key money for the letting of almost-beachfront accommodation. 'The one who gets it can clean it up. Ta for your trouble, Sergeant. So long.'

Sitting in the hut's stifling gloom so many years later, Sarah thinks of Lizzie whom she hardly knew, and Rose who lies here now, so dear and so dead. Rose cared too much, she thinks with bitter hindsight. But Africa got her, just as it got Lizzie. It's something Gordon will never understand, with his business-man's talk of progressive politics and improved social benefits and encouraging the black middle class. They're exercises in futility. Africa gets us all one way or another.

5

Gordon was not feckless; he was shrewd, hardworking and lucky. A death and a retirement in the shipping company meant that within two years he had become manager of a division, with a salary to match. He had taken pains to join the right cricket and golf clubs and stand the right people beers afterwards, and he was surfing less often. His old South Beach cronies had metamorphosed from boisterous cavaliers of the waves into sluggish bronzed lizards who seemed to want little more from life than to sprawl on the sand, squinting at the sea and passing girls out of eyes stopped down to f 22. Gordon was ambitious. He wanted money, and he wanted very badly to show Sarah's parents that he could do better than they had done by the daughter whose life they said he had ruined.

He hated the claustrophobic flat and the shabby furniture they had bought in sale rooms, and the limp curtains and bedspread Sarah had made on her sewing machine from cheap Indian-shop cotton. He hated making love in stealth while Rose slept a few feet away, and the cooking smells that greeted him when he came home, and the mildew that infiltrated shoes and cupboards and damp linen in the humid summer months like some virulent fungus. He wanted to live out in the suburbs where the other managers lived, to have space and a garden round him. He fine-combed the *Daily News* and *Natal Mercury* property sections for a house they could afford.

It was the end of 1959. Rose was three. Dr Verwoerd had been in power for a year, and the mesh of restrictive laws he had woven was beginning to tighten round 'undesirable' political organisations like the African National Congress and the Liberal Party. Helen Suzman was one of twelve MPs who broke away from the staid opposition United Party to form the Progressive Party. The talk in Durban social circles, however,

37

was of Gary Player's triumphant golfing win in the British Open, and the new musical *King Kong* with its explosion of exuberant African jazz and dance that told the tragic story of a black boxer who drowned himself at a farm prison. It was a new experience for white people actually to listen to and enjoy township music; Miriam Makeba had an amazing voice, they all said.

Of more remote interest was the bushy-bearded guerrilla with his trademark cigar whose people's army of cane cutters and school teachers had swept Batista and his military cronies out of Cuba. People scoffed, 'Castro'll never last, I'm telling you.' Twenty-five years later, his troops were facing their sons and grandsons across the Angola border.

When Gordon came home early one afternoon waving a torn-out property ad for 'A Brand New Kosy Kottage On One Full Acre In Westville's Newest Housing Development!', he was astounded by Sarah's lack of interest. 'Why don't you want to move?' he repeated for the third time. 'I thought you hated this hovel as much as I did.'

'I'm not talking about the flat. I'd love to move from here.' Sarah had been sitting at the pine table reading a story to Rose when he walked in. Now she stood near the sink where the breakfast and lunch dishes were still soaking in cold scummy water. Rose had crept away to twist herself into the curtain that screened her bed.

'But why not to Westville? It's really nice out there. Remember the Freemans' place? You said you loved it.' He was walking up and down, bombarding her with arguments. It was the quality they called drive at work, making the hieroglyphic on his personnel file that signified: Watch this young man, he's going places. Sarah thought of it as his bulldozer mood.

She said, knowing they were weak excuses, 'Westville seems so far out. I've got used to living near the beach and the shops. Rose loves the playground and the paddling pond. All we really need is a bigger flat.'

Gordon looked confused. 'Are you serious? Don't you want a house and a garden and a better quality of life? I thought all girls did?'

And he really had. Faithfully following the well-trodden male paths of school and sporting competition, of peacock blazers and convivial beers and talk of girls as a potentially hazardous foreign sub-species, he had assimilated as part of the air he breathed the prevailing wisdom about them. Women were magpies who wanted nests full of pretty things where they would be happy to breed and make homes for the father magpies, who must naturally be free to flit about at their pleasure in return for shouldering the burden of maintaining the nests. This cosy vision of domestic felicity was reinforced in glorious Technicolor by the films he took Sarah to see when Doris could stay on to baby-sit in the evenings. The fifties was a good time to be young, white and male.

'I'm not all girls.'

The way she said it, leaning against a sink full of dirty dishes with paint all over her hands and her lovely blonde hair in a lank plait, irritated him to sudden anger. 'That's for sure! Most girls would have had the dishes washed by now, and this pigsty cleaned up.'

She said tiredly, 'I've been painting most of the day, and you're home early. It would have been cleaned up by the time you normally get back from cricket practice.' She had wanted to read to Rose first, to distract her from Doris's going.

'I *missed* cricket practice so we could drive out to Westville and have a look at this place.' They had recently bought a green Morris Minor on hire purchase.

'I wasn't to know that. Be reasonable, Gordon.'

'Reasonable!' His face was scarlet. 'I'm not the one who's being unreasonable here. It's you! It's those damn art classes, isn't it? Or is it someone who goes to them?' His anger made him ugly, turning his smooth tanned boy-man's face into a snarl of knotted muscle and pinched flesh that Rose, the silent watcher of many quarrels, thought must be some other person who lived inside her daddy.

Sarah said, 'Are you just saying that to punish me for not tidying up in time, or do you really believe it?'

He shouted, 'Painting's becoming a bloody obsession with you, that's what I'm saying! How do I know there isn't a boyfriend tucked away behind the tea urns at that hall, some arty fart with long hair and paint all over his jeans?' He turned to throw his suit jacket down on the bed, and added in a choked voice, 'God, even the bed isn't properly made. You've just pulled it up.'

She turned towards the sink so he wouldn't see her tears. 'I was in a hurry to get to class this morning. Mr Sneddon doesn't like us to be late.'

'*Us?*' Gordon sneered. 'You haven't answered my question

yet. What's the real attraction – some budding Picasso with a nice line in perspective points?'

She could hear him fighting his tie as he always did when he got home, as though it were a boa constrictor. The shipping company insisted on the wearing of suits and ties, even during the hottest summer months, and Gordon often came home grumpy and red in the face.

She thought, The ways of businessmen are as alien to me as my involvement with painting obviously is to him. Maybe I am getting too wrapped up in it, neglecting things I shouldn't. She squeezed her eyes shut to try and force the tears to stop, and said, 'You know that Mr Sneddon is over seventy, and he teaches retired people and interested housewives like me, not art students.'

Gordon changed tack suddenly, coming at her from a different angle. 'And what does my daughter do while her mother indulges herself in all this intense creative activity, might I ask? Sit still in a corner?'

'Of course not. If it's Doris's afternoon off, she plays with another little girl whose mother brings her along.' She had managed to stop the tears, and turned back to face him. 'But you know all this.'

'I'm beginning to wonder just how much I do know. What are all these lessons costing, for example? Oils and canvas don't come cheap.'

'I've told you that too. Dad's been helping. He says it's part of my education.' Which I wasn't able to finish because of you. It was a thought that came more often now, specially when he spoke to her with the arrogant edge of a degreed person towards lesser mortals.

'Dear darling Daddy! What would we do without him?' He was standing by the window, staring out at the brick wall. 'Do you think he'd come up with the cash for a deposit on a house, by any chance?'

Money. It always cropped up somewhere in their fights. She had a patrician indifference that came of never having had to worry about it, until recently. Even now she did not question the amounts he gave her, merely asking for more when she was short. But Gordon wanted lots of money and resented people who had it. Since setting his sights on owning a house, he had become stingier with her allowance and begun hoarding as much of his salary as he could in a savings account. She had to dip into the ever-useful building society account for extras like Doris and painting materials. That it was in her name, available only to her, irked him too.

Her father had kept it faithfully in credit, and came visiting the flat on occasional afternoons when he knew Gordon would not be there. They would drink tea together at the pine table while he held Rose gingerly on his knees, trying not to wince as she dribbled milk and dropped soggy biscuit crumbs all over his immaculate suits. 'I'm not good at small talk, I'm afraid,' he had mumbled on one of his first visits, not really knowing how to speak to this daughter who seemed to have grown up and disappeared from his home between the end of one financial year and the next. But as she spoke of her life and he responded with halting news of his, and fingers of afternoon sun crawled over the cheap teacups and the scarred parquet floor, under-standing and friendship had grown between them. Her mother had taken up bridge and the organisation of charity evenings for the Durban Community Chest, he said, adding, 'She misses you a great deal, Sarah, though she'd never admit it.'

'Dear darling Daddy' Gordon had just called him in the sarcastic voice he used during their worst arguments. She saw her father in her mind's eye, the pale blue eyes and the sparse grey hair combed severely back, and the gentleness with which he kissed his granddaughter when he left, saying, 'Be a good girl, Rosie, and look after your Mummy for me.' And she thought, Isn't it funny, I never would have known him if it hadn't been for all this.

'All this' was how she had labelled her sudden marriage and her too-early child and her break with her mother; lumped together and labelled and filed them away in the place where she kept other regrets under lock and key so they would not intrude too often on the life she had made for herself. Which right now included a sinkful of dirty dishes, a husband like a pressure cooker about to reach critical heat, and a child who was trying to wriggle under her bed with her doll and her baby blanket.

She said, 'Dad will help, if it's what we really want,' and went to pick up Rose, who was hiccuping with sobs and covered in dusty fluff. 'It's all right, lovey, it's all right now,' she soothed, holding the little body close to hers with her hand cupped round the curly blonde head, and rocking her from side to side.

Gordon turned back from the window, transformed. 'You sure? It definitely looks like a good proposition, this house. I've checked it out with the agents and they say it's fantastic value for the price. Let's go and look at it right now! You'll change your mind when you see it, I swear. Bugger the dishes and the bed, let's just go.' His anger was dissipating as his enthusiasm surged back: the male on a quest for his own territory, an unstoppable force. 'It'll be lovely to have a real home of our own, with space to make a garden and for Rosie to have a sandpit and a swing.'

He's already forgotten the hard, hurting things he said, she thought, but Rose won't forget. What are we doing to her? Perhaps a proper home is what we really do need, all of us, and I'm just being selfish. 'Of course I'll come and look.' She tried to smile.

'That's great! I'll go and get the car.' He came over and gathered them both into a hug, once more the ebullient boy she had married. 'Sorry, babe. I didn't mean to get mad.' And he was gone.

Chameleon, she called him privately, and the likeness went deeper than khaki eyes that could look green one day and brown the next. He could switch from loving endearments to cutting sarcasm in one breath; he was articulate and sharp, with a tongue that could flick rings round an argument, and a retentive memory for facts that would take him a long way in business. As would his ability to take on the colour of his surroundings, adapting easily to new ways of thinking and new technologies.

It took Sarah time to find the words she wanted to say, to change homes and environments and to make new friends. She never made any at Westville, and she hated on sight the brash new house and the greedy red earth all round it that rejected all her efforts to tame it. There were no painting classes nearby, no buses, and while Gordon was at work, no car. She had to struggle on alone with her painting, clearing her mess away in good time before he got home in the evenings because (predictably) the long hot drive from the office into the setting sun made him tired and grumpy.

It was different for Rose. After a period of mourning for Doris and the beach and the paddling pond, she began to enjoy her new home and the wonderful new friend who came with it: Mfayedwa.

6

Sarah sits in the hut with her dead daughter remembering the black boy who was Rose's first real friend. She can see him still: the agile five-year-old body seemingly held together by rubber bands, striped T-shirt, grubby khaki shorts, bitter chocolate eyes and a smile that would split his face with delight. She thinks, Mfayedwa was another who led her towards this terrible place where masked men bring death in the night while people are dancing.

She gets up with an effort, a large woman whose hair, once as blonde as her daughter's, is now a pale fine silver caught back in a lumpy bun. Her hands are heavily veined and rough in patches, washed often but not creamed and cared for. There is still paint under her fingernails, and the dress she is wearing is not the conventional easy-care shirtwaister with matching bag and shoes that white women of her age and class usually wear. It is a loose floral cotton shift in colours that seem to have leapt off Van Gogh's palette: sizzling yellow and acid green and a hot Mediterranean blue. Her feet are in brown leather sandals and, again, they look uncared for, with calluses and chipped toenails. She goes slowly over to Gordon who stands angrily swatting with his hat at the bluebottle flies buzzing outside the window.

'Shit!' he curses. 'I can't stand this. I'm going to go back and ask that bloody official –'

'Gordon.' He turns, and at the look on her face moves quickly to put his arms round her. They stand there for some minutes, weeping together in the sweat-prickling heat. Sad things have always made her cry easily; she still walks out into the cinema foyer with damp pink eyes after a film with a sad ending. But today's tears are different. They seem to be drawn up by a dark artesian force that she feels helpless against.

He has not wept since he was a child ('Big boys don't cry'), and his tears feel like the painful ooze of pus from a boil. He lets go of her to brush them away with the back of his hand, and putting his arm back round her shoulders to try and steer her away from the terrible sight on the floor, says, 'Come with me, babe. You need to rest, and something to drink.' His voice is burred, as though he has been shouting for a long time.

She shakes her head. 'I won't leave her. Don't try and make me.'

'Sarah, there's –'

'Don't try and make me!' She is no longer the apologetic bride, the dutiful 'fifties wife deferring to her husband's better judgement. She has learned, in the thirty years they've been together, how to deflect his male persistencies like a cricketer angling a powefully delivered ball past the stumps, redirecting the momentum. 'I can't leave her now, don't you see? Not until she's decent – until they're decently –' Her voice falters to a disbelieving whisper. 'Oh God, how could anyone do this?'

She begins to weep again. Because he has also learned things in those thirty years, and is a lot less certain who is right now than he was then, he leads her to the wooden chair and helps her to sit down again. 'I'm going to see if I can find you a drink of cold water. Are you all right on your own, sitting here?'

'I'm not alone.' She wraps her arms around her stomach, begins to rock her body backwards and forwards, remembering.

He pushes open the cracked door to a furnace blast of heat and the upturned faces of two children who almost fall over with fright at his sudden appearance. Before they scuffle away across the stamped earth yard, he sees that they have been crying too; tear-paths run down their cheeks and twin trails of mucus glisten on their upper lips. Under the midday blanket of heat, the village huddles as still and silent as an empty church.

Doris lived in a distant township and her husband was not willing to allow her to work for Sarah in Westville as a live-in domestic. Who then, he said, would see to his meals and general comfort, and look after his children, and clean his house?

Doris and Sarah had both cried when they said goodbye. Sarah because she had come to rely on the black woman's discreet and comforting presence, and Doris because it meant losing the blonde child she had loved and nurtured, and because she would not easily find another madam so appreciative and little apt to interfere. She wondered if Sarah would change as she grew older, with a larger house and more children, into the usual sort of madam who screamed out the back door if you were a minute late from breakfast, and kept the tea and sugar and mealiemeal under lock and key, doling out the week's rations on Mondays.

Rose howled on and off for days after Doris left, dragging her baby blanket into corners and sitting hunched over it with her thumb in her mouth, sobbing, 'Want Doris! Where's Doris, Mum?'

Though Sarah took her to the park or to the paddling pond every day during the week before they moved, it wasn't the same as going with Doris. Sarah walked briskly and hurried her through her turns on the swings and the roundabouts, anxious to get back to the flat and an unfinished painting of the sea. 'I won't remember the colours if I don't get them down on canvas,' she'd apologise, putting down a glass of milk and some of Rose's favourite zoo biscuits as a guilt offering.

But even being able to nibble into as many sweet pastel lions and elephants and monkeys as she liked didn't make up to Rose for the loss of Doris. Their walks had rambled on for whole afternoons, and she missed the other flat children and their coterie of nannies who had sat comfortably chatting on the benches while they played. Nannies never flew into rages like mothers did if you got wet or dirty, just laughed and said, 'Hawu, look at you! Come, we better go home, eh?'

Like the waves that crashed over and licked up the beach, Doris's face came to Rose in dreams for months after they had moved out to the bare plot at Westville with its stark Kosy Kottage whose newly painted walls were already mud-splashed at the bottom.

The house sat in the middle of a patch of red earth, one of several identical rows served by gravel roads that petered out at one end into grassy hillside. The new development had been built on cheap land some way out of Westville, and there was no bus service. Unless a family could afford two cars (unlikely for the income group for whom the Kosy Kottages had been designed), the wives who stayed at home were marooned without transport from Monday to Friday, while the husbands who had been seduced by the wide-open spaces ('We'll be able to have a decent-sized garden! Go for walks! Fly kites! Breathe fresh air instead of petrol fumes!') drove back into their city offices every day along a traffic-choked highway that was an invisible river of petrol fumes.

Glumly contemplating the debris of their morning meal in her new white Formica breakfast nook, Sarah thought, I'll have to learn how to paint landscapes.

She had not reckoned on the intrusive Kosy Gardens housewives. The excitement of decorating their new houses soon wore off. There were no shops close by. Since each Kosy Kottage had a back-yard servant's room most of them had domestic help, which meant that the hours between waving the breadwinner off in the morning and welcoming him home at night had to be filled with other diversions.

In her first week, Sarah was asked to join two discussion groups and a sewing circle. After one morning of insipid instant coffee, three kinds of cake and conversation that ran the domestic gamut from childbirth to dressmaking, she declined further invitations. She was an artist working towards an exhibition, she told them. The other wives spent their next get-together discussing the way she dressed and her standoffish manner. The only woman who had managed to get into her house reported that it was sparsely furnished with, 'Not a single homely touch, not one! Just unframed pictures leaning against the walls.'

'A bohemian,' one of the older wives said.

'I suppose you've got to make allowances for the artistic temperament,' her next-door neighbour said. 'But that poor child!'

Sarah thought it herself sometimes, watching Rose play her solitary games. Since she had opted out of the Kosy Gardens social round, she could hardly expect Rose to be included in the junior gatherings that took place. Surely my responsibilities as a mother don't extend to endless trivial conversations just so Rose can play with other children? she thought. Or am I being selfish?

At least Albertina made her feel less culpable. Gordon, correctly assessing a threat to his creature comforts in Sarah's continued passion for painting, had insisted that they hire an experienced full-time maid for the new house. When Doris had been unable to come to Westville, Gertrude had offered to find someone else.

Sarah told her, 'I need someone who can do the housework and plain cooking, as well as look after Rose some of the time. A sort of Jill of all trades.'

Gertrude gave her head a dubious shake, agitating several chins. 'I don't know anybody by that name Jill, Nkosazaan. Where she's coming from, eh?'

Sarah flushed. She was always forgetting the language gap. 'I meant – sorry, Gertrude, don't worry about Jill. If you could find me someone as nice as Doris, I'd be grateful.'

'Doris, she is crying too much now you go away,' Gertrude said with satisfaction. 'I'm telling her first of first when I bring her to you, that you number one top madam, you give her no trouble. But she never believes me. Now she knows I talk the truth.'

As Gertrude's chins went into a fandango of chuckles, Sarah thought, I'm going to miss them both terribly. Without a mother to fall back on for advice and help, she had come to rely on Gertrude and Doris, and tea round the pine table had become a regular thing. Over the emptying cups they had told Sarah about their lives, and she had begun to realise what a cocoon of privilege she had been living in. These women and their friends had suffered fires and beatings, had been wrenched out of school after a few years to slave for widowed fathers, had watched children die in their arms for lack of a bus fare to get them to hospital. Why didn't I know about all this? Sarah would ask herself, remembering the well-ordered plenty of her sunny childhood in the big house on the Berea.

Saying goodbye to Gertrude and Doris had been hard. She had hugged them both, and been generously hugged in return. In the emotion of the moment she had tried to hug Miss Hodgkiss too, but had been rebuffed by the rubber-tipped cane and the old woman's smell underlying the aura of Chanel No. 5 which, according to Gertrude's sworn testimony, she wore in place of the panties she considered unhealthy. 'Look after yourself, girlie,' she had said with a green olive glare. 'And remember what I said. Don't let anyone push you around. Least of all that jumpy little husband of yours.'

Jumpy little husband? Sarah had laughed, thinking how furious Gordon would be if she repeated it. He always said he was five foot eight and a half when asked about his height, as though the half inch made a difference.

Gertrude had brought Albertina to apply for the job during

the week before they moved. 'Here's Albertina, Nkosazaan. Guaranteed number one top references.'

Sarah had got used to Doris's tall, silent presence and had not expected her opposite, a worried-looking, loquacious little woman, neatly dressed in black with a hand-crocheted collar, steel spectacles on her nose and a fine sheen of sweat that made a mirror of her face.

'I'm Albertina, Madam,' she said with the respectful bob she had been taught in mission school. 'I would like to work for you too much. Please Madam, I need the job.'

'Her man's got TB bad, they put him away in hospital last year already,' Gertrude said. 'And now her madam's moved away. She needs the job for sure, with five kids to support.'

'TB? But isn't that catching? I couldn't let anyone look after Rose who'd been in contact with a serious illness.' Sarah saw Albertina's trying-to-please expression fade, and added quickly, 'Really, nothing personal.'

'She's OK, Nkosazaan, never to worry,' Gertrude boomed, giving the smaller woman a hearty clap between the shoulder blades that nearly sent her crashing into the passage wall. 'You think would I bring you trouble? Aikona! Already they check Albertina and her kids for TB there by the clinic, and they all number one OK, no sickness.'

'A clean bill of health, the doctor said.' Albertina's hands were tightly clasped round a black umbrella. 'I can show you a certificate, Madam.'

Her eyes and posture had been so anxious that, after checking the health certificate, Sarah had felt unable to say no to her. She pushed the niggling worry about TB to the back of her mind and showed Albertina's excellent references to Gordon, who had agreed at once that she sounded like the right person.

' "Albertina is clean, polite and honest, and her work is always satisfactory. We are sorry to lose her," ' he read out. 'Can't beat that. Maybe we'll get some decent meals for a change. I presume she can cook?'

'She says she can and Gertrude confirms it, so you shouldn't starve.' Sarah was learning to counterattack with humour when Gordon made sharp comments; it was a strategy that sometimes made him laugh with his head thrown back, as he used to before Rose came and life got serious.

Their relationship was touchier now, more circumspect and wary. He was finding that she wouldn't automatically do what he wanted, and that she was very different from other wives. She didn't care about clothes or doing up the house or the formal dinners their friends were beginning to give, self-consciously dressed up, with candles on the table and Lieberstein chilling in the fridge. The rock'n'roll parties they had whirled through with her blonde ponytail flying seemed a thousand light years away. Marrying early and having a child and the brutal break from her mother and home had given her a stubborn strength that surprised him. He sometimes thought he did not know this vague, paint-obsessed stranger in his bed at all.

He had changed too in ways that were unexpected: become more ambitious and fixed of purpose, determined to show everyone who had predicted disaster after his forced marriage that he was a better person than they were. The tanned boy who drank too much beer at parties and made love once too often in the back of his mother's car was giving way to a pale, tense young man Sarah hardly recognised. A man who cared about where they lived, what kind of car he drove, and the size of his office carpet. Who insisted, 'We're going to make this marriage work, dammit,' at the end of every argument. Who wanted to put his daughter's name down for Durban Girls College at the age of three.

He gave Sarah full credit, however, he said graciously one Saturday morning, for finding Albertina. They were sitting over breakfast in the L-shaped lounge/dining room (A New Kosy Koncept!) with the morning sun making chequered patterns through the cottage window panes. 'She's a hell of a cook. Look at these scones.' He had eaten six.

'Yes, she is.' Sarah thought, This is the moment to ask him. 'She's asked if we'd mind if her youngest boy came to stay with her for a few weeks. He's five. The sister who usually cares for him is going into hospital for an operation.'

Gordon looked annoyed. 'Hasn't she got anyone else who can look after him? We don't want kids hanging around. It's a bit much of her to ask, so soon.'

'She's got nobody, and she's desperate.'

Sarah remembered the way Albertina had cried in the kitchen when she asked, tears sliding under her spectacles and the dish towel twisting in her hands. 'I've got nobody on God's earth, excepting for my sister,' she had said. 'Oh Madam, I ask you nicely. He won't be any trouble, he's a good boy.'

'I'm sure it's illegal to have kids staying in the back yard,'

Gordon was grumbling, 'not to mention a damn nuisance. Why is it that whenever you find a good girl, they have complications?'

Sarah thought, She's nearly forty, with five children, and we still call her a girl. She said, 'What difference does it make to us if she has him to stay for a while?'

'It's the thin end of the wedge, you know that.' He pushed his chair back and got up from the table, his pleasure in the scones evaporating. 'Next thing you'll find she's moved in half a dozen relatives, all eating us out of house and home.'

'You talk as though they're parasites!' Sarah's voice was rising now. Sometimes it flew right up the scale when she was angry. 'Albertina is a decent, law-abiding, respectable woman who does a good job for which we don't pay her nearly enough, and all she's asking is to have her child with her for a few weeks. It won't affect us at all.'

'It bloody will, and you know it. He'll sit around looking pathetic and half starved until you feel so guilty that you let him eat himself silly at our expense. I'm not having it. Tell her there'll be no extra rations if he comes.' Gordon was not gracious in defeat, though he knew better now than to oppose taking in an urchin Sarah was determined to help. He thought, It's time we had another kid. That'd stop her getting involved in everyone else's problems to the exclusion of our own. He was looking out the window at the wilting tufts of kikuyu grass he had planted a few weeks before. She had forgotten to water them again.

Sarah said, 'Sometimes I wonder what crap-hole your mother found you in,' and went out, slamming the door.

He was right about one thing. The small boy who dragged his feet into the back yard behind his aunt several days later looked unutterably pathetic. They had had to change buses three times and walk six miles to get to Kosy Gardens. His shoelaces had unravelled, his feet were blistered, his shirt was grimy, and the skinny little legs sticking out of too-large khaki shorts were grey with dust and fatigue. Albertina ran out of the kitchen to scoop him up against her white apron.

Rose, watching from the window, said, 'Who's that boy, Mum?'

'That's Albertina's little boy, Mfayedwa. He's coming to stay with her for a few weeks.'

'Can he come and play with me? Can he be my friend?' Rose

50

started to climb down from the breakfast nook bench where she had been standing. 'I'm going to ask him. Maybe he can climb trees. Maybe he likes dolls too. Maybe –'

'Not now, darling.' Sarah bent to hug the determined little body from behind, to stop her running out the kitchen door. 'Let him be with his mummy for a while. They haven't seen each other for a long time, and he's very tired.'

'But I want him to come and play with me.' Like her father, Rose was single-minded and did not like to be held back. Standing on one foot, she kicked Sarah's shin with a small red sandal. 'I *want* him to come.'

Sarah snatched her up as the red shoe flashed again, so that her plump legs flailed in the air. 'No, you don't. Nasty little girl.'

'But I want him! I want him!' Rose wailed. 'Please, Mum.'

'I said no, Rosie, and I mean it. When he's had something to eat and a good rest, we'll go and say hullo. Then you can ask him if he'd like to play.'

Rose began to sob, her small round cheeks flushing into angry pink splotches just as Sarah's did. 'But I want him now, Mum. Please?'

Sarah looked down into the blue eyes like wet plumbago flowers that Rose used shamelessly to get what she wanted, and thought, She's lonely, and it's my fault. Rose was still too young to run up and down the road making friends by herself, and the mothers who pitied her over their coffee had not invited her to come and play with their three-year-olds. She had seemed happy enough with her dolls and toys and afternoon walks with Albertina, but Sarah remembered now, guiltily, seeing her pressed against the picket fence watching other children.

'I promise we'll go and talk to him as soon as he's feeling better.' She pushed the damp curls off her daughter's petulant face. 'I'm sure he'd like to be friends.'

After half an hour's looking at each other sideways over mugs of orange juice, Rose and Mfayedwa had become inseparable companions.

He loved playing with her dolls and teddy bears in her infinitely clean white bedroom, and watching the water run out of the taps and swirl down the lavatory bowl in the bathroom. Together they dropped in and flushed away, yelling with delight at each disappearance, seven pairs of her panties and were trying to help his belt round the bend with the lavatory brush when

51

Albertina, alerted by the constant flushing, rushed in and stopped them.

He was two years older than Rose, an induction coil of energy and *joie de vivre* as yet undampened by school, and she followed him like a disciple. He showed her how to mould clay oxen from the red mud under the garden tap, and they made a whole herd to graze among the mint leaves by the kitchen steps. He could perform marvels like making his ears waggle and sending spitballs soaring over the fence. With Gordon's pliers, he twisted some abandoned wire into a skeleton car with shoe-polish tin wheels. It had a long steering column so they could walk upright driving it along roads they smoothed in the dust with their hands.

He was not, as Albertina had promised (and to her great embarrassment), a particularly good boy, just a boy. He and Rose stole packets of jelly from the pantry and cough sweets from the bathroom cupboard. He took Rose into Albertina's room to show her how the bed's iron legs had been raised on bricks, out of reach of the malicious earth spirits called tokoloshes, and gave her nightmares for weeks by asking why her own bed wasn't similarly protected.

She learned from Mfayedwa one of the great advantages of being a boy when he pulled down his shorts to pee. His little brown willie jutted out at the top of his legs like a magic finger that he could wave around and use to make patterns of droplets in the dust. When she pulled down her own shorts, all she could achieve by thrusting out her hips and squeezing was a curving jet that dwindled all too soon to a trickle on her red sandals.

'Why haven't I got a willie like Mfayedwa's?' she asked her mother in the bath that night.

'Because you're a girl, and girls don't have willies.' Sarah soaped the vulnerable little neck where wet curls clung like delicate seaweed. 'Girls have other things that boys haven't got,' she added carefully.

'But I *want* a willie.' Rose pursed her lips and frowned and commanded her mother, 'Get me a willie, Mum.'

Perhaps Gordon is right, and it's time to have a brother or sister for her, Sarah thought. She's far too used to getting her own way. I give in easily when I'm busy and don't want to be disturbed. She said, 'I'm sorry, darling, I can't get you one. You have to be born with one.' She was smiling to herself, thinking, This is our first serious sex talk.

Rose started to howl and splash the water with her feet and hands. 'I want one! I want one!'

Gordon put his head round the door, just home from work. 'What's wrong with Rosie?'

Still smiling, Sarah looked up at him from where she knelt holding the yelling child's arm so she wouldn't slip and bang her head against the bath. 'She wants a willie like Mfayedwa's.'

'What?' He came into the bathroom. 'What was that you said?'

'Oh, all girls want one at some stage.' Sarah reached for a towel and scooped Rose out of the water before she could splash any more on to the floor. 'I remember seeing a boy at my kindergarten peeing all over someone's sandcastle, and wishing that I could have a willie too, to – '

'Has that little black bastard been pulling down his pants to show himself to Rosie?' Gordon was crouching in front of them, his eyes narrowed to khaki arrow-slits.

She said stupidly, 'What do you mean?'

'You know bloody well what I mean!'

Sarah felt the child shrink back against her, a little wet body jerking with sobs. She said, 'Stop it, Gordon. You're frightening her,' wrapping her in the towel and turning her round and holding her close.

'I won't stop until I get an answer! Have you allowed that – that little kaffir to get familiar with Rose? What has he been doing with my daughter?' The furious questions ripped through the steamy bathroom like chain saws.

'Nothing! They're just children, for Pete's sake!' Her voice was rising to match his. Rose began to scream, butting her head repeatedly against Sarah's shoulder.

'He's black, goddammit!'

'He's a child! So is Rose! You're being ridiculous.' She was gasping with the shock of what he was saying.

'Am I? *Am* I? Didn't you read in the papers last week about the six-year-old in Durban North who was molested by a garden boy who had been working for the family for ten years? You can't be too careful where blacks are concerned, babe. Take it from me.'

'But they're just kids playing together –'

'Playing, hell! I won't bloody well have it! Not with my daughter!'

He looks like a toad, she thought, a big red bloated toad in a city suit and a half-loosened tie. Rose's piercing screams were rising and falling between them like an air-raid siren. Holding her tightly, Sarah yelled, 'Our daughter, had you forgotten? Do you think for one moment that I'd ever let her come to any harm?'

'You don't even know she exists while you're wrapped up in a painting, so how can you tell what's going on behind the garage? Or what that little bugger is doing to her when nobody's watching?' His anger was being fuelled by a mental image of black hands on his daughter's soft pale pink body. 'You know there's nothing these township kids haven't seen, sleeping packed like sardines in the same rooms as their parents, who probably screw each other every night. I should have stopped the whole thing at the very beginning and not let the kid come and stay at all.'

'I keep telling you, he's only five!'

'That doesn't mean a thing. These kids grow up fast.' He reached towards the screaming child. 'You can see she's upset.'

Sarah turned her head away from the sickly-fond look on his face to remember the children as they had been that afternoon: Mfayedwa's tight black curls bent next to Rose's blonde wisps over one of her picture books, both pointing and laughing at the cow jumping over the moon. She thought of his bright little face, and his skilled fingers that could make clay oxen and wire cars and scoop a blob of jam so fast out of the jam dish that you wouldn't believe it had ever been there. She thought of Albertina too, neat and fussy and respectable as a brown hen. She would die of shame if she heard this.

Gordon was saying to Rose in a cozening voice, 'Shush now, Rosie. Tell Daddy. What games have you and Mfayedwa been playing?'

Sarah was engulfed with loathing. She got up, snatching Rose out of his reach, and yelled, 'It's you who's upsetting her! You make me sick! You've got a dirty, sick, disgusting mind!'

The movement made the steam swirl round them and Rose cry even louder. Sarah saw the look of a much-tried man blooming on his face, the look she had seen often on her father's face, and thought with horror, Is this how it was between him and Ma? Am I getting like her?

Gordon said in a hard voice, 'I don't care a stuff what you think. I want that kid out.'

He sounded like her father too. She grabbed the moisture-beaded doorknob with her free hand to steady herself. 'If he goes, I go. Rose too.'

'What do you mean?'

Over the child's agonised sobbing, she cried, 'It means I am revolted by you! I don't want to live with you any longer! I hate this bloody house anyway!'

It was not the first time she had slammed the bathroom door, dislodging bits of the sub-standard plaster that characterised all the Kosy Kottages and had helped to make their builder rich.

7

More than twenty-five years later, Sarah thinks, We did a lot of shouting and door-slamming that year, each so pig-headed and convinced we were right. It wasn't only Gordon, bigoted by his upbringing. It was me too. And we fought in front of Rose, which was unforgivable. No wonder she grew up to see herself as a one-woman League of Nations dedicated to keeping the peace.

For the first time she forces herself to turn her head and look steadily at the bloodied face of her daughter. Are you still there, Rosie? Can you forgive us? Did we make up adequately later for our stupidities? Whatever we did wrong, we always loved you. Always. And we were learning to like Jake.

Her eyes move to the face of the husband, Jake, staring sightlessly up at the roof of the hut. It is scored with deep grooves that do not usually belong on the face of a young man. The animation of intelligence and humour that was there in life has gone; he looks stern and unforgiving now, his mouth twisted in a rictus of pain. Next to Rose's morbid greyness, his skin has the honeyed warmth of old yellowwood, the colour of his Malay and Hottentot grandmothers liberally mingled with that of their white masters.

Sarah thinks, Your colour was the least of the things that worried me about you, Jake. Skin colour is like soil colour, where the mineral content and trace elements and pigments may vary but the basic structure is the same. It's what falls on the soil that really matters: how much rain, how much sunlight, how long and how harsh the drought.

It was your hatred I feared, the inevitable contagion of years of injustice and anger. I was afraid it would spread like a fungus to Rose and the child, dimming their brightness. But it was they who infected you with their gentle bacilli of domestic happiness, and other men's hatred that killed you.

Just – why did it have to kill her too? How can anyone possibly

56

condone the murder of women and children by saying, 'It's all in a good cause – the few must be sacrificed for the many'?

Killing innocent people is negating our most basic belief: that life is worth living. Killing women and children is killing off the future. The end can never, ever, justify those terrible means.

The first serious crisis in their marriage lasted all of an unpleasantly hot and humid Durban evening, long after Rose had been comforted with hugs and kisses and put to bed.

Sarah had not wanted to talk any more. It seemed pointless to go on wrangling with Gordon when she felt more and more alienated from him. She felt guilty about upsetting Rose so badly, and longed to crawl into bed herself and pull the covers over her head.

But he had insisted that they talk, bulldozing her (as usual) into agreement with an undeniable, 'It's too important to leave until morning. Our whole marriage is at stake.'

'I think it's run its course, such as it was.' She sat hunched into the corner of the boxy modern couch in the new living room, her jeaned legs and bare feet pulled up underneath her as if shrinking from any possible contact with him. 'It's over, Gordon. You've changed and I don't like you any more. I don't like this nasty little house either, or the desert outside, or the dreadful people who live all round us. I want out.'

'You want. Operative words. You haven't changed at all! You're still the spoiled only child of rich parents, used to getting her own way, full of nice liberal sentiments about the underprivileged but well cushioned against their hardships. Where would we be without Daddy's discreet financial help?'

He had changed from his business suit into shorts and a T-shirt and thonged Indian sandals which flapped against the soles of his feet as he walked up and down: flap flap flap-flap flap, a dragging sloppiness that had always irritated her.

She said with scorn, 'Money. That's all you ever think about.'

'I have to, that's why! Somebody's got to earn enough to keep food in our mouths and a roof over our heads, even if it's beneath you. And I've done all right so far. You could at least give me credit for that.'

'It's not enough! You're exactly like Dad used to be, so consumed with your work that you can't see what's happening under your nose at home. *I'm* happening, Gordon. I'm growing and changing and learning that I'm not entirely stupid and uneducated, that I have a talent worth developing and –'

'That's happening to me too, can't you see?' he burst out. 'You're not the only one with a newly-discovered talent. I'm damn good at what I do, however low an opinion you may have of business.'

She said, almost too weary to speak, 'I know you're good at it. I'm not knocking that. I just don't like what it's doing to you, what it's making you want and need. They're not the things I want and need any more.'

There was a silence, then he said in a gruff voice she had not heard before, 'Maybe we ought to compare notes. We started off in such a hurry that we never had time to sort out priorities.'

'That's just psycho talk.'

'Bullshit! At least I'm trying, which is more than you are. This marriage means a lot to me.'

'You don't like failing, that's why.'

It was close to the bone. He thought, Is that why I want to keep it going? Or is it because I really like this girl I got landed with for a wife? She sat in a defensive huddle in the corner of the couch, not looking at him, fiddling unhappily with the arm rest. Her jeans bulged at the upper thigh where before there had been a smooth curve. Her blonde hair was dragged back into an elastic band, her face pale. She had lost the bloom of beach walks and the sea wind, become a hermit crab in an unwanted shell. He said, surprised at the revelation, 'Do you really dislike this house?'

'I loathe it.' Her voice was on the edge of tears. 'But even more, I loathe the way you yelled and shouted in the bathroom tonight over a child who's no different from the other kids around here, except that he's black. You've turned into someone I don't want to live with.'

'You can't live with anyone else, had you forgotten?' He slid out his trump card as he had been taught to negotiate in business, keeping an unexpected trick hidden up his sleeve. 'You're saddled with me, babe, so we'd better make the best of it.'

She remembered her father saying, 'I expect you to stick to your word too. And while you do, I'll help you when I can.' Having persevered with his marriage, he would not support her if she left her husband, and she had no way of earning a living. She picked at a loose thread on the arm rest. 'Go on.'

The bargaining lasted all evening. At the end of it they had agreed to move closer to the city, where she could take painting lessons again, and to put Rose into a nursery school where she would have other children to play with. 'But if Albertina comes with us, I won't ban Mfayedwa from coming to stay with her.' Sarah made her last condition belligerent with exhaustion.

Gordon shrugged. 'It's a mistake to encourage that sort of thing. I'm not as starry-eyed about blacks as you are.'

'Don't start again!'

'Pax.' He came to her, sandals flapping, and put both hands on her shoulders, trying not very hard to conceal a victor's smile. 'Ref's whistle. Come to bed now, babe.' He made love to her as though he were celebrating his prowess in battle, with scant concern for the conquered. Sarah held her tears back until he was asleep. He would not have understood them anyway.

Despite its lack of homely touches they made an unexpected profit on the sale of the Kottage, which gave Gordon his first sweet taste of a tax-free capital gain. David was conceived a few months later, after they had settled into a red-tiled bungalow with an established garden overlooking the sea in Durban North.

Sarah need not have bothered with her last condition. Mfayedwa came only once to visit his mother in the new house. Rose was happy to see him, but they did not play together again. She had made new friends at her nursery school, and he could not go on to the beach with them in the afternoons. The only black people allowed on the broad stretch of sand were nannies. Small boys with longing bitter-chocolate eyes had to wait on the gritty pavement with the tethered dogs and the green-painted oil drum rubbish bins and the WHITES ONLY/ALLEEN BLANKES signs.

Albertina sent him away to boarding school near Mtubatuba the next year.

8

Gordon walks down the middle of the rutted track that runs through the village, kicking up spurts of red dust with his velskoens. He walks with the assured tread of the landowner he has become in retirement: three hundred hectares of prime Natal Midlands on which two managers run a herd of Herefords and a small race-horse stud, and rotate the fodder crops used to feed them – lucerne, oats, mealies, teff. He is not a gentleman farmer who sits back and lets others do all the work, however. It is not in his temperament to rest on his laurels, or to allow employees less motivated than he is to make what he calls 'stupid bugger-ups' that cost him money. He keeps a tight grip on the farm's reins and is not afraid to get his hands dirty mending tractors or helping at the births of new calves and foals.

He is also used to commanding attention, even in his farm clothes. Walking from the hot sunlight through the public entrance of the government building into the main office, where an old-fashioned ceiling fan is revolving so slowly that it could be stirring thick soup rather than air, he takes off his hat and says, 'Where can I get some water, please?'

There is nobody there. Just a wooden counter worn smooth on the outside edge and several chairs like the one his wife is sitting on in the hut. On the wall is a calendar with a photograph of King Moshoeshoe beaming under a conical straw Basotho hat worn with third world panache above a well-cut navy suit and club-striped tie. The pages of the calendar have curled inwards and are spattered with specks of fly shit. Flies are clustered like ticks on the unpainted fibre-board ceiling, too lethargic to fly or even to crawl in the sweltering heat.

Gordon goes up to the counter and bends over it to peer down the corridor that runs off to the right and left, leading to other offices. 'Is there anybody here?' he calls, feeling like the traveller knocking on the moonlit door. 'I need some water, please.'

There is no answer, not even approaching footsteps. No voices, no telephones ringing, not even the typewriter he had heard earlier that morning. The building feels deserted, a cement-block and corrugated iron *Marie Celeste* abandoned by her crew of civil servants and doomed to sail the bare stony peaks of the Malutis for ever. He will have to find water himself.

He goes round the counter and down the right-hand corridor, looking for a door that could lead to a washroom or lavatory. Or kitchen; there must be a kitchen somewhere from which the steel trolley on wheels is pushed at morning and afternoon tea-times, clinking with thick white cups of strong tea that slops into the saucers. He was offered one on his earlier visit by a harassed woman with muddy eyes, who clucked her tongue saying, 'Shame, poor Rose, eh?' He had declined it, not wanting to listen to commiserations from a stranger and knowing how strong and sickly-sweet it would be. He is sorry now that he didn't ask for a jug of water instead.

He pushes open a likely door and walks into a small canteen where people are sitting on both sides of a long metal table, eating phuthu and stew from enamel plates. There is a stainless steel urn seething in the corner, and a smell of meat that has been kept too long before being cooked.

To the double row of masticating faces turned towards him, Gordon says, 'Could I have a jug of cold water, please?'

The official he spoke to earlier, the one he asked for ice, looks up and says, 'I already told you, we have no possibility of a fridge here.' The rest continue to eat as though he is not there.

'Could I have some tap water, then?' Gordon tries not to let his impatience and irritation show. He is not used to begging.

'Over there.' The official waves towards a stone sink with two taps, but shows no sign of getting up. Except for the woman who had offered him tea, who looks up and smiles, none of the others acknowledge Gordon's presence. The only sounds are the clink of cutlery on enamel and the vibrating hum of the urn.

He goes over to the sink and looks round for something to carry water in. There is a brown teapot standing on the draining board, which he checks inside and then swills out and fills from the tap marked C, though the water running out is as warm as blood. When he turns back carrying the teapot in one hand and one of the white cups and his hat in the other, all the heads are bent over their plates again.

He feels the violent anger which he has been suppressing all morning out of concern for Sarah explode like a grenade in his chest, and bursts out, 'Thanks for bloody nothing!'

One by one they stop eating, look up at him and grow still. The woman who had offered him tea says quietly, 'We are all sad for them, can't you see? You are not the only one. Rose was like our daughter.' There are tears in her muddy eyes.

'Yet you didn't protect her!'

'From your people, who cross any border they feel like with assault rifles, to kill who they like?' The official's voice has an answering anger. 'Can mud walls stop bullets? We are not the murderers here!' He was risen from the bench he has been sitting on, and strains forward across the metal table.

'I didn't say you were! But my daughter came here to help you, and what thanks does she get?' Gordon is shouting now. 'A death sentence!'

'It is not our fault!'

'I'm not talking about whose fault it is! It's too late for that. She's dead, man! Dead!'

'This is shameful.' The woman who had offered him tea gets up and walks round the table until she is between them. 'Stop, now.'

'She's lying dead in a hut with flies at the window and a dirty sheet over her legs. How can you people sit here eating?' Gordon is choking with the frustration of not being able to do anything about his daughter's torn body, or to ease his wife's anguish, except fetch water. In his head fumes the thought, If this had happened at home, the police would have sorted things out hours ago. But what do you expect in a country run by blacks?

'I told you before, we have already telephoned for the undertaker. We are not responsible for the fact that he does not come.' The official is still leaning over the table, looking as though he wants to pick it up and hurl it at Gordon.

'Vans are not available at this moment, Mr Kimber. You will have to be patient.' The woman comes closer to him and puts her brown hand on his deeply tanned arm. It is one of the ironies of sunny South Africa that they are almost the same colour, give or take a shade.

'But the heat,' he says, and finds himself pleading after all, 'the heat in that hut is terrible. I'm afraid they'll – they'll –'

'We will try to arrange another extension cord and a second fan,' she says. 'And we will telephone through to Maseru again when the exchange opens after lunch. People have to eat, you know.' Close up, he can see that her eyes have the yellowish-brown look of chronic liver disease. 'We are the living.'

'Yes. Well, thank you. I appreciate your concern.' Gordon is beginning to feel embarrassed by his outburst. It has led to an undignified scene with a black man in which he, a white guest in the black man's country, has been shown up badly. He half turns towards the table of silent people. 'Sorry. It's just been too much.'

The official glares his passionate dislike, but sits down again with an angry thump. Several of the others murmur in Sesotho, looking at him sadly, and he sees that he has mistaken their sorrow for indifference.

Back in the empty main office, he rests the cup for a moment on the counter while he puts on the green felt hat with its incongruously jaunty guinea fowl feather. The sweat-drenched headband feels cold on the skin of his forehead. He picks up the cup again and goes out into the hammering heat.

High above the village, so high that only the keenest eye can pick them out, five dark bird-specks are planing in wide slow circles. Death is never a secret kept for long in Africa.

In the hut with the body of her daughter, Sarah is remembering the first child she mourned.

David was born two weeks before Rose's fifth birthday at the end of 1961. That was the year John Fitzgerald Kennedy was inaugurated President of the United States, the year of the Berlin Wall, the Eichmann trial, Yuri Gagarin and Alan Shepherd soaring in space, thalidomide babies, and the evacuation of Tristan da Cunha because of a volcanic eruption. It was also the year the Union of South Africa fulfilled a long-held Afrikaner dream by spurning the Commonwealth (and its members' criticisms of the 1960 Sharpeville shootings) to become a republic.

The new State President, C. R. 'Blackie' Swart, wore a black top hat and a blue, white and orange sash over his dark suit as he addressed the nation from the steps of the Palace of Justice in Church Square, Pretoria, flanked by Dr and Mrs Verwoerd.

Few of the cheering crowd were aware that their immensely dignified new head of state had once acted in a Hollywood cowboy movie. The three-day stay-at-home campaign organised by the African Action Council under the leadership of Nelson Mandela fizzled out everywhere except in the Johannesburg area.

David's birth brought Sarah's mother to the nursing home with an expensive model train set and a stiff smile that hid her trepidation. 'I'm sorry it's been so long, Sarah,' she said.

'I'm glad you've come.' Sarah burst into tears.

But they were not easy together, though they both tried hard to pretend things were back to normal. It was like smashing a porcelain cup, Sarah thought. The integral strength of their bond had been broken and no matter how carefully they tried to patch and glue it, the cracks still showed.

Her mother had become Chairman of several charity committees and a bridge fanatic who played five afternoons a week. Sarah learned that her father had a new secretary who lived in a smart flat on the Esplanade near the Durban Club, which provided him with an excuse for being absent from home on certain evenings. Yet the marriage persisted with a surface amity that made her wonder if love had ever been part of it. Maybe it's mutual possessions that really count, she thought, and that huge house and all their beautiful things hold them together.

David was a chesty baby who seemed to have a continual cold, even in Durban's midsummer heat. Rose adored him, and had to be restrained from picking him up every few minutes. 'Can I hold him, Mum?' she would beg, longing to play with a real doll that moved and smiled and blew bubbles with his mouth.

To make feeding times less fraught with refusals, Sarah would ask Albertina to distract Rose by taking her out for a walk, or into the garden to splash in the blow-up plastic paddling pool. David was a much more difficult baby than Rose had been, fretful and colicky, waking often during the night and draining all Sarah's energy. Sometimes just sitting on the veranda looking at the sea seemed to be too much effort. Her easel gathered dust on top of the wardrobe in the bedroom. She had never been more grateful to have help in her home.

Albertina's feet had fallen arches and hurt when she stood ironing for too long, or had to walk too far. She preferred to sit with her crochet work watching Rose play rather than go on the long rambles Rose had enjoyed with Doris. She had a compensating gift, however, that made her the nanny Rose would remember best: a genius for storytelling.

With the child tucked into the crook of her arm, Albertina would recount in a soft voice the many stories her grandmother had told her, stories about wild animals that talked and the ways of nature and the things she had done as a little girl. Sometimes the whole afternoon would go by in stories. One of Rose's favourites, which she had to repeat often, was the one about the young Zulu girl who had tricked a notorious mamba which bit passersby on the head, by walking underneath the tree where it lay in wait with a pot of boiling phuthu on her head. Another was the story of the crocodiles, which Albertina swore was true.

'In the olden days,' she would begin while Rose pulled the brown arm closer round her, 'there was one time in the year when the big chief of the Umfolozi Valley would make a sacrifice to the crocodiles.'

'What's a sacrifice, Tina?' Rose would ask.

'You know,' Albertina would say, rather embarrassed by the bloodthirsty practice now that she was a Christian. 'When they pick one girl to give to the crocodiles to make them happy. So this way they will not eat anybody else going down to the river to wash clothes, or to get water.'

'Was it always a girl?' Rose would ask with a delicious shudder.

'For sure, a girl,' Albertina would say, mouth pursed and steel spectacles glittering. 'Those crocodiles, they don't like tough-meat boys. Nyaniso, is true what I say. They like nice soft girls like you and me, those crocodiles.' She would tremble then, remembering a glistening mud-brown snout that had surfaced once next to some reeds while she was dipping a paraffin tin into the river for water, and her heart-clutching terror before scrambling in panic up the bank.

'So each and every year,' she would go on after a moment, 'the people make a big party with plenty of meat and beer, and then they walk up the Umfolozi River to where the two rivers join into one big river –'

'The Black Umfolozi and the White Umfolozi,' Rose would prompt, picturing the black river purling over its rocks like molten liquorice, and the white river like milk being poured from a jug.

'The people walk singing and dancing, with the cowskin

drums making a big noise Boom! Boom! Boom! and the men smacking their fighting sticks on their shields, and all the women making like –' Albertina would break off to give a high-pitched ululation from the back of her throat that would make Rose's skin crawl. She could almost feel the procession winding through the bush along the riverbank: the dust clouds from trampling feet, the sun burning through the leaves, the people singing loudly to cover their fear, as she did when she ran from the bathroom down the dark passage to her bedroom at night.

'Until they get to the place where the two rivers join.' Albertina would lower her voice at this point to a thrilling whisper. 'And there they are. Too much crocodiles, Rosie, boiling up in the water like green beans cooking in a pot. Just like green beans, only much bigger. And much more –'

'Ugly!' Rose would burst out. This was the best part, even better than the great grey-green greasy Limpopo River that Sarah read about sometimes. 'With their mouths opening and closing, and all their horrible pointy teeth showing, and their horrible scaly tails swishing backwards and forwards –'

'And then they give the nice fat girl to the crocodiles and they all go home again.' Albertina would gloss over this part, having seen when she was nine what a crocodile had done to a herdboy who had not been able to resist the lure of the river one brutally hot day.

'Tell about when they tricked the crocodiles,' Rose would say into the silence.

After a moment Albertina would go on, 'But when the white men they come, the English and the Boers and the missionaries, they tell the chief, "This is no good, Nkosi! You can't give all these nice fat girls to the crocodiles, what a waste," and make the chief stop. So, no more parties.'

'No more parties,' Rose would sigh, thinking of ice-creams and jelly oranges and the grinning clown cake Sarah had made for her fifth birthday.

'No more parties,' Albertina would confirm, thinking of the days spent brewing beer in calabashes, and the long bloody task of slaughtering and cutting up an ox.

'Until one day many, many years after, a white hunter comes to the Umfolozi Valley. And he talks to the people there and they tell him the story of the girls and the crocodiles, and he says to the new chief, who is the grandson of the old chief, "These

66

crocodiles, Nkosi, how much you think they remember? Let us make a party for them once more, to see what will happen. But not using any girls, of course," he says quick before the chief gets the wrong idea.

' "OK," says the chief, "me too, I like to see." So he says to the people, "Let us make a big party for the crocodiles, to see what those spook-a-spooks will do." "Aikona!" all the people say. "Nothing doing, Nkosi. We need our daughters for their lobola, their bride price, not to make tasty snacks for crocodiles." So now the chief is getting cross, and he's shouting, "What kind of a no-good chief you think I am, to waste our nice fat girls on the crocodiles? I'm not attending mission school up to Standard Six for nothing! No, me and this white man here, we just want to trick the crocodiles to think we are giving them another party, to see what they will do. He says he will give us an ox to slaughter for the occasion. It will be a completely free party, my people. This is what kind of chief you have, a man who organises free parties for you. All you have to do is make the beer." '

'And then what happened, Tina?' Rose would ask, knowing full well. This was the best thing about favourite stories, that you knew what was going to happen. She would turn her head up then to watch Albertina's face as it took on the look of revelations about to unfold that she wore on Sundays to church.

'And so they make a big party and they go shouting and singing up the river to where the two rivers join, smacking the drums Boom! Boom! Boom! and making plenty of noise. My grandmother was there, Rosie, and she told me this her very own self. Her heart is beating here inside,' Albertina clamped her free hand dramatically to the middle of her chest, 'like a mad dog as they get closer and closer, closer and closer, with the chief and the white hunter walking in front and all the kids running and laughing behind. Until they get to the join in the river, and then everybody goes dead quiet.' Her voice would drop so low that Rose had to snuggle closer. 'Dead quiet. Because you know what they see?'

'Crocodiles,' Rose would whisper.

'Crocodiles,' Albertina would breathe. 'Too much crocodiles. Crocodiles like you never see before, boiling up in the water like green beans in a pot, waiting for the nice fat girl. For all those years, the crocodiles are waiting for the noise of singing and drums and the nice fat girl to come. Like Ndhlovu, the elephant, they never forget. They wait there even now, some of the people they say.'

'Even *now?*'

'Even now. And that is the story of the crocodiles,' Albertina would end up, hugging the child before freeing her arm with a brisk, 'Now I must get back to my kitchen and make some tea for Mummy. You play nicely by yourself, OK?'

'I'm not a nice fat girl am I, Tina?' Rose cast an anxious downward glance at the small round pot belly pushing out her sun-dress.

'Never.' Albertina gave a decisive shake of her head. 'Not in a hundred years, Rosie. Those crocodiles, they take one look at you and they run away double quick, s'true's bob.'

From the bedroom window, Sarah would watch the two of them sitting on the white bench near the amatungulu hedge, Albertina talking and Rose listening with her thumb in her mouth, taking it out only when she needed to answer a question. Sarah had asked the doctor about the thumb-sucking on one of his frequent house visits to David, but he'd said, 'Oh, don't worry about it. She'll stop when she no longer feels the need of it. At the moment it's a sign that she still wants attention, and an excellent antidote against jealousy of the new baby.'

'But what about buck teeth?' Sarah's were inclined to curve outwards more than they should.

'Highly unlikely,' the doctor said, but he was wrong. Whether it was because she sucked her thumb in bed at night until she was ten or because of the tendency inherited from Sarah, Rose had to wear orthodontic braces for two excruciating years in high school.

But that was a later worry. David at a year old had continual chest trouble, sometimes wheezing so badly at night that Sarah would take him into the bathroom, turn the hot taps on and sit with him in the warm steam that made his breathing easier. The doctor talked about asthma and advised them to buy a croup kettle. It was only when David was nearly two that he was tested at Addington Hospital and confirmed as having cystic fibrosis, by which time his lungs had been badly damaged.

'It's an inherited disorder,' they were told. 'You must both have recessive CF genes. It causes the mucus in the lungs to thicken and become glutinous so it is hard to expel, distorting and damaging the air sacs. His life expectancy –' Sarah's hand tightened in Gordon's '– is not much over twelve years. If that.'

'Twelve years.' It went on echoing in her head like a prison sentence being called out in court. 'Twelve years – twelve years – twelve years –' until she thought of Rose with sudden dread. 'What about our daughter? Could she develop it too?'

'No.' The specialist grew pedantic to cover his distress at always having to be the one who told the parents. 'People can't develop it. They're born with it. Your daughter is only affected in so far as she has two chances in three of carrying the recessive gene too. It will be imperative for her to have genetic counselling before she marries. The incidence of carriers in the white population in this country is one in twenty-five, which means that statistically speaking, one marriage in sixteen hundred will involve two carriers. Of these marriages, one in four children may be born with cystic fibrosis, as David was. I'm sorry.'

They were stunned for weeks, all through David's initial lengthy treatment in hospital, the demonstrations by physiotherapists showing how to treat him at home, and the endless journeys to and from hospital. 'You were right. We should have found a bigger flat instead of moving to Westville,' Gordon said late one night as they followed the familiar road back to Durban North. 'We could have walked to Addington then.'

'It's no comfort to have been right. We couldn't know this would happen.' She lapsed again into the withdrawn silence that seemed to have absorbed all her joy in being alive, all the intensity of feeling she had tried to distil in delicate strokes of her sable brushes on canvas. She was like a shell that had lost its mysterious sea-sound.

David came home with a carload of medical paraphernalia supplied by the hospital: face masks and antibiotic sprays and a padded A-frame over which he had to be bent twice a day while they pounded his bony little back to make him cough the mucus up. He was a thin, brave, stoic child with steady grey eyes and the hunched-in look about his chest that lung sufferers get.

Rose's feelings for him alternated between motherliness and resentment. Some days she would happily play nurse, bringing him orange juice and biscuits on her dolls' tea tray and playing games with him for hours. But there were other days when she wanted to run and shout and swim with her friends far away from his small stuffy room. Days when she hated the sound of his wretched coughing and his sad little calls of, 'Rosie, play with me.'

She became exasperated with her parents' increasing inattention to her needs, with the way they said, 'Very good, darling,' when she did well at school, not really noticing her marks. Desperate for an audience, she would read stories to David in the afternoons when Albertina was off and Sarah was resting; he was a rapt listener and never interrupted.

Sarah was grateful for the break. She had not found the energy to start painting again. David's needs, the twice-daily physiotherapy and the clinic visits and the vigilant nursing, took up nearly all her time and strength. She was twenty-five, and felt fifty. Not caring what she ate, she put on weight and began to solidify like the matrons in doek-covered curlers who forged through the new supermarket down the road, scattering lesser shoppers with their formidably loaded trolleys. Her world contracted to David and Rose and Albertina, with Gordon a wandering planet whose orbit intersected with hers fitfully.

He had been promoted to manager of a bigger department, a position which rated a company car, so Sarah was able to use the Morris during the day. Ambitious as ever, he worked long hours and came home late. He and Sarah had become almost strangers, communicating only when they needed to discuss the children, or money. He was too busy and too intent on the next promotion to look for romantic involvement elsewhere. For David he felt more sorrow than love. Gordon was a logical man, and logic demanded where the percentage was in putting emotional capital into someone who would not be around for long? He hoped it didn't show in the way he greeted Rose, the child who would live.

There were many times when David, in crisis, had to be rushed back to hospital. They became accustomed to his sudden acute setbacks, his weeks of intensive antibiotic treatment and his long slow recoveries. So accustomed that when he died at the age of six during a severe bout of pneumonia, the shock was absolute. It was as though a giant hand had reached down and torn a black hole in their lives.

Her gaze turned inward now, Sarah remembers the small white coffin lying in a gash of red earth in Stellawood Cemetery, and Gordon pushing away the man in the obsequious black suit, saying, 'Give me the spade. I'll bury my own.' Except for the sound of clods falling on hollow wood, she does not remember anything more about David's funeral or the months that followed. She knows, because Gordon has told her, of the time spent in a nursing home for acute depression, and she has a vague memory of helping Albertina pack up the household for their move to Johannesburg, but that is all.

It's not fair! she thinks now, feeling a first rush of anger under the numbing sorrow. I've had to bury one child already. Not fair that it should happen again!

Prickles of sweat break out all over her body. The face she turns to Gordon as he pushes the door open is furious with accusation.

9

He takes his hat off and says, 'I've brought you some water,' holding out the teapot.

But she wants answers, not water. 'Why?' Her face is red with heat and sweat and anger. 'Why both our children? Couldn't we have been left with one?'

'I don't know why.' He pushes the door shut with his elbow. It is only marginally cooler in the hut than outside in the full blast of the sun. The fan that stands on the floor next to the partly sheeted bodies swinging first one way and then the other moves the air sluggishly, but does nothing to cool it. He tries not to look in their direction as he goes towards the chair where she is sitting.

Some of the silver hair has come loose from the bun and droops against her cheek, giving her a dishevelled look. She flares up at him, 'It's retribution, that's why! Our family is the scapegoat. We've been chosen to pay for all the white sins that have been committed. But why us? Why not the real sinners, the ones who make the lunatic laws and shoot people in the back and imprison children? We've never done anything like that. We never even voted for them. It's not fair!' The words spill from her mouth like prickly pears, barbed with fine needles of pain.

He says, bending over her, 'Sarah, you can't go looking for a reason to this kind of madness. You've got to believe it just happened, and Rose was in the way.' Still bent, he pours some of the blood-warm water from the teapot into the white cup he holds in the other hand. 'Have some water.'

'I don't want any!' She turns her body away from him like a petulant child. 'I'd choke.'

'Please, babe. Please drink some. You've got to keep drinking in this heat.'

'Don't mother-hen me! I'll drink when I need to.' Her face is

72

scarlet. Because of her weight, her blood pressure is higher that it should be and she has had two dizzy spells recently. Firming his voice, he says, 'Don't be silly. Here. Drink. You'll be in trouble otherwise.'

She hesitates a moment as if trying to decide whether protest is worth the effort, then meekly turns back to him, accepts the cup and drinks. It is a sign of their finally mellowing relationship that he does not see her capitulation as a victory, but merely thinks, That's good. Now I must get her to lie down.

But she is too deep in memory to hear his suggestion. The warm metallic taste of the water has reminded her of the water she and Rose had to drink from the sloshing glass container in the corridor of the train up to Johannesburg, after Gordon had been promoted to head office. The train journey to a new house in a new town three months after David's death had cauterised the wound, but not healed it. It would be a year before she picked up her paintbrushes again.

Albertina helped Sarah to pack up the Durban North house in a betrayed silence, unable to understand why she could not go with them. Gordon had applied at the Bantu Affairs office for permission for Albertina to travel up and work for them in Johannesburg, only to be told, 'Ag sorry, we can't give it, sir. All these girls want a Jo'burg pass, but there's too many of them already out of work up there. We daren't let any more in.'

'But she's been with us for nearly nine years,' Gordon insisted. 'Doesn't that make her a special case?'

'Ten, and I could of done something maybe.' The Bantu Affairs official picked up a newly sharpened pencil and, very delicately, slid it through his hair to scratch the place that had been itching all morning. 'But nine? Forget it. Sorry, hey?'

'That's a highly unreasonable attitude!' Gordon had had experience in dealing with underlings by now, and knew how to ginger his indignation with the hauteur of a superior who will not be messed around with. 'The woman in question is a trusted servant, not just anybody. I'd like to take this matter further.'

But he had not yet had enough experience with the civil service, or the laws that were beginning to keep black people more and more confined to their home areas – unless, of course, their labour was needed somewhere. 'You can take this matter up as far as you like, sir.' The official gave him a smile with hard edges as he carefully withdrew the pencil. 'But you won't get that permission, believe me. Jo'burg is closed this year to applications from Natal female Bantu, finish and klaar.'

Gordon went a week ahead to look for a new house, and Sarah's parents took her and Rose to the station soon after the removal van arrived. Albertina could not believe they were really leaving her behind until they said goodbye. Sarah hugged her and whispered, 'Thank you so much for everything.' Rose, twelve now and almost the same height as the capable little woman who had looked after her since she was three, sobbed, 'Goodbye, Tina. I'll never forget the crocodiles, never.'

Albertina's voice failed her for the first time since they had known her. She stood forlornly on the pavement shaking her head in helpless loss as they drove away. Her severance pay had been generous and Sarah had arranged another job for her, but she would never quite trust another employer. She was thinking, White people! You work for them your best, you look after their kids like your own, and for thanks they just go away one day and leave you behind.

Whenever she heard a domestic worker boast about being called 'part of the family' after that, she would laugh and say, 'Only until that time they don't need you any more. Then you are rubbish to be thrown away.'

Rose had not expected to like the big bad city of Johannesburg, but the koppie behind their new home in a northern suburb changed her mind.

A koppie is a small rocky hill sticking up out of the veld. This one had always provided good shelter and a high vantage point: for the early men who hunted with stone axes, for the bushmen who hunted with bows and poisoned arrows and, much later, for the men who travelled in ox-wagons and hunted with guns. Seldom for women, however, since there was no water and very little fuel there. Scrubby bushes, aloes and a single wild olive tree were the only plants that found a root-hold in the eruption of sandstone rocks that reared up like a sudden infection of the earth's crust, weathered by time. It was a place to steer by, a place to stop and rest for a while in the scant shade before moving on to camp by the reed-fringed river half a day's walk further on.

Then gold was discovered, and the mining camps grew and spread into towns and cities; a more virulent, man-made infection that metastasised into suburbs and shops and factories and schools where children were taught things of extraordinary irrelevance to the soil they walked on or the gradually souring air they breathed.

In the 'thirties, the land round the koppie was surveyed, mapped and carved up on a drawing board into equal-sized segments. Earth movers and graders scraped a perfectly circular road round its base, dynamiting a magnificent stone buttress that would have interfered with its symmetry. In the sentiment of the times, all the roads in the area were given names associated with British royalty.

The wedge-shaped pieces of land that sloped up from Buckingham Circle towards the koppie were sold to a developer who built on them identical tile-roofed three-bedroomed houses with small front and back stoeps whose red granolithic floors had to be buffed daily by servants on their hands and knees. Each prim home faced the street, ignoring both the view and the sun which would have warmed them in winter. Had the houses been built forty years later, they would have climbed much higher up the koppie to incorporate its boulders in dramatic brick and glass living rooms, and the stunted bushes and aloes in a rash of indigenous rockeries.

In Buckingham Circle, however, it was the kitchens and screened back stoeps, the washing lines, dog kennels, laundries and servants' quarters that faced the koppie. The developer, an enlightened man for his time, was proud of his servants' quarters which he had equipped unusually handsomely with stone sinks, running cold water and squat lavatories whose porcelain foot rests were flush with the cement floor. 'They're just not used to using white people's toilets, lady,' he explained earnestly to the only woman who asked to see them.

The new residents of Buckingham Circle planted privet and hakea hedges all round their properties which grew so densely that in time the koppie almost disappeared from sight, and certainly from the minds of the people who lived round it. Life was focused on front rooms and neat front gardens, with only occasional forays into the back yards where the servants gossiped and ate sitting with legs stretched out in the sunshine, throwing their scraps to the dogs.

Buckingham Circle was considered rather a good address for a long while. But fashions change, and the houses were not designed for easy alteration to a more open-plan style of living. The roof tiles couldn't be matched. The solidly built distempered walls resisted hammer blows. The back yards were too small to accommodate even a modest swimming pool and braai area. Families with children tended to move away to more spacious gardens and houses with picture windows, though many of the older residents stayed, unwilling to uproot their prized roses and their elderly dogs.

When the Kimbers moved into Buckingham Circle, Rose was the only child in the street.

She soon became used to being alone. Sarah had begun to suffer from migraines, and spent a lot of time in her bedroom with the curtains drawn. Rose came home from school to a quiet house except for the sounds of the new maid, Agnes, making the supper, which she would put on the table at seven when Gordon's automatic-transmission Ford came zooming up the short driveway. Sarah's lassitude gave him a good excuse to work late in the grey tower where the shipping company had its offices.

It was 1968, a troubled year. Martin Luther King and Robert Kennedy were assassinated, Czechoslovakia was invaded and students were on the rampage everywhere. Jackie Kennedy married Aristotle Onassis, the first manned orbit of the moon took place and, closer to home, Jim Fouché became State President. Rose was in her first year of high school. The move to Johannesburg had helped her to get over David's death, but it did not appear to be working for Sarah. When her English teacher discussed *La Belle Dame Sans Merci* with the class, she recognised her mother at once in Keats's Knight at Arms, 'alone and palely loitering'. Sarah was sad and withdrawn and had not unpacked her painting things; David's short, attention-consuming life seemed to have numbed both her feelings and her need to express them on canvas.

Rose filled her time with library books, desultory homework, and dreaming about how famous she would be when she grew up. In an old ledger Gordon had given her with 'Journal' in gold letters on the cover, she kept detailed notes on what it was like to be an unheralded genius trapped in a suburban backwater. She had no special friends; the school was in a newer suburb, and her classmates lived too far away for regular visiting. All they talked about anyway was boyfriends and makeup and who was going to bioscope with whom on Saturday. Not knowing any boys, Rose managed to convince herself that friends like that were far too trivial for a famous person-to-be.

Most afternoons at four she would have tea and biscuits with Agnes on the back stoep steps. Agnes was a large, bossy woman with a face like a friendly potato and heavy legs knotted with varicose veins. Her conversation centred rather boringly on her children as she sat squinting down at the pillowcases she embroidered to sell in the township for extra money. Rose would talk about school or read in companionable silence, dipping biscuits in her tea and leaving trails of drops across her shorts.

Like the rest of the Buckingham Circle residents, she didn't really see the koppie until the day its winter shadow crept earlier than usual across the yard and crawled over her bare feet, blocking off the sun.

Shading her eyes as she looked up, she said, 'That koppie's quite high. Have you ever been up there?'

'Nobody goes there.' Agnes was scornful. 'It's nothing there. Just big stones and rubbish.'

'Kanchenjunga on my back doorstep.' Rose had recently been reading her way through Arthur Ransome, and was deeply envious of the way English children could roam the countryside, having adventures. Gordon would not allow her to walk round Buckingham Circle by herself, let alone ride her bike to her nearest friend's house. 'You never know who's hanging around in the street,' he said, though the only people Rose ever saw there were Agnes's friends, who sat together on the grass verges in the afternoons.

'I wouldn't even need to use ropes,' she mused.

Alerted by the tone in her voice, Agnes said sharply, 'You don't want to go up there, my girl.' She put her embroidery down and gave her head an emphatic shake. 'Never.'

'Why not? I mean, is it dangerous?'

'Not so much dangerous.' Anges's forehead crumpled into a network of frowns. 'But is not a good place to go by yourself. Where there's stones, there's also snakes. Or maybe you fall down and get a blood knee. Remember what I say, you hear?'

But Rose was gazing upwards to where the setting sun haloed jutting black rocks and a single wild olive tree. A sense of daring would be an essential quality for an unheralded genius, and her life at the moment was singularly deficient in adventure. A climb up the koppie would fulfil many needs.

Next day after school she changed into jeans and tackies, and armed herself with her father's knob-headed walking stick in case of snakes. As soon as Agnes had gone next door to spend her off-hour with her friend Beauty, Rose crossed the yard to the narrow alley between Agnes's small dark room and the back hedge.

The hedge was well past its prime, and in parts had died back to expose jagged fragments of the wire mesh fence that had once marked the boundary of civilisation. She wriggled through easily, despite a rusty wire that scratched a long white scribble on her arm.

Agnes was right about the rubbish. Banked up behind the hedge was an ugly midden of rusting tins, garden debris and sorghum beer cartons, thickly overgrown with khaki weed and fat fleshy stinkblaar. Beyond it, though, was an unexpected belt of tall veld grass, greenish-blonde and glistening where it caught the sunlight. Rose pulled up a sweet-tasting stalk to suck, wanting to lie down on her back and look up at the sky as she had as a little girl, through curving green leaves and heavy seed-heads and softly ticking insects to where the clouds billowed against an infinity of blue.

But she had come to climb the koppie, and sternly put childish thoughts out of her mind. The rocks began where the veld grass ended, in a tumble of small frost-split boulders. The going was easy at first with no frightening rustles to make her grasp the walking stick tighter. When she reached the bigger boulders she found a sort of pathway between them, though it soon petered out and she had to climb, grasping with her free hand for finger holds in the hot rough rock, glad of the firm grip her rubber-soled tackies gave her. Towards the top a sheer face reared above her, and wondering what to do, she looked left. There was a ledge in the sandstone that had been invisible from below, and flaring back from it, a shallow sandy-floored cave.

The jolt of delight Rose felt made up for all the solitary afternoons, all the envious reading of other children's adventures. Breathless and sweating, she worked her way over to the ledge and poked at the debris in the cave with the walking stick. No sign of snakes. No bats. A few small spiders. A lot of busy black ants going in and out of an anthill.

It had been occupied before, she saw at once. There was a ring of blackened stones cupping a long-dead fire, a bed of dry grey grass in the corner, and the faint outline of an eland drawn in red pigment where the roof sloped down.

She felt from the beginning, however, that the cave was her

own secret refuge. The inspection over, she climbed down the koppie and toiled up again with some rags and the balding hand broom that had been banished to the laundry cupboard. That first day she cleaned and swept it out as though the tokoloshes that Agnes spoke about in knowing whispers were after her. In fact, Agnes would have been astonished to see how hard she worked, being used to spending a good part of her day picking up Rose's clothes and books and cleaning her room.

When she had finished, she tucked the brush into a sheltered crevice where it would not get wet if it rained. Next day she would bring up some cushions and a blanket and turn her cave into a real house, a secret private eyrie where she could read and write in her Journal and dream undisturbed of fame.

So circumspectly did she furnish and visit her new hide-away that even Agnes did not find out about it until she came back early from a Sunday afternoon church meeting to catch Rose pushing her way through the hedge behind the dust-bins with a thermos of tea and a whole new packet of ginger-nuts.

'Where you going, my girl?' she said in a bossy voice honed by hymns and redemption.

'Just, oh, just up there. Sort of.' Rose tried to hide the incriminating evidence behind her back.

'You going up there on the koppie when I tell you no?' Agnes bustled towards her.

'Honestly, it's quite safe, please let me go.'

'Aikona, Miss Rose. Your mother will be mad with me! And your father too!' Agnes seemed to fill the narrow alley like the wrath of God. 'How can I look after you nicely when you not under my eye?'

'Agnes, oh please, I've made a house up there and it's quite safe. *Please* don't stop me.' Rose was almost sobbing with the dread of losing it. 'It's my special place. Please don't tell anyone. Promise I'll be good.'

Agnes softened. Rose was as pale as a sheet. The pity she felt for the child's sedate friendless life, so different from the noisy camaraderie of her children's township home, swelled in her throat. Sighing, she said, 'OK, my girl. Where is it, this house of yours? Come there with me so I can see for myself, eh?'

Agnes gave her consent on the strict understanding that Rose was not to do anything dangerous, *ever*, and with the fervent hope that she would never have to climb up there again. Her heart had been thumping quite alarmingly by the time she reached the cave. But it seemed innocuous enough, and was well within calling distance of the back yard. There was no evidence of snakes, and since the koppie was almost totally barren and had been surrounded by suburban gardens for a good many years, she presumed they had all been killed with garden spades by now. It was quite a small koppie after all, she told herself, just a pile of rocks really. The child could not possibly come to any harm other than grazing her knee in a fall, and it would keep her happy and occupied. She, Agnes, would keep a close eye on her comings and goings.

Rose climbed up every day during the hours Agnes permitted, furnishing her cave bit by bit with tomato-box bookshelves, tea things, old cushions and a pair of binoculars 'borrowed' from Gordon, which she used to scan the suburban landscape and, more particularly, the back yards that lay exposed below. In a few months she learned more about the way people live than she would learn in years to come, and it all went into her Journal.

She learned that Beauty's husband slipped into her room late every afternoon and left early the next morning, unknown to her employers. She learned that Mr Louw two doors away slipped into his maid's room every Saturday afternoon while his wife was out playing tennis, and understood at last why the maid's baby had skin the colour of creamy coffee when hers was the deep brown once called nigger. She learned the bitterness of women who clean and clean homes that can never be theirs, however hard they work and save and hope. It was a different Buckingham Circle to the one she had known, and she filled page after page of her Journal. When writing palled, she would make tea with condensed milk and sit with her feet hanging over the ledge, reading or gazing out over her kingdom, dreaming of greatness.

The faint red eland on the roof painted by some long-dead bushman artist made her feel safe and protected. She thought a lot about him, and got books out of the library which explained how he had mixed and carried his paints. Sometimes she thought his friendly ghost must have come visiting while she was not there, so strongly did she feel the presence of someone else in the cave, some other dreamer who watched and wondered too.

So she was not so much surprised as vindicated when she climbed up to the cave one early spring afternoon to find a man lying there, fast asleep.

80

Very quietly, she crept on all fours along the rocky ledge to where she could see him better. He lay on the sand with his head on her cushions and his back huddled against the rock, a black man dressed in shabby clothes that smelled musty even at a distance. On his sockless feet were worn shoes too big for them. His mouth was open and his breath wheezed in and out as though he had a chest cold, or perhaps smoked a lot.

She sat back to study him, intent on writing an exact description of him into the Journal. It was quite possible that the nature of her genius was literary, and she would need all the true observations she could collect for the books she would one day write.

After a while she thought, I should be writing it down while he lies there, and moved cautiously towards the ledge where her Journal lay. The movement woke the man to a wary stillness, his breath caught in his throat, sparks of reflected light under his eyelids.

Rose said, quite reasonably she thought, under the circumstances, 'What are you doing in my cave?'

He sat up like an old man, keeping his back against the rock. Now that his face was turned towards the light, she saw that it was filmed with sweat and dragged down under the eyes and at the sides of the mouth with exhaustion, as though he had been running in the hot sun for a long time and started to melt.

'Your cave?' His voice was hoarse.

'Yes, mine. I keep it clean. I brought all these things up here. Of course it's mine.'

'Your cave.' He tried to laugh, but it became a bubbling cough that forced phlegm up into his mouth which he leaned over and spat on to the sand next to the cushions. It lay there obscenely quivering as he wiped his mouth with his hand and turned back to her.

'How can you do that?' she burst out, furious at the desecration.

'What, sleep in your cave or spit on your floor?' Now that he had coughed the phlegm out, his voice was clearer. He did not speak like Agnes as she had expected, but like Father Dunwoodie, with the same thin cold smile that was not amused.

'Spitting's disgusting, even Agnes says so.'

'Agnes being your maid-of-all-work, yes? If even a servant says it is disgusting, it must indeed be so. Therefore, I apologise.' He bent over and scooped up the phlegm with a handful of sand, throwing it past Rose and out over the ledge. 'See, it's gone now.'

Some of the sand had stung her arm. 'That doesn't make it undisgusting! That's just getting rid of the evidence.'

He gave a sarcastic laugh. 'A policeman's mentality already, and so young. It must be catching.' He shifted position to make himself more comfortable, keeping his back to the wall, and added, 'Are you the Byron reader, then?'

Rose was confused. Not only had the strange man taken over her cave, but his words were completely at odds with the dirty old clothes he was wearing. Only tramps and men looking for work off the street wore clothes like that; Agnes always gave them a cup of strong sweet tea before she sent them away, muttering 'Shame!' under her breath. And Rose had never heard a black man speak as though he were giving a church sermon.

'Who are you?' she demanded. 'Why are you dressed like that? And why are you sleeping in my cave?'

He sighed. 'And so the inquisition begins. Could we not discuss Byron instead?'

'If you don't tell me, I'll call Agnes.' Rose gestured down at the house. 'She's just down there. She told me to scream out loud if I ever wanted her, and she'd come double-quick.'

'If Agnes is the large woman I saw crossing the yard this morning, I doubt she'd make it in under twenty minutes, and I'd be gone before then. So what's the point? Rather we talk, Miss Rose.'

For the first time she felt a niggle of fear. 'How do you know my name?'

'It's written inside the cover of that book in your hands. Rose Kimber, 24 Buckingham Circle, Windsor View, Johannesburg, Transvaal, South Africa, The World.'

'You read my Journal – oh!' Rose jumped up, fear forgotten in the rage of invaded privacy. 'You had no right to do that! It's private! It's like reading other people's letters, only worse.'

The man put up his arm in mock defence. 'Please, don't tear me into little bits. Again I apologise. It was unforgivable, reading your private notebook. But I wanted to know the name of the person who had cleaned and furnished my cave so nicely.'

'Your cave?' She was ready to burst into tears at the thought of a stranger reading her inmost thoughts, and now he was claiming her secret place as well. 'But it's mine! I found it first!'

'And brushed away the ashes from my last fire, yes? You white people are all the same. Push everybody who gets in your way out of sight, and what's left is yours by default. QED.'

The anger in his voice was so much greater than hers that it stopped the threatening tears. 'There was a fire here once,' she admitted, 'but that was long ago. And if it was your fire, you weren't the first anyway. There's a bushman painting up there.'

'Of an eland, yes I know. I found this cave when I was about your age, you see. My mother was a servant down there like your Agnes, and I was permitted to visit her for one week at Christmas time, to be given my Christmas box.' The thin smile appeared again. 'One pound and a new shirt, with a bag of sweets and a cooldrink and some Christmas cake thrown in.'

'Is she still there?'

'Oh no. Died of a heart attack some years back. She was overweight, of course; ate too much putu and the cheap fatty meat you people so picturesquely call 'boy's meat'. But I thought of the cave when I needed somewhere to – stay for a few days. I hope you don't mind, as its new occupant,' he added formally.

'I mind about your reading my book. I mind that badly. It's very private.' She blushed, thinking of some of the things she had written.

'Look, I said I was sorry about that.' He leaned forward and patted the sand near her feet. 'Sit down, please, and let us talk like two civilised people. I'm sorry about sleeping in your place without asking, and I'm sorry about reading your book. But you write very well. It was hard to stop.'

'I do?' She sat down a little further away than he had indicated, feeling the blush deepen.

'It is the notebook of a sensitive person who observes and stores things away to use another day. You spend a lot of time by yourself, yes?'

'Well, yes. Up here sometimes. Reading on my bed some-times, or with Agnes. My mother's often sick.'

'No brothers or sisters?'

'No. I used to have a brother, but he died before we came here. I miss him quite a lot.'

He seemed to relax, settling his back against the cave wall and stretching his legs with their bare ankles and too-big shoes out in front. 'You wouldn't if you had as many brothers and sisters as I did. I could never get away by myself – until recently, that is.'

'Where do you come from?'

'Oh, Tembisa. Fort Hare. Wits University. Robben Island.' He gave her an enquiring look.

And then she knew, and knew that he wanted her to know. He was a terrorist on the run from the police. He was going to keep her there, holding her to ransom or as a hostage. She was transfixed by a surge of fright. What if he killed her to keep her quiet, then –'

'It's OK, Miss Rose,' he said softly, watching her. 'I am not a violent man, just another thinker with a big mouth. You're quite safe. I won't hurt you.'

'How do I know? You said –'

'Robben Island, yes? The barren place of seals where they condemn men to a lifetime of prison gardening and regrets. People don't escape from there, you know. It's too far to swim to the mainland, through dangerous currents. But they do complete their sentences.'

'You were let out?'

'I was, and then I opened my big mouth again and so –' he opened the mouth and gave a shout of laughter '– here I am, on my way to places north. I'm tired of seals and prison gardens. I want to live again.'

The laugh lifted the dragging lines of exhaustion on his face and she saw that he was much younger than he looked. Of course, tiredness makes people look old, she thought, seeing her mother's face in the darkened bedroom. And then, He must be hungry too, and thirsty. She said politely, 'Would you like some tea?'

'If it's not too much trouble.'

She fetched the basket she had brought up with her from the house and poured some out for him. 'Here you are. More condensed milk? Some biscuits? I don't really feel like any.' She handed him a brimming plastic mug with a teaspoon sticking out of it and the packet of biscuits she had been intending to eat, but kept a careful distance. What if he snatched her arm?

His nod of acceptance was understanding. 'Thanks. Yes to the biscuits, no to more milk.' He dunked and ate the biscuits first, swiftly, one after the other, then sipped the tea with closed eyes. When he passed the mug back, she saw that his hand

84

shook like an old man's. 'That was good. I don't suppose there's a drop more?'

It was strange. They could have been sitting on the chintz sofa in the living room sipping out of her mother's best porcelain teacups, instead of on a sandy cave floor drinking out of plastic mugs. Mrs Dunwoodie had said exactly the same thing when she had come visiting after they moved in: 'I don't suppose there's a drop more in the pot, Rose dear?'

After three cups, he patted his stomach and said, 'Thank you kindly, my friend. Best tea I ever had. I appreciate the fact that your hospitality overcame your fear; it's a comforting thought that I'll take with me. Maybe there's hope for us all in this country yet.'

'You're not staying here, then?'

'Hardly. The police dogs are well trained, and I smell rather too much of *me*, if you see what I mean. No access to soap and water for some while.'

Rose swallowed. 'Can I help?'

'You've decided to trust me now that we've broken bread together, so to speak? Yes, you can. By going home and pretending you've never seen me. I don't exist. I'm a chimera. Can I trust you not to say a word to anybody about seeing me here?'

She blurted, 'Please tell me first, are you a real terrorist?'

'Terrorist. There's a thought.' The thin smile was back. 'But I have never carried a gun. I don't believe in killing people. My crime in the eyes of this government is to believe that I am as good as any white man. Or woman.' He inclined his head to her. 'Wouldn't "political refugee" be a more appropriate term?'

Rose blushed again. 'I didn't mean to insult you, I'm sorry.'

He nodded. 'Apologies accepted. Now we've got that little point cleared up, you promise you won't tell anybody about me?'

'I promise, cross my heart.' She was thinking, If the police really are after him, I won't be able to write anything in my Journal in case they find it. I'll just have to store it all up in my mind. Concentrating on his face so she would remember every detail of it, she said, 'I won't tell anyone, honest. But can I write about meeting you one day?'

'Done. It's a bargain. Your silence in return for permission to publish an exclusive interview with a wanted person – but not too soon, please. I'd like to be some distance away before it appears. And try to be charitable about appearances. I don't always look like this.' He plucked at the crumpled, threadbare coat. 'I favour Levison's suits when I can afford them. Italian leather shoes. Silk ties. Quite the dandy.'

'I'll remember.' She gave a businesslike nod.

'Shall we shake on it, then?' He held out his hand, and this time she was not afraid to go closer to him. She saw that his eyes were a deep soft fringed brown, the colour of an eland's eyes. She looked into them as they shook hands, and she remembered them with vivid clarity when the police came and questioned her and Agnes about the traces of occupation in the cave up on the koppie.

'What man?' she kept saying, looking as blank and bewildered as only a thirteen-year-old can when she knows she's cornered. 'What man? I never saw anybody up on the koppie, it was only me who ever went up there.'

She kept her end of the bargain faithfully while her father raged and her mother wept and Agnes flustered her denials and the police combed the koppie, bringing down a cardboard box full of her cushions and tea things and books. 'I wouldn't let your kid go up there again, sir,' they said to Gordon. 'You never know how safe it is with so many vagrants around. And one of our sergeants killed a night-adder by the fence this morning.'

But her Journal was under her mattress, and the koppie and her cave were written into its pages, to be joined after a discreet interval by the man with the fringed brown eyes and the big mouth and the voice like Father Dunwoodie's that said, 'Are you the Byron reader, then?'

For months afterwards she half-expected to hear from him – a postcard from 'places north', perhaps, with a cryptic message on it. She had no way of knowing that the brown eyes had closed finally and in agony during what the army public relations officer called 'a shooting incident' on the Border two weeks after the encounter on the koppie. QED, as their owner would have said.

10

There is a knock at the door of the hut, and a woman's voice. 'Ko-ko. May I come in?'

Gordon goes over to open it. Standing outside is the woman with muddy eyes, holding a second fan and a coiled extension cord in her arms.

She is a large woman in an indigo print dress, hand-embroidered round the neck. Her head is wrapped in a cloth of the same print, a dark swathed oval against the bright rectangle of the doorway. She says, 'I've brought the fan from my office. I don't want you to think we've forgotten about Jake and Rose. We have telephoned through to Maseru again, and they've promised to send a van by mid-afternoon.' When she moves her head there is a glint of tears in the shadow-pits of her eyes. 'This is a terrible thing.'

'Yes,' he says, inadequately, 'yes. Please come in. I don't think you've met my wife yet?'

Sarah looks up from the chair where she is sitting, her broad cheeks too red, her blue eyes hostile. The woman puts the fan and the coil of cord down before going over to her and bending to touch one of the hands that lie inert in her lap, cradling the teacup. 'I'm Cordelia Motaung, school circuit inspector for this district. We are truly sorry about Rose. We loved her very much. She was so good to our children, such a wonderful teacher. I don't know what we'll do without her.'

'What *you'll* do? She was the only child we had left! They've both been taken now.' Sarah's grief blazes up into accusing anger. 'You people used her, but you didn't protect her! She gave so much, gave up so much, and in return she got – this.' She gestures in fury at the bloodstained sleeping mat with its burden of death. 'It's not fair!'

Cordelia kneels down beside her, first tucking the hem of her dress under her knees to protect them from the coarse dung-

87

smeared surface of the hut's floor. She says, 'No, Mrs Kimber, life is not fair, specially for people who live in mountain villages like this one. But you must know this?' She looks at Sarah intently, as if to prise the answer out of her. 'Or did you think that Rose would be protected from the hard realities of her life – our lives – by her whiteness?'

Sarah has always been honest, even when she is most angry. 'I suppose I did,' she admits.

'Maybe that is the whole crux of the racial problem.' Bracing herself with one hand on the floor, Cordelia stands up, brushing the dust off the front of her dress. She speaks to both Gordon and Sarah. 'For whatever reason, white people seem to feel that they have an invisible aura around them that separates them in some way from the rest of humanity. The coffee-coloured majority.' She grins unexpectedly, a brief glimpse of teeth in the stifling gloom. 'The better ones try to explain it away by giving self-deprecating reasons. "Of course, we've had more advantages than you people, we've just been lucky, our backgrounds have been more privileged, we've been given a better education, more skills. Forgive us, we can't help being better than you are." The worst ones rest their arguments on superior genes. But they are both saying the same thing.

'Rose was different. She is the only white person I have ever known who did not have that aura. From the day Jake brought her to our village, she was one of us. She spoke plainly. She entered the poorest of our huts without the surreptitious sniff of people who live in more hygienic conditions. She picked up and cuddled our children even when they were dirty, with snot all over their faces. When she fetched water from the tap, she didn't care if her feet got muddy. She was a truly good woman, Mrs Kimber. You must remember this.'

'Then why was she so brutally killed? You tell me! Is there no justice? What is the point of being a good woman if your reward is a hail of bullets and a terrible death?' Sarah gets up from the chair, letting the tea cup crash on the floor, her face blooming like a great red hibiscus. 'It's such a God-awful waste!'

They both move towards her, Gordon saying, 'Don't upset yourself, babe.'

'Don't upset myself?' Sarah blunders towards the half-open door as though the hut can no longer contain her furious grief. 'I'm outraged! I could kill with my bare hands! To see Rose –' Her foot catches in the coiled extension cord, and before they can reach her she has tripped and fallen in an explosion of dust, banging her head against the door frame.

Gordon rushes forward and bends over her. Her eyes are closed, her breathing ragged. He looks up at Cordelia in panic. 'She's knocked herself out! Is there a doctor in the village?'

'Only at the mission, half an hour away, but we have a clinic sister. I'll run and fetch her.'

'Tell her my wife's got high blood pressure, besides the head injury. It could be dangerous.' With shaking fingers he is feeling the weal on her forehead.

'I'll run.'

Gordon sits down in the settling dust and lifts Sarah's head and shoulders up on to his lap, smoothing the dishevelled silver hair with his hand. Her face is alarmingly red and sweaty, smeared with dust up one side. The weal on her forehead is swelling into an egg.

The clinic is not far away, and within minutes there is a sound of hurrying footsteps and the door is pushed open. Cordelia says, 'This is Sister Quthing. Sisi – Mr Kimber. Rose's father.' The two women kneel swiftly beside Sarah. As the sister bends forward to feel her head and pulse, Cordelia looks at Gordon, breathing heavily from her run. 'I hope it wasn't what I said that caused this. I'm so sorry.'

'No, of course not. What you said was true.' He is anxious to reassure this woman who has been Rose's friend. 'Sarah seemed all right when I left her to go and get water, but by the time I got back she had worked herself into a state. Delayed shock, I suppose. And she's not been very well these past few months.'

Cordelia looks down at the unconscious woman. 'I can see she is Rose's mother. You are lucky to have such a wife.'

'Yes. And we were both lucky to have such a daughter.' His eyes are drawn across the hut to Rose's still, staring, bloodied face. 'Even for a while.'

'There is nothing so terrible as losing a child.' The way she says it makes him turn to her, recognising the anguish of another bereaved parent. She goes on, 'But of course you still have Hope, the baby. She is sleeping now, down at the clinic.'

The baby. In the horror of Rose's death, both Gordon and Sarah have been too overwhelmed to think of the new grand-daughter they have driven all the way up from Natal to see, arriving too late last night to continue along the badly rutted road to the village. The news of the tragedy reached them at their Maseru hotel early this morning, conveyed by a nervous policeman who could not look them in the face. On the back seat of the car, which is parked now in the narrow strip of shade next to the government offices, is the body of a new pram piled with presents of baby clothes and a menagerie of soft toys presided over by a cheerful button-eyed teddy bear. The wheels are in the boot.

'The baby,' he says, dazed by the thought. 'Rose hasn't left us completely, then.'

'No.' Cordelia smiles. 'She's a lovely little thing. You will be taking her home with you?' There is a curious note to the query, as if she is not as sure of his answer as her words imply.

'We haven't even thought –' he begins, then says more firmly, 'Naturally we'll be taking her home.'

'She has other grandparents?'

'A grandmother only. Sarah has met her. I don't think she's likely to mind if we – '

The sister, who has been checking Sarah's vital signs, says without looking up. 'She's quite deeply unconscious. Sweating. Pulse too fast. I'll take her blood pressure.' She lifts the apparatus out of the bag she has brought with her, wraps the cuff round Sarah's arm and frowns as she reads off the figures, listening to her pulse with a stethoscope. Letting the air out of the cuff, she says, 'Higher than it should be, I'm afraid. I'd like to keep her under observation in the clinic. We'll need the stretcher and some carriers.'

'I can carry one end,' Gordon volunteers.

Sister Quthing looks at him, assessing, then says, 'I think better four men. She's heavy. Can you call some from the offices, Delia?'

'If you could hold Sarah and tell me where the stretcher is, I could go and get that.' Gordon is anxious to help.

'Better I go.' The sister is brisk, snapping her bag closed and getting up in one movement. 'I need other things too. Are you all right here for ten minutes, Mr Kimber? Listen to her breathing, please. If it slows down –'

'I'll shout. You'll hear me at the other end of the village.' The look on Gordon's face leaves no doubt that they will.

'Very well. We'll go now, then.'

The door closes and Gordon is alone with his injured wife and his cruelly dead daughter and son-in-law. The working fan is still swivelling its round head patiently from side to side; the other fan stands motionless next to a tangle of extension cord, part of which has coiled itself round one of Sarah's sandalled feet. A large bluebottle fly that slipstreamed in as the door was closing buzzes round and round, high up under the conical thatched roof.

He thinks, Sarah and I began life together so carelessly, so unaware of what it held for us. And here we are on the floor of a hut in the middle of nowhere with our dead. Except for Hope.

Gordon recalls that Jake had wanted to call the baby Daisy – all his sisters had flower names, he said, maybe that was why he had married a Rose – but Rose had insisted on Hope. 'Hope Daisy, if I like, she says,' Jake had told them on the phone with the irrepressible laugh of a new father. 'It's a bit of a mouthful. I'm going to call her just Meisietjie.'

Hope Daisy. Word association makes Gordon remember the bright yellow and orange Namaqualand daisies that bloomed next to the Buckingham Circle driveway towards the dusty end of each highveld winter, and getting home late every day from the office. I was an ambitious little shit then, he thinks. What was it all for?

Having policemen in her home questioning her daughter about a wanted terrorist shocked Sarah into the realisation that she was giving her very little attention. I'm too busy wallowing in my own miseries, she thought. I've got to pull myself together and be a better mother.

She saw a neurologist about her migraines, and with the new medication he prescribed soon had them under control. He sent her on to a psychiatrist, saying, 'You need help with your depression too, Mrs Kimber. Mourning can easily slide into quite debilitating illness.'

'You don't mean madness?'

He gave the tight-lipped smile she had come to associate with medical specialists during David's long illness, as though they had to be careful not to let any professional secrets slip out. 'No. I mean an entirely understandable depression that you haven't been able to shake off. Depression has an effect on body chemistry that we don't fully understand yet, or perhaps it is vice versa. Whatever the cause, psychiatrists have a battery of chemical anti-depressants at their disposal now that are extremely efficacious, used in conjunction with counselling.'

She did not tell Gordon about the psychiatrist until she had been to him several times, thinking that she knew what Gordon would say: 'What do you need a shrink for?'

But to her surprise he insisted on going with her to her next appointment, saying, 'I want to know how he's worked the miracle. It's good to have you back with us again, babe.' How we misjudge each other, she thought, reaching for his hand in the car afterwards.

Tentatively Sarah began to paint again. She took out one of the blank canvases she had put away when David's illness worsened, cleaned her time-stiffened brushes in turps and a bowlful of soapy water, and sat on the back stoep for several mornings painting the koppie rearing up behind the hakea hedge and the peeling tin roofs of the servants' quarters.

Agnes said, bending over the canvas and clucking her tongue, 'Why you make a picture of that bad place?'

'Because it's an interesting contrast. And because it's there.' Sarah was smiling. It was good to feel a brush in her hand, to cover the bland white rectangle with subtle dabs of colour using the sure strokes she had not forgotten.

Agnes clucked her tongue again. Her repertoire of clucks punctuated the Buckingham Circle days, expressing by their different little explosions of air against her palate a range of negative responses from disapproval to annoyance. 'Why you not make a picture of flowers, eh?'

'Because I prefer landscapes – pictures of places,' Sarah explained. 'They're more of a challenge than flowers.'

'But not so pretty.' Agnes wondered what a challenge was. Sometimes the Madam was hard to understand. Though she came from Natal, she did not use the pidgin Zulu once known as kitchen kaffir, but now that the word 'kaffir' was acknowledged as insulting, called Fanagalo. She had asked Agnes at the very beginning not to call her 'Madam' but 'Sarah', though of course this was out of the question. A madam was a madam, however lightly the reins were held.

She was also the vaguest madam Agnes had ever worked for, with little interest in household matters. Sarah didn't lock things up or run her finger along shelves to check for dust or ostentatiously count her silver once a week as Beauty's madam did, and she came into the kitchen only to discuss meals. Agnes had been rather shocked at first by this indifference, but had grown to appreciate the autonomy it gave her.

Sarah seemed to have shaken off her lethargy during the past few weeks, however. Ever since those policemen with eyes of stone came, Agnes thought with a shiver, asking questions, questions, like I'm a bad woman. When I don't know nothing. She hoped fervently that the Madam would continue to spend her time reading or painting as she was doing this morning, leaving her, Agnes, to carry on with the serious work of cleaning the house and cooking. Doing things her own way gave her a feeling of independence and pride in her own handiwork that she had never felt with previous madams who ordered her round all day, and shouted when she got things wrong or mixed up.

But Agnes was not one to butter people up for favours. She looked down at the painting of rocks and tin roofs and said doggedly, 'It's not so pretty like flowers, Madam. I got some in my room, you like them to make a picture?'

'Not as pretty maybe, but with a lot more impact.' Sarah sat back and looked at the nearly finished painting with critical, half-closed eyes. She had been drawn by the contrast between the primeval wild place and the dingy back yards which had encircled it; the koppie was like an ancient fossilised insect trapped in suburban amber. I've got to get more yellow into those browns, she thought, pleased with the image. 'I like painting people too, Agnes,' she added. 'Perhaps I could do a portrait of you next? Would you like that?'

'Me? A picture of me? You make a joke, Madam.' Agnes turned away. 'I don't like people to make jokes with me. Aikona.'

The indignation in her voice made Sarah reach out for her arm and pull her back. 'No, really, I'm not joking. I'd like to paint you, Agnes. It would help me very much. I'd pay you extra, of course.'

Agnes burst out, 'But I'm not pretty, Madam! I'm fat, look here! And I've got bad things on my face.' She lifted her hand to touch the discoloured patches on her cheeks and forehead which had bloomed like malignant lichens after two years of diligent application of skin-lightening cream. 'I am too shame.' She started to cry.

Oh God, Sarah thought, she thinks she's ugly. I've put my foot in it again. She knocked over the kitchen chair she had been sitting on as she got up to put her arm round the weeping woman. 'Honestly, you've got a very strong, interesting face, Agnes. I'd really like to paint it. That is, if you want me to.'

'I want, but I'm not pretty. I'm just black,' Agnes sobbed.

The words burned like acid into Sarah's mind for days afterwards. She kept thinking, My contribution to this family compared with Agnes's has been almost nil for months. Yet she says 'I'm just black'. Is this how we make them feel?

She managed to convince Agnes that she was serious about the portrait, though not that it was better to have an interesting rather than a pretty face. 'Don't talk, Madam. I know what I know,' Agnes said. 'But if I say OK to the picture, you won't show these bad things on my face?'

'I won't show them, I promise.' Sarah had a lump in her throat as she turned back to her easel.

The newspapers were beginning to publish articles about the rights of domestic workers, one of which appeared a day later. Reading the suggested conditions of employment made Sarah realise how inadequate Agnes's were. She had glanced into the mean little room in the back yard where Agnes slept only once when Gordon had first shown her round the house, and had no idea whether it had an electric plug or a place to sit and eat. Guiltily she asked to see it, and was reproached by Agnes's valiant efforts to alleviate its cheerless gloom.

The bed had a pink candlewick bedspread on which, lined up precisely against the wall like cancan dancers before a firing squad, was a row of frilly embroidered pillows. A rickety table bore several spindly pot plants arranged on crocheted doileys, photographs of relatives staring unsmiling out of nickel frames, a cluster of patent medicines, and a glass ashtray that shrieked *Lion Lager* several times round its rim. The only other space in the room was taken up by a hideous plywood 'servant's wardrobe' with plastic gilt handles, piled on top with bulging cardboard boxes. Not quite covering the damp patches on the walls where the paint was flaking away were a bottle store calendar, torn-out magazine pictures of beautiful black women, a wall hanging made from an old sheet embroidered with deformed but jolly-looking birds, and the orange feather flower arrangement that Mrs Dunwoodie had brought and Sarah had given to Agnes to throw away. The cement floor was bare.

In the shower room next door, water dripped from the rusted shower head on to a slimy duckboard. The window above the squat lavatory was broken. The peeling green doors of all three rooms were rotted through at the bottom. A backless kitchen chair stood next to the row of dustbins outside, where Agnes could sit to catch the brief rays of afternoon sunlight that managed to penetrate the gaps in the hedge.

And we live in eight bright, clean, warm rooms that look out over the garden, Sarah thought.

She finished the painting with a surge of energy that carried her into the refurbishment of Agnes's rooms, dipping once again into her building society account, which had grown during her years of inertia. As she supervised the stripping and painting, and helped Agnes choose new curtains and a carpet and a two-bar heater for winter, she had a feeling of coming alive again. It was like cleaning a dirty window, brushing away the dragging cobwebs of depression to let in the sunlight.

The Sunday after it was finished, Agnes brought her husband and children from Soweto to admire it. Sarah was called out into the back yard to be formally thanked. Agnes, beaming, announced, 'My Madam, she is too good, nè? Say thanks too much for the Madam,' and the four solemn, neatly dressed children did a shuffling little dance and clapped their hands and said, 'Happy! Happy!' in dutiful voices, clearly anxious to impress the white woman on whose continued goodwill their mother's job depended.

Sarah was embarrassed by the fulsome display of gratitude with its *Gone with the Wind* undertones. She asked them into the kitchen for tea, calling Rose from her bedroom to meet the black children, but it was not a success. Rose had been sleeping and was flushed and grumpy. The black children were intimidated by the echoing spaces in the white people's house, and by the delicate china cups which they held in both hands and sipped from with round unblinking eyes, putting them down on the saucers as though they were eggshells, taking care not to clink too loudly. Agnes's frequent admonitions to sit up nice and straight and not to spill a drop strangled any impulses they may have had to speak.

The only person who seemed to enjoy the occasion was Harrison, Agnes's husband, who sat with his polished brown leather shoes side by side talking to Sarah about his work and where his family came from. He was, as so often with men married to large women, thin to the point of boniness; his shirt collar stood away from his neck and his checked sports coat hung off his shoulders, obviously a hand-me-down. 'I'm lucky,' Agnes had confided once. 'Harrison, he is a very good husband, he doesn't drink or play the numbers. Only sometimes – ' She did not elaborate, and Sarah, watching him stir his tea with genteel precision, wondered what it was that he did only sometimes to make Agnes's face grow secretive.

'You could have tried a little harder,' she said crossly to Rose as they watched Agnes shepherding the children down the road in a tight pack so none of them would stray in the unfamiliar white territory.

'I hate it when you're being all condescending,' Rose mumbled.

'What do you mean?' Sarah thought she had been absolutely charming to them all – and she was going to have to wash up all the tea cups herself.

'You know.' Rose kicked the doormat with her sandal. 'Putting on the gracious lady act. I felt embarrassed.'

'It wasn't easy for any of us, but at least I tried.' Sarah was annoyed. 'I didn't notice any attempts at conversation coming from your direction.'

'I didn't know what to say. I mean, it's all right with Agnes, you can talk to her and she talks back. But those kids just sat staring at me and at you and all round the kitchen as though we were Martians on the moon or something. I kept feeling I wanted to say sorry to them for having so much more than they did.'

Sarah thought, Join the club. But all she said was, 'Well, try a bit harder to be nice next time, will you? You've got to learn how to talk to all kinds of people if you want to get on in life.' It was only after the parental cliché had rolled effortlessly off her tongue that she realised it was one of her mother's.

The newspaper article on the rights of domestic workers had suggested higher monthly wages than Sarah was paying Agnes, or a reduction in the number of hours worked. Higher wages Gordon would not sanction. 'She's getting a hell of a lot more than most servants get,' he said, quite correctly. The best way to reduce her hours, Sarah decided, would be to let her go off earlier, leaving the prepared evening meal in the warming oven. It paid a dividend she had not expected. Without Agnes bustling round the table and banging things in the kitchen, keen to get the dishes done and to be off, their suppers became far more relaxed and convivial.

Sarah began to feel that the family ship was back on course again, after years of lying becalmed. Her confidence had been very much restored by the painting of the koppie, which Gordon admired and Rose begged to be given to hang in her bedroom. She joined a painting class and was soon working towards a group exhibition. Rose was doing well at school. The wind was in both their sails: Set Fair for France! Sarah thought, smiling.

When Gordon's years of overtime finally paid off and he was made General Manager of the shipping company a few months later, it was like foundering on an unexpected reef. At supper that night he was euphoric. 'We can afford to move to a really good suburb now!'

Sarah felt the sickening crunch of keel timbers on rock. 'Not again!' she wanted to howl into the high wind of his ambition. But she said only, in a tight voice, 'Honestly, Gordon, we'd have done better to buy a mobile home instead of that awful Kosy Kottage. Then we could have moved it round from place to place as your promotions materialised.'

'Will I have to leave my school?' Rose demanded.

'How about setting your sights a bit higher, Rosie?' He beamed at his daughter with the benign certitude that a rise of a thousand a month brings with it. 'You can go to Kingsmead or Roedean or St Winifreds now. Be educated with the cream of the crop.'

'But I like it where I am.' For the moment Rose forgot the inadequacies of her classmates. 'Besides – '

'Besides what?' Gordon pounced on her hesitation. He was thinking, If I'd had the chance of a private school when I was a kid, I'd have jumped at it.

'The cream of the crop sounds horrible. I mean, they're probably all stuck up rich kids who live in huge houses. I'd feel out of place, Dad.'

'We can afford a huge house too now, that's what I'm trying to say! You'd be the equal of any snotty northern suburbs miss. I've worked damn hard for it, too.' He planted both elbows on the table and glared at them with the exasperated puzzlement of men through the ages who say to themselves, What more do women want, for God's sake?

Recognising the warning signs of the bulldozer mood, Sarah scanned his face for indications of its intensity. His face was paler and puffier than it had been when they lived near the beach. Too many cigarettes had shortened his breath, and daily business lunches with whisky and wine had thickened his stocky body to what his tailor trenchantly described as Portly Short. Only his hair had thinned. He was not yet forty.

She said in her most diplomatic voice, trying to stave off the inevitable, 'You work too hard, Gordon. You never seem to have time for other things.'

'Like your precious painting?'

She forced a smile. 'Like my precious painting. And you deserve this promotion, I know that. But – '

'But what?'

'I don't know that we need to move to a bigger house. With only the three of us, this one's quite adequate.'

'Adequate!' From the way he seemed to toss the word up so that he could blow holes in it, she knew that they were going to have to move again. 'I'm not bloody doing all this so we can live in an adequate house with Rose going to an adequate school! It doesn't have to be big, but we're going to live in a really nice place for once, in a suburb where people can't look over our fence or through our windows. You're going to get the best education I can buy you, Rosie. Choose your school, I don't care which one as long as it has a good academic standard so you can go on to university.'

'But Dad –' Rose wailed. Sarah was silent, knowing it was futile to argue. She would have to go through the whole thing again: the search for a house that fulfilled Gordon's expectations, packing and moving, finding a new school for Rose and a new painting class for herself. She thought, And we've just fixed up Agnes's room. I wonder if she'll want to come with us? Having to start from scratch with a new maid would be the last straw.

Gordon looked at his daughter across the table. She was fourteen now, almost as tall as her mother, with the same blonde hair and blue eyes and high cheekbones, but with his strong jaw that gave the lower part of her face a determined jut. They had grown closer during Sarah's depression, and he had begun to enjoy the feeling of being father to an almost-grown, intelligent daughter.

'Rose, love,' he said in a softer voice. 'You're the only one now, and we want to do our best for you. A private school will have more advantages than your government school: better teachers, smaller classes, extras like dancing and riding.'

'But I don't *want* to dance and ride! And what about my friends?' Rose could feel the inevitable descending on her too, but she wasn't going to give in easily.

'You can make new ones, surely? Better ones,' he said,

brushing aside the long and often lonely year it had taken her to build up acquaintances in the school.

'I don't want to. I like the ones I've got. And I like this house, and I like the koppie, and –'

'You haven't been up there again?' Sarah said sharply.

'No, of course not. I said I wouldn't. But there's no harm in looking at it, is there?'

Sarah shivered. 'The koppie's the one thing that could make me leave this house. I don't like the idea of a convict having sat up there watching us. It's a lawless sort of place.'

'Mum!' Rose felt betrayed. 'You didn't paint it as though you were frightened by it. You painted it as though it was a wild, special place stuck in the middle of all the houses.'

Sarah thought, pleased, She saw what I was getting at. I haven't forgotten how to paint. But she said, 'Painting's one thing. Our only child being endangered is another.'

'You're damn right.' Gordon seized his opportunity. 'I'm going to make sure our new house is fitted with burglar guards and a security gate before we move in.'

Rose heaved a theatrical sigh. They'd ganged up on her using their most potent weapon, the fact that she was an only child. Only children had to work extra hard at not being a disappointment to their doting parents. Only children had to be overprotected and lavished with advantages like being sent to fancy schools, she thought with despair. I'll have to face a new class and make new friends again.

Both were skills she would need often in her short life.

11

Moving Sarah to the clinic turns into a procession down the stony track that leads through the middle of the village. The sister walks in front carrying her bag like a priest with the sacraments, followed by four men stumbling under the burden of the stretcher on which Sarah lies in her bright crumpled shift like a dead queen being paraded in state. Gordon walks next to the stretcher, shading her face with his hat. Within a few steps of leaving the hut his sensitive scalp starts to burn as though a hot iron is being held there, but he hardly notices. All his attention is fixed on holding the hat's shade steady over Sarah's jolting flushed face.

Behind them come Cordelia Motaung and a straggle of children attracted by the drama. They walk quietly with wary faces, expecting any moment to be shooed away. Some are wearing adult clothes that fall off their shoulders and hips and droop in swags near their ankles. Most of the boys wear just khaki shorts that bear the stigmata of constant mending.

The only other sign of life in the village is a shaggy brown and white goat shambling down the track in front of them, dragging a frayed rope from a collar round its neck. Passing the government offices, Gordon sees that the public area is still empty, the fan still revolving. The patch of shade his car is parked in has dwindled; he will have to come back soon and move it.

The procession comes to a stop outside the tin-roofed village clinic while the sister opens the door. It is too narrow to admit two men and a stretcher side by side, so the front bearers have to turn round and shuffle in backwards. Behind the stretcher, Gordon gestures towards Cordelia. 'After you.'

He follows her into a large whitewashed room with a row of iron beds along one wall. Each has two plump pillows, a white cotton bedspread smoothed and tucked in with hospital corners, and a locker next to it. Ranged round the other walls are an assortment of old wooden PWD cupboards, tables and a desk, all recently painted in a bright green enamel that gives them the look of a furniture family – each one different, but related. Behind the desk are shelves holding medicine bottles marshalled into battalions according to type and size. The black cement floor is polished to the high gloss of boots awaiting inspection. Sister Quthing believes in fighting disease with all her forces in parade order.

She puts her medical bag on the desk and says briskly in Sesotho, 'The bed in the corner, please.' She goes before them to turn the bedspread and sheets down in exact parallel folds, then shows them how to lay the stretcher on the bed, to slip out the wooden poles and to roll the canvas sling under Sarah's body and out the other side.

Gordon shakes each man's hand by way of thanks. He is not sure whether he should tip them too, as he always does with black shop assistants who carry purchases out to his car. But they are from the government offices, dressed in the shirts, ties, dark trousers and shiny cotton jackets of the civil service, and he decides that to tip would be insulting. 'I appreciate your help,' he says instead, 'specially in this heat. My wife is not well. This has been a terrible day for her.'

'For us, too,' one of the men says. He could be the prototype of a clerk: prim mouth, neat head, buttoned waistcoat, desk-frayed cuffs. His eyes peer from behind round glasses like small wet drawer knobs. 'Rose and Jake were my friends. I was at the party last night where it happened. The men with guns –' His voice falters to a stop.

'Tell me.' The black rage that Gordon has been suppressing all morning boils up like hot tar. They have not yet been told how the shooting happened, but now he wants to know every detail: how many men, what they wore, how many shots, what they said, exactly how long Rose took to die. He wants to hear the horror while it is still raw in this man's mind, and while Sarah lies unheeding on the white bed with the sister bent over her, wiping the dust off her face with a damp cloth.

He grasps the clerk's arm and pulls him away towards the cupboards. 'Tell me!'

Cordelia follows. 'I don't think you should hear this, Mr Kimber. It is too soon.'

'I must know!' The face he turns to her is florid from over-exposure to the sun, with the prosperous jowls that indicate

101

good living attended by well-trained servants, and perhaps more brandy at night than he should be drinking. It is the white South African face of the TV newscasts, seen against flags and rows of party faithful in best dresses and dark suits, each with its buttonhole carnation bound in a twist of silver foil with a sprig of fern that shivers when its wearer speaks. Or seen pontificating about Communist agitation against frozen shots of fire and mob violence whose very stillness makes them untrue. It is an instantly recognisable face now, good for at least ten minutes' righteous condemnation in snug TV rooms all over the world.

But there is a fury in the puffy-lidded khaki eyes that tells a different story. Cordelia has seen it before in Rose's eyes, and it reminds her that this is no standard white farmer. Gordon's years in business and farming and with Sarah have acted on him like fine sandpaper, smoothing the roughness off his prejudices and exposing a grain that is hard but true. Rose has told with some amusement how he opened his home to her leftwing student friends though he abhorred their fervently debated socialist politics and their flea market clothes and their bare feet, and of his struggle to accept Jake as the man she loved and wanted to marry. Cordelia has underestimated him, she realises. Beneath his solicitude for his wife and the tough-but-reasonable attitude he parades, he is ready to kill for the death of his girl.

She turns to the other men who have helped with the stretcher. 'Let's go. We've done what we can. I must phone through to the mission to see if the doctor can come to Mrs Kimber.'

They go out the door and as it closes behind them, Gordon demands, 'Tell me, man!'

The clerk lifts off his glasses to massage his eyes with a palm that is stained with violet stamp-pad ink, then settles them back on his nose, prodding them into place with his forefinger. He looks away through the window so he doesn't have to see Gordon's expression.

'There were three of them, very big men, very quick to move. They wore camouflage overalls and gloves and black rubber-soled boots, with balaclavas pulled down over their faces –'

Gordon listens frowning. Outside, the children who followed the procession have got bored sitting on the clinic steps waiting for something else to happen, and are scuffling in the dust with a bald tennis ball.

The sun has gone past its zenith but the furnace heat has not abated. Small clouds are gathering along the rim of the rocky peaks of the Malutis to the east, precursors of a thunderstorm. The goat has wandered into an open hut and stands looking out the door as though he owns it, surveying the afternoon through cynical black slits in eyes the colour of warm beer.

Gordon bought a five-bedroomed double-story house in Houghton that just missed being a mansion. When it had been repainted, carpeted in wall-to-wall Wilton, curtained by a decorator and burglar-proofed, they were moved in by professional movers.

'You're not going to lift a finger this time, babe,' he told Sarah, wanting to please her after having got his way about moving. 'It's all going to be done for us. One of the company perks. They like their top men to live in a certain style.'

Rose said to her mother later, 'What's it going to be like living with a Top Man, d'you think?'

'Exhausting, probably,' Sarah said, with feeling. She was wearing one of Gordon's old shirts, with a scarf knotted round her head to keep her hair out of her eyes. 'Business dinners and boring cocktail parties where the men get together to talk about money, and their abandoned wives are forced to make conversation about their kids. I'm dreading it.'

Rose laughed. 'You are funny, Mum. Other women would jump at the prospect of parties.'

'Not me. I'm not cut out to be a Top Wife, Rosie. For one thing, I've got out of the habit of making small talk. Like a foreign language, it has to be continually practised or it atrophies.' Her capacity for social conversation had shrivelled after David was born to brief pleasantries exchanged with doctors and nurses, and it seemed to have died with him. 'For another thing, I've let myself go, rather. Rubens would have adored my figure. I must have the biggest bum in town, a monument to the fact that nibbling stimulates creativity.'

'You're not that overweight.'

'Loyal Rosie. Too much for a Top Wife, though. Top Wives are svelte, willowy creatures who look as though they live on smoked salmon and caviar and champagne, not dumpy housewives.'

'Or painters who take part in exhibitions. That's much more noteworthy.'

She said it so earnestly that Sarah could not laugh. Rose sometimes used old-fashioned words and phrases out of the books she read that made her sound like a pedantic schoolmarm, when they weren't mispronounced. She was a gangling fourteen with braces on her teeth and straight thick eyebrows that met in the middle and gave her face a serious, considering look. It turned into a thunderous scowl whenever she thought about her new school.

Gordon's secretary had managed to wangle an interview with the headmistress of St Winifreds, the most exclusive girls' school in town. Rose was to go there in January. 'At least you don't have to face a Top School,' she said gloomily now to Sarah. 'I'm going to hate it, I know.'

'The tuition's supposed to be very good.'

'You and Dad think that's so important, but it's not! Friends are. Why can't I stay where I am?'

'You know why.'

'But why do we always have to do what Dad says? Why can't we do what *we* want sometimes?'

'Because he cares so much about doing the right thing. And he's the breadwinner, Rosie.'

'That doesn't give him the right to dictate to us!'

Sarah looked at the mottled pink patches on her daughter's face and thought, She's like me in some ways, but there's a lot of Gordon in her too. They're pig-headed enough to become enemies if I don't keep the peace between them. How can I explain him to her so that she sees the good things, even when he's doing his utmost to conceal them? She said, 'Dad wants the best for us, and he's worked very hard to achieve it. It would be like throwing all his hard work in his face if we said we didn't want the perks it brings.'

'He's not doing it for us, he's doing it for himself! Can't you see? He wants you to have a big house and me to go to a smart school because we reflect his success like two mirrors.'

'It hasn't occurred to you that he may be doing these things because he loves us?'

'Oh Mum, really! You know that the only person Dad loves is Dad, and the horrible old company comes second. We're just household pets he's fond of because we belong to him.'

Sarah thought, Fifteen years of marriage, and our daughter is playing psychologist backed by her vast experience of life. With some irritation she said, 'You don't paint a very flattering portrait of me. Do you really believe I'd have gone on with a marriage that had turned into some sort of high-class kennel?'

Rose gave the brittle cough of laughter she had heard in an old Bette Davis movie, and perfected in the bathroom mirror. She had been waiting for this opportunity for months. 'I used to wonder why you and Dad ever got married in the first place, until I compared my birthday with your anniversary and realised that you had to. My friends think it's glamorous to be a shotgun baby, but I'm not so sure. Would you still have married him if I hadn't been inconveniently on the way? I mean, I'd like to know how close I came to not existing.'

Sarah had known she would have to explain one day, but not that it would be to an adolescent on the edge of tears asking questions that were no less urgent for not being put into words. She thought, I must get my answers right, or I'll sour her view of marriage.

She took Rose's hands in both of hers so that they were facing each other. 'If you want the plain truth, Rosie, I don't know. We were spoiled, ignorant children. All we knew about life was parties and beach picnics and having fun; lectures were mildly interesting weekday interludes that one attended to justify being at university. Your Dad and I were one of the big romances on campus that year: handsome Gordon and pretty blonde empty-headed Sarah. When you made your presence known, much to everyone's surprise, it seemed the most natural thing in the world to marry – specially as it made your grandmother so angry. She was furious at being done out of the big white wedding she had planned for me. Dad and I were like two naughty kids saying "Nyeeeeeah!" to her and waggling our fingers in our ears. It was the first time I ever stood up to her, and Dad helped me do it.'

'Is that why Granny hardly ever comes to see us?'

'Granny had got used to running my life.' Sarah thought, with sudden insight, My leaving must have left almost as much of a hole in her life as David's death did in mine. I was so angry with her that I never saw it. She went on more slowly, 'We lived with her and Gramps after the wedding because Dad was still studying and we had no money. One night when you were about a year old, she and I had a dreadful fight. Next morning Dad and I packed our bags and moved out with you howling in your carrycot. It was all very dramatic and silly, but that's when our marriage really began.

'Dad and I were thrown together in a tiny flat with very little

105

money, having to learn about life together. And we did, but it was hard. Hard for me because I'd never had to lift a finger at home, and didn't know the first thing about keeping house or looking after babies. Hard for Dad too, because he felt he had to prove to everyone that he could look after you and me as well as my parents had – better, in fact. That's when he started working such long hours, and caring so much about appearances.'

'You've never told me any of this.' Rose was already planning how to write the thrilling story of her origins into her Journal. *I Was A Shotgun Baby!* would make a good heading. 'But I don't understand about Dad. Doesn't this business of trying to prove he's better than other people confirm what I just said: he only cares about what *he* wants?'

Sarah thought, Life is so simple when you're fourteen and over-sheltered and sitting in judgement on your parents. She said with a sharpness she seldom used towards Rose, 'If that had been the case, Dad would never have married me. He didn't have to; Granny was against it. But he did. He took on responsibilities long before he was ready for them, and he's carried them out faithfully. I don't think you have the right to criticise.'

'Don't bite my head off! I was only asking. And you still haven't answered my question.' Rose was every bit as persistent as her father. 'Would you and Dad have stayed together if it hadn't been for me?'

'I honestly don't know. But I would like to say one thing, Rosie. Don't ever, *ever* try and judge a marriage from the outside. Dad and I may have our disagreements, but we have our good times too.' She thought, Kids think marriages are expressly designed for them. And she calls Gordon self-centred! She was smiling. One of the bonuses since her depression had lifted had been a surprising upsurge in her need for physical loving, and Gordon's enthusiastic response. Making love was different now, no longer the urgent grappling of two healthy young bodies in a hurry to reach nirvana but a slower, deeper pleasuring of the senses that brought sleep like a benediction.

Rose watched her smiling to herself and knew that her question had been answered. It wasn't a yes but a maybe, and perhaps judgement on her father should be reserved for a while. How would I stand up to hardship, if I had to? she wondered, and was so intent on puzzling out an answer that she did not feel the ghost walking over her grave.

12

In the clinic, the clerk is crying. 'They had pistols with silencers. When they stopped shooting –' he falters, then goes on '– one of them shouted, "Anyone moves, they get shot too!" We did not move, not one of us. The baby was crying in the next room from all the noise, and the music was still playing – oh God, *Sunshine Reggae*. Then they ran out into the darkness, and we heard a jeep going away fast. I went straight to Rose, but she was dead. It was quick for her, Mr Kimber, I'm telling you.'

'How quick?' He can hardly get the words out for the pain in his throat.

'Quick like she just fell down, and did not move again.' It is a lie. She took agonising minutes to die, jerking in frantic arcs on the cement floor, frothing blood. He will not, ever, forget the noises that she made, or forgive himself for not defying the deadly black eyes of the guns to run forward and comfort her. She was my friend, and I just stood there, he mourns. She had spent months coaching him in English for his civil service exams. But he can repay a small part of his debt by comforting her father.

'You're sure?' Gordon's eyes are almost worse than those of the guns.

'I'm sure. It was very terrible, but it was quick.' He lifts off his glasses to stanch with his shirt sleeve the rivulets of tears that vein his cheeks like the back of a leaf. He is not ashamed of crying because it is a sincere tribute, but he does not want the white man's eyes to pierce the soft shell of his lie by watching his face too closely.

'You'd recognise the men again?'

The clerk shakes his head. 'No. The faces were all covered. They used English, but not well. Maybe the voices – '

'Were they black or white? Nobody has said yet.' It is the question that Gordon has been asking himself from the moment he learned of Rose's brutal death. This is the first time he has felt able to ask it aloud. He dreads the answer.

'I don't know.'

'But you must! Good God, man, you *must* know!'

The clerk looks at him now with the shiny round eyes that remind Gordon of drawer knobs. They falter away again as he says, 'We suspect, of course, but we never saw these men in the light. That is the very terrible thing, Mr Kimber. Nobody knows for sure who they were.'

Rose did not take to her new school, and the feeling was mutual. As an only child she was used to being asked her opinions and having them listened to. At St Winifreds the teachers issued their opinions disguised as gospel, not to be questioned or debated. She was continually in trouble for answering back. The biology teacher said she was too pert for her own good. Miss Ramsden, the headmistress, wrote at the end of her first report: 'Rose will have to learn to curb her wilful obstinacy if she is to profit by her time with us.'

A large proportion of the staff had been recruited from upper-crust English girls' schools, which gave St Winifreds a cachet that did wonders for its fees. What the Board of Governors did not realise was that many of them were only available because they were too old-fashioned and had been encouraged to retire early. They were easily persuaded to accept exile from Cheltenham and Brighton in exchange for the privilege of continuing to teach, unaware that they were joining the stream of indifferent actors, musicians and entertainers who take their meagre talents to the colonies where they can be big frogs at last, albeit in small ponds.

The English teachers at St Winifreds took to tweed suits and twinsets and leather brogues as winter approached, and sweltered in the unexpected heat of the midday winter sun until they learned the highveld art of layer-dressing. In summer they wore clumpy-heeled white sandals that were all straps and buckles and patterns of holes. They sat together during tea in the staff room talking in cultured English accents to impress the local teachers, and were offended when the local teachers did not make any effort to befriend them.

The school uniform was a grey flannel blazer and tunic and a grey felt Breton hat with a badge that had to be worn straight on the head, not tilted (even fractionally) back or sideways. Blazers and hats had to be worn at all times outside the school grounds, even on the hottest day. 'We want people to know that St Winifreds girls are always neat, smart and well-behaved,' Miss Ramsden said in her pep talk at the beginning of each term. 'We aim to turn out young ladies who can tackle anything that life throws at them, without losing their femininity.' If anyone sniggered when she said that, she would quell her with a single laser beam from eyes that missed nothing.

Rose begged to be allowed to leave after the first week, but Gordon would not hear of it. 'Just stick it out, Rosie,' he said. 'St Winifreds is the best, and it'll be good for you in the long run.'

'But I hate it! I hate everyone there!'

'New schools are always difficult to get used to, like new jobs. Believe me, I know all about it. You'll soon settle down.'

Rose was more lonely in the big quiet Houghton house than she had ever been. Her friends from the old school lived too far away to visit, Gordon worked late and was often away on business, and Sarah painted all day in her new studio off the veranda. Desperate for someone to notice how unhappy she was, Rose made an ostentatious effort not to settle down. She argued with the teachers, served endless detentions and wore her socks defiantly round her ankles. She burned every dish she made in domestic science. When told to tie her hair back, she used knotted black elastic with frayed ends.

Towards the middle of her second term, Miss Ramsden asked Gordon and Sarah to come and see her, and called Rose out of class to be present at the interview. After a catalogue of Rose's misdemeanours, shaking her iron-grey bob with solemn relish, she said, 'I'm afraid your daughter's behaviour has been entirely unsatisfactory. Unless she pulls her socks up – and I mean literally as well as figuratively, since she goes out of her way to look like a dog's breakfast – I shall have to ask her to leave.'

Gordon said, 'I don't blame you. I'd do the same.'

Miss Ramsden was used to parents who blustered and begged, and Gordon's reply threw her off balance for a moment. 'Well!' she said. 'Well, I appreciate your bluntness, Mr Kimber.'

'I must add,' Gordon went on in his best General Manager's voice, 'that I think the failure is as much the school's as my daughter's. She's a bright, stubborn girl with passionate convictions who has a lot to offer anyone who uses the right key.'

Miss Ramsden was a good match for him. She said with an acid smile, 'If she put as much energy into her schoolwork as into her attempts at anarchy, we locksmiths would be more motivated. But I see no point in trying to find the right key if the lock refuses to admit it.'

'It's up to her, then.' Gordon turned to Rose. 'Don't cut off your nose to spite your face, Rosie. Give it a fair try before you decide it's not right for you. I'm not a complete fool, you know, and I do have your best interests at heart.'

'I wish we had more parents like you, Mr Kimber,' Miss Ramsden sighed.

Sarah said afterwards when Rose came home crying betrayal because she had not joined in the discussion, 'I'd rather stay out of it, if you don't mind. Sorry. I can see both your points of view, but I refuse to choose between them.' She was busy with a still-life and did not take her eyes off the canvas.

'Mum, you can't opt out just like that!' Rose was shocked. 'My whole *future's* at stake.'

'Exactly. That's why it must be your decision, not mine. You're quite old enough to decide these issues for yourself now. I wish I'd been given more choices at your age, instead of being so absurdly mollycoddled. I'd have been a much less näive eighteen.'

'And made fewer mistakes like me?'

Sarah turned to smile at her then. 'Sometimes a mistake is the best thing that could have happened.'

But Rose was in no mood to be placated. 'Don't soft-soap me! I need you to tell Dad's he's wrong.'

Sarah put her brush down with reluctance. She had been enjoying the quiet afternoon and the way the sun came slanting through the window to fall on the bowl of apples she was painting. There was an interesting contrast between the sharp, glowing red where the sun fell on each apple and the dull russet on its shady side, and she wanted to go on exploring it with variations of crimson alizarin and cadmium red and burnt sienna, not to agonise over Rose's school troubles. More and more she found herself escaping into the studio, away from the demands of the big house which would soon need two maids to cope with Gordon's ambitious social programme.

'You won't need to lift a finger,' he had repeated grandly when he told her that they would be entertaining at least once a week, if not twice. 'We'll get a housekeeper, and the company will pay.'

But of course she would have to plan the dinners and luncheons, and order in the food and drink, and worry about flowers and names and what to wear, when all she really wanted to do was paint. 'Do we have to, Gordon?'

'Yes, we have to. It's part of the deal. Big job, big house, big car, big parties, big money. Life at the top is tough, babe.' He had been grinning with triumph. 'Who would have guessed all this fifteen years ago?'

Now a flushed and angry Rose was demanding her involvement, and she did not feel like arguing away the peaceful afternoon. She said, 'Can't you talk it over with Dad yourself?'

'No, I can't! He won't listen to reason. He just wants his own way, as per usual.'

'Which of course you don't?

'It's my life! Can't I decide what to do with it?'

'That's exactly what we're asking you to do,' Sarah reminded her gently.

'If I do what I really want, I'll never hear the end of it from Dad.'

Rose kicked off her school shoes and slumped down into the old armchair that Sarah kept in the studio for sitting and reading in; she often had lunch there now that Rose was away at school all day, munching and sipping in comfortable silence over the newspaper or a book. Rose lay in a sulky slouch with her feet in their ugly grey socks over one arm of the chair and her head propped up on the other, fiddling with a new pimple on her chin. 'At that age they like to spend most of their time in a horizontal position, draped all over the furniture,' Sarah recalled the wife of one of Gordon's colleagues saying of her own teenagers. 'The only time they ever move with the faintest sign of alacrity is to answer the telephone, and then they lie draped all over the floor for hours talking to their friends.'

She thought with a rush of guilt, The phone hardly rings at all for Rose these days. We've torn her away from her friends and she hasn't even tried to make new ones. No wonder she's been so unhappy. It's mean of me to begrudge her my time. She said, 'Let me ask Agnes to make us some tea, love, and we'll try to talk it out logically and calmly.'

'I don't want to be logical and calm! I just want – I just want –'

Rose started to cry, and the afternoon dissolved into tears. By the end of it, she had agreed ungraciously to stay at St Winifreds at least until the end of the year. 'But I'm not going to be a meek and mild yes-girl, I'm warning you!' she said with an angry blue look from swollen eyes.

'I should hope not.' Sarah hugged her. She was nearly the same height now.

Rose wore her hair that year in a single thick blonde plait that hung straight down her back, reminding Miss Ramsden irresistibly of a scorpion whenever she walked behind her in the school corridors. The girl seemed to lurk under stones in unexpected places too, and gradually gathered other malcontents round her to form a guerrilla group who questioned authority at every opportunity. They drew up a petition against 'unnecessary, childish rules' and lobbied for the abolition of school hats, a request which was unexpectedly granted when an epidemic of head lice swept the school. It was traced not to the black cleaners (as expected by most parents) but to a child who had picked up her nits in a posh European ski resort while on an overseas holiday. 'Head lice that live on black people's hair won't go near white people's hair,' Rose reported with glee to her new cronies after reading it in the newspaper. 'St Winifreds lice are a specially imported strain from the snowy slopes of the Alps, guaranteed racially pure.' They began to call themselves The Louse Club, and Rose typed out a manifesto committing all members to fight for student equality and freedom of speech. By the end of the year she was having such fun ruffling the placid waters of St Winifreds that she wouldn't have dreamed of leaving.

Besides a good, if rigid, education and excellent experience in opposition tactics, the school gave her an unexpected bonus: a best friend. Ursula Ginsberg was an effervescent Jewish girl with a mind honed on constant argument in a large family, and a wild bubble of curly hair the colour of the scrap steel her father had grown rich on. Ursula was afraid of nothing and revered nobody but her grandmother, a brittle old woman with the sad foreign elegance of an Afghan hound and hooded eyes that had watched her whole family die in the camps, with the exception of the son she now lived with.

Ursula and Rose fomented rebellion wherever they went. They devoured *Future Shock* while their classmates were swooning over *Love Story*. They scorned the spotty youths who congregated at parties to discuss rugby and motorbikes at length, then broke up to find a girl each to hustle into a corner and kiss with slack wet mouths like puppies. Ursula and Rose went to plays and foreign films instead of parties, and wore long black skirts with silk shirts and black berets when everybody else was in bell-bottom jeans and skinny fluorescent sweater tops that buttoned uncomfortably under the crotch.

When Miss Ramsden asked them to be prefects in their Matric year, they were astonished. 'I thought we were abominations and a pox on the school,' Ursula said, recalling a painful episode from the previous year.

'You're also two very strong individuals with a certain following that I am anxious to – '

'Control?'

Miss Ramsden gave them her most acid smile. 'I would prefer to say "influence".'

'No, thanks. We're not going to shop our friends.'

'It wouldn't be nice,' Rose said. This was one of Miss Ramsden's favourite admonitions: 'Now, girls, that's not nice.'

Miss Ramsden closed her eyes and plunged her fingers through the iron-grey bob that had gone white at the temples. Rose and Ursula liked to think it was because of them. She said, 'You won't consider it?'

'We'd rather not.'

'It'd ruin our reputations.'

Miss Ramsden's eyes snapped open again. 'Don't think this changes anything. If it comes to a showdown, I'll win. You're in your last year at school now, and it would be very inconvenient to be expelled.'

'We're not fools, Miss Ramsden.'

'No, you're not, either of you. But you're going to find one day that it's not enough to protest against and undermine a system you find inadequate or unjust. You have to have a better system to offer in its place before you destroy it, or you will leave a vacuum. Which nature abhors, as you will have learned in physics.' She nodded at her study door. 'You may go now. Just one request: try and make your final year with us a constructive and fruitful one. Agitation is fun, I know, but it won't produce the good Matric you will need to get into university.'

'We have to follow our consciences,' Ursula said. Rose showed her now-straight teeth in a smile that promised better-orchestrated and more sustained confrontations now that they were experienced seniors.

Roll on the end of 1972, was Miss Ramsden's fervent wish as the door closed behind them. She would not have believed how much she would miss them after they had gone on to Witwatersrand University. St Winifreds was a duller place without them.

13

Gordon stands in the clinic doorway watching the clerk stumble down the dirt track towards the government offices. He is still crying, but Gordon does not dismiss his tears with a shrugged 'Bloody sissy!' as he would have once. He wonders instead why little white boys allow themselves to be persuaded from their earliest years that crying is unmanly, and that it is necessary to keep their distance from other boys except when they're fighting or playing rugby. He has learned from working with farm labourers these past few years that black men are not ashamed of tears, and that black male friends sometimes hold hands or link little fingers while they're walking and often touch each other to make a point while they're speaking.

He thinks, Rose and Jake would touch each other all the time. I couldn't stand it at first. His hand like a lizard on her soft pink skin. His dark fuzz of hair next to her silky blonde. His broad yellow-brown nose nuzzling into her neck where the skin was so pale and fine that the veins showed through. But the more you saw them together, the less you noticed their differences. His hand was just a hand: five fingers, writer's bump on the middle one, clean trimmed nails, pink palm. Just like mine except for the writer's bump. And we had no alternative, of course. We had to learn to accept Jake, or lose her. Funny joke. We lost her anyway.

He turns round and goes inside, closing the door behind him. Sarah is still unconscious on the bed in the corner, her loosened hair muddled on the pillow. Her face is as white as the cotton sheet Sister Quthing has pulled up and tucked in round her, as if to obliterate the riot of colours she is wearing. Anarchy has no place in this disciplined room where battle is relentlessly waged against illness and disease.

It is more than an hour since Sarah tripped and banged her head against the door frame of the death hut, and she still hasn't

115

come round. If he doesn't start agitating for a doctor as he has for the undertaker, nothing will happen in this backwoods mountain village where all the doors close at midday, and tomorrow is time enough to do things.

Though I don't know about the backwoods bit, he thinks with an irritable glance out the window at the stony hillside where rock shadows are beginning to crawl sideways like spreading ink blots as the sun moves past its zenith. What a fucking awful place. There can't be a tree for miles. No shade and no wood. These people make their fires with dried cow pats and their walls with stones or mud; their floors are trampled earth hardened with ox-blood and wet dung. How could Rose stand living here after the beautiful homes she's been used to? Gardens with bright flowerbeds and lawns spread out like full green skirts. Trees that give shade and scale to our lives. Clean water running out of taps, and electricity, and smokeless winter warmth. Sprung beds and polished furniture and chairs that cradle your body with respect. How could she choose this harsh skeletal Third World instead of our comfortable First?

A cloud shadow slides across the corrugated iron roof of the clinic, making it tick as it cools down. Sweat trickles down Gordon's back as he says to Sister Quthing, chin jutting, 'I want a doctor. Now!'

'He has been called already, Mr Kimber.' She straightens up from her umpteenth checking of Sarah's pulse and looks at him with an expression that is not constrained by the fact of being employed by him. Both at work and at home he has been lord of all he surveys for many years, and he is not used to being looked at like this, except by Rose and her friends and sometimes by Sarah. And Gloria too, he thinks suddenly. That's strange. I haven't thought of her for years. She used to look just like this when you gave her an order.

He insists, 'My wife has been unconscious for over an hour. Do something, for God's sake!'

'Should I try waving my magic stethoscope?' Sister Quthing's black eyes glint like iron pyrites.

When they moved from Buckingham Circle to Houghton, Agnes moved with them. This time Sarah had inspected the outbuildings first, finding a warren of grim, airless, smoke-blackened little rooms that smelled of cooped-up living. A builder was brought in to install a proper bathroom and cooking facilities, and to alter a row of small rooms to make three bed-sitting rooms: one for Agnes, one for the housekeeper Gordon was talking about, and one for a gardener.

Agnes, being the first to move in, took the corner room with two windows that looked out over the mulberry tree in the back yard. Once again she brought her family from Soweto one Sunday to admire her new room and thank her Madam for being so good to her, but Sarah did not make the same mistake as last time. She had tea and cooldrink in plastic mugs waiting on the table under the mulberry tree, where Agnes ate her breakfast, and a cream cake to make up for not asking them into the house. I just want Harrison and the kids to feel comfortable, she told herself, but it had been she who had been most uncomfortable last time, sitting in her large kitchen with its built-in cupboards and gleaming fittings while the six of them probably had to shoehorn their whole existence into an area half its size.

The increasing frequency of dinner and cocktail parties soon grew too much for Agnes to handle alone, and Gordon spoke to a domestic employment agency about hiring a housekeeper. He was told that they didn't have blacks at that level on their books.

'We could do you a nice live-in girl with good references and a Jo'burg pass, you'd be surprised how many we've got,' the voice on the telephone said. 'Or alternatively a white house-keeper who's been looking after this divorced guy's kids, but she comes expensive.'

Gordon put on his General Manager's voice. 'I am looking specifically for a black woman who can take over the running of my house and cook well enough to handle fairly top-level dinner parties. I already have a good all-round maid, but she needs help.'

'Shame, your wife passed away?'

'No, she's a very busy artist, actually.' Gordon wondered why he sounded so defensive. He was proud of Sarah's paintings and liked to show them to visitors, though her awkwardness in company continued to niggle him. She had decided that caftans were the garments most flattering to her shape and size, and had asked a dressmaker to run up half a dozen in the same style and different fabrics: Finnish cottons and rustling silks in the bold colours and splashy designs she loved. They didn't help her to feel more at ease, however. At the parties they gave and went to, she was like a tongue-tied macaw who has gatecrashed a convention of chic egrets, and doesn't know quite what to do with her gaudy wings.

The voice on the phone said, 'A artist, hey? Ag, that's nice. So long as it's pictures where you can see what they getting at. Know what I mean?'

Gordon thought, I know exactly what you mean; Tretchikoff. He said, 'Can you suggest where I should look for the sort of housekeeper I need?'

'I'd try advertising in the *Star* Smalls if I was you.' The voice on the phone took on a confiding tone. 'Put it under "Domestic Vacancies". You never know what'll come out of the woodwork when you run a ad in the papers. I advertised "Lonely widow seeks sincere companionship, no chancers please" once and the phone never stopped ringing. Honest to God. I had to take it off of the hook after a while. They was pestering me like you wouldn't believe, guys from all over the show. Even schoolkids some of them, by the sounds of it.'

Gordon thought sourly, The woman runs like a broken tap, and accountants wonder why company phone bills are always so high. He said, 'Thanks for the advice,' and rang off before she could proffer any more.

In answer to his advertisement for a housekeeper/cook, among the dozens of misspelled beggings for employment written in pencil on paper torn out of school exercise books ('I am a good clean girl sir and no troble can I come nexweek?'), only Gloria's letter stood out. It was on Basildon Bond embossed with an address in Illovo, and she wrote in a neat convent school script, 'I have been trained by a madam who writes books about cooking, therefore I know how to cook very well and serve too. She is going to live in Cape Town, which is why I apply for this job.' He asked his secretary to telephone her and arrange an interview.

On the Saturday morning that Gloria was to come to the house, Sarah made a last-ditch stand. 'Do we really need a housekeeper? Agnes looks after us quite comfortably.'

Gordon looked up from his morning newspaper with annoyance. 'Taking on another servant has nothing to do with our own comfort. Hell, Sarah, I respect the fact that you'd rather be painting than cooking or arranging flowers. I don't *mind* your not wanting to get involved in the business entertaining, but it's got to be done by someone. Hiring a good housekeeper is the best solution for both of us.' There were beads of sweat on his forehead and nose. He was working longer hours than ever, and had no time even for golf now.

He was being very reasonable, Sarah knew. But she hated the idea of having another woman in the house, another personality to adjust to whose needs had to be considered, whose feelings not hurt. Agnes's uniformed bulk was a friendly presence in the house, her discoloured face above the white apron as familiar as the china pattern they had used ever since they were able to afford something better than bazaar cups. A housekeeper would be bound to upset their equilibrium. Sarah sighed. 'I know you're right. I'm just not mad about the idea.'

'It's either that or pull finger yourself, babe.' He folded his newspaper at the page with the stock exchange prices and went to his stinkwood-panelled, tax-exempt study to go over them before tackling the reports he had brought home.

Agnes knocked at the half open door an hour later. 'Here's a girl to see you, Master.'

'Send her in.'

'The Master, he want me to come too?' He looked up. Agnes was looming in the doorway, blocking the person standing behind her.

'No, it's all right, thanks. Just send her in.' He had asked Sarah to explain to Agnes why they were taking on a housekeeper so that her feelings would not be hurt, but by the look on her face Sarah had not succeeded. He said, 'You know this is for my business, Agnes.'

She gave her most disapproving cluck and moved slightly sideways to reveal the head of a young black woman wearing a red felt hat that slanted forward over one eye, carefully matched to the glistening red lipstick on her full lips.

He said, 'You may go now, Agnes.'

'You want tea?'

'Please. Come in, Gloria. Let her through, Agnes.'

'With biscuits or no?' Agnes stood unbudging.

'It doesn't matter! Just go, will you, so I can interview this lady standing behind you.' Gordon felt the sweat pricking out again on his forehead.

'Lady!' Agnes turned her head and raked Gloria's straightened hair, red nylon blouse, grey skirt and high-heeled red shoes with a look that would have drawn blood if it could, but she moved at last, lumbering away down the passage with a face like thunder.

Gordon got up and walked round his desk. 'I'm sorry. Agnes is a little upset this morning.'

In the doorway, the young woman nodded. 'It's understandable.' Holding a red plastic handbag in both hands, she looked round the study with considering eyes.

'Won't you come in?' he said, rather unnerved by her self-possession.

'Thank you.' She walked in and stood in front of him, taller by several inches, dark as molasses, with her hand stretched out. 'I'm Gloria Nosiswe Ntuli. Pleased to meet you, sir.'

Her letter had impressed Gordon and he had been expecting a servant who was a cut above the rest, though not this poised young woman who was offering to shake hands with him as an equal. The only time he ever shook hands with black people was at the company's long-service award ceremony every Christmas, when painfully polite middle-aged employees in threadbare suits would hold their hands out shyly for the supreme accolade from the boss: a brief handshake, murmured congratulations and a cheque that came nowhere near rewarding them for their years of toil. He thought, I'll give offence if I don't, and shook her hand with only a moment's hesitation. 'I'm pleased to meet you too, Gloria.'

'I hope you will find me satisfactory, sir.' She was looking at him from under the red felt brim with the expression of nun-like seriousness that seldom varied during the months she was to work for them. 'I want very much this job as a housekeeper.'

'Why?' His curiosity was tinged with amusement. 'We haven't even begun the interview yet. You don't know what sort of an employer I'll be, or what salary I'm offering.'

'I want this job, sir, because it will help me to better myself. This is my main aim in life.' Her voice wobbled. 'I will never be poor again, never!'

Her intensity astonished him. He had never given more than a passing thought to the lives of the black women they employed; all that was Sarah's department. He read the newspapers, of course, and made the usual noises about how badly black women were treated ('By their men as much as by society – they can be bastards when they're drunk'), but it had never occurred to him that a black woman could have the same aspirations as, well, Rose, for example. He suddenly remembered his mother yelling at his father once, 'My family may have been poor, but I won't be! You take that job, or I'm leaving!'

He said, 'I appreciate how you feel, but could we just get on to a few details first, such as – '

'Sir, you cannot know how strongly I feel, how hard is this life for me!' Her words fell over themselves in her passion to convince him. 'But I can show you my work and how nice I do things, according to how my Madam is teaching me. See, she gives me this reference.'

She looked down to rummage in the red plastic handbag, mauve-rimmed brown eyelids lowered over two port-holes into depths he had not imagined. Close up, she was less attractive than she looked from a distance. Her face was broad and flat, with a heavy nose buttressed by wide nostrils, too-big lips and pockmarked cheeks. The makeup she wore, however, had been applied with skill, and her cheap chain-store clothes had been put together with an eye that clearly devoured the fashion pages of women's magazines. She looked smarter than Sarah or Rose ever had, on a fraction of their resources. Quite a gal, he found himself thinking.

The mauve-rimmed eyelids snapped up like released blinds. 'Here, Mr Kimber. My reference. You see that I can do many things for being a housekeeper. What I can't do, I can learn. I learn extra-quick.'

He sat down behind his desk to read her employer's letter, indicating the visitor's chair to her. As he lifted his eyes from the letter, she launched into a catalogue of dishes she could cook and things she had been taught by her current employer, who sometimes catered for small parties. 'So you see, sir, I can be the best housekeeper for you. You will try me out?'

Gordon thought, If only all the people I have to interview were so keen to get the job. He said, 'Your reference is excellent, and it sounds as though you can cook to the standard I need. I'll go and call Mrs Kimber, if you don't mind waiting a few minutes.'

Gloria looked surprised. 'There is Mrs Kimber? But I was thinking – '

'Mrs Kimber is an artist. She's too busy to cook.' He was jarred into annoyance again. Because of Sarah's reluctance to go to business functions, people were always assuming that he was divorced. 'Or are you queer?' a woman with donkey teeth had brayed at him once. 'How divine! I adore queers.'

Gloria's full red lips quivered. 'Then I will not be doing all the ordering from the shops, running the house and so forth?'

He remembered the assessing glance as she came into the study, and thought, I wonder exactly how far she hoped her duties would go? In his driest voice he said, 'As Mrs Kimber is working full-time towards an exhibition, you will be doing exactly that. Plus the planning, organising and cooking of at least two business dinners a week, and a monthly cocktail party. This job will be hard, challenging work, I promise you.'

She looked down at the red-tipped fingers knotted in her lap. 'I like to work hard, sir, but maybe Mrs Kimber will not like me. Or the mama who brings me to you.'

At which apt moment Agnes came barging in with a tray holding the stainless steel kitchen teapot, two chipped cups and a plate on which two small biscuits lay in splendid isolation, defying anyone to eat them. 'Here's your tea, Master, and some for that one too.' She banged the tray down on the desk, indicating Gloria with a jerk of her head.

Gordon said, pointedly polite, 'Thank you, Agnes. I suppose you know that Gloria may be coming to work here?'

'The Madam, she says.' Agnes's face seethed with what she thought of the idea.

'We hope she'll take some of the load off you, as well as helping the Madam with the parties and the general running of the house.'

'What's wrong with Agnes, eh?' Agnes planted her hands on her considerable hips.

'There's nothing wrong with you, Agnes. It's just that there's too much work for one – ' he was going to say servant, but changed it quickly to '– person to do in this house. So we thought we'd bring someone in to help you.'

'That one? To help me? You think I'm stupid, Master, that my eyes can't see what is in front of them?'

Gloria, who had sat very still since Agnes came into the room, said something quietly in Zulu.

Agnes swung round at her like a Sherman tank, guns blazing. 'Thula, wena! For five years now I work for the Master and the Madam, they never complain. They never say, "That's no good, Agnes". They treat me nice, I treat them nice. I work hard. I clean all over this big house, no trouble. And now you come to tell me what to do? Suka! Better I go.'

'Agnes, please.' Gordon got up to stand between them.

'No, Master! No "Agnes, please" any more!' She mimicked his placatory tone exactly, tears running down her face. 'Agnes, she is finish here! Agnes must go out with the rubbish!' She put her hands up to her face and began howling into them, 'Ai! Ai! Ai!'

Gordon thought, The bloody's woman's gone berserk. Where the hell is Sarah? He said loudly, 'Stop that!'

But Agnes was rocking herself backwards and forwards so the fat shuddered on her heavy brown arms and thighs, howling, 'Ai! Ai! Ai!' into her hands in a rage of betrayal.

It was the beginning of months of feuding between the older woman, whom Sarah persuaded to stay on by raising her salary and saying she couldn't do without her, and Gordon's young usurper. Gloria was more than good at her job, and the house ran smoothly as long as Agnes confined herself to the cleaning and washing and ironing. The trouble came when Gloria felt her domain had been invaded, or Agnes balked at helping her with dinner preparations. Sarah had been right: the equilibrium of the house was disturbed. Rose made things worse by sympathising with Agnes in Gloria's hearing, and occasionally dressing up in high heels and one of Sarah's hats to sashay up and down the drive imitating Gloria on her day off.

'Agnes is very unhappy,' Sarah told Gordon at the end of the first month. The house reverberated with her clucks and sighs and dragging varicosed legs.

'She'll get over it. Gloria's doing a damn good job, and tries to keep the peace.' Sarah had to agree. Gloria was hardworking and tactful, and had taken a great burden off her shoulders. She did not mention Agnes's unhappiness again.

Agnes had won the first battle in the feud. On the day Gloria moved in, she demanded the corner bed-sitting room with two windows as her housekeeper's right. Agnes said since she had been there first and longest, it was hers by right. Both appealed to Sarah, who said that of course Agnes must stay in it, since she'd been given first choice. Agnes was buoyant with triumph and the vacuum cleaner whined all morning as she attacked every speck of dust, every lurking fluffball in the house. *That* one would not find fault with her work. Gloria sulked and burned the first lunch she cooked. Sarah shut herself in her studio all day.

When Gordon came home for the third evening running to the sound of raised voices in the back yard, he called both women into his study and read the riot act. 'This is no good! You've got to learn to work together, or you can both leave – yes, Agnes, you too,' he added as she opened her mouth to protest. 'Nobody's sacred here. I pay you both damn well, and I expect you to do a good job. It's the same at work. If people don't do the job I'm paying them to do, I fire them. How you feel about each other is none of my business, but as long as you're in my house I expect you to behave.'

Both women were silent. Agnes stood with her hands clenched under her apron, glaring at the floor as though trying to melt a hole in it. Gloria was looking straight at him with the expression Rose had perfected in early adolescence: a look of total incomprehension that anyone could be so unreasonable.

Gordon felt the blood rising in his neck as it did so often now when he got annoyed, a feeling of engorgement that made him momentarily dizzy. 'I want a commitment from both of you! No arguments. No fighting. No trouble. Understand?'

Redirecting her glare upwards, Agnes appealed, 'But Master, this one, she – '

'No bloody arguments, I said!' They were both standing there looking at him now, two pairs of eyes brimming with injustice. Like a dark yawn at his feet he felt the chasm that separated his secure white world from the uncertainties and hazards of their lives: pass arrests, buses that ran late, men who robbed people of their wages in the dark Friday night streets, shoebox homes – employers who demanded the impossible. But the chasm closed as abruptly as it had opened, and he said again, 'Understand?'

Agnes's eyes sank to the floor like stones. 'Yes, Master.'

'I understand, sir.' Gloria's lips shook like two scoops of red jelly. He would have to speak to her about wearing too much makeup.

'You may go, then. I don't want to have to speak of this matter again.'

Gloria used her free time methodically. She attended night school in the local church hall twice a week. She nagged Sarah to get her reading books from the library, and could be seen during her afternoon breaks at the table under the

124

mulberry tree puzzling over the written English that was so different to the English everyone spoke. On her weekends off she would take the bus to town carrying a large brown cardboard suitcase. After a two hour sewing lesson at a self-help centre, she would take another bus to her sister's home in Alexandra township, where she would change into the lime green spangled net ballgown with matching high-heeled sandals that she had saved for six months to buy, and spend the evening at a community centre learning the syncopated swoops and twirls of ballroom dancing. She never danced with the same partner twice, though there were plenty of offers from sharply dressed hopefuls in pointed black Italian shoes.

'I don't have a boyfriend,' she told Sarah once when they were sitting at the kitchen table over cups of coffee, discussing the week's menus. 'All they want is to get on top of you in bed and take your money.'

'Surely you'd like a husband one day?'

'What for? To come home drunk every night and beat me up and give me ten kids? No ways, Madam.' The full red lips firmed into a compressed oval. 'I want to better myself. Next, I'm learning to drive. Then I can truly be a housekeeper, going to the shops too.'

Sarah thought, She's like Gordon in so many ways. Ambitious and determined to make her way, to make a mark on the world. That's why he chose her, I suppose. They're soul mates. What if – ? But the thought was quickly suppressed.

Gloria's competence at orchestrating dinner parties became a talking point at them. 'You'd better watch it, old man. Someone'll steal her from you,' his business colleagues said to Gordon with winks that implied, Bully for you, if you're getting it too.

Sarah felt sick when she saw them. She was enjoying very much the freedom from domestic worries that having two servants – three now with Joseph, the new gardener – gave her. A small gallery had offered her a solo exhibition, and she was working full time, often late into the night if they weren't entertaining or going out. Having Gloria meant that she could work untroubled, and she was grateful to her for it. But hearing the men's snide remarks and seeing the way women guests sized Gloria up when she served the meal in the black skirt and white satin blouse Gordon had decreed, her red lips and nails and mauve eyelids shining like jewels in the candlelight, Sarah wondered if she was not paying too great a price for her freedom.

I know Gordon's not like that, she thought, or I think I know. But they don't. They're giving me the supporting actress role in the crude jokes about sex across the colour line that white men banter about in pubs, and in huddles at parties.

She asked Gloria to wear her floral uniform with matching apron and doek for dinner parties, telling Gordon it was more appropriate.

The feud in the back yard simmered for months, flaring up into accusations of stolen meat rations, unsanctioned visitors, newly-ironed laundry dropped deliberately on the floor, and favouritism.

'You give her the best room because you like her best!' Gloria accused Sarah one day in the middle of a wrangle over who should wash the lettuce for the salads she was preparing for a large buffet dinner.

'That's not true, Gloria. She was here first, that's all.'

'But I am the senior member of staff! I do all the important work. It should be mine.'

'Aikona!' Agnes shouted, swinging round from the sink where she was scrubbing last night's pots that Gloira had left soaking, another bone of contention. 'You come *last* in this place!'

'Anyone can clean. Anyone can wash and iron.' Gloria's scorn would have scorched milk. 'Not anyone can cook like me. Is true, Madam?' She looked at Sarah with an expression that dared her to deny the fact.

It was not the first time Gloria had challenged her on grounds she could not quite put her finger on. She thought, It can't be Gordon. He comes home late every night, and either works or sleeps all weekend. I'd know if he was – doing anything with her. But it wasn't impossible. Sarah was in the studio for long stretches when Rose was out and Agnes away on her day off, and he could be doing what he liked in the spare bedroom. Tasting dark honey. White men were supposed to love it.

She pushed the thought away and said, 'You're a very good cook, Gloria. Agnes is a very good helper too. I'm grateful to both of you. But it's got nothing to do with who sleeps where.'

'Madam, I can't better myself in such a small room!' Gloria burst out. 'There's no place for me to study with a desk and a light and a place for books, like Rose. Black people never get a chance like white people.'

She had come to resent with a passion the white girl with the long blonde plait who was given so much, while she had to work so hard for so little. Rose had beautiful clothes in her cupboard and a big sunny bedroom to herself with a bathroom opening off it, and she went to a school where the buildings looked like a Hollywood film castle and the teachers were English ladies. Gloria had had to share a narrow mattress in a tin shanty with two restless younger brothers, and listen to her father making brutal love to her mother every night when he came home drunk from the shebeen. At school, she had sat on the concrete floor with a scratchy slate among seventy other children trying to listen to over-burdened teachers who would be lucky to have Standard Six certificates. Her only clothes had been a black gym and two white school shirts and a new dress every Christmas. Rose was rude to her too, mocking her behind her back to make Agnes laugh. Why? would boil in Gloria's head whenever she thought of Rose. Why her and not me?

Sarah was thinking, It's quite true. Black people don't get the same chances. It had never occurred to her to provide either maid with a reading light; she suspected that Agnes couldn't read but had never quizzed her about it, for fear of hurting her feelings. Then she thought of the narrow store-room at the far end of the outbuildings, part of the original warren, which would probably take a small table and chair if the old bottles and news-papers that accumulated there were cleared out. 'Would you be happy if we made a place for you to study in, Gloria?' she said.

'Oh Madam, I will be so happy.' Yet she could not resist casting a sideways look of triumph at Agnes that said, You see? I'm the most important here. I'm educated.

Joseph, the gardener, whitewashed the small room and fixed an electric extension cord under the eaves from Gloria's room. Sarah found a table and chair that just fitted in, and an old lampstand that had nothing wrong with it but a mild case of the wobbles. On her next trip to town, Gloria bought a pine shelf kit and a length of floral cotton from the Oriental Plaza for curtains, which she sewed by hand. By the following weekend when Sarah came to see the room, trailed by Agnes, the curtains were hanging from a piece of wire stretched between two nails. The shelf had been fixed to the wall. On it Gloria had put her books from night school, a jam jar with a match-impaled avocado pip in its mouth, and a doll made of leather and fur scraps with a beaded apron and tiny brass wire bangles.

At the sight of the doll, Agnes jumped back as though she had been bitten by a snake. 'Thakathi! Thakathi!'

'What's wrong?' Sarah thought, Now I suppose she's jealous because I haven't done anything for her.

'Thakathi, Madam! That dolly is from a sangoma, a witchdoctor. She makes big trouble.' Agnes's fat cheeks were still quivering from her sudden movement. Her eyes looked frightened. '*That* one wants for me to go, Madam. She wants my room.'

Gloria said angrily, 'This is nonsense, Madam. My sister, she gives it to me. For good luck, she says. This mama is trying to make trouble for me with this rubbish talk of sangomas and so forth. Is nonsense!'

'Is not nonsense! That dolly is a bad thing, Madam. She must throw it away.'

'No ways I throw it away! You know nothing! You can't even read!' Gloria began shouting at Agnes in Zulu. Agnes began to yell back.

Sarah was furious. After all her efforts at peacemaking and fairness, here she was trapped in a room barely bigger than her wardrobe with two screeching women who would be tearing each other's hair out any minute. And why? Because one thought she was superior because she was educated, and the other thought she was superior by right of longer tenure. And I've got myself into this because I feel guilty about living in a big house and employing them to do work I should be doing, Sarah thought. This is crazy.

She shouted, 'Be quiet, both of you! I won't have fighting. Go to your rooms. I'll talk to the Master when he comes home.'

The threat quelled them both: Gloria sullen under her fashionably tied doek, Agnes with wide wet crescents along the gaping under-arm seams of the outsize nylon overall she was wearing. Since Gloria's assumption of the more glamorous duties in the house, Agnes had become increasingly sloppy. You could often see the assortment of old clothes she wore under her overalls because she never mended them. She would come with a doleful face, pockets torn off and buttons missing and say, 'Madam, she must please buy me a new uniform,' as though Sarah was wilfully keeping her in rags.

Sarah thought, They're becoming more trouble than they're worth. She said crossly, 'I wish you'd try to work together without fighting all the time.'

'But Madam, she wants my room!'

'*She* wants to pull me down!'

'Oh shut up, both of you!' Sarah walked out, fuming. There was silence for the rest of the day from the back yard.

Gordon came home to cheese on toast and Sarah's exasperated account of the strife. She had not been able to paint all afternoon. He said, 'Can't you handle it this time? I'm tired tonight. I don't feel like talking to them. My advice is to tell Agnes to go.'

'How can I, just like that? She's been with us for over five years.'

'You know my philosophy, babe. Shape up, or ship out. One of them's got to go, and logically it should be Agnes, whose skills are easily replaceable.'

Logically. Gordon all over. She said, 'Rose would be very upset if Agnes went. She was so good to her when I was ill.'

'You want to go on like this?'

She looked down at her hands, which for once had cheese instead of paint under the nails. 'No.'

'Then get rid of Agnes. Rose will get over it. She's a big girl now. Don't waste your sympathy on a jealous old woman with her nose out of joint because someone younger and better looking does a better job.'

Better looking. He sat across the kitchen table with the bright overhead light cruelly highlighting his thinning hair and the sagging skin pouches under his eyes. She launched a missile from a deeply buried silo pit where it had been building up pressure for months. 'I sometimes think Gloria's becoming more useful to you than I am.'

'What do you mean by that?'

'Just what I say. She's slotted so neatly into the Gordon Kimber support team: your secretary, your driver, your board of directors — and the gifted Gloria to keep things running smoothly at home.'

'She's damn good at what she does! Efficient and capable. I like that, specially when my job's on the line.' He hunched his shoulders and moved his head from side to side to relieve the tightness in his neck. 'You seem to forget that I hired Gloria in the first place to take the pressure off you.'

'I'm grateful for the kind thought, Gordon, but it isn't working. Mainly because Little Miss Efficiency has her beady eyes on a bigger prize than being a housekeeper for the rest of her life.'

'What prize? You're talking in riddles.'

She felt the pressure in the silo pit beginning to build again, fuelled by the many irritations of the day: the fight in the back yard, not being able to paint, grazing her fingers on the unaccustomed cheese grater while she was making supper. She said, 'I'm beginning to feel as though I have a cuckoo in my nest who could push me out at any minute.'

'Don't be bloody ridiculous!' He slammed his hands on the table. Thick ropes of veins pulsed in his neck. 'She's a black servant, goddammit!'

'And therefore untouchable? You wouldn't think so from the way men's eyes follow her over our dinner table. Yours too, sometimes.'

'Are you accusing me of fucking her, Sarah? Or just fancying her? Or has your fevered imagination got something more exotic in mind?'

'I'm only telling you what I see. And feel.'

He shouted, 'You've got a bloody nerve! When would I have the time to get involved with other women – let alone the inclination to break the law with a black one? You know as well as I do that company directors have to be legally lily-white.'

She felt a relief valve open down in the silo pit, but the steam it released burned her. She thought, I was wrong. I should have known the company always comes first. She mumbled, fighting tears, 'I had to know.'

'You should have known. We go back a long, hard way, Sarah.' He looked old and tired, and he had only just passed forty.

'I'll give them both one more chance,' she said, getting up to go so he wouldn't see her crying.

After Sarah spoke to them the next day, Gloria said, 'Please, I would like to talk to Mr Kimber about this matter, Madam.'

'He's too busy, I'm afraid.' It gave her a shameful satisfaction to say it. 'He asked me to say that he'd give you both one more chance. We can't go on with this continual bickering.'

'It's not my fault, Madam, you know.' Gloria had swollen eyelids like her own this morning; she must have been crying too. 'I try to do my utmost best all the time. But this old mama, she pulls me down. I don't know what more I can do.'

Agnes muttered, 'This is a bad woman, Madam. She has bad things in her room.'

Sarah raised her voice. 'I'm not interested in how you feel

130

about each other. I just want peace in this house, understand?'

Gloria closed her swollen eyelids. 'I understand only too well, Madam.'

On three consecutive days off after that, Sarah saw her walking to the bus stop down the road in the red and grey outfit, the red felt hat slanted low over her eyes, the red shoes stumbling on the uneven pavement. She was not surprised when Gloria submitted a neatly written note of resignation the following week. 'I must go,' she said. 'There is no place for me here.'

'Mr Kimber will be sorry.' Sarah felt she owed her at least that. 'Where will you be going?'

'To a business canteen in Booysens, Madam.' Glora's mauve-slicked eyelids were still puffy. 'It is not so nice a job like this one. I won't have a place to study or so much time off, but the pay is good and I can get promotion quick, if I work hard.'

'I'm glad for you, Gloria.'

The black woman's full red lips parted in a faint smile. 'The old mama will be glad too. She can sleep with no more worries about my sister's dolly coming to catch her in the night.'

Sarah said, trying to mean it, 'I'm sorry things didn't work out for you here.'

'No, excuse me, Madam, but you are not sorry.' Gloria shook the glossy pageboy that had taken a salon stylist in town three hours to straighten, coax into smooth curves and lacquer stiffly in place. 'But I take it for a compliment, like the good reference Mr Kimber is giving me to get this job.'

Sarah had not known Gloria had even spoken to Gordon. He had said nothing to her about it. She said, 'I'm sorry for a lot of things, really.'

'I don't want your sorry, Madam. I want for you to understand.' Gloria's pocked cheeks were burning. 'I try to pull myself up, not to be poor, not to be ignorant. It is so hard, but I must keep trying. Mr Kimber, he understands.'

Sarah thought, He's behaved much better than I have. She said, 'I wish you luck in your endeavours, Gloria. I'm not unsympathetic, you know.'

'But you must look after what is yours.'

On the day she left, Gloria put out a slim brown hand with red-tipped nails. 'Thank you for the study room, anyway. I was happy for it.'

The handshake was brief. 'Goodbye, Gloria.'

'Goodbye.' She added as an afterthought, 'Madam.'

Gordon had sent his driver to take Gloria to her new job. All three of them watched her leave: Sarah from the studio window, Agnes and Rose through the window of the kitchen where they were having a giggly celebratory tea together. Gloria was wearing the red felt hat with a tight red sweater, black trousers and spiky red sandals; the need to make a ladylike impression had passed. She carried the cardboard suitcase in one hand and the lime green spangled net ballgown on a hanger in the other, with its matching sandals dangling by their heel straps from the hook. Inside the suitcase was a cut-glass scent bottle from Rose's dressing table which she would never even notice was gone. Gloria did not look back at the house as the long black Chrysler Imperial swept down the drive.

Sarah went out later and bought two new extra-outsize uniforms for Agnes.

Gordon said next day, 'Find a good caterer to do the dinners, will you? I'm sorry Gloria wasn't a success. I liked her.'

Fifteen years later in the tin-roofed clinic where Sarah lies unconscious, he remembers the expression on Gloria's face and thinks, I hope you made it where you wanted to go, Ms Ntuli.

14

Sarah has to fight her way through shoals of dissolving purple shapes behind her eyelids to understand what the voices above her are murmuring. Her head is throbbing like a beaten drum.

'It's been too long. You've got to call a doctor.' Gordon. In his bulldozer mood.

'We've tried, I told you. He's not there.' A voice she does not know, and a rustle of cotton. She feels a hand on her forehead. 'I wouldn't worry too much. The vital signs are good. Her eyes have been moving. She'll be coming round soon, I think.'

'How do I know you're right?' Gordon again. 'Concussion can be bloody serious. I'll go and find a doctor myself.'

'By all means go, if you must.' The unknown voice, very polite. 'You'll discover that there's no doctor closer than Maseru at the moment, and that's an hour's drive away and an hour back. Our doctor is out at one of the mission clinics, but they expect him back soon.'

'I'll go and fetch him.'

'You will not! You will rather wait for his phone call and ask if he is able to come,' the voice says sharply. 'We don't like being ordered about in these parts, Mr Kimber. We are no longer a colony.'

'This is an emergency!' Gordon's voice goes into the speed wobble that presages rage. 'My wife is lying there badly hurt, and I want her seen by a doctor. I haven't got the time or the inclination to pussyfoot round your susceptibilities right now, Sister. Sarah's more important to me.'

Sister. I'm lying on a bed. Where? Sarah tries to move her head, and a bolt of pain smashes through the top of her forehead and rips downwards to force its way out of her mouth in a moan.

'I do not – ' the unknown voice is saying, but it stops abruptly. Sarah feels someone bending over her, the warmth of a face near her own, the hand on her forehead again. 'Are you awake, my dear? Can you hear me?'

Gordon is bending over her too. She can smell the sweat on his shirt; he always smells like this when he comes in from the lands on a hot day. It's not unpleasant, just very much him. Essence of Gordon. He is calling. 'Sarah? Sarah?'

Another bolt of pain, and she moans again. There is something pressing down on her brain, a heavy, terrible weight that will not let her open her eyes.

'She's definitely coming round. I'll get some water. Keep talking to her.' Footsteps going away, brisk crêpe soles on polished cement.

Sarah feels her hand being picked up and kneaded by strong fingers with calluses where other people's fingers are softly cushioned. Gordon is saying, 'Can you hear me? It's all right, love. I'm here. You're safe.'

Love. He never called me that in the beginning. Only 'babe' . . . What is this heaviness? She mouths, 'What – '

'She's trying to talk!' Gordon calls out to the unknown person, and the loudness sends another burst of pain through her head. She lifts her free hand to the weight pressing down so relentlessly on her eyes.

'Lie still.' He captures it and crushes her two hands together in an excess of relief. 'Don't try to talk. Thank God you're all right.'

She feels as though the bones in her hands are birds' bones, frail breastbones and clavicles and fine brittle wing bones that will snap in an instant. 'Don't,' she whispers.

'Don't what?' He is so close that she feels his breath on her face. It is hot and anxious, like a berg wind.

'Don't hold – my hands so tight,' she manages to get out before the next flash of pain. It is worse than the others, and spins the purple shapes behind her eyelids into a whorled maze into which she is falling. But she can't fly. I'm a bird with a leather hood over my head and jesses on my wrists, she thinks frantically.

Gordon loosens his grip but does not let go. 'Lie still. There's water coming.'

She moans and mutters, 'Two birds on the hand are worth one in the bush.'

'You mustn't try to talk, love.'

But she must. It's not only the hood over her eyes; there's

something outside it ramming bolts of pain down through a hole in the middle of her head. 'Get this thing off me,' she begs. 'I want to open my eyes, and I can't.' She begins to tremble and move her head from side to side, trying to free it.

He says urgently, 'Lie still, Sarah! Just for a few minutes while you get your bearings. You've had a hell of a knock.'

'Get them off!' She pulls her hands away from him and claws upwards. Pain strikes again in sledgehammer blows that feel as though they are breaking open her skull like a ripe pomegranate to expose the sticky wet redness inside. And then she remembers Rose lying in the sticky wet redness of her own blood. Rose so deathly pale and torn. Rose dead. Sarah feels a howl of rage and loss building up inside her, knows it will hurt if she lets it out, knows it will shatter her tenuous hold on the reality of a bed, Gordon, an unknown voice and a hand on her forehead – and lets it burst out anyway.

After concerted pleading, Sarah and Gordon agreed to allow Rose to join Ursula in the university residence. 'I won't be able to get properly involved in varsity life if I have to schlep home every day,' she kept nagging. 'I'll miss all the fun. Everybody says so.'

It was Sunday morning, one of the rare times when all three of them were able to sit down to a meal together. 'I remember it well.' Sarah looked across the table at Gordon to see if he too remembered.

But he was wearing the frown that always appeared now when he was annoyed: three deep grooves coming to a knotted arrow-point above the bridge of his nose. He said, 'I'm not sending you to varsity for the fun, Rose. I'd rather you stayed at home.'

The frown did not seem to have the same effect at home as at the office, however. Rose said, 'Because you know only too well what I could get up to, is that it?'

'What do you mean?' Gordon put down his knife and fork and turned to her, investing the frown with the additional hunching of his shoulders, a combination which could make grown men quail across his office desk.

Rose hardly noticed. She banged her own knife and fork down. 'You weren't exactly a model of rectitude yourself at varsity, were you? I mean, I'm the living proof of that.'

She could have been Sarah during their early fights in the

Durban flat, Gordon thought. She had the same furiously mottled cheeks, the same blue eyes that seemed to stare right through you when they were angry. Her blonde hair was cut in a bob now where Sarah's had been long, but it had the same tendency to fly out in electric wisps. He had a dizzying sense of the past interlocking with the present in a female conspiracy that excluded him. 'What do you mean?' he repeated. 'I worked damn hard there.'

'And played hard. Ma's told me how – how I began.' Rose had been able to fling 'shotgun baby' at her mother, though the words seemed to stick in her throat now. She was as knowledgeable about the mechanics of sex as any seventeen-year-old who hasn't yet experienced it could be – Miss Ramsden had made sure that St Winifreds girls would not go into battle ill-equipped with the facts of life – but it wasn't something you discussed with your father. Nor was the hurt she had felt when she first realised that her conception had been the unwanted by-product of a back-seat teenage grope that went too far. I would have been another abortion statistic if Granny had had her way, she guessed. The whole edifice of this marriage between her parents, the homes they had made, the arguments and makings up, David, her mother's long depression – all had been consequences of the conjunction of one stray sperm and one unfortunately available egg. Me.

Gordon, still feeling dizzy, turned the frown on Sarah. 'You told her?'

'She asked a long time ago. She can add and subtract as well as anyone else.' The smile had faded on Sarah's face.

Watching it die, Rose felt a rage she had never felt before towards her father. 'Do you think I'm a complete fool? I know what happened! I know I wasn't wanted! I know you had to get married because of me! How do you think that makes me feel?'

Sarah said, reaching across the table, 'Darling, if you hadn't been very much wanted, you wouldn't be here. Don't let it worry you.'

Rose snatched her hand out of reach. 'I don't! It's Dad's attitude that worries me. He's so pompous and insensitive!'

Her birth was such a long-past event in his life that he had almost forgotten it, yet here she was blazing at him as though he had deliberately tried to harm her. He said irritably, 'Why dig up old bones, for hell's sake? All that was over and done with long

136

ago. I'm sorry if you feel bad about it, Rosie, but it's quite irrelevant to what we're discussing now, which is what's best for you. I don't understand why you should want to go and live in some grim institution with hordes of females and indifferent food, when you could be much more comfortable at home.'

Rose gave him her favourite Bette Davis look, withering scorn. 'But that's just why I've got to get away, can't you see? Neither of you understands the first thing about me!' She stood up, knocking over her chair, and flung her arms out in a dramatic gesture before running out of the room.

Gordon said in the silence that followed the slam of her bedroom door upstairs, 'Am I?'

'What?' Sarah could not look at him. She hated quarrels, specially between Rose and Gordon who were so alike in their persistence that they would keep on picking and rubbing at each other's raw places until they bled.

'Pompous and insensitive.' The dizziness in his head had settled into a familiar tight ache above his eyes, with the frown at its epicentre.

'A bit of both, I suppose. Neither of us is perfect.' Sarah was fiddling with the ornate silver salt cellar, chosen by his secretary, that Gordon had given her for Christmas. 'I do think we should let her go into residence. It'll be far more fun for her than having to stay at home with two boring middle-aged parents.'

Gordon gave a cough of laughter. 'Boring and middle-aged too. How am I going to face myself in the mirror any more?'

Sarah looked up at him then, and saw the pallor of too many meetings in closed rooms reeking of cigarette smoke, of endless tense phone calls and confrontations and decisions that had to be made at once, though they needed more thought and care. The folds of his neck had begun to sag over his shirt collars; the stocky surfer's body was submerged under a succession of soft bulges. This morning there was a thin white edge to his mouth that she had not seen before. She said, 'Are you feeling all right?'

'Bit of a headache,' he admitted. 'Trying to get some sense out of our daughter in one of her more belligerent moods is no easy task.'

'Really, I think we should let her go into residence. She needs to be with young people.'

He shrugged. 'Who am I to deny her the pleasure, if you both feel so strongly about it? I just hope she keeps her head there,

137

and doesn't get sucked into all that bleeding heart nonsense students seem to go in for these days. She's being sent there to study, not to indulge in demonstrations and airy fairy politics.'

'She's going there to Experience Life, she told me.' Sarah's smile crept irresistibly back. 'Do you remember how adult and sophisticated and important we felt as new students, and what babies we were, blissfully oblivious that it wasn't real life at all?'

'You and I found out soon enough.' He got up and came round the table to her and picked up her hand with its paint-ingrained fingernails. 'Do you have many regrets, babe?' He had not called her that for several years. It was not a word that fitted easily into their life in this grand house that had never felt quite like home, except when she was among the familiar things in her studio.

She said, 'Some. Inevitably,' and was surprised when he squatted awkwardly down beside her chair to see that his eyes were moist.

'We haven't had much time together these past few years,' he said. 'It's my fault. The job always seems more important than anything else. Maybe we could get away for a few weeks when Rosie goes into residence – to the Cape, perhaps. A good beach hotel where we can unwind completely, swim, lie in the sun, talk. And go to bed without being too exhausted to do anything but sleep. Would you like that?'

Her first wary thought was, This isn't Gordon. I wonder what he's trying to compensate me for this time. Another promotion? Another move? She said, 'What's the occasion?'

'Do we have to have one?'

'I don't know any more. Do we?' His face was very close. She was looking down on it, seeing the thinning hair on his forehead and the puffiness round and under his eyes. She thought, What strange chance is it that chooses our mates for us? Why did I get this man, and not another? And what have we created together that is good, besides Rose? David doesn't count now.

He said, squeezing her hand, 'I hope you still like what you see. It isn't the first fine flush of youth any more, but this too too solid flesh can offer auxiliary attractions. Such as first class hotels, and the odd mansion.'

She felt a bubble of laughter rising and thought, He can still make me laugh. Maybe that's reason enough to be glad we are still together.

His secretary booked them into the Beacon Island Hotel for

two weeks in March, when the rush of the financial year-end in February was over. He slept for most of the first week and was called back to a merger crisis at the beginning of the second, leaving her to paint her seascapes and eat her crayfish dinners alone. She came home to find that his secretary had arranged for the house to be filled with flowers as an act of contrition, though not for the broken holiday. Gordon had been called to London.

Sarah held her second solo exhibition a few months later. But the favourable critical appraisal she received was marred by a phone call from her mother, whom she had not seen for over a year. 'Your father's dead,' she said. 'He had a heart attack while he was with his floozy, and by the time she stopped screeching and got him to hospital, he was dead.'

'Ma – ' Sarah wanted to say, 'Are you all right?' but the cold fury in her mother's voice chilled her to the bone, so she said instead, 'I'll come down for the funeral.'

'No, don't. I'm having him privately cremated this afternoon, no mourners. I can't run the risk of *her* turning up in front of all my friends.'

'You can't! I want to be there.'

'What for? He's gone now. He won't know.'

The words were like a lash across her face. Sarah gasped, 'Because I loved him! Because he loved me.'

'And I didn't?'

Sarah was silent.

'You betrayed me.' It was an old woman's spiteful quaver. 'I gave you all I had, all I could offer, gave it to you on a plate. And you betrayed me.'

Sarah felt her throat swelling with pain and tears. 'I just made a mistake,' she whispered. 'Anyone could have. I wasn't deliberately trying to hurt you. And it all happened so long ago – '

'You took everything I ever cared for! And always for a minimum payment, like the Catholics, who can sin all week and get forgiven for two Hail Mary's on Sunday. But I'm the one who's had to do the penance, Sarah. You shamed me in front of everybody.'

Standing in the hallway of her big quiet house, Sarah said, 'Your penance was self-inflicted, Ma. And I've had to do plenty of my own. Did that ever cross your mind?'

'I forgave you when David was born. I tried to mend things

between us. But you worked on your father behind my back.' The cold voice sharpened to needle point. 'He's left you everything, with only a small annuity to me. I'm contesting it in court. You won't get your hands on a cent as long as I can help it. The floozy, I'm glad to say, got nothing.'

Sarah was stunned. Her mother was talking about money, not the rift begun so long ago by the arrival of Rose. She stammered, 'I – I didn't know.'

The laugh at the other end of the phone was not quite sane. 'Don't try and play the innocent with me! I won't be taken in again.'

Sarah felt herself turn to stone. She said, 'When I do get my hands on Dad's money, and I'm sure I will since he always had good lawyers, I'll make sure the floozy gets some of it too. Thank you for phoning. I'll send flowers for the cremation.'

She put the phone down on her mother's scream of rage and went to her studio to mourn her father. The money when it came went into a trust fund in case Rose should ever need it. She got the woman friend's number from her father's office and phoned her later on the day of his death. Her answer was, 'Thanks for the offer, dear, but I couldn't accept it, you know. He saw me right with this flat long ago, and a good endowment scheme besides. He was a lovely gentleman, your Dad.' Her voice was heavy with tears.

What better epitaph? Sarah thought as she wept for him, and for the mother she had now irrevocably lost.

15

Poor things, Sister Quthing is thinking. She stands by the bed holding an enamel mug of water and watching Rose's father trying to comfort her mother, who is sobbing against his shoulder with her mouth open like a stricken child. Grief consumes her body like a fever, in long racking shudders. Tears are coursing down his sun-reddened face and falling with hers in dark splotches on his checked shirt.

Sister Quthing remembers the young man who came to the village a few months ago on a recruiting drive for the *Free Azania Now!* movement. 'We must fight their violence with our violence!' he had shouted from the schoolroom platform to a silent audience more used to church services. 'Our children are dying like flies in the townships! Their children must die too, so that they know what it feels like to see their future bleeding and burning and lying in the dust full of bullet holes! An eye for an eye and a tooth for a tooth – it is their Bible that tells us so!'

If this is what he means, I want nothing of it. Sister Quthing's capable brown hand tightens round the enamel mug. Evil is not stopped by doing more evil. It is stopped by people like Rose and Jake, who cared so much for others. These people care too, even if the man talks rudely sometimes. They are parents like I am a parent. Their sadness is my sadness.

She puts the mug down on the green-painted locker by the bed and says, 'It is good that you can cry, my dear, but try to lie back on the pillows. It will be better for the swelling.' When Sarah shakes her head, she bends over to embrace her too and says, 'Please?'

'It's unbearable, the way she died,' Sarah keeps repeating. 'Unbearable.'

When Gordon finally manages to lower her on to the pillow, he says in a hard voice, 'I'll kill whoever did it. I'll track them

141

down and bloody pull them apart with my bare hands, if I have to.'

Sarah is still weeping. Sister Quthing strokes her hair away from her sweaty forehead where the swelling is already turning blue, thinking, I should get a cold compress on to it. She says, 'Don't cry. It would be better to think of Hope now, Mrs Kimber.'

'Hope? Oh God, what hope?' Sarah turns her swollen face up to the whitewashed ceiling that sags in places where rainwater has leaked through the nail holes in the tin roof above, and howls.

It is a terrible noise, the recognition of death's finality. The fine hairs on the sister's arms rise up in goose bumps. The last time she heard it was when her father died, and her mother and his other wives wailed all night in his hut over his cold blanket-wrapped body. Trying to banish the memory, she says, 'But of course you have Hope. Rose's baby. She is in the next room.'

Sarah's sobbing breath catches in her throat. 'What?'

'The baby was not hurt at all.' Sister Quthing fusses unnecessarily with the pillow under Sarah's head, trying to keep her voice matter-of-fact. She prides herself on her professionalism, on always upholding the high standards of nursing conduct she was taught at Baragwanath Hospital, even in this poor village where the facilities are so inadequate. 'At the time of the shooting she was in the bedroom. The Lord was watching over that little one, for sure.'

'The baby? Rose's baby?' Sarah tries to lift her head, and cannot. She turns it sideways on the pillow and says urgently to Gordon, 'I hadn't realised. Hope's alive!'

'Would you like to see her?' The sister pulls the rumpled sheet up to Sarah's chin, folds it over at the top and smooths it flat in the reflex action common to all nurses. 'She's sleeping now after a mid-morning feed, but I could bring her to you in her carrycot.'

'Please.' Sarah begins to cry again, but softly now. 'Please bring her. We've never seen her.'

'If you will just take a sip of this water, Mrs Kimber.' Sister Quthing is expert at blackmailing her patients into doing what is good for them. 'We don't want you to get dehydrated in this heat. Then I'll bring the baby, and when you've had a good look at her we'll get a cold compress on to that bump on your head.'

Sarah nods, unable to speak for her tears, and reaches for

Gordon's hand. He leans down to kiss her as the sister goes briskly into the next room.

University was a revelation to Rose and Ursula after their schoolgirl years at St Winifreds. At university they were treated as adults, called Miss Kimber and Miss Ginsberg at lectures and tutorials, and were free at last of maths prep and grey flannel uniforms.

At university, they were told in the Vice Chancellor's introductory lecture for new students, you chose what you wanted to study and it was up to you whether you attended lectures or not. 'Of course, if you decide not to, you will not receive your Duly Performed rating at the end of the year, and without a D. P. you can't write exams,' he went on with the mild twinkle under bushy grey eyebrows for which he was famous, and which hid the cynical wit without which he could not have survived academia. 'Which would be a great pity, as we would find it difficult to accept you back again next year.

'I would like to drop a further word of warning into your shell-like ears,' he went on. 'First-year failures are rising at an alarming rate. We are not quite sure why. It could be due to residual malaise from the flower child era,' he twinkled again, 'to a superabundance of pocket money from more affluent parents which has made the fleshpots of this city more available to students, or simply to a general increase in sloth. Whatever the reason, I would remind you ladies and gentlemen that you are highly privileged people in our society compared with your black fellow citizens, of whom we have recently been graciously permitted by the government to enrol a small number.' He twinkled at the small group of black students who sat together towards the front of the Great Hall, looking self-consciously studious in new clothes.

Rose whispered to Ursula, 'D'you think he always talks like this? Do they all?'

Ursula followed her gaze along the row of brightly gowned, velvet-hatted and mortar-boarded professors who sat on the floodlit stage behind the Vice Chancellor, blinking slowly amid the dazzle of their finery like bedizened old tortoises enjoying the sun. 'I hope not,' she whispered back. 'You'd get writer's cramp taking notes.'

They soon discovered, however, that most of the professors

were too grand to be bothered with the general run of first-year lectures, confining themselves to one or two major performances a month. First-year students got the nervous new lecturers and the faculty workhorses who ploughed on year after year turning the callow undergraduate soil and planting their seeds of knowledge in the grim certainty that only a small percentage would germinate, take root and flourish. The rest would fall on the stony ground of ignorance, commercial careers and the good marriages in which so many parents of daughters believed they were investing their university fees.

It was only when Ursula had battled her way to Senior Lecturer in sociology and was banging on the gate of the inner keep where old professors retreat behind their tenures to fight off the onslaughts of decrepitude and feminism, that she realised how apt her vision of old tortoises had been.

Their first year was 1973, the year of Watergate and the Yom Kippur war in Israel, the year when the oil price gushed out of control and the last troops left Vietnam, and those two waspish old geniuses Picasso and Noël Coward died. The major events in South Africa were the first mass strikes by black workers in Durban, and the first boxing match between a white man and a black man. Afrikaans boxer Pierre Fourie fought Bob Foster of the USA for the world lightweight title which Foster won, to jubilation in the townships. It was a rare treat to see a black man beating a white man in public.

Rose and Ursula had interlinking bedrooms with a shared washbasin in Sunnyside, the oldest women's residence. It was a venerable stone building covered in Virginia creeper with stone steps at the entrance on which there was nearly always a knot of senior girls sitting. During their first few months new students had to steel themselves to run this gauntlet, knowing that their clothes and hair would be discussed in detail, often before they were out of earshot, and soon painfully aware that the mix'n'match 'college clothes' fond mothers had helped them to buy were not worn on campus. It took time to develop the requisite degree of student tat, or if you moved in the social set, casual chic.

Inside the front entrance was a waiting room with a black woman seated at a switchboard who would call students on the intercom when they had a visitor or a phone call. Beyond it was a network of dark passages that had been painted a glossy cream to make them less forbidding, but whose cold granolithic floors struck a chill through sandals even on the hottest summer day. The passage floors were polished weekly with stoep polish by black men in khaki kitchen suits bound at the edges of the sleeves and short pants with red; shuffling along with polishing cloths under their hands and knees, their upturned bare feet were a pale, vulnerable beige. At mealtimes they would change into white cotton waiters' uniforms and tackies, and squeak about the dining room serving the vegetables and collecting dirty plates, still smelling of stoep polish.

Residence students were required to wear academic dress to dinner on Fridays, and Rose and Ursula soon learned how to conceal their rolled-up jeans under a demure façade of white blouse and black undergraduate gown. They tilted their heaters back to toast marshmallows in winter, and brewed illicit pineapple beer under their beds. They learned to make scathing remarks about the curfew hours and the prim and proper House Committee and the food, though Sunnyside was like paradise after St Winifreds.

Rose had kept up her Journal during her early high school years, but the entries dwindled as her rebellion flowered and her friendship with Ursula grew. Going to university aroused her ambition to write again, and she chose to study English and history while Ursula took the very different direction of sociology. They enjoyed and did well at their studies, managing to escape the pitfall of first-year failure they had been warned against.

Maintaining their image as interesting rebels was much harder at university than it had been at school, however. The student body divided quite neatly into four factions: the studious, the rugger buggers, the social set and the lefties, of whom most considered themselves interesting rebels. Lefties wore beards and beads and leather sandals and clothes that looked as though they had just come out of a trunk in the attic. Lefties talked politics and French films and bean sprouts and worker communes, and had minds so wide open to other people's sensitivities that you sometimes felt uncomfortable draughts in their presence. Lefties were stridently anti-racist, and indeed it was easy to be friendly towards the occasional black student sitting outnumbered in lectures and at socials. When he disappeared at the end of the day into the labyrinth of the townships, who could blame anyone for not getting to know him better?

For three years, Rose and Ursula's world was the magic closed circle of university where few are troubled by the necessity of earning a living. Life began and ended on campus; parents were boring old wrinklies; politics was a drag, except when someone they knew got banned or jailed. Then the campus would erupt with protest meetings passing furious resolutions whose net result would be a fuzzy photograph of upraised fists on page five of the evening paper, followed by a spate of angry letters from taxpayers demanding that the government's student subsidy be cut forthwith. The government, apprehensive over the unaccountably lily-livered behaviour of the Portuguese which was leading rapidly towards independence for Angola and Moçambique, was too busy refining and setting in legislative concrete its vision of a white South Africa dalmatian-spotted with black nation states, to pay much attention to the ravings of either students or taxpayers.

At the beginning of their third year, Ursula began to talk a lot about a new sociology lecturer called Isidore Frankel. Walking up to the library one hot afternoon in March, she asked Rose to go with her to that evening's meeting of the socialist discussion group he had started. 'He's such a good speaker, you wouldn't believe. The best lecturer we've got this year.'

Rose said, 'Forget it. You know I'm not even mildly interested in socialism. Plus I've got an English tut tomorrow and I haven't done any preparation for it.'

'Oh come on, Rose! Since when did you lose any sleep over a tut?'

'The answer is no. N–o, no. I've got work to do.'

'Please come. I know you'll enjoy it. They're an interesting bunch of people, everybody says.'

She was being unusually insistent. Curious to know why, Rose said, 'Do you really want to go? I mean, is it a matter of life and death?'

Ursula's sallow face was urgent with her need to convince. I will positively die if I can't go to that meeting. Say you'll come?'

Rose thought, It must be a guy. They had both had several boyfriends, though no one serious. She said, teasing, 'I just might, if properly bribed.'

'Name your price. I could do your next House Comm duty? Double chips at the cafeteria? Free ironing services for a month?'

Rose laughed. 'Don't worry, I'll come. Free, gratis and for nothing. But just this once, OK?'

Ursula turned and enveloped her in a hug that included the exuberant tangle of curly hair, into which many a comb had sunk its teeth without trace. 'Unreal! O friend without peer! You won't be sorry.'

And she wasn't. Isidore Frankel's discussion group changed the whole direction of her life.

His flat was several streets away from the university in a dingy Braamfontein building that had suffered generations of students and poorly-paid junior lecturers. Thick beige paint peeled off the walls of the stairs and passages like gum tree bark, and the Meccano fire escape jutting off the back wall had almost rusted through in places.

An earnest mutter of voices drowned the sound of Ursula's tentative knock on the door of Flat 23. 'Knock on, Macduff,' Rose said.

'I'm nervous. You knock.'

Rose had never known Ursula to be nervous. She thought, There's definitely more to her sudden passion for socialism than meets the eye, and was about to knock with a flourish when someone pulled the door open, leaving her hand poised foolishly in mid-air.

A slight, pale man in jeans and a red shirt and round John Lennon glasses grinned at her from a thicket of beard and said, 'Don't break my door down, Delilah.'

Isidore Frankel, Rose was to learn, came in two modes: intense and jokey. When he wasn't listening with what seemed like all his being, or talking with passionate chopping gestures of hands that stuck too far out of his sleeves, he would be teasing someone. A bald patch at the top of his head made him look older than his late twenties. In contrast, a dark brown beard rampaged over the lower half of his face like the stuff that comes out of coir mattresses, and the backs of his hands and arms were tufted with the same coarse glossy brown, as though he had torn pieces off and stuck them there with super-glue. He had impeccable socialist credentials: his father was a plumber, an emigrant from Lithuania in the 'twenties, his mother was a shop steward in the Garment Workers' Union, and he had gone to primary school barefoot.

Seeing Ursula behind Rose, he said, 'I'm glad you could come, Ursula. And this is?'

147

'Rose, my best friend.' It sounded schoolgirlish, and she blushed. 'Rose Kimber. We were at school together. She's doing third year English and history.'

'Ah, literary arty rather than fine arty. Come in, come in, then.' Isidore pulled them in so he could close the door again. 'We mustn't make things too easy for the Special Branch. They'd think I was slipping.'

'What does he mean?' Rose whispered to Ursula. 'Is this meeting illegal?'

'Not as far as I know.' Ursula's eyes were on Isidore as he made his way across the room. 'He says his brand of politics isn't too popular with the government, so they sometimes keep him under surveillance when they've got nothing better to do.'

Rose felt a shiver run down her back, as she had on the koppie so long ago when she had realised that the man in her cave was a terrorist. No, political refugee, she corrected herself quickly, wondering again what had happened to him as she looked round the room. It was full of people sitting on the arms of chairs and on the floor and overflowing into a kitchenette at the far end where someone was pouring boiling water into rows of coffee mugs, and others were arguing over the remains of a cooked chicken and an unstable pile of dirty plates. At least a third of the people in the room were black. Rose found herself counting them with her eyes: three young men in workers' overalls, a woman knitting in an armchair, an older one with grey hair and cat's eye glasses, a tall young woman jiggling a baby on her hip to stop it from crying, and a man with a face like a puzzled owl. They were scattered among the whites and everyone looked completely at home, either talking or listening with the intent expressions of those waiting to pounce on a shaky argument or with their own, better, opinions.

She said to Ursula, 'Who are they?'

Ursula was still watching Isidore, who was talking to a girl in an ethnic print pinafore. 'I'm not sure. I know he teaches at an adult education centre in the evenings, and some of them are probably his students. He also goes into Soweto quite a lot.'

Rose thought, It's him, and said, 'Are you in love with Isidore, by any chance?'

'From afar,' Ursula admitted. 'It's one-sided, I'm afraid. He's the brilliant up-and-coming academic while I'm just another reasonably bright third year student.'

'What are your chances there, d'you think?'

148

'Nil, I'm sure.' Rose had never seen Ursula look so glum. 'He doesn't seem to have a social life. It's all meetings and classes and discussion groups. I admire him so much for what he does, but I wish he'd occasionally look at me like other guys do. You know, letting his eyes wander a bit.'

Rose laughed. 'You're not supposed to say that. It's your mind he should want you for, not your body.'

But Ursula was not to be teased. 'I just want him to want me, period. I don't care what for.'

Someone had moved up for them, and they were sitting on the floor with their backs against the wall. Rose said, 'You should work at it. I can see he likes you.'

'It's not enough, I want more! And I know damn well I'll never get it.' She turned on Rose a startling look of her grandmother with the hooded eyes. 'He's one of those people who have to be fully committed, or they feel they aren't properly alive. That level of commitment excludes irrelevancies like girlfriends.'

Rose thought, She's always so desperate about the things she cares about. No sense of proportion. She said, 'How can you know this when you hardly know him?'

'I know.' Ursula turned back to watch Isidore handing out steaming coffee mugs and getting people to pass them along. 'I haven't done socio for nearly three years for nothing. If I'm to get close to him at all, I have to make his cause my cause. Only more so.'

The discussion began with a short talk on socialism for those who had come for the first time, after which Isidore invited them to ask questions and discuss the answers he gave. Apart from the owl-faced man, who turned attentively to each speaker but did not speak himself, the black members of the group were not hesitant about joining in, as black students so often were in tutorials. There was a feeling of ease in the crowded room that came partly from the way people were sitting, so close together that they could not avoid touching each other, and partly from Isidore's firm handling of the discussion. He was careful, Rose noticed, to allocate as much time to the stammered queries of one of the young working men as to the smooth exposition by a graduate student of the iniquities of capitalist-oriented history.

When the formal discussion was over, Isidore picked his way through groups of people who were still arguing to where Rose and Ursula were sitting, and said, 'I'm pleased you came, Ursula.

And your best friend too, of course.' The beard thicket parted to expose a smile. 'Come and meet some of the others.'

They stayed late, talking hard, then had to run all the way back to Sunnyside to be in before the midnight curfew. The Braamfontein streets were badly lit and deserted, with a hot city wind rustling paper rubbish in the gutters, but they were too exhilarated to notice.

'Thanks for dragging me along,' Rose said. 'It was really interesting.'

'You'll come again next time?'

'Try and keep me away!' She was thinking, It's the first time I've talked to black people on an equal level, not as servants. And they were so surprising.

The woman with grey hair, Sebenzile, was a sister tutor, and the one with the knitting, Nyemzele, a social worker in the prison service. 'My name means "keep a stiff upper lip, things aren't going to be easy",' she chuckled between smoker's coughs, 'and they haven't. My parents were realists.' The tall young woman with the baby was Pinky Bhengu, a law student who wanted to become an advocate. 'My granny looks after Mpho for me during the day,' she confided, 'but there isn't anyone at night if my sisters are out. Our parents are both dead.' The baby had a warm shiny skin like melted chocolate and looked up at them out of calm round eyes, sitting quite still on her mother's lap.

Rose kept thinking during the following days, Our society pulls us so far apart that we can't see each other as people, only as different coloured symbols.

She and Ursula went together every week to Isidore's meetings, where the discussions spiralled inevitably from socialism to Marxism to revolutionary theory, at which point they lost the young black working men. 'You talk, but you know it cannot happen!' their leader Ben Tsolo shouted. 'Not here. Not now. This government is too strong. We have no chance!'

Sebenzile gave her grey head a reproving shake. 'Talk costs nothing, and all the time we learn.'

'Learn for what, Mama?' Ben rounded on her angrily. 'To stand up in front of police shotguns and be killed, like at Sharpeville?'

'Learn the ways to fight their force with our brains, my son, like Isidore says. Our time will come. That is what I've learned in my years of nursing: a patient is well named. We must prepare well and be patient for things to get better.'

'Not me! I'm tired of listening to big talk, of learning, of waiting. I want to go where I can do something for myself.' He and his friends left, making a lot of noise with their steel-capped boots.

Though they didn't come back, his outburst changed the group's focus. Instead of quibbling over theories and definitions, they began to explore avenues of legal protest. Ursula and Rose became accustomed to standing with placards at the university gates as the heavy traffic along Jan Smuts Avenue swept past, most drivers with averted faces, though there were always those who jeered and hooted. Neither admitted to the other that she was secretly enjoying the sense of public martyrdom, specially as its only consequence was sore feet, which could be alleviated by a long soak in a hot bath afterwards. Rose was thrilled when Gordon's Chrysler drew up at the robot once and he saw her standing there. She met his glower with a radiant smile and a proud lift of her chin that blazoned her disdain for his air-conditioned comfort while others suffered. His driver could not understand why the boss barked at him to drive on when the light was still red.

It was 1975, the year the Suez Canal re-opened, the Decade of the Woman began with such high hopes, South Africa was finally granted the boon of television, and David Protter ran amok with a rifle in the Israeli consulate in Fox Street, Johannesburg, killing one and wounding thirty-four passers-by. Chiang Kai-shek and P. G. Wodehouse had died and the British government had decided to terminate the Simonstown Agreement that allowed their Navy to come calling at the Cape. In Soweto high schools, children and their parents began to hear rumours that the Department of Bantu Education had decided that certain subjects would in future be taught only in Afrikaans, the language of the Boers.

The clouds were gathering.

16

Sister Quthing's crêpe soles make a noise like grapes being crushed as she comes towards the bed holding a small red carrycot in her arms. Propped up against a pile of pillows that Gordon has taken from other beds and tucked in behind her, Sarah waits with hands that fumble with the edge of the sheet. The pain in her head has settled to a dull hard throb; her face looks less lividly white. Gordon stands beside her with one arm across the pillows. The cloud shadow over the clinic has moved away and is crawling up the rocky hillside. The corrugated iron roof above the sagging ceiling ticks like a metronome as it heats up again in the sun's blaze.

'Here she is, still fast to sleep.' The sister bends over and settles the carrycot on the bed next to Sarah. 'We had trouble feeding her from the bottle this morning. She didn't like it, poor little thing, though she took nearly two ounces.'

She looks apologetic as she says this. Her sister tutors had been most insistent about metric measurements during her training. 'Ounces are an outdated colonialist measurement, a thing of the past,' they had said. Which made life difficult when English baby equipment donated to Lesotho arrived with everything marked in pounds and ounces that had to be laboriously reconciled with the kilograms and millilitres employed by the local baby-food industry. Good baby care, she feels, should not depend on mathematics.

Sarah bought the carrycot a few months ago to send up to Rose, choosing red canvas for its cheerfulness, and this particular one (mindful of its dusty destination) because it has a red and grey pin-striped cotton lining that can be zipped out for washing. Now she sees, lying under a crocheted coverlet, her granddaughter: round head, dark hair and a small sleeping face that glows against the white baby pillow with a honeyed radiance, like a lamp seen through net curtains on a hot summer evening. She's beautiful! is her first thought, followed by, And it's not just because I'm her grandmother.'

Sarah lifts her hand to touch the child's cheek. It feels infinitely soft, like silk. Black eyelashes sweep down from peacefully closed eyes. Her small eyebrows are well defined arcs, unusual in a new baby. Also unusual is the quantity of hair on the small head, dark curls with a gleam of red where the strong light from the windows catches them. Sarah's eyes move over each feature, seeing a button mushroom nose, an ear like a crumpled rosebud, a pursed mouth on which a milk bubble trembles. Tightly clasped next to the determined little chin is a doll's hand that looks as though it has been carved in palest amber by a master craftsman.

'Gordon, can you see she's got Rose's chin? Your chin.' Sarah's hand moves to stroke the child's curly head. 'Jake's hair. I can't believe she's so lovely.'

'It can't be my chin then.' Pleased by the idea of being a grandfather, Gordon has not given any thought until now to the physical fact: a small, real person who carries his gift of life in her tiny body, flesh of his flesh. One quarter anyway, he thinks, looking down at her. I hope it's a good legacy. I haven't been any greak shakes as a father. Maybe I can make up for it now. He swallows to dispel the deep ache in his throat.

'I'd love to hold her. May I, Sister?' Sarah begs.

Sister Quthing has hoped Sarah will not ask, knowing it will plunge her into a familiar conflict in which her mother's instinct pits itself inconveniently against cold fact: holding the baby will help Sarah, but wake the baby. Having spent a good hour this morning first calming the screaming child, then lulling her to sleep tied to her back in a blanket as she has always done with her own babies, she is in no hurry to do it again. She says reluctantly. 'I'm afraid that waking her up will only upset her, Mrs Kimber. Look how nicely she sleeps.'

Sarah turns pleading eyes upwards. The rims are red and puffy and they still weep at the inner corners, but they are less anguished now. 'Please? I need her.'

'If she wakes – '

'I'll look after her.' Sarah leans back into the shelter of Gordon's arm. 'We'll look after her. Hope.'

Jake came to the first meeting of the discussion group after the mid-term break in September. When Rose saw him hesitating in the doorway she said to Ursula, who was washing coffee mugs, 'Look, a new recruit. Doesn't his face look familiar to you?'

'Not really.' Ursula was watching Isidore flipping through one of his thick files of notes and photostats, looking for a paper he wanted to quote from. She had been unusually quiet during the past few months, acting as though she were in suspended animation between group meetings and his sociology lectures, surprising Rose with her dogged efforts to make him notice her.

'I'm sure I've seen him somewhere before. Not recently, but somewhere.' Rose had a good memory for faces, thanks to the years spent observing people to put in her Journal.

Ursula dragged her eyes away from Isidore for another look at the man in the doorway. 'He looks like Harry Belafonte.'

'Maybe he's one of Izz's socio students.' Rose was cutting bread for sandwiches. Most of the black members of the group came to the meetings straight from work, and Isidore always made sure there was something to eat with the coffee.

'Who?' Pinky Bhengu had come over to them and picked up a knife to spread margarine on the cut slices.

'The new guy over there.' Rose gestured with the bread knife towards the door.

'The coloured, you mean?' Pinky scorned the delicacy with which group members avoided racial terms during their discussions. 'I've got no hang-ups about being black,' she'd shrug, 'or being called "kaffir" or "coon". It only dirties the person who calls me those things, not me.' She was tall and thin with a small close-cropped head on a long graceful neck. 'Like a giraffe, nè?' she'd say, turning her head this way and that like a giraffe does, peering over thorn trees. Her long limbs looked as elegant in jeans as in the stylish ethnic-print skirts and jackets she often wore, made by her sister, a Soweto dressmaker. 'I'm her walking advertisement,' she'd say with the throaty laugh that burst out often in law lectures, disconcerting students and professors alike with its mockery. Tonight her small daughter Mpho was dressed in a tiny matching blouse and wrap-around skirt, a corner of which she was gravely sucking as she sat in a chair near Isidore.

'Do you know him?' Rose persisted. The man in the doorway was slouching against the door frame, trying to look casual as he

154

covertly scanned the room. He wore the same clothes as the other students, a sweat shirt and jeans and velskoens, but they looked too neat and well cared-for, a self-conscious effort to look like a student rather than clothes thrown on for comfort.

'Oh yeah, that's Jake Van Vuuren. He's a poet.' Pinky was slapping on the soft margarine and scraping it off thinly with the expertise of long hours spent in the kitchens of a fast food restaurant, eking out her scholarship. 'He's at varsity repeating first year.'

'He looks much too old for first year.'

Pinky looked amused. 'Most likely it took him a while to save up the fees.'

'Oh. Yes.' Rose felt herself blushing and thought, Why do I always put my foot in it?

Pinky's laugh was a small explosion above the hum of voices in the room. 'Ag Rose man, don't be so sensitive about your old man's money. We don't hold it against you. Would you like to meet Jake? I'll call him over.'

'Oh no don't, please. I just thought I'd seen him somewhere before.'

Pinky turned and looked at her, large dark eyes in the long narrow face of Coptic paintings. 'You have, in Sunnyside. He was there for nine months last year.'

'Sunnyside? You mean Women's Res?'

'The very same. He signed on as a kitchen boy and graduated to house boy and dining-room waiter, big deal.' She chuckled. 'He used to go to lectures between meals, changing out of that ridiculous uniform in the toilet on the way. The other workers covered up for him as long as they could – he was always polishing the other passage or fetching supplies when the matron asked for him – but she caught him one day coming in the back door with a file of lecture notes. She fired him on the spot, and of course he lost his room in the varsity compound. Wasn't allowed to write his exams either. Shame, Jake.' Pinky shook her head. 'He's a good guy. Clever too.'

When the coffee and sandwiches had been handed out and the discussion began, Rose sat where she could watch him, trying to picture him in a khaki kitchen suit toiling on hands and knees over his polishing rags in the residence passage, and later squeaking about the dining room serving the chattering women. She thought, Sometimes we don't even lift our heads to say 'Thanks' when they put the dishes down or clear them away. We

155

see them, yet we don't see them. What does he know of me, besides feet going past and a blonde head stuffing itself from plates of food?

Afterwards, Isidore brought him over to her, saying, 'Have you met Jake Van Vuuren? He's also doing English and writes damn good poetry, they tell me.'

Had Isidore been watching her watching him? She felt herself blushing and said, 'Hullo.'

Jake nodded but said nothing, looking down at her with green eyes like swamp water, fringed with stubby black eyelashes. He's not *very* coloured, was her first thought. His skin was a pale smooth tan, breaking into fine wrinkles at the corners of his eyes. Her second thought was, He's all contrasts. His nose was broad and his hair was an Afro fuzz with red glints in it as though a fire smouldered in its depths, but his cheekbones were high and slanted, unmistakably Eastern, as was the angled set of his eyes. Two deep vertical grooves bracketed his full mouth, making it look as though he held it under tight control, damming up words that wanted to escape.

'Like what you see, Rose?' Isidore teased.

She said, 'It's not the first time we've, well, encountered each other.'

'I didn't know if you'd recognise me.' Jake spoke with an Afrikaans accent, his words abruptly clipped.

Shall I pretend I remember, or shall I be honest and confess and make myself look like all the others who don't really see the face above a servant's uniform? Rose stood hesitating.

'You wouldn't hurt my feelings if you didn't.' An ironic smile twisted the tight mouth. 'Being invisible has its advantages.'

Rose thought, He's categorised me already as a spoilt rich whitey, and felt a hot red tide creeping up her neck. She said, 'But I did recognise you. I just couldn't remember where from until Pinky told me.'

He gave her a ferocious grin. 'Ag, it's not surprising. When I polished the passages my face would have been about knee-level looking downwards, and all us coloured folk tend to look the same, don't we?'

'I'm sorry.' Rose wished that Isidore's frayed carpet would open up and swallow her.

'I'm not hassled.' He shrugged.

Isidore said, 'Do you mind if I leave you two children to explore each other's sensibilities on your own? I said I'd help

156

with the next lot of coffee.' He went off, leaving them standing awkwardly side by side.

'I'm sorry, really,' Rose said.

'What for? It happens all the time. Why should you be any different from the rest?' Jake turned away, looking for someone else to talk to.

She protested, 'But I don't want to be like the rest. That's one of the reasons I come to Izz's meetings, to be able to talk to people I wouldn't otherwise meet.'

He turned back, the swamp water eyes narrowed. 'Slumming in darkest Braamfontein, are we? I'm impressed. You win this week's hands-across-the-colour-bar badge, Miss Rose Kimber.'

'You know my name?' She wondered if he had found it out when he was working at Sunnyside, and watched her from afar with hopeless longing.

The flatness of his answer dispelled her fantasy. 'Izz told me when he brought me over to you. Forgive the intrusion by a humble first year student.' He gave an ironic bow. 'I'll drag my unworthy carcass elsewhere.'

'Please don't be like that,' she said.

'Like what?'

'So sarcastic. Most of this is new to me. I didn't mean to upset you.'

'I'm sure you didn't. Liberal whites are *so* well-meaning.' Scorn deepened the grooves round his mouth. 'They don't like rocking the boat with people like me. We're educated just well enough to sound like we could belong if they close their nice blue eyes.'

Her embarrassment began to give way to irritation. 'Why did you come here tonight, if we bug you so much? To find someone to pick on?'

'Nooit! I wouldn't even try with this bunch of Uncle Toms.' His gesture dismissed everyone in the room.

'That's not fair!' she burst out. 'You're cheapening what Izz is trying to do here, get people together to talk to each other.'

'I'm definitely not fair. I'll grant you that.' He began to walk away.

Rose remembered some lines from a poem that her group had been discussing in an English seminar that morning, and quoted at his retreating back,

' "Why do I sap my powers in singing songs
Of Nature's beauty or of untroubled bloodless things,

157

When I should break like thunder on the wrongs
That bind humanity in chains of maddening
   stings?" '

'Who wrote that?' He had stopped.

'Herbert Dhlomo, a Natal journalist.' She willed him to turn round and say something nice about it, something complimentary about her interest in black writing. 'We were studying his poem *Renunciation* in our Af. Lit. seminar this morning.'

'Af. Lit.!' He did turn round then, a venomous backward whip, the way a puffadder strikes. 'Af. Lit., sies! Nice new-smelling set books that you people condescend to study in spite of their bad grammar, while the writers run dry of words because they're starving! I'll quote you something to discuss in Af. Lit., Miss Rose:

' "He hits God's heart with screams as hard as stones
   flung from the slingshot of his soul." '

She said, 'You can't catch me on that one. It's by Oswald Mtshali. And Herbert Dhlomo died in 1956, so he's hardly running dry of words any more.'

'That doesn't change what I'm saying! You people talk so easy, so smooth, about Af. Lit. as though it's just another study subject, useful for passing exams and getting good marks in. Liewe God, these are our hopes and sufferings you're picking over!' He was furious.

'Would you rather we didn't study African writing at all, in case we sully it?' Rose was equally angry now. 'Who are you writing for, anyway, if not for us? To make us feel guilty about you? I'm an African too, you know!'

'You don't say.' He gave her another ferocious grin. 'Who would have guessed? And with a skin so Persil white.'

'My skin's got nothing to do with it!'

'Your skin's got everything to do with it! It's your passport to a nice home, a good job, a ballot paper.' He held up his hand, ticking the items off with tense, trembling fingers as he named them. 'Not to mention first class trains with your backside on leather cushions instead of wooden benches, restaurants, movies, the best beaches, the best – '

'None of this is my fault!'

'Then whose fault is it?' He was shouting now. 'God's? Our ancestors'? The government's? It's just too easy to shift the blame, Miss White Rose. Too damn easy to sit there in your fancy houses and – '

'Jake. Rose.' Isidore's voice cut in. 'I won't have this kind of thing here.'

'What kind of thing? The truth?' Jake turned on him. 'What's the point of these meetings, then?'

'The point is that we're trying to build bridges here, not pull them down.' Isidore put his hand on Jake's arm, where the sweat shirt sleeve had pulled up. 'We come together to talk about a common ideal, socialism, and to try and create among ourselves a community of spirit that – '

'Don't talk shit, man!' Jake shook the hand off like an ox does a fly, with a shiver of hard brown muscles. 'You're just like all lefties, full of shit talk about brotherhood and equality and common ideals. And you expect us to swallow it like cockroach bait and roll over with our feet in the air.'

'If that's how you feel, my friend, why did you come here?'

'I'm not your damn friend!'

'Would you mind leaving, then? This is my home.'

'It would be my total pleasure.' Jake's mockery was savage. 'These northern suburbs chicks give me the shits anyway. They think the sun shines out of their dainty white arses.'

In six months of coming to the meetings, Rose had never seen Isidore even mildly ruffled. Now she saw that the jovially rampant beard and watchful eyes behind the John Lennon glasses could conceal an anger at least as vivid as Jake's. He said, 'Get out! I won't stand for foul language any more than the racist dreck you've been talking. We don't need your kind here.'

'Moenie panic nie, I'm going. My kind know when they're not welcome.' The room had gone quiet at the sound of raised voices, and he looked round with contempt. 'Enjoy your party, sellouts.'

Pinky's laugh rolled out from the other side of the room like a red carpet. 'Don't be such a mompara, Bra Jake. These are good people. They're OK.'

'They're do-gooders. I shit on do-gooders!'

'Get out!' Isidore said again, louder.

Pinky put down the tray she had been holding and came towards them, picking her way with a giraffe's lanky grace through the people sitting on the floor. She said to Jake good-naturedly, 'Listen, man. You're wrong this time. Say you're sorry and stay for some coffee. We have good talk here.'

'And good other things too, they tell me. Do your people

know what you do with this so-friendly white man after hours, when everybody else goes home?'

The words seethed out of him before he could stop them, hurled as much at the watching faces as at Pinky, whom he had thought he loved once. Rose saw her quick glance at Isidore and thought, shocked, But she's black! and then, But she's nice too. I like her. No wonder Izz does, and then, Oh God, Ursula. I hope she didn't hear.

But of course she had. When Rose turned to look at her, she was pouring boiling water from the kettle all over the table instead of into the ranged coffee mugs, staring at Isidore with a face like marble.

'What's it like, eh, sleeping with a white man?' Jake went on as though, once uncorked, he could not stop. 'Is he the same as us, big and hard and good, or is it like one of those fat white worms you find in shit heaps, creeping around like blind things?'

Pinky was saying, 'Stop it, Jake – ' when Isidore hit him. Rose was astonished at the force with which the hair-tufted fist of the smaller man clenched, drew back and whammed into Jake's mouth, scattering blood and spit. Jake staggered back, putting his hands up to his face.

Isidore hit him again, shouting, 'I told you to bloody go, and I meant it!'

Jake stood swaying and spitting blood. Pinky reached out to steady him, saying furiously to Isidore, 'You stop it too!' and in a lower voice, 'Why did you do that? Jake's just mixed up, not a bad guy. He never means what he says when he gets mad.'

'He's a foul-mouthed bastard!' Isidore's voice came from very deep in his beard. He was massaging the hand he had used, looking down at it with surprise as though it had shot out of its own accord. 'When he started dragging you into it, I – '

'You didn't have to hit him! He would have gone in a minute. And now look.' Jake's lip was cut, dripping blood in thick slow drops on to his shirt. A red mark on one of the slanted cheekbones was beginning to swell. 'It's like they carry on in shebeens, all this hitting. Suka!'

The buzz of voices, which had stilled during the argument, began again as people turned their heads away and carefully resumed their conversations.

'I've never hit anyone before.' Isidore looked almost as dazed as Jake. 'Sorry, Pinks. It was stupid of me.'

'Stupid? It was crazy, Izz, man! These people see you as

somebody different, somebody to look up to who thinks and understands big things, not – ag, somebody like them who hits out when he gets mad.'

His eyes crinkled and the beard parted. 'Then it hasn't been a complete fiasco. That's exactly what I've been trying to get over to the group all these months, the fact that I'm *not* somebody different. You of all people should understand.'

Rose saw the look he gave her, and knew that this was not a new relationship. She thought, I wonder how long? As long as Mpho? Though she's very dark. I thought mixed-race kids were lighter . . . Poor Ursula. She never had a chance. Rose looked over towards the kitchenette. Ursula was pouring coffees and handing them out as if nothing had happened, though she was still very pale.

'No, I don't understand.' Pinky clucked her tongue crossly and turned to Rose. 'Hey, Rose. Help us get this silly man into a chair.'

They helped Jake shuffle towards a chair. As they neared it, Pinky said, 'If we can just get him sitting down with his head back, we can get some ice on before he swells up too much. Ursula!' she called. 'Get some ice out of the fridge and put it in a plastic bag. If you can't find one, wrap it in the dishcloth.'

Ursula managed to smile at Pinky when she brought the ice, a strained smile that carried her through the rest of the evening's awkwardnesses: Isidore's apology to Jake with its man-to-man handshake (wincing), Jake's swaying apology to the room mumbled through swollen lips and a blackening eye, and the subdued way everyone drank their coffee and left.

As she and Rose were going down the stairs, Nyemzele, the social worker, caught up with them. 'It's quite a relief, knowing that Izz is normal,' she said. 'I always thought he was just too good to be true.'

'Are you coming back?' Rose asked her. There had been a feeling during the last part of the evening of concealed truths simmering below the surface. Of crocodiles like green beans boiling in a pot, she thought, remembering Albertina with remorse. I never wrote to her even once, and I loved her stories so much.

'Sure, I'll be back.' Nyemzele's voice was ravaged by too many cigarettes. 'Where else can I talk to whites face to face, same-same, with free coffee and sandwiches thrown in?' She went through the swing door into the street in front of them, looking both ways as they came out. When she saw it was empty, she dropped her voice and said, 'Only trouble, Izz and Pinky better watch out for the cops now the cat's out of the bag. So long, eh?' She waved goodnight and walked down towards Park Station to catch a late train home. Her knitting bag bulged with the packet of left-over sandwiches Isidore had pressed on her for the families of prisoners who would queue endlessly outside her office next day.

Rose said to Ursula, who was walking head down into the gusting September wind with her hands in the pockets of her jeans, 'Will you be going back?'

'I can't not.' Ursula's windblown hair looked like a black tumbleweed rolling from one pool of street light to the next. 'It would look as though I disapproved of Izz and Pinky, which I don't. Only it'll be hard. I really thought he liked me.'

'He does.'

Ursula looked sideways at her. 'Like he likes everybody he gathers into his flock. Izz has a definite shepherd complex. Maybe it's a Jewish national trait.'

Rose thought, That's the first joke she's made for months. She said, 'You're not being entirely fair. I've always felt Izz really means it when he says equality is one of the principles he lives by.'

'Intellectually, yes. But he also enjoys playing the all-wise guru dispensing eternal wisdoms to those who have not yet reached the pinnacle of enlightenment on which he sits. Oh, I'll go back, until the exams at least. But it won't be the same. This little sheep isn't going to be lured back into the fold.'

Three weeks later, just before their final exams, the newspapers carried front-page stories about the Wits lecturer arrested and charged under the Immorality Act with 'one of his black female students, who was discovered hiding naked in his wardrobe during a police search of his Braamfontein flat. "We were acting on a tip-off," a police officer said this morning. "She tried to make out she was his servant girl, the usual. I don't know what these people take the police for. Morons?" '

There was a photograph of Pinky being hurried into court with a coat over her head, and a flash shot of Isidore that managed to make him look like Rasputin. Pinky was sentenced to six months in prison; though she was allowed to take Mpho in with her, she was unable to write her exams and failed the year.

Isidore was sentenced to two years suspended and dismissed the same day by the dean of his faculty, who said what while he had the utmost sympathy with his dilemma, the university's policy precluded employing convicted people as lecturers. Students were young and impressionable, after all.

Isidore held a final group meeting at the Braamfontein flat to tell them that he had applied for an American study grant, but been turned down. 'I hope the British will see it differently,' he said with what tried to be a laugh deep in the beard thicket. 'They're partial to lame ducks. If I leave, though, I'll have to go on an exit permit. The police took away all my files when they searched the flat, and now they've withdrawn my passport.'

'What of Pinky in jail?' Sebenzile asked.

Izz looked harassed. 'I've protested, of course, but I haven't been allowed to see her. My mother has promised to visit and help her when she gets out. I don't know what she'll do then.'

'Who ran to the cops?' Nyemzele growled. 'For future reference, we should know.'

'I think we can guess. He's not here tonight.'

Rose thought, Of course. The owl-faced man. He had never opened his mouth, but always looked intently at the people who spoke.

'We'll fix him if we can find him.' Sebenzile had a look on her face that Rose tried to forget afterwards, and could not.

Some of the women cried as they hugged goodbye, though not Ursula. 'I'll miss the other sheep,' she told Rose, 'but not the shepherd. He can wash his own socks by night.' By the following year she was back to her ebullient self, though more wordly-wise and cynical as befitted a sociology honours student. She was going out with an archaeologist famed for his eccentric hats and passion for caves.

Looking for a reason to stay on at university and put off the evil moment when she would have to think about getting a job, Rose decided to do English honours that year. Early winter flu swept through the English department in April, and several of the honours students were asked to substitute for afflicted lecturers at undergraduate tutorials. Rose drew the Wednesday one on African poetry and spent two anxious days preparing for it. She walked into the room with its long table buzzing with students, settled her books in front of the chair at its head, and looked up to find Jake sitting on her right.

A shock of recognition passed between them as though their glances were live wires that had touched, then he smiled quite pleasantly and said, 'Morning, teacher.'

The relief of his reaction broke the tension of her dreaded first time in charge of a class. When it was over and he asked her to have coffee with him at the cafeteria as a peace offering, she agreed. Partly because of the residual awkwardness she still felt over their first meeting (He's coloured and bitter, she had thought often, what did I expect?), but also because the smile had made him look for a moment like someone very different from the furiously angry young man she remembered.

It is just as well that Sarah, cradling their daughter now in the tin-roofed clinic, does not know that their lives hung on a single smile. It would make her howl again.

17

Gordon stands looking out the window near the bed where Sarah talks softly to the baby lying in the hollow between her arm and her body. The child's dark eyes, the newborn's blue already deepening to brown, are open and gaze up at her unblinking, as though trying to puzzle out this new, strange face.

It is the sound of hooves that has drawn Gordon to the window. Riding past the clinic towards the government offices are three Basotho horsemen, sitting deep in the saddle so that they bump up and down with each step. Despite the heat, each is swathed from neck to knee in a traditional blanket patterned in brilliant colours – blue, deep red, yellow, purple, brown – and fastened high on one shoulder with a blanket pin. Blanket designs have a special significance for the wearer, Rose has told them: crocodiles symbolise the Bakwena tribe to which King Moshoeshoe belongs, for example, while freedom torches celebrate Lesotho's independence in 1966. Underneath the blankets, the men wear trousers and shoes that bear the scuff-marks of endless mountain paths.

Each man carries a wooden fighting stick held with the reins in his right hand. Tucked under the left arm of the man in front is an orange plastic sjambok that tapers to a blunt point. Its use is demonstrated almost immediately. A dog with ribs like a rake and sparse bristly sand-coloured hair runs out from behind one of the huts towards the horses, barking with panic-bared fangs. The front horseman reaches for the sjambok under his arm, leans over and lashes in a casual arc at the dog, sending it yelping. The men ride on, their shadowed faces stippled with rows of tiny sun spots thrown by the lacy pattern of their conical straw hats. The horses are pot-bellied from the quantity of grass they have to eat to stay alive. Grain is scarce and expensive in Lesotho, needed for people, not horses.

Gordon watches them, thinking, It's a damn good thing

these people have horses or they'd never be able to get around this place. It seems to be ninety-five per cent rock and the rest pot-holes. Not far from the village is a mountain pass called Molimo Nthuse, God Help Me.

The Basotho must be one of the most adaptable peoples in the world. They first saw horses in 1825 when the white man who had trekked north in search of land began to nudge aside the people who already lived there; they were natives whose ownership didn't count, and anyway men on foot with assegais and fighting sticks are no match for men on horseback with guns. Similar dispossessions were happening all over the world as the European empires expanded into pastures and prairies new. But the dark-skinned tribesmen who were gradually driven into the barren mountains of Lesotho with their families and long-horned cattle were able to slip among the horse lines of the usurpers at night with ease. By 1870 the Basotho men were not only mounted, but had beaten off the Boer army of the Orange Free State and petitioned Britain successfully to become a protectorate. It is said that King Moshoeshoe sent a message to Queen Victoria asking if his tiny nation might become one of the fleas in her imperial blanket.

The three horses Gordon is watching are Basotho ponies, which have a good percentage of Arab blood in their veins thanks to the stallions that stand at the Livestock Improvement Centres and the Government Stud near Maseru. They are working horses, not cosseted pets; hollow-hipped, bony, flea-bitten and covered with saddle-sore scars. The Arab grace is still there, however, in their long full manes and calm eyes and sturdy temperament.

The men ride up to the hitching rail in front of the government offices and dismount, slipping their reins into iron hooks like short squiggly pig's tails. Now that they are standing, their blankets fall almost to their shoes like long capes. It is impossible not to look dignified in a Basotho blanket. Like three kings, the men go up the steps and disappear through the public entrance.

Jake was silent during the walk to the cafeteria, and Rose was not sure how to open the conversation. She felt awkward in her role as teacher to this older man who had not been able to contain his impatience with the other students in her tutorial,

166

dismissing several of their statements with a brusque, 'That's kak, and you know it.' He had said this to a girl with a freckled face who had suggested that the ungrammatical English of a particular poem was 'part of its charm'. He'd added, 'The guy's writing about the war in Biafra, not modelling school.'

The girl went pink. 'I didn't mean to say that war was charming, only that the poet's use of odd words made his language more –'

'Please don't say evocative, miss,' Jake said, 'I beg of you. If I hear that word again, I'll vomit.'

It was clear by the way the girl's blush deepened that she had been going to say 'evocative'. Rose said, trying to change the subject, 'What would you say the poet's intention was, Mr Van Vuuren?'

'It's obvious.' Jake had gone on to give a succinct analysis of the poem that showed he knew the poet's work well. The other students round the table had sat listening to him with bemused expressions, though the keener ones were soon picking up their pencils to scribble notes in the margins of their poetry books.

She had thought, He's much too good for this lot. The Prof should have put him in with the advanced group. I'll have to do something about it. She said now as they neared the cafeteria door, 'The tutorial was rather wasted on you, wasn't it?'

He shrugged. 'I didn't learn anything new, if that's what you mean.'

'I'm sorry, that was my fault. It was my first time in charge. I've never had to take a class before.' She heard herself babbling excuses and thought, Admit it, you were lousy. 'I was lousy,' she said. 'I don't think teaching's my strong point.'

He pushed the cafeteria door open and held it for her. 'You weren't bad, you know? Nervous, ja, but you knew what you were talking about.'

'Two days solid I've been working on those poems.' Rose stopped in the doorway and clapped her hand to her heart, trying to make a joke of it to make him smile.

'I've been crazy about his poems ever since our high school English teacher read out his very first one in class. I couldn't believe it. He was saying all the things I was thinking.' Jake had not smiled, and now he jerked his head sideways. 'You going in? Or are we going to carry on the conversation here in the doorway?'

'Oh, sorry.' Embarrassed, she went in ahead of him and

looked round for an empty table. There was one by the window. 'Shall we sit over there?'

'Anywhere, I don't mind. You sit down and I'll get the coffee. Milk? Sugar?'

'Milk, thanks. No sugar.' She watched him go towards the serving counter, looking from behind like any other student with a summer tan, except for his hair.

He came back with two cups, slopping coffee in the saucers as he put them down. 'Ag, clumsy,' he muttered, pulling out his chair to sit down.

Rose thought, Where do we go from here? I mean, do we talk about poetry or do I ask him where he comes from? Can I do that without seeming intrusive? I've never really talked to a coloured person.

He said abruptly, 'Listen, I'm sorry about that last time. I'd had a phone call from home that my Pa was sick again, and it always makes me mad.' The eyes she had thought of as swamp water were a clear, cool green in daylight with brown flecks in them like grass seeds. They kept moving away from her face as he looked to see who was coming and going through the cafeteria door.

She wondered if she should challenge him on his betrayal of Pinky and Isidore, but decided it was not the right time and said instead. 'Where's home?' She had several black friends on campus, some of whom she'd invited to Houghton for meals, though she'd never been to any of their homes. They hadn't asked, and anyway she would have been nervous to go into a township.

Jake was tapping his teaspoon in a restless rhythm on the saucer of his coffee cup. 'Home's in Bosmont. You know, across the cemetery from Industria. All the long roads in Bosmont are called after South African mountain ranges and all the short ones after indigenous trees, to make us indigenous folk feel at home. Thoughtful of the city council, nè?'

Rose in her insulated northern suburbs existence had no idea where Bosmont or Industria were. She thought, I must look them up on the map, as she said, 'Does your family live there?'

'Most of the coloured branch, ja.' He gave his ferocious grin.

'What do you mean?'

'I'll give you three guesses.' He leaned back and took a packet of Texan cigarettes out of his sweat-shirt pocket, holding it out to her. 'Smoke?'

168

'No thanks, I don't. Do you mean that some of your family, well – '

'Pass for white? Sure.' He put a cigarette into his mouth and lit it with a flaring match between cupped hands. 'Until the government passed the Population Registration Act in 1950, giving everyone a number with a letter at the end of it to show their race, us coloureds used to slip through the cracks easy if our skins were light enough. Take a look at your average Pretoria civil servant and you'll check what I mean: he'll have krissy hair, a little black moustache, dark skin, the works. I don't think there can be many Afrikaners that haven't got little black Sambos hiding in their family trees. Hell, they started the whole gemors when they couldn't keep their hands off their slave women.'

Rose said, 'I can't imagine what it must be like.'

'To be coloured?' His voice was suddenly harsh. 'It may come as a shock, poppie, but we function much the same as you paler versions of Homo so-called Sapiens do. Eat, sleep, fart, piss – '

'Please don't, Jake. Don't start being sarcastic again. I really do want to know who you are and how you live. I'm so ignorant of other people in this country, and I hate it.' She was talking fast, trying to stop the look of indifference she saw rolling down like a blind over his face. 'Talk to me! How will I ever know anything about you if you don't?'

He sat looking at her, thinking, She pleads with all the winning charm and confidence that money and a good education gives you. And that milky skin and hair like winter grass and the blue eyes like iceberg shadows . . . I don't know. She's just so damn different. Is there any point in trying to get through?

'I'm not so different,' she said, and he thought he must have spoken aloud and felt discomfited. She saw his expression and went on, 'That's why being students together at varsity is so good, don't you think? We meet on common ground.'

He said drily, 'Idealism rules,' and it was on the tip of his tongue to add, 'Nice try anyway, white chick,' and push his chair back and go.

She thought, He's in two minds about trusting me. What more can I say? and remembered the lines of a poem that an English honours student from Zambia had brought back after his last vac, written into a notebook in which he was assembling an anthology of African liberation poetry. She said, 'Quote:

169

"If you don't stay bitter
and angry for too long
you might finally salvage
something useful
from the old country." Unquote.'

After a moment the deep grooves on either side of his mouth relaxed, and he said, 'Always the apt quotation, hey? You must have one hell of a memory, teacher. So who is it this time?'

'Charles Mungoshi, a Rhodesian. I think the whole poem is very good. Very strong. Life-affirming.'

'He must be a bridge builder like the famous Izz.' There was a riffle of sunlight across the swamp water eyes. 'Fists like rocks, that guy's got. I asked for it, though, I admit.'

'Poor Izz. Poor Pinky. How could you do that to them?' There, it's out, she thought.

'Do what?'

'Tell everyone about them.' She felt herself going pink. 'Maybe nothing would have happened if you – '

'Don't kid yourself. Everyone else in that room knew, even if you didn't.' Jake was scowling. 'It was only a matter of time. Pinky should have known better than to think she could buck the Immorality Act.'

'Why only Pinky?'

'Because she knew damn well she'd be the one to get punished! It's OK for the Izzes of this world; those lefties know how to look after themselves. It's the Pinkies that get hurt. She's lost her bursary now.'

'What will happen to her when she gets out?'

'Who knows? At least she's got family, and the kid.' Rose watched Jake trying to shrug away his anger, and not succeeding. He said in a rough staccato, 'Listen, you really want to hear the Van Vuuren family saga?'

All around them was the clatter of students eating, laughing, arguing, scraping their chairs on the floor, throwing chips and rolls at each other – behaving more like chimpanzees at a zoo tea party than the end product of a superior education denied to so many like Jake, Rose thought. She nodded and said, 'My turn to buy coffee,' and went to the serving counter before he could say no.

When she sat down again, passing him a fresh cup, he said, 'Thanks. This should last us through the coloured branch.'

'I'm listening.'

He lit another Texan and drew the smoke in deeply before he spoke, using the fast light voice of a comedian trying too hard to raise a laugh. 'The family at home in Bosmont first, then. Pa works as an upholsterer and suffers from asthma' – he pronounced it 'azma' – 'made worse by the kapok he works with. Ma stays by the house. My older sister Violet left home when she got pregnant at school and had to get married, but her man died in a factory accident last year, so she and the four kids moved back. They stay in the garage. My second sister Marigold is a hairdresser at Black Beauty, a salon in town. It's a good job, but she lets her boyfriend drink most of her wages. My youngest sister Yasmin (she was born after Pa converted to Islam) runs with a tsotsi gang from Newclare, and Ma says if she gets pregnant too, she needn't come home because there isn't any room. Her real problem is she's a lot darker than the rest of us. I'm the only son and the white hope of the family, excuse the pun. Saint Jacob the First, our future provider.'

She thought, No wonder he resents over-privileged people like me. Curious to know more, she said, 'Where did you go to school to get this education that has you writing poetry and speaking – '

When she hesitated again, he cut in with an aggressive, 'Like a lanie? I'm flattered.'

'Stop putting words in my mouth, Jake. I was going to say, so articulately.'

'Why do I get the feeling I'm being patronised, not to mention pitied?' He stubbed the second cigarette out in his saucer, squashing it down into a mess of ash and spilt coffee until the paper split.

Rose thought, He's so touchy. He takes everything the wrong way. 'Because you're looking so hard for it! You wait like a – like a housewife with a broom outside a mousehole for some poor unsuspecting mouse to stick its head out so you can flatten it. But maybe the mouse isn't trying to steal your food. Maybe it just wants to sniff the air or something. You've got to give it the benefit of the doubt.' She leaned towards him across the table, anxious to make him understand. 'I'm not sitting here deliberately trying to offend you.'

'You may not mean it, poppie, but some of the things you say are damn offensive.'

'Such as?'

'Such as paying me compliments about the way I talk. Shit,

you're assuming that anybody with a darker skin than yours is going to massacre your precious English! No matter that they might speak fluent Afrikaans or Zulu or Tswana which you don't even begin to understand. It's these thoughtless put-downs that make you people so hard to take. Another perfect example is calling us "non-whites". It's like saying "non-kosher" or "non-entity". How would you like to be called "non-black"?'

'Not much, I'll admit.' She tried a rueful smile.

Which he ignored. 'Then would you kindly stop commenting on my amazing ability to express myself in your language as though it were some rare fucking phenomenon?'

She thought acidly, He sits there using four-letter words and thinks he's the immaculate conception when it comes to offending, and said, 'If you'll kindly stop crashing your broom down on my head every time I stick it out! The mouse just wants to look into the room, not steal your cheese. Or maybe you just don't like white mice? If so, tell me now so I can go back into my cosy little mousehole lined with chewed-up rand notes.'

He sat looking at her for a long moment, then said, 'You're good at extended metaphors, I'll grant you that.'

'An actual compliment! I'm overwhelmed.' She thought, Sarcasm must be catching. But I don't want to push him away. She said in a softer voice, 'Look, can we try starting this conversation over again? I'm really sorry if I've offended you. I didn't mean to. I'll try harder not to. Just let's keep talking.'

'You really want to?'

She nodded. 'Tell me more about your family.'

'My family.' He picked up the coffee spoon and began tapping it on the table top. 'I don't think there's time to do the white branch this afternoon, but I could do you the Sophiatown episode. That's quite picturesque.'

'Sophiatown?' She remembered the history teacher at St Winifreds pinning up a series of black and white photographs of people being moved out of their houses, and the dazed expressions on their faces. 'But that was before I was born. You must be – '

'I was six when they moved us out, but it's surprising how much kids remember.' His green eyes had gone dark and still, looking back twenty years. 'Oupa had this upholstery business on Gold Street. We lived in the house across the yard behind the shop, one of those old corrugated-iron shacks with wooden floors and a stoep in front with criss-cross trellis under the rails.

172

I used to play for hours with my toy soldiers on the stoep, marching them up and down the floorboards, tonk tonk tonk tonk. Hang, but I loved those soldiers! Oupa had brought a whole box of them home from Egypt after the war, where he'd been a sergeant with the Native Military Corps. They must have belonged to some English kid, because the paint had chipped off the lead in places. Some were in khaki uniforms holding guns, and some in bright red jackets and black trousers, with those high round black hats –'

'Bearskins', Rose said, and could have bitten her hasty tongue off.

But he was too lost in memory to be annoyed. 'Ja, bearskins. They had shiny black boots and gold buttons and little pink faces with even the eyes and mouths painted on. I used to lie on my stomach and march them one by one through the hole in the front of Ouma's basket chair, making her move her fat old legs to one side. That was their barracks, see, where they slept at night in rows. In the morning I'd wake them up and put them on parade for Oupa to take the salute before he went across the yard with Pa to work. It wasn't so long after the war then, and soldiers were still heroes to us.'

'You all lived together in the same house?'

'There were three bedrooms, as I remember. Oupa and Ouma slept in one, Pa and Ma and us kids in another, and Pa's sister Aletta and her son Ivan Rabie, who had just started working as a reporter on *Drum*, in the other. Ma only had me and Violet then, and she used to work in the upholstery shop whilst Ouma looked after us. Her job was sewing on the buttons. Often she would bring left-over buttons and bits of upholstery material and sponge rubber home for us to play with. Violet used to cut out dresses for her dolls and tie them on with bits of piping cord. I used to cut out squares to make blankets to cover my soldiers at night. Magtig, but those soldiers slept well! Brocade, taffeta, velvet – nothing but the best for Jacob's army.

'I suppose you always remember your favourite toys, but other things I remember too. Like going down to Balanski's bioscope once to see *Shane*, the first time I ever saw a bioscope, and a guy peeing off the balcony in the middle of it, all over Ouma. You've never heard such a racket as she kicked up! And the old mealie mamas who used to go past in the street with big bulging sacks on their heads, calling 'Meeeeealies!' And the tsotsi gangs you had to run from if you met them in the street, and the vetkoek

173

Ma used to buy us from the fish and chip shop, all fatty-crisp on the outside and hot and doughy in the middle. And the leaky tap under the grapevine in the yard where we got our water, and the long-drop – '

'I've always wanted to try a long-drop,' Rose said. 'People who've used them get so nostalgic, like it was some sort of religious experience.'

'You wouldn't if you'd known this one. It stood by itself across the yard like a corrugated-iron coffin up on end, with a rotten wooden door with rusty hinges that screamed like it was in agony every time anyone went in. Inside, it was dark and scary. Cobwebs would drag against your face and there'd be soft sounds of spiders scuttling into cracks. The toilet paper was torn-up squares of newspaper pushed on to a wire hook. The stink in there would stay in your nose long after you came out, no matter how much Jeyes Fluid Ouma used to clean it. For a kid, climbing up on the wooden bench was terrifying. You had to drop your broeks and sit down quick so as not to look down the hole into the blackness, though your eyes were always pulled to it.' He shivered, even in the cafeteria's fuggy warmth. 'The hole was grown-up sized, much too big for a skinny little backside like mine. You had to sit with your arms out stiff on both sides to prop yourself up, and be quick about your business before they started to shake. I had nightmares about falling through and drowning in that terrible pit, with only the bluebottle flies buzzing round my shit-covered head as witnesses. And I really believed the kid next door who told me that there was a nest of snakes living down there that could rear up and bite me, this trembling little bum hanging over the void.'

'Point taken,' Rose murmured.

But he was remembering, not listening, his coffee spoon unconsciously tapping out the kwela rhythms of the noisy Sophiatown streets. 'There was a faded curtain that used to hang between Ma and Pa's bed and Violet's and mine, and it used to sway backwards and forwards, backwards and forwards in the early morning with the shadows of vine leaves sliding up and down. It's the most peaceful feeling I've ever had, lying in bed with the blankets and sheets tucked safe around me and the sunlight coming in the window and the vine-leaf shadows doing this quiet, slow dance up and down, just for me.'

Rose thought, Now I know why he's a poet.

'Then Oupa got the first letter about the removals. He'd

bought the shop and the house freehold with his demob money from the army, but the Nationalist government that got into power in 1948 was just beginning to get moving with their apartheid plans. First they passed the Group Areas Act, then the Natives' Resettlement Act, which said that anyone with a skin that wasn't lily white must be shifted away from the cities out of sight, but with plenty of buses and trains available so they could come in to work. I mean, we couldn't have the white man getting his hands dirty, could we?'

Not knowing what to say, she shook her head.

The grooves on both sides of his mouth deepened. His eyes seemed to be looking into the far distance. 'Sophiatown had to go first because it was a slum and its mix-up of races made it a black spot on the fair face of Johannesburg, where all the money gets made. Also because there was always a lot of noise and trouble coming out of there. Black people demanding votes! Black people owning land! A crazy white priest letting black kids use his swimming pool, sies!'

'Father Huddlestone,' Rose said, remembering the photograph of the thin-faced priest swinging down a pot-holed street in his long cassock with several children hanging from each hand, laughing up at him.

'So they sent letters telling us we had to go and they started building rows of little brick houses, in Meadowlands for the blacks, and in various other places for the coloureds and Indians and Chinese, who weren't so many. A lot more noise came out of Sophiatown then. I remember looking out the shop window at mobs of shouting men with sticks marching up Gold Street, and the GG cars that went up and down with the letters. There were cops everywhere: in trucks, on street corners, walking in twos – they never went alone. People used to call them ginger-cakes because of the khaki uniforms they wore, and they weren't laughing when they said it.

'Anyway. It was cold and raining the day they came to take the first families away, two days early so troublemakers would be caught on the hop. There were a thousand cops with automatic rifles, somebody said, moving up the streets and banging on doors and shouting, "Maak julle oop! Maak julle oop!" Behind them were the army trucks. People had no warning, no time to pack. They had to get their stuff on to the trucks in a hurry, pulling their washing off the line and piling up their furniture any old how, chipping corners and getting cushions wet and mud all over everything. We watched the trucks pull away in one long line with people sitting on top of their things looking like Judgement Day had come. Maybe it had.'

He fell silent. Rose prompted, 'They just walked in and moved you out?'

'It was all over so quickly.' The child's disbelief that his world could crumble overnight showed on his face now. 'Ouma sat in her chair crying all the next day. "Dis die einde vir ons, die einde," she kept moaning, and she was right. Oupa couldn't find a house for us all to stay in, so we had to split up when the trucks finally got to Gold Street. He'd lost the shop and didn't have enough money to rent one closer to town, so he lost most of his business. And then he got pneumonia and lost heart and died. Pa had to go and work in a furniture factory, and Ma too. Ouma came to live with us in the small house we were renting in Vrededorp, but she wasn't much help. Often she sat in her old chair crying until she nearly drove Ma crazy. It was better when she took to her bed after Marigold was born, and wouldn't get up. Then we just used to carry her food in and the covered potties out until the day she stopped eating and died. Ma said she'd turned her face to the wall. Shame, poor Ouma with her fat legs.'

He sat tapping his spoon, remembering her. When he spoke again, his voice was very low. 'I don't remember too much about the day we were moved. I know Oupa went round to the police station to find out the exact time, and we were ready with everything nicely packed when they came, even Ouma's beloved dahlia bulbs dug up and wrapped in newspaper and tied in a sack. Oupa made us all go on to the stoep to say a prayer, but the funny thing was he said it in English. We'd only ever talked Afrikaans, all of us, but Oupa said, "From this day forward, this family talks only English." Pa bent down and explained to Violet and me what he was saying, and he had tears in his eyes, Pa who never cried. "You better say goodbye to the house and the shop and the yard now, quick," he said. "I hear the trucks coming."

'I didn't have time. I had my own thing to do before we left. I went to Ouma's chair and lifted it up and took out the shoebox I'd put my tin soldiers in, each one rolled in his blanket of scrap material. Then I carried it to the long-drop and threw it down the black hole. Those soldiers were too like the cops in the streets, and I didn't want them any more.' Jake gave the coffee spoon a final tap and said, 'I didn't cry. It was one of the best moments in my life.'

176

The cafeteria was emptying. The lights went off over the serving counter. Rose sat stunned, not knowing what to say.

'So it goes.' Jake pushed his chair back. 'I must go too. Ta for the coffee. I'm sorry I didn't do it full justice.'

Rose said, 'Can we have coffee again?'

'You enjoyed the saga?'

'Not enjoyed. I'm appalled.'

'What by? Surely you knew all this? You majored in history, didn't you?' He was impatient, clearly anxious to be off.

'I'm ashamed at how little I really know. I want to know more. Will you tell me?'

He laughed. 'The student teaching the teacher?'

'I mean it. I'd like to read some of your poetry too.'

He made a dismissive gesture. 'Ag, it's all unpublished. You wouldn't be interested.'

'Try me.'

'I'll think about it.'

'Promise?'

He nodded. 'Listen, mind if I go now? I've got a bus to catch.'

She thought, And still I do it. Because I have my nice little car Dad gave me for my eighteenth birthday sitting outside in the parking lot, I'm totally insensitive to the fact that he has a bus to catch. She said, 'I'm sorry. Of course, go.'

He got up and pushed the chair neatly under the table. 'You don't have to keep apologising. I know third world living conditions must be hard to visualise when you're used to living in Houghton.'

She looked up. 'Now who's condescending?'

For a moment she thought she had gone too far, and that he would leave in a huff and not speak to her again. But he said, '*Touché*, teacher. Check you, OK?' and went out pushing the cafeteria door so far open that it swung backwards and forwards several times before settling.

She swallowed the last of the cold coffee in her cup and picked up her books thinking, Could I call him a friend? I wonder what his poetry's like. I must speak to the Prof about his tutorials.

She walked down to Sunnyside feeling the glow of an earthling who has reached out and made successful contact with a Martian. And would have been amazed to know that Jake was feeling exactly the same.

18

Gordon is still standing by the window when he sees a metallic blue BMW coming very fast down the dirt road on the far side of the village. It pulls up in front of the government offices in a surge of dust that sends the horses at the hitching rail jostling sideways. A heavy-set black man in khaki trousers and shirt gets out, stretches briefly and goes up the steps two at a time to disappear through the door. Gordon thinks, That must be the doctor. Minutes later the man comes out with Cordelia Motaung and they walk up the road towards the clinic, talking. He makes his points jabbing at the air with his forefinger; she answers with nods.

Not wanting them to break into Sarah's communion with the baby, Gordon goes out to meet them, closing the clinic door behind him. 'Sarah came round about half an hour ago, thank God,' he tells Cordelia. 'She's got her baby with her now. Is this the doctor?'

'Do I look like one? I'm flattered.' The man's broad lips part in a faint smile. His face could have been carved from the stratum of dark granite running along the base of the sandstone cliff above the village, which traps water and gives the village its name: Place of Stones Weeping. He is older than he seemed at first from the vigorous way he moves. Small ears lie flat against a bullet head with grizzled hair. His eyes are hard black pebbles under heavy brows; his massive neck rears out of a barrel chest like a baritone's. Even standing two steps below Gordon, his presence dominates.

Cordelia says, 'This is Maxwell Tshabalala, Mr Kimber. He is the unit commander.'

'Maxwell Livingstone Tshabalala,' he corrects her, emphasising the 'Livingstone' as if daring to be mocked for it. 'My father was a sucker for the colonial myths.'

'You must have a Zulu name as well?' Gordon has recognised

his surname, which is common among black men in the Natal Midlands, and wants to start off on the right footing with this obviously important person.

'You probably wouldn't be able to pronounce it.'

Gordon's chin goes up at the reminder that few white people in Africa bother to learn a black language. 'Tell me anyway.'

'Mgwetshana,' he says. The faint smile is gone.

'I see you, Mgwetshana Tshabalala,' Gordon says in Zulu, and they shake hands as they exchange the formal greetings required of two strangers meeting for the first time. Gordon has learned to speak fluent Zulu by asking his farm labourers to talk to him only in their own language, and by studying the difficult grammar at night. The only thing he misses about Johannesburg and his executive job is pitting his wits against the interesting problems that came up. Now he pits them against Zulu grammar, farm implement salesmen and racehorse pedigrees. Being able to impress this powerful black man with an unexpected facility in his own language pleases him.

'I came as soon as I could. This atrocity will not go unpunished.' Tshabalala switches smoothly back to English. 'My organisation offers you and Mrs Kimber our most profound sympathy. Rose and Jake were good fighters in the struggle.'

Gordon has assumed that he is in command of a local unit of the Lesotho army. But the word 'struggle' indicates that this must be Jake's superior in Umkhonto we Sizwe, Spear of the Nation, commonly spoken of as MK. This is the military wing of the African National Congress, specialising in sabotage (or terrorism, depending on which side you are on). Gordon flares, 'Don't call her a fighter to me! Our daughter was passionately opposed to the violence on both sides in this country.'

The massive khaki shoulders begin to lift in a shrug, then remembering the occasion, drop again. 'Fighting does not necessarily imply violence, Mr Kimber. Rose may not have used a gun or explosives, but she certainly fought for better education and living conditions for our people, and for this we honour her.'

'Honour!' Gordon's voice is bitter. 'What can that possibly mean to a dead woman, or a child who will never know her parents? Pardon me if I don't sound grateful.'

'I'm not asking for your gratitude. I'm stating facts. Though Rose did not belong to MK or even the ANC as Jake did, we honour her for the beliefs she held and her good work, and the way she supported Jake. And we will continue to do so, whether you like it or not.' Beads of sweat like ball bearings are beginning to coalesce on the granite face and slide down under the khaki collar. 'That is what I have come for, to discuss funeral arrangements. We will be giving them both full military honours. I've just had word from Lusaka.'

'Ah, the wonders of modern science. Lusaka arranges the burial before the bloody coffins get here.' Gordon's fists clench. He wants to hit someone, anyone.

Tshabalala swings on Cordelia. 'No coffins have been supplied yet?'

'We've been trying all morning, Max. Both the mortuary vans are out on call. Maseru is trying to find a replacement.'

'Where are the bodies?'

'In the empty hut, with two fans – '

'In an empty hut, lying on a grass mat with a filthy sheet over their legs, for fuck's sake!' Gordon rages. 'In this heat!'

'We must do something straight away, then. This is a legitimate complaint.' Tshabalala jerks his head towards the government offices. 'Delia, go and phone Maseru police headquarters. Tell them to send a police van with the coffins if a mortuary van still isn't available.'

'I'll go now. Meantime – ' Cordelia hesitates.

'Meantime what?'

'Please,' she says, looking at both men in turn, 'please don't make this terrible thing any harder than it is already.'

Gordon thinks, I like this woman. She really cares. And we owe it to Rose and Jake to get through the funeral with dignity. Making an effort, he says, 'We would have liked to take Rose home, but she should be with Jake. I suppose that means here in the village. Can we discuss the funeral arrangements down in the offices? My wife mustn't be disturbed. She needs to rest.'

'We'll all go, then.' Tshabalala turns and walks away down the rutted road, calling back over his shoulder, 'Make it snappy. I haven't got much time.'

Gordon says to Cordelia, 'Hang on a sec, will you? I'm going to tell Sarah I have to go down to the offices and make a phone call, though she's so taken up with Hope that she probably wouldn't even notice I'd gone.'

'She's a lovely child. Rose and Jake adored her.' Tears well

180

up in Cordelia's muddy eyes. 'I had a daughter too. She died some years ago.'

'I'm so sorry.' He thinks, We are legion, the bereaved parents. 'You'll wait?'

'I'll wait. And listen, Mr Kimber, don't pay too much attention to Max's bark, eh? He's doing a job he doesn't like, and he's very upset about Rose and Jake. You remember him from the old days, maybe?'

Gordon shakes his head.

'I'm sure you will when I remind you. He used to play sax with the Golden City Jazz Kings back in the 'fifties. He was a composer too – remember *My Good-time Baby? Bloemfontein Blues? Sweet Sibusise?*'

The song titles take Gordon back to university days and the rock'n'roll parties that ended with a slow dance to the saxophone solos that wailed of smoky shebeens and unfaithful city women and gangsters in zoot suits. He says, 'Good God. Was that Max the Sax?'

'The very same. He left South Africa on an exit permit soon after Todd Matshikiza, and played in jazz bands in England for years, but then Soweto happened. His music was shot dead along with the kids, he says. He joined MK and he's never played since then.'

Gordon goes into the clinic thinking, How we lay to waste our best talents in this country. How we squander and plunder our only resource that really matters – people.

Walking down the road with Cordelia to the government offices a few minutes later, they talk of the network of school huts deeper into the mountains that she visits weekly as circuit inspector. Diminutive Lesotho has a higher proportion of school attenders than any other African nation, and she is proud to be part of the system. It is a conversation between two professionals, and he remembers with shame how long it took Rose to convince him and Sarah that she had black and coloured, as well as white, friends.

'That left-wing bunch of yours,' he called the student friends she brought home to swim and lie sprawling round the pool in the garden, eating his food and drinking his beers, talking and arguing for hours. He came home rumpled and tired from the office late one afternoon and went out into his garden, to be

181

greeted by a babble of raised voices over the blare of music from a portable radio. There were two black girls lying among the bodies round his pool, wearing bras and wet nylon panties that he could see right through.

Called into the house, Rose answered his furious protest with a calm, 'They're my friends, and they can't afford swimming costumes, Dad.'

'What will Joseph think? Have you given any thought to his feelings?' Joseph, the gardener, was a dour, silent, slow-moving man whose tribal earlobe plugs were a symbol of his conservatism.

'I should think Joseph would be pleased for them,' Rose said, giving him her Bette Davis gooseberry glare. 'I mean, imagine it, black girls actually being able to fraternise with whites, not to mention swim in our meticulously chlorinated pool! It's a step up in the world for them, isn't it?'

Gordon felt the blood pounding in his neck. It had been a bad day, crowded with meetings and confrontations with a frantic contractor who was going into liquidation. He said, 'You're deliberately distorting what I'm trying to say. It's not their colour I object to, it's those – those unsuitable undergarments. And I'm not sure if having black visitors to a house in a white area is legal. I don't want the police breathing down my neck.'

'Can't have our Top Man rocking the boat, can we?'

'It's my bloody house!' he shouted. 'I'm entitled to decide who comes here!'

'And my bloody home!' she shouted back. 'I'll have whatever friends I want!'

The poolside became a meeting place for a shifting population of bearded and sandalled young people with frizzy hair and ethnic shirts and Indian cotton skirts whose fraying hems dipped and swayed round their ankles. They lolled about in heaps looking like refugees from a United Nations rock concert, rolling their own cigarettes and smoking what Gordon was sure was dagga, and talking, talking, talking. Socialism seemed to be the favourite topic, and he would hear phrases like 'it's a matter of class, not race' and 'we've got to keep up the struggle' and 'surplus value' floating like bees over the clipped hedge round the pool and through his study window, innocuous enough in a summer garden but concealing hidden stings in their tails. He and Sarah became acquainted willy nilly with the repertoires of Bob Dylan and Fleetwood Mac and Ricky Lee Jones and David

Bowie, at a decibel level that made the constant clatter of typewriters and duplicating machines at the office seem genteel by comparison.

Like locusts, Rose's friends ate their way through any food they could find, and could make two dozen Castle beers disappear in a trice. When the sun grew low and the pool-side cold, they would move en masse into the kitchen and casually empty the fridge and half the pantry, leaving a mess of coffee mugs and biscuit crumbs and, if there were no ashtrays within easy reach, cigarette ends stubbed out in Sarah's porcelain saucers.

More than once, Gordon pointed out the irony of Agnes having to clean up after the socialists who so fervently advocated equality, yet thought nothing of leaving their considerable debris behind for others to deal with. 'You and your friends want to tear down this capitalist society, but you're not averse to enjoying its benefits,' he grumbled.

'Our family has more than most of theirs do,' she said. 'We can afford to share.'

'If all this were yours to give away, you'd be welcome to indulge your principles.' He gestured round the elegant living room where they were sitting watching a boring programme about the Canadian tundra on the new TV, still a novelty after its tardy arrival in South Africa the year before. 'But it's mine, Rosie. Mine and your mother's. We've worked hard to get here. It didn't all fall into our laps. We don't feel obliged to share what we've earned with anyone, least of all a bunch of hippies we hardly know.'

'You don't make any effort to *get* to know them! You just dismiss my friends because they don't conform to your idea of how "young people" should behave – bowing and scraping and calling you "sir" and standing up when Mum comes into the room.' Rose's face was flushed in the familiar mottled patches. 'We don't think those things are as important as being honest and caring and sensitive to the feelings and aspirations of others.'

'Good manners never go amiss.'

'Good manners are irrelevant in a world that's rotten with racism and poverty and hundreds of nuclear warheads crouched in pits waiting to be set off! Your generation is so blind and selfish and smug.'

She doesn't realise how smug she looks, he thought. He said, 'We don't claim to be perfect –'

'You aren't!'

'– but we aren't arrogant enough to think we can change the world overnight by applying pie-in-the-sky academic theories. Life isn't like that. It's tough and hard and heartbreaking.' Gordon leaned forward in his armchair with the blue light from the television flickering on his face. If only he could wrap this prickly, passionate, beloved daughter in an invisible layer that would protect her against the difficulties and sorrows she would have to face in her life. 'You're so sheltered, Rosie. I don't know how to prepare you for what's coming.'

She was exasperated by the sheen in his eyes. Older people seemed to get emotional so easily. 'But I don't want to be prepared. Your dire warnings mean nothing to me, Dad, nothing! I've got to make my own mistakes, to create my own place in the world. And I badly want it to be a better world.'

He thought, You pass on your genes to your kids, but you can't pass on what you've learnt because they close their minds to advice. Even when they know it's good. He said, aggrieved, 'You could at least listen.'

'You're not the world's greatest listener yourself.' Rose had got up and was standing in front of him with her hands stuck in her jeans. 'Have you taken in any of what I've been talking about these past few years? My experiences and thoughts and feelings? Mum and I have long talks in her studio. She likes my friends.'

Gordon thought, Fathers miss out on so much, being away at work all day. Yet we never seem to get credit for the sacrifices we make. We're just the grey toilers at the rockface who earn the money and come home grumpy every night. He said, 'What, specifically, am I supposed to be hearing about your life that I don't know already?'

'What it's like to be young and white and feeling guilty about people who don't have my advantages because they're black,' Rose said, kneeling in front of him, urgent with the need to convince. 'The injustices that don't get into the papers. The way workers are treated. Dad, you wouldn't believe some of the wages my friends' parents are paid! I hope your company doesn't exploit its employees like that. You talk about how tough and hard life's going to be for me, but it can't be a quarter – a hundredth – as tough as it is for black people.'

He reached out to touch her wispy blonde crop, silhouetted against the Canadian tundra. 'I hope you're not getting mixed up with anything illegal.'

'You haven't been listening to a word I've said!' She pulled away, impatient with him.

'I have. And I'm glad that you care about other people. But I'd hate you to run foul of the security laws, Rosie. Going to jail sounds very noble, but the reality is boredom and frustration and mental stress.'

'I know. I've talked to people who've been in jail. One of them told me about a student called Stephanie Kemp who used to go to Cape Town Varsity. She spent eighteen months in Kroonstad Prison after she was convicted of sabotage in 1964. She said later, "What kept me going is that you no longer feel isolated as a white unable to tackle the system. You are transformed into a South African, part of a mass movement. That sustains you." I can't forget it.'

Alarmed at the glow of admiration on her face, he said, 'But you can't take the whole world's troubles on yourself! Specially not here, not now, with the security laws we have. Are you doing or planning anything illegal with these friends of yours? Tell me!'

'We've just been holding demonstrations.' It was a relief to be able to unburden herself of a confession she had been meaning to make for some months. 'You saw me at one, outside the Wits gates. There have been others too, outside the John Vorster Square police headquarters and the Supreme Court. It's not illegal to protest – ' *Yet*, he thought, '– though there are usually policemen sitting in cars across the road watching us and taking photographs with zoom lenses. They never photograph the white yobbos who come past in carloads to spit and swear at us. One of them – ' She turned away, embarrassed.

'What happened? Tell me!' he repeated, feeling his stomach drop into a pit.

'One of them came up to me and started fondling me and making disgusting suggestions,' she said in a low voice. 'It was awful. I didn't know what to do, whether to keep standing there being dignified and holding my placard and pretending nothing was happening, or whether to bash him over the head.'

'I wish I'd known this. You should have told us!'

'I couldn't. I thought you'd take me away from varsity.' Rose looked back at him, trying to gauge the extent of his anger. She'd been waiting for an opportunity to let her parents know of her increasing involvement in anti-government protests, without alarming them so much that they over-reacted. Judging by the look on his face, she'd have to make a joke of it. 'Anyway, one of our guys saw what was happening and came over and told him to bugger off, then kicked him in the backside so hard that he lifted off the pavement. It was really funny. Even the cops in the cars across the street were laughing.' She gave her father a winning smile. 'Demos aren't so bad. They have their moments.'

'Does your mother know about this?' He wondered how much more he hadn't been told.

'Some, not all. She's pretty wrapped up in her work. When I go into the studio sometimes and it's quiet and peaceful and Mum's humming while she paints, I don't have the heart to spoil her good moment.'

He thought, How lucky we've been; she's a daughter in a million. We've got to stop her from getting too deeply involved with this left-wing bunch and inevitably drifting into something illegal and getting hurt. There are cases every day in the papers of students being arrested and detained, often without being charged, for months. I couldn't bear to think of her in jail, this sheltered, idealistic child of ours who doesn't begin to know what degradation it would mean. We've got to stop her *now* without letting her think we're interfering.

Trying to hide his panic, he said, 'Will you promise me on your honour not to do anything illegal? I mean it, Rose. I'll even offer a handsome bribe.'

Her smile faded to scorn. 'Trying to buy me off, Dad? That's a real Jo'burg solution: all problems solved if enough silver crosses enough palms.'

'I make no apologies for trying to keep you out of trouble, young woman.' He leaned forward in his easy chair so that his face was inches from hers, jowly and serious in the reflected blue light. 'Listen to me. We care about you. We don't want you to get into trouble. Sitting in prison for years would be a waste of your talents, and muck up your life. It seems to me that you could do far more good by turning your honours degree to some practical use that helps the people you care about. When I talk of bribes, I'm thinking in terms of another year at university or further training overseas, and I'm trying to be honest with you. You owe it to us to consider the offer carefully before you dismiss it.'

Rose thought, I can see why he's an effective boss. He's very persuasive and logical, and knows how to dangle a clever carrot. She and Ursula had made tentative plans to go to Europe on a working holiday at the end of the year, and to study in England or America would be fun – but irrelevant. With her new eyes that saw beggars and glue-sniffing children and ragged vendors selling pathetic little bundles of shoelaces in the streets where before she had seen only well-dressed shoppers, she saw that her English studies had become the occupation of a dilettante, a well-off white girl with nothing better to do than become a perpetual student. If I want to help people, I'll need skills, she thought. What am I good at, besides writing essays and arguing?

'How about a trip to Europe at the end of the year?' Gordon said, as if mind-reading. 'I'm not kidding, Rose. I don't mind your being involved in student politics on a reasonable level; in fact, I'd be disappointed if you weren't concerned for others. But setting yourself on a collision course with the government is bloody stupid.'

'Europe would be fun.' She thought of skiing and London shows and walking down the Via Veneto and climbing worn steps up to the Parthenon, to sit with her back against marble quarried thousands of years ago, looking down on Athens.

'I'll book a return ticket for an indefinite period tomorrow, and another for Ursula, if she wants to go. You could leave after your exams in November,' he said, pressing home the idea.

The temptation was great. She longed to go and see the places she had read about in books: Arthur Ransome's Lake District, Georgette Heyer's Regency London, Hemingway's Paris, Isak Dinesen's gothic Denmark. But her parents, by the time they were well off enough to consider it, had not wanted to go on tourist holidays. Gordon's overseas business trips were exhausting, and Sarah had become immersed in her painting to the point where she felt bereaved without her studio.

Rose thought, But I'm not going to be bribed. She said, 'Nothing doing, Dad! Though I take your point about putting my degree to practical use. Maybe – ' she thought of Jake Van Vuuren saying 'You weren't bad, you know?' of her handling of the poetry tutorial, '– maybe I'll do a Higher Education Diploma so I can teach in black schools. You could give me another year at Wits, instead of overseas.'

'In return for certain promises?' He was thinking, Now what have I done? Teaching in black schools!

She flared, 'I won't give up my friends, if that's what you mean! Or stop taking part in demos. Dad, can't you see that if nobody protests about the security laws Vorster's pushing

187

through Parliament, we're also responsible for them? I mean, one of the things happening right now is that the Bantu Education department is trying to make black high school students do some of their subjects in Afrikaans. The Soweto Students Representative Council is organising a big protest for next month.'

'I'm just asking you to stay on the right side of the law, Rosie.' He tried to make it sound reasonable. 'Not to compromise your conscience. Your safety is extremely important to us.'

She thought, He's putting on the only-child pressure again. Sneaky. 'I'll try,' she said. 'No promises.'

The feature on the Canadian tundra was dragging to its dreary conclusion. He thought, What more can I say to make her think twice before she gets mixed up in something serious? He reached for the whisky and soda that had remained untouched on the table by his side, and said, 'You might try considering our problems and concerns for a change. Your mother may be reasonably happy now, but it took her a long time to get here. And I'm beginning to find that there are more and more times at work when I look out the window and think, "What the hell am I doing here? I'd rather be farming." '

'But I always thought you loved your work. Specially now that you're running the show.' She was astonished. He had been promoted the previous year to Managing Director, and asked to join the Boards of several large companies. His photograph had appeared more than once in the *Financial Mail*. He was one of a small group of top executives considered to be in the running for Businessman of the Year for 1976.

The surprise on her face made him think, Kids are so busy hacking their way through their own jungle of problems that they never see ours. Maybe that's the way to get to her. He said, 'Top management isn't easy, however glamorous it may seem. I spend a lot of my time doing unpleasant things like reprimanding people who've made mistakes, and sometimes firing them. Have you ever thought what it's like to have to fire a man in his fifties when you both know he probably won't get another job, and his mouth quivers, and helpless tears slide down his face? Sometimes I spend all day criticising poor work and picking holes in arguments, until I feel I haven't a good word left in me to say.'

She looked at him more closely then, and saw that his face was puffy and his eyes very tired. 'Capitalist bosses are supposed to be unfeeling pigs,' she said, 'but you don't sound much like one.'

'I've got a boss too, don't forget.' He thought of the Chairman's petulant pink face and silver hair and over-fondness for Dimple Haig, and the way his pompous drone could keep a meeting going all afternoon until it was time to re-open the Board Room's liquor cabinet. 'He's not a man I can admire, yet we're paired together in a relentless tango swooping between profits and losses, unable to stop for a minute to rest our feet. I'm beginning to feel that the rose in my teeth is plastic.'

She laughed, but she was thinking guiltily of all the times she had mocked him for being a Top Man, and wondered why she had not tried harder to see the person her mother had married. 'Why did you go into business in the first place, anyway?'

'It was a means to an end. I had to show your grandparents that I was better at looking after Sarah and you than they were. And I can't say I haven't enjoyed my business career. It's been interesting on the whole, as well as lucrative.' He looked round his living room again, seeing the sleek brass lights arching over Sarah's canvases, the leather lounge suite imported from Italy, the expensive Danish hi-fi system. 'But recently it hasn't seemed to be enough any more. I get so tired by the end of the day that I just want to crawl on to the sofa in my study and sleep.'

'So that's why you look so grouchy when you come home, and glower at my friends?'

'I feel they're leeching off me,' he admitted. 'Though I suppose you'll say they're only being true to their socialist principles. Share and share alike.'

She said, 'What are capitalists for, if not to be leeched off? It's only restoring the balance.'

'I'll grant you that socialists always have excellent reasons for relieving the wealthy of their supposed excess,' he said. 'I used to belong to a political discussion group before I met your mother, mainly because they had good socials after their meetings, though the girls were a bit grim.'

'You never told me.'

'You never asked. We don't seem to know a hell of a lot about each other, do we? Did you know I used to be a damn good surfer once?'

'A surfer?' Her disbelieving eyes went to his paunch. 'Now you're kidding!'

'I'm not. I played a good game of cricket, too. Your mother used to go all gooey when she saw me in my whites. She's got a thing for the feel of skin under a cricket shirt.'

Rose had never heard any of this. Her parents had left their Durban life completely behind them when they moved away after David's death, and Gordon was a man who believed in looking forward rather than back. She tried to picture her awkward, overweight, paint-spattered mother and this unexpectedly accomplished father being young and kissing each other, her hands sliding under his shirt, and failed. Of her early childhood, Rose remembered only Albertina talking loudly of crocodiles to cover the sound of quarrelling, and a tall silent woman walking next to her along a beach. She thought, He's a different father underneath to the one I always thought I knew, and said, 'Do you often find that people are different underneath to how they appear at first?'

Good God, she's actually asking my opinion, he thought. Rose had made it plain for some years that they were not to try and tell her anything; what they knew was probably out of date, and anyway she was perfectly capable of finding out for herself. He said, 'Sometimes, not often. One of the things you have to learn fast in business is how to sum people up. Your job as a boss is to choose the right people for the work that has to be done, and to make sure they do it. So you're always asking yourself, "Will this man be up to the work I'm going to give him? Or will he let me down?" You soon learn to sort the bullshitters from the doers.'

'But how do you tell, just from meeting him or her a few times – ' she laid stress on the 'her', mindful of her feminist reading ' – what sort of person they are? I've lived in the same house with you all my life, and I didn't know you could surf and play cricket.'

'You develop an instinct after a while.'

'That's too glib, Dad! There must be things you watch out for, things you notice?'

He thought with a pang, She's got a mind that likes to get to the nub of things, and a sympathetic heart that'll lead her into trouble. We'll have to keep a bloody close eye on her. He said, 'I suppose I look for men – people,' he corrected himself carefully, 'who will fit into our business culture. People with reliable work records and references, to start with. People with open faces who look at me directly when they're talking, and who speak well about their subject without being smarmy. People without irritating mannerisms; a man who keeps clearing his throat can drive everyone round the bend.'

'What about black people? Do you employ them in white collar jobs?'

'Worried about your old man letting you down in front of your left-wing friends?' He grinned at her. 'Yes, we do, as a matter of fact. We pay them well too. A good shipping clerk is worth his weight in gold.'

She smiled back. 'You're not a bad old Dad, you know?'

'Not quite the iron-hearted industrialist you thought I was?'

'Not at all. Full of surprises, actually.'

'We should talk more often. I've enjoyed it.'

'Me too.' Rose leaned forward to hug him as a cold sun set on a flat TV vista of grey-green tundra. 'And you don't need to worry about me. I won't do anything silly, I promise.'

Walking down the dusty Lesotho road with the black woman who has been her friend, Gordon thinks, She didn't do anything silly, and even then she couldn't escape those bastards. I will find out who did it, and I'll kill them.

19

Gordon sits facing Maxwell Tshabalala across a scarred teak desk with legs like tree trunks, relic of the British colonial administration. The government offices are full of such elephantine relics: massive stationery cupboards, sets of pigeon-holes, filing cabinets whose heavy sliding drawers could fell an ox, wooden chairs built to last a century, hat stands the size of palm trees, giant benches that clog the narrow passageway, all marked or stamped PWD, for Public Works Department. Most of the cupboards and pigeonholes are empty now, or used as temporary resting places for an extra pair of shoes, yesterday's newspaper from Maseru, an umbrella in case of rain, half-eaten packets of biscuits. It is surprising how well a country can get along without snowdrifts of meticulous paperwork.

Cordelia Motaung sits on a chair near the window looking out over a bare earth yard where people are sitting in the long thin strip of shade thrown by a fence made of chicken wire and thatching grass. Most of them are women from outlying villages, come to register births and deaths in the absence of their men who are away working on the gold mines, or to collect pensions for old people who can no longer manage the mountain paths. They sit patiently waiting their turn, moving only to swat at flies or to jiggle a baby to sleep again. They don't talk to each other. Cordelia thinks, This terrible apathy. How can we expect the children to achieve anything when their mothers are so beaten down?

Tshabalala stabs a thick forefinger at Gordon and says, 'You have no right to accuse me! We are in a state of war, as you well know, and in wartime innocent people get killed. Your daughter's death is not unique.'

Gordon sits back, folding his arms to keep his anger contained. He will not lose his temper again with this man. Rather, he must find out what Tshabalala knows or suspects about the killers by goading him into letting information slip.

'I'm not accusing you personally,' he says. 'I'm stating the obvious: if your organisation has the backing of the local people, as you claim, how could this murder have happened in their midst?'

'You know damn well how! We're not far from the border here, and the men who usually guard this village are no defence against highly-trained killer commandos.'

'Yet you send instructors like Jake to live here with their wives and children. Don't you care what happens to them?'

'Of course we care.' Tshabalala's voice is like the grating of stone chips sliding out of a tipper truck. 'We care about all our people. The kids who get gunned down for throwing stones. The families who are bulldozed out of their homes, then dumped in the veld with a few sheets of corrugated iron. The workers who are put out on the street for daring to strike. The old people who slowly starve because their pensions aren't enough to buy even basic food for a month, let alone pay for the roof over their heads. We care so much that we've dedicated our lives to fighting their oppressors, by any means we can. Your daughter was just one of millions, Mr Kimber.'

'One who offered more than most,' Gordon says, keeping his voice under tight control to stop it shaking. 'For purely practical reasons, I'd have thought that you'd protect your key personnel better. Good qualified teachers prepared to work under these conditions can't be too easy to come by.'

'We don't subscribe to elitism.'

'I'm not talking elitism, I'm talking usefulness. You've lost two people who made a real contribution to this country because you did not give them sufficient protection. Was it slipshod administration, or just plain lack of caring? I have a right to know.'

'You have no rights here! This is an atrocity committed by your people, not mine!'

'Who says?' Gordon challenges. 'The clerk who was there when the shooting happened told me that no one could tell who the killers were. It was dark. They wore camouflage overalls and balaclavas. Exactly the way your men dress.'

'What insinuation are you making?'

Gordon feels Tshabalala's growing fury across the desk like a dragon breath from a blast furnace. Throwing more petrol on the flames, he says, 'It's no secret that when he knew the baby was on the way, Jake asked to be relieved of his training job here. He told us he wanted to resign from Umkhonto we Sizwe altogether. Was this your way of helping him along?'

The word Tshabalala uses as he surges out of his chair with his fist drawn back is one that Zulus use only under extreme provocation, and in battle. 'No, Max!' Cordelia cries. Gordon lifts his arm, elbow outwards, to protect his face. Sweat is pouring down his back. Across the desk, Tshabalala's heavy-set body is trembling with outrage, the tendons under his chin standing out like steel cables. From the passage outside the office door comes the mundane clattering of the tea trolley.

'You shouldn't do this, Mr Kimber.' Cordelia's quiet voice comes from above and behind him. 'The situation is bad enough without trying to create enemies out of people who are on your side.'

It is a long moment before the big man across the desk drops his hand to his side and thuds back into his seat. Gordon lowers his arm and says in his most reasonable voice, 'I have to know who killed them. All else is secondary. If I'm treading on some sensitive toes, too bloody bad.'

'It was not my people. That's a disgusting suggestion.' Tshabalala holds his voice down with an effort, still very angry.

'If you espouse violence as a means to an end, it would be a logical way of getting rid of those who get in your way,' Gordon says calmly. 'And Jake was getting more and more uneasy about the way the ANC is fanning the flames in the townships. Did he talk to you about resigning?'

'Four months ago, he asked for a transfer to Tanzania.'

'But you didn't see fit to grant it?'

'It takes time to train instructors. They would have been allowed to go as soon as the new man arrived.' Tshabalala plunges his hand into the breast pocket of his khaki shirt and pulls out a neatly folded handkerchief, which he uses to wipe his face. It is a method he has been taught at an advanced interrogation psychology course to calm himself and create time to think. 'We are not insensitive to the needs of our people. It's a definite problem, this question of trained men who want to be taken off active service as they grow older.'

'You can't find enough people who enjoy murder?'

'Mr Kimber!' Cordelia says in despair.

But Tshabalala's black pebble eyes just look at him this time. He is well in control again. He says, 'I'm not going to keep rising to your bait. I understand what you are trying to do now. You are trying to make us accept some of the guilt for your daughter's death. We will not! This is an act of war.'

Gordon is beginning to feel very tired. 'I don't care a sweet fuck what you think,' he says. 'What matters is that I've lost my only child, and I want to know who killed her. You can't deny that the ANC's policy of violence was the prime cause.'

'You accuse us of violence! That's rich, after the centuries of physical and emotional abuse my people have been forced to suffer for the past three centuries. What do you whites expect us to do, keep turning the other cheek? Wait until Kingdom Come for our place in the sun of our own country? No way, Mr Kimber. We are tired of waiting, of being reasonable. Now we fight.'

Cordelia puts in, 'Albert Camus said, "What is a rebel? A man who says no." What Max is trying to tell you is that black people are finally saying no.'

Annoyed at being lumped with other unfeeling whites, Gordon bursts out, 'Nobody is disputing your right to do so, but you're using the wrong weapons! No civilised person can condone violence. Killing and maiming innocent people is wrong, whether you call it an armed struggle, justified violence or terrorism. There can be no exceptions. A line has to be drawn somewhere, don't you see?

'Violence in our situation is counter-productive anyway. It has no hope of succeeding against a government with the support of a solid majority of the electorate, plus a well-trained, well-equipped, loyal army. Be realistic, man! The Nationalists are not going to be stampeded into handing over power by a few land mines and car bombs. You people forget that you're dealing with a nation whose history resounds with stories of outnumbered settlers battling hordes of savage warriors. Just like the American settlers, only they were more successful at decimating their indigenous population than we were.'

'I should have known you would talk of savages. All whites do, sooner or later. It is so much easier to see us as a howling mob than as people with individual faces.' Tshabalala speaks with contempt. 'I have nothing more to say to you, Mr Kimber. Not now, and not at the funeral. Rest assured that your daughter will be accorded every respect.'

'You're evading the issue! You haven't given me the bit about sacrifices having to be made for the good of the whole. I'm not just another white bigot, Tshabalala. I'm personally involved, with a coloured grandchild who gives me a stake in our common future – if there is a future after your cohorts and our government have finished chucking bombs and grenades at each other.'

'It is you who are evading the issue, I think. Do you know the motto of the Jewish fighting unit, the Palmach, that fought against the British in Palestine?' Tshabalala glares the question and Gordon shakes his head. 'It is *Ein Breira*", which means "No Alternative". That is exactly our position.'

'They were a bunch of thugs too!'

Tshabalala leans forward, hands splayed on the desk, shoulders knotted into great bulwarks of muscle. 'I see no point in carrying on with this interview. You are just trying to provoke me. Next thing, you'll say what all the busybody politicians from overseas say when they come to South Africa to flaunt their concern for human rights. "Be patient, chaps. Build a political structure. Negotiate. We'll help you with advice and scholarships. We are your friendly big brothers." Paternalistic shit! The battles of Africa must be fought in Africa, by Africans, face to face. This country is our indaba, not anybody else's. And while we blacks may not have a police force and an army backed by tanks, we do have the numbers. Five to one, Mr Kimber, increasing every year. We have the weapon of our labour, on which you whites depend. We have the weapon of righteous anger because our birthright has been stolen from us. We are well infiltrated in the very heart of your society, in your homes, making your tea in the morning, bringing up your kids. And we have endless patience. Make no mistake, we will win in time.'

'But at what cost, man? There's got to be a better way!' Each word from Gordon is a groan.

'At any cost.' Tshabalala's hoarse whisper spreads through the office like used sump oil, leaving a black silence. Cordelia shivers. There is a distant rumble of thunder.

Gordon gets up and leans on the chair's curved wooden back, feeling the tiredness in his back and legs. 'In that case, we have nothing more to say to each other. I would like to make two more points, however. One: if you find out who killed my daughter, I want to be told. And I want your solemn promise on that.'

'I give it.' The grizzled bullet head gives a decisive nod.

'Two: I believe your saxophone was a bloody sight better way of getting your message across than bombs ever will be. I was a great fan of yours once.'

'And now you are not.' There is a hint of amusement on the granite face across the desk, quickly suppressed. 'Go well, Mr Kimber,' he says formally in Zulu.

'Stay well, Mgwetshana Tshabalala. Mrs Motaung.' Gordon smiles at her, grateful for her calm presence that runs like a silver thread through this terrible day. He walks out of the office, green hat in hand, footsteps fading down the passage past the rattling tea trolley.

'He is a good man, Max,' Cordelia says.

'So are we all, all honourable men.' He is thinking of the young man lying dead in the hut up the hill, and of all the young men who have gone before him, and all the young men still to go, and the sound in his head is a dirge played on a saxophone. 'I wonder what he would have done in my place.'

Rose and Jake had six weeks to get to know each other before the maelstrom of the Soweto riots which began on 16 June 1976 tore them apart for four years.

She had spoken to the English professor about Jake the day after her poetry tutorial, and he was transferred to the accelerated group the following week. He was waiting outside one of her honours lectures to thank her, adding, 'It makes a hell of a difference, being with people who know what they're talking about.'

'It was nothing, honestly. You were way ahead of the other students in my group.' She stood by the door with her lecture file and a pile of books in her arms, smiling up at him.

'Would you like to come and have coffee with me again?'

'Very much. You promised to tell me about the white branch, remember?'

The swamp water eyes looked wary. 'Ag, I always talk too much. You don't want to hear that stuff.'

'But I do! You promised, Jake. You can't wriggle out of it now.'

Other students were brushing past them in the corridor, coming out of a nearby lecture theatre. Above the sound of trampling feet, she heard a voice saying, 'What's she doing with that bushy? Sis, I wouldn't let my sister – ' The rest of the sentence was lost.

Jake's mouth tightened. 'You're the one who should be wriggling out. Sorry I asked.' He turned and started pushing his way through the crowd.

'Hey, what did I do? Jake – wait!' She hurried after him. 'What's wrong?'

'You heard.' He didn't slow down.

'Heard what? Don't be so mysterious.' She had to run to keep up with him. They were through the crowd now, walking under an archway and out into an empty quadrangle. 'How can I know what's upsetting you if you don't tell me?'

He stopped and turned to face her. 'Never heard of a bushy?'

'No, I haven't. What is it?'

He put his hand up to his fuzz of dark hair and grabbed a fistful. 'This is a bush, see? And I'm a bushy. Not quite black and not quite white. Neither fish nor fowl, but something in between that nobody knows what the hell to do about. Shit, I'm sick of it!'

'I'm sorry.' What else could she say? 'It won't stop us having coffee, though, will it?'

'You don't mind having coffee with a bushy?'

'No,' she said. 'I did it before and nothing terrible happened. No reason why I shouldn't do it again.'

The deep grooves bracketing his mouth relaxed, but there was no smile. 'What you shouldn't do, poppie, is underestimate the power of people to make you feel uncomfortable when you're with me.'

'I'll ignore them.'

They began walking more slowly in the direction of the cafeteria. He reached into his jeans pocket for a crumpled packet of Texans and lit one inside cupped hands, drawing the smoke deep into his lungs.

'I don't know why you let stupid remarks like that bother you,' she said. 'You know it's not the majority feeling on campus.'

'Is that what you think?' His voice was bitter. 'It's the image so-called liberal univerisites like this want to project, but it's not the reality. Take it from me. I get remarks like that every day, dropped quietly so I'll hear but nobody else will. And they sting like hornets every time. Learning how to take insults is one of the skills a bushy's got to have if he wants to survive.'

198

'If the word upsets you, why do you keep on using it?' He's like a child who keeps picking at a sore place, she thought. 'I'd like to have a conversation with you that doesn't mention race for at least ten minutes.'

'You're asking for the impossible.' They had reached the cafeteria door, and he pushed it open.

'But why? There's so much else to talk about. Poetry. English. Families.'

'That's why.' He jerked his head at the crowded tables. People were turning to look at them, leaning heads together, saying things.

Her chin went up. 'It doesn't worry me. Where shall we sit? In the middle?'

'If you want to prove your point. Me, I'll settle for a quiet corner. I'm not going to be anybody's cause, not even as a thank you.' He had gone towards the counter to get the coffee before she could answer.

She chose a table next to the window, away from the chattering crowd but in full view, and sat watching him. He had a slouching walk that she was to realise was part of his attempt to fit in and look like a student. But he was too tense, too defensive, too ready with acid comments for other students to feel comfortable with him. He was older than most undergraduates, with a corrosive cynicism that came from having had to work for several years at a grinding job to earn his tuition fees, which most students took for granted as a parental obligation. His sense of being different surrounded him like coils of razor wire, making it almost impossible to get close enough to see the real man inside the defences.

When he came back with the half-smoked cigarette dangling from his mouth and a cup of coffee in each hand, she said, 'Does this table suit your royal touchiness?'

For the first time that day, the ferocious grin appeared. 'Pass with a push.'

She took the full cup he handed her, and waited until he had sat down before leaning forward. 'I'm not trying to do anything but be friends, OK?'

'Friends.' He said it as though it was a word from a foreign language. 'Do you really think that's a proposition, under the circumstances?'

'We could try.'

He took two spoons of sugar and sat stirring his coffee,

looking down at it, the smoke from the cigarette rising in a thin spiral past his broad nose and slanted cheekbones and half-closed eyes to founder against the tightly curled dark mass of his hair, and vanish.

He said, 'When I first came to varsity, I tried. I thought it would be different here, a meeting of true minds and all that jazz. I should have known better. When I joined the rugby club because I was quite fit and wanted to try the game, they couldn't figure out what the hell to do with me. Put me in the fourth team at first, playing wing because I could run fast, but I didn't know which way I was supposed to be running most of the time. The other guys had been playing school rugby for years. When we went to away matches, I meant trouble because I couldn't go into the pubs with them afterwards. Somebody had to order beer and take it outside and sit there with me so I wouldn't feel left out, which of course made me feel more of a freak than ever. So rugby was out.

'But all the other clubs I tried to join were the same. There'd be a small percentage who tried hard to be nice to me – I used to call them the Heavenly Hosts. You could almost see the haloes they wore, actually going so far as to sit and talk to this weird coloured who insisted on trying to play their white men's games. But for most of them I was just the bushy with the big ideas. You saw it in the poetry tutorial. When whites look at me they don't see Jake, the man. They see Jake, the coloured. I worked my guts out in a boring job to save enough to get into this palace of learning, but now I think I'm wasting my time.'

Rose thought, What a travesty of our education system if a man like this gives up. She said, 'One thing I can tell you, you're not wasting your time in English. The Prof was raving about your essay on the new directions township poetry is taking. He read it out to us in a lecture, and we had a whole discussion on performance and protest poetry.'

'Oh, that.' He dismissed a week's hard work with a shrug. 'I can grind that sort of thing out any time. What I really want is to be taken seriously as a poet. It's much harder to write a good poem than an essay for the Prof. A poem that talks to people via their guts, not their intellect. What's the point of writing stuff only academics and smart people can understand?'

He's opening up at last, she thought. I'm getting somewhere. She said, 'I hate intellectual poetry.'

'You'll like mine, then. I write about ordinary things, ordinary people. My people.' There were sparks of sunlight in the swamp water eyes. 'Talking of which, I'd better stay off the subject of the white branch of the Van Vuurens. It's sub judice, so to speak.'

'Oh, please tell me,' Rose begged.

He shook his head. 'Family secret. I never should have mentioned it.'

'But you did. You must have wanted to.'

'It slipped out. I can't – '

'Trust me with it?' By his defensive expression she knew she had guessed right. 'But you can, honestly. I keep secrets very well.'

'How can I know that? There's too much at stake to risk things being blabbed to the wrong people. Sorry.'

She thought, We're really getting through to each other. I can't let the opportunity slip away, and said, 'I'll trade you, then. I'll tell you a secret I've never told another living soul, and you can decide how good I am at keeping my mouth shut.' For ten minutes, speaking quietly so her voice would not carry to the nearby tables, she told him about the man she had met on the koppie when she was thirteen, drawing on the account she had written in her Journal and re-read only last month. 'I never heard from him, and I never even asked him his name, so I don't know how to find out what happened to him,' she ended. 'But I kept his secret until now.'

'Impressive,' Jake said. 'And you reckon you can keep mine? Cross your white heart?'

'It's no more white than yours!' She was offended by his teasing, knowing that he was using it as a shield against her.

'Everything's relative in the matter of colour in this country.' He looked down at his hand curled round the coffee cup, enjoying its ceramic warmth. 'Specially coloured relatives. In one family you can have every shade from ebony to peach pink, and the ones at the darker end of the spectrum like me have got to be damn careful they don't bugger things up for the ones at the paler end. We can envy their luck, but we don't rock their boats.'

'Nor would I,' Rose said. 'Please tell me more about your family, Jake. I really want to know.'

The pause before he started speaking again was a long one, and she thought she had failed until he said abruptly, 'If I didn't like my Auntie April so much, I'd say what she did was the worst thing that could happen to any family. But Auntie makes it OK. She hasn't cut us dead like most of the other try-for-whites do when they make it to the other side. If you only knew the number of people who stand in the streets of white suburbs at night, looking in at houses that they daren't go into – at cousins and grandchildren basking in the glow of their pale skins and blonde hair. Then turning to go home with the bitter comfort that at least somebody of the same blood has bucked the system.'

'Do you still see your Auntie, then?'

'Oh, ja.' The ferocious grin again. 'She's in the papers every time they have the opening of Parliament. We even saw her on TV in January. She married an MP who's now a cabinet minister.'

'You're kidding me!'

He shook his head, enjoying her shock. 'It's the honest truth. Only it's not for publication, ever, you hear? Auntie isn't ashamed of who she is, or of us, but like she says, she's got her kids to consider now. One of them's at Stellenbosch University, studying law. He doesn't know about the niggers in the woodpile, of course.'

'Jake, don't start now – '

He went on as though he hadn't heard. 'You'd like my Auntie April. She's a real practising Afrikaner: church twice every Sunday without fail, and sex across the colour bar at home. You could make a fortune if you sold this story to the papers.'

She felt herself going pink. 'You should know me better than that.'

'I don't know anything about you, except that you're damn quizzy.' He lit another cigarette from the stump of the first one.

She thought, He smokes too much, and said acidly, 'I'm a northern suburbs chick with a rich daddy and a passion for slumming, and I think the sun shines out of my dainty white arse, don't you remember? You said so the first time we met.'

'Ag, I was mad that night. Didn't mean it.' For the first time since she had met him, he was at a loss for words. After a long pull at his cigarette, he said, 'Do you want to hear the whole story?'

The offer was clearly by way of an apology. She said, 'Of course I do. Don't keep me in suspense.'

'Auntie April is Ma's sister – ' he began.

The Fiemies family lived in a suburb of Cape Town where

202

historic whitewashed plaster gables rubbed shoulders with ram-shackle corrugated iron, and the back yards filled up with old cars and lean-to shacks and fowl hoks in the make-do anarchy of places where too many people live.

Pa Fiemies mended shoes and rented half a house from Achmet Spons, who lived in the other half. There were three Fiemies girls. The first two, Hester and Miriam, were born with their parents' reddish-brown krissy hair and dark eyes and skin the colour of scrubbed new potatoes, a fresh pale brown. They had nearly identical moles on their faces that would grow prominent with age and sprout thick black hairs.

But April, the last-born, was unexpectedly gifted with the genes of a distant Dutch forebear: Delft blue eyes, hair like smooth farm butter, skin the colour of full-cream milk that would easily pass for white if she was kept out of the sun. 'You've got an opal there,' Fatima Spons said when she first saw the baby. 'Good insurance for the old age, nè?'

Ma Fiemies was like a terrier the way she nipped and worried at the family over April. The two older girls had to make sure that the child kept her deep-brimmed cotton kappie and her shoes and socks on at all times, and never rolled up the long sleeves of her pinafores, no matter how hot the sun. They kept vigil with irritable resignation. April would have her chance to melt into the white community whose boundaries were still expediently blurred, but they would exact a price for it. 'You owe us, April,' they would say when their mother wasn't looking, pinching her pale plump little arm, so different from their sinewy brown ones. 'Don't forget, hey?'

What money could be spared in the grim years after the Depression was spent on getting April polished and ready. She had dancing lessons to discipline the chubby little feet that would rather have run wild through the Cape winter puddles. She had elocution lessons to teach her the difference between the giveaway singsong Afrikaans they spoke at home and the rounder, slower, more cultured cadences of the radio announcers on the B programme. There were extra lessons in English and the subjects in which she was weakest at school.

'A well-educated person gets the best jobs,' Ma Fiemies would say when April whined about the long hours of study. Ma took in washing to help pay for the lessons, and her back was never free of pain.

'But Ma –'

'Don't complain, child! As ye reap, so shall ye sow,' Ma said, while her sisters hissed their jealous refrain, 'You owe us, April.'

Pa Fiemies took a chance and enrolled her (by telelphone) in a deportment course for young white girls run by an ex-ballet teacher with pretensions. It was held in Claremont, and whoever took her there was under strict instructions to walk behind her so no one would guess anything. When she had completed the course and obtained her certificate without incident, they grew bolder and applied (again by telephone) for a place at the Technical College. If admitted, she would be able to write the white Junior Certificate and follow it up with secretarial training in both official languages. The transfer papers required from her previous school were forged by an out-of-work white artist for a fee of KWV brandy. Such was the demand for his services in the coloured community in those days before a person's race was enshrined in a reference number given at birth, that the brandy killed him before he reached forty. He advised them to change her name to April Fillis. She was accepted at Tech without any questions being asked.

Mixing by day with white girls, envying the nice clothes they wore and the homes they talked about, April began to see the point of her parents' endless nagging. She set herself to work harder than the white girls and passed out first in the class. Her parents were not able to be present when she went up to the dais in the Tech hall, wearing her mother's best church outfit, to receive her diploma, but they stood in the street outside. It was handed over by a white Member of Parliament who had been invited to pronounce the usual platitudes to the newly fledged secretaries. He was much taken by the shy, well-spoken seventeen-year-old in the old-fashioned navy crêpe dress who had come first, and phoned the college principal the next day to offer her a job in his office in Parliament.

For a year she took two trams to work: the coloured tram into the Station, and the white tram from the Station up to the top of Adderley Street. She could easily have walked from the Station to her office, but it was worth the extra penny tram fare to be able to sit on the spacious leather-padded seats of the white tram and listen to the conversations around her, after the crowded wooden seats and raucous chatter of the coloured tram. She sometimes worried that its fug of smoke and sweaty bodies and musty second-hand clothes would cling to her and give her away to the white people she sat next to, but she was never challenged.

If an occasional keen eye noticed that the folds where her skin creased were darker than usual and the half moons of her finger nails were tinged with blue, there was no great surprise. Cape Town is a city where for three centuries a melange of races co-existed under the great blue bulk of Table Mountain without laws to keep them out of each other's beds. The people who live there do not, as a rule, feel the need to compute physical differences with a flickering up-and-down glance as those further north do.

April had become friendly with one of the older girls in the office, who shared a flat in Gardens with her cousin. When the cousin moved back to Johannesburg, Helene asked April if she would like to move into the flat with her. The rent was reasonable, but Pa Fiemies was not.

'She's only eighteen!' he shouted. 'She can't go and live on her own yet, it's not right!'

'It's the next step up the ladder,' Ma said calmly. 'She's got to take her chances when they come. You can't say no.'

'But eighteen! What about men who'll take advantage of her, and the wages that she gives us? This is the first year in nearly twenty that we haven't had to worry about next week's bread.'

'I'll take in washing again,' Ma said, trying not to remember the permanent ache in her back. She was so adamant that he had to give in.

Hester and Miriam helped April pack her smart office clothes in the small bedroom they shared, sullen with envy. 'Don't forget, you owe us, April,' they said.

'How could I forget?'

'You've got your freedom. You'll forget.' Hester wore her dark hair in a bun already; she was soon to marry a bricklayer who lived in the next street.

April looked up from the suitcase, her blue eyes like chips of summer sky. 'God will strike me dead if I ever forget, Hester. I know I'm getting a big chance in life, and I know who helped me to get it.'

'But you're so different from us already!' Miriam burst out. 'You won't want to come home any more.' She was a machinist in a clothing factory, working ten hours a day with her feet on a cold cement floor.

'Maybe I look white, but I'm still coloured inside,' April said.

She had learned how to separate her two lives like a schizophrenic and slipped easily into the family's accented Afrikaans at home, so that she certainly sounded coloured. 'I promise you both now on the head of Baby Jesus that if you ever need help from me, I'll give it. Anything. We'll always be sisters.'

April kept her promise, even after she had met and married Tertius Tulbagh De Wet, a wealthy farmer's son who had been elected to Parliament. She was taking a huge chance, she knew, but prayed that God's help and Tertius's pale pink and blond colouring would counteract her darker genes. She gave birth to three (thankfully) blond children called Willemien, Chris-Jan and Barend, and become renowned for her koeksisters and springbok biltong and clever adaptations of old Cape Dutch recipes for the modern table, but she did not forget her promise. The elegant outfits she wore to meetings of the Vroue Federasie and parliamentary functions were run up by Miriam for a generous fee, at least until she married Jake's father and moved to Johannesburg. April recommended Hester's husband's building company to anyone who asked, and became known as the right person to consult if you needed a good little upholsterer or dressmaker who wouldn't charge a fortune, or an honest maid. April De Wet had a way with coloured people, it was generally agreed. She was commended every year from the pulpit by the dominee of the local Nederduitse Gereformeerde Kerk for her charitable work among the poor of Woodstock.

To run her Constantia home she chose the capable, ugly daughter of Achmet and Fatima Spons, since she was nearly thirty and unlikely to get married. Farida was sent to various domestic science and cookery courses until she was able to orchestrate any social occasion from a working breakfast of parliamentary colleagues to a dinner for fifty. Her presence also enabled April to invite the family to visit her, masquerading as Farida's relatives, but only when her husband and children were out of the house; side-by-side comparisons were too risky. It was understood that they were to enter and leave the property by the back gate, and the house by the kitchen door. Pa Fiemies came seldom, intimidated by the echoing spaces in his daughter's house. But Ma would put on her best dress for the occasion and walk through each room in her dumpy black shoes, drinking in April's good fortune. She would run her fingers over the fine furniture and the curtains and the silver-framed photographs on the shiny black grand piano of the blond grandchildren she would never know, and think, Ja, my child, it was worth it. It was well worth it.

When Hester's eldest daughter Magdaleen was old enough, she was taken on to help Farida in the kitchen. The arrangement did not last. Magdaleen became more and more resentful of the blue-eyed cousins who dropped all their belongings on the floor for her to pick up, and who ordered her around like lordlings. 'It's unbearable!' she hissed at her mother. 'I want to kill them for not being dark like me.'

'But Auntie April only wants to help us.'

'Nooit! She can find herself another slave.'

April shrugged when she was told. 'She's losing a good chance, Hester. You've got to work for your chances in life. They don't just fall into your lap. Nobody knows this better than me.'

'She doesn't have your advantage,' Hester said. They were sitting at the breakfast table in April's kitchen drinking coffee together. Like her father, Hester felt uncomfortable in the other rooms that seemed to open out like huge balloons when you went into them, instead of settling in round you like a familiar blanket.

'I've tried to make it up to her. To all of you.' So bountifully blessed in their eyes, April could never tell them what it cost her to live a divided life, in constant, dreadful fear of discovery. Her husband was a hard man who exacted his toll for the comforts his family enjoyed. The blond children were cowed by an iron set of rules, even minor transgressions of which merited a beating and a session on their knees begging a stern Almighty for forgiveness. Since their teachers wielded the same weapons, they were equally submissive in school, never questioning the word of authority which came tightly laced in Christian National corsets. The only people on whom they could vent their normal childish spleen were servants and, very occasionally when she had come home tired from her charitable work, their mother.

Hester sighed. 'You've done your best, April, I know. But it doesn't make it any easier for our kids.'

When Jake was twelve and ready to go to high school, Miriam sent him down to Cape Town to stay with his grandparents. Auntie Hester took him to meet Auntie April one afternoon when Tertius Tulbagh De Wet was in Parliament and the blond children were busy with school sports. Jake was flabbergasted by the big white double-storey house with Cape Dutch gables that stood in a hectare of lawned garden where two gardeners could be seen working. Great clouds of blue hydrangeas bloomed under the oak trees lining the stone-paved drive up which they were walking. Rising behind the house was a massive grey stone buttress whose lower slopes were clothed in a deep forest green that his highveld eyes, used to sparse thorn trees and grass that turns quickly from pale green to gold, could hardly believe existed.

'Table Mountain,' Auntie Hester said, seeing his awed upward look.

'But it's not the right shape, Auntie. That's not how it looks in my geography book.'

'This is the other side of Table Mountain, Jacob.'

All the Cape Town family called him Jacob, which he hated because it sounded too biblical, too goody-goody. He had chosen Jake from an American cowboy movie whose hero had been somebody like Gregory Peck, strong, good, handsome and silent, with wise eyes that saw into the far distance.

Auntie April opened the back door. 'So you're Jacob,' she said, and led him inside so she could bend down and hug him. Her hair had faded from butter to cream with the years, and her face was like a powder puff, soft and pink and velvety. Even the creases of her neck smelled of soap and expensive perfume, where Ma's smelled faintly of sweat and Ouma's of old woman.

'Jake, please, Auntie April,' he said when she had disengaged, her gold chain clanking against mother-of-pearl buttons. 'That's what I like to call myself.'

'Allewêreld, a rebel, is it?' she said, and gave a fat woman's chuckle. Jake loved her as the most special person in his life from that moment on, and when he began to fall behind in school because the classes were so big, it was Auntie April who came to the rescue with money for him to go to St Barnabas College, a good private school for coloured boys near his home in Bosmont. 'Don't ask me where it comes from,' she told his mother Miriam over the phone. 'Just see it as part of what I owe you.'

'You've been a good sister to us, April,' Miriam wept in gratitude.

'I pay my debts,' April said, and told her husband that her gold chain necklace must have been stolen from her jewellery case, along with the children's Kruger rands. The insurance was paid without demur, but she was not given another gold necklace.

Jake looked up from his empty coffee cup. 'So that's how I got my superior education, from a Nationalist Member of Parliament via Auntie April. Satisfied?'

'It's an incredible story.' Rose had tears in her eyes. She was thinking, What else has been happening all these years in this country, my country, that I haven't known about?

Having coffee together in the cafeteria became a regular habit after morning lectures. Jake told her more about his family, and they argued about poetry, the Prof's lectures, campus politics and the perfect hamburger, just the two of them leaning across the plastic tablecloth. Ursula joined them once, after which she said to Rose, walking back to Sunnyside, 'Careful, kiddo. You're getting involved there.'

'I *want* to be involved! I've never met anyone like Jake. He's so different. He tells me things I've never heard or believed existed.'

'He's so coloured too. You haven't forgotten what happened to Izz and Pinky?'

Rose went red. 'It's not like that. It's a friendship. I like him. He likes me. We have coffee together sometimes. That's all.'

Ursula looked at her out of her sad hooded eyes. 'I know you won't listen to me, but I'll say it anyway. Jake's offside. Out of bounds.'

'That's just what's wrong with this country, we're always putting up barriers when we should be breaking them down!' Rose was furious. 'I wouldn't have thought you'd be one of the bigots. So much for sociology.'

'You know I'm not a bigot, but I am a realist. Chatting someone up over coffee is one thing. Breaking laws with him that could land you in jail is another.'

'Who said I was going to break any laws?' But she had thought about doing so. Ursula read it in her face, and sighed.

With trepidation, knowing that Sarah would be doubly alarmed by her friendship with a young Afrikaans man who was also coloured, Rose invited Jake home for lunch. 'Don't expect anything smart,' she warned him. 'My mother's not your average Houghton matron. She paints all day and won't change out of her jeans unless she absolutely has to.' To Sarah she said only, 'Jake will interest you. He's a coloured poet.' She was thinking, If I say any more, she'll imagine things.

They sat eating Agnes's cold pickled fish and salad off plates on their laps in the studio, talking about painting. Sarah was charming to Jake and said over coffee, 'As one artist to another, I'd really like to read your poems. Would you let me?'

'Ag, they're in a terrible mess, Mrs Kimber. All jumbled up in a file, some hand-written, some typed by my sister. You wouldn't find them very impressive.' Jake looked sheepish, an expression Rose hadn't seen before.

'You speak about them with such hesitant pride. Has anybody else seen them?' Sarah seemed really interested; Rose glowed.

'Not seen, exactly,' Jake said. 'I've done some poetry readings in the townships, that sort of thing. Sitting in small halls in front of small audiences, everyone very serious, nodding like they agree with me when they think anyone else is looking. But I haven't had anything published yet.'

'Does the Professor know you write poetry?'

Jake shrugged. 'He hasn't asked to see any of my work. He's a Dickens fundi, you know? More interested in Victorian slums than the ones under his nose.'

'After talking to you, I'm interested,' Sarah said. 'In fact, I'll make a deal, Jake. One of my paintings for a read of your poetry. Fair exchange.'

Jake sat looking at her, surprised and wary. From the way his full lips firmed and the grooves appeared on both sides of his mouth, Rose could see that he was wondering whether Sarah was making a genuine offer or being condescending, the lofty white artist to the lowly black scribbler.

Sarah insisted, 'I mean it. I've had a head start in my chosen work, and I'd like to see if I could help you in yours. Gordon and I know several publishers.'

'I don't know. I'll have to think about it. They're very private to me.' Jake got up and put his plate on the table. 'Ta for the lunch, Mrs Kimber. We'd better be getting back to varsity.'

'I understand. My paintings are private too. I always feel as though I'm taking off all my clothes and walking round naked at my exhibitions.' Sarah was smiling up at him through the paint smudges on her broad face. 'But I'd be mortified if no one came and looked at them. So I suppose I do them because I want to communicate what I'm thinking to others. Painting in a vacuum where you have no outlet, no feedback from others, must be a very sterile experience.'

'Writing too,' Jake said. 'I'll think about your offer, OK?'

He went home with Rose again one afternoon a week later, taking Sarah a folder of his poems, neatly retyped by Violet. He was elated that someone should want to read them and with the prospect of possible publication, and did not notice Rose's sulky annoyance that he should be showing them to her mother before her.

In return for the poems, he chose a small painting Sarah had done of Rose sitting reading on the windowsill. 'I'd like that one, if you don't mind, Mrs Kimber. It's a very good likeness.'

Sarah sent Rose to the kitchen to ask Agnes to bring tea, and said in a low voice as the door closed behind her, 'Are you in love with her, Jake?'

His head went up like a buck startled by an unexpected sound in the bush. 'Ag no, we're just friends,' he managed to say. He looked at the pink blotches on her face and thought, What happens to white women when the greenhouse breaks and all the balmy air escapes?

He heard her saying, 'If it should go further, I must ask you to consider the consequences carefully. Will you? I don't want my daughter to get caught in the conscience trap, doing something because she feels she ought to, rather than because she really wants to.'

He saw the icebergs in her pale blue eyes and thought, furious with himself, Being with Rose has made me soft. I didn't see this coming. He said in a cool hard voice, 'Moenie panic nie, Mrs Kimber. I'm not looking for charity.'

'We understand each other, then.' She gestured at the painting he had chosen. 'I'm very happy for you to have that, Jake. I'll give your poems to Rose when I've read them through.'

His pride would not allow him to reject the gift now. He took it home wrapped in newspaper and pushed it under his bed so he did not have to look at it. Before Sarah could return the folder of poems, Soweto erupted and Jake disappeared.

20

Back at the clinic, Sarah hands her now-sleeping granddaughter back to Sister Quthing, who settles her in the red carrycot on the next bed.

'Right, Mrs Kimber. Now let me put on that cold compress.' She leans over and touches the swelling on Sarah's forehead. 'You've got quite an egg here.'

'I think I fell.' Sarah looks up at her through eyelids that are still swollen from crying. 'Do you have to put anything on it? I'd like to get back to – to that place where Rose and Jake are. I must be with them.'

'Friends are with them now. It is our custom. You should rather rest.' The sister fusses with the sheet, pulling it up and tucking it under the mattress on both sides as if to restrain her physically.

'But I'm her mother. I must!'

'I don't think it would be a good idea for you to get up and walk just yet, Mrs Kimber. One, it will make your headache worse. Two, you may have concussion. I would like to keep you under observation for a while.'

'The headache's much better,' Sarah says quickly.

'You will have a cold compress and some aspirin,' Sister Quthing says in a firm, no-nonsense voice. 'I am responsible for you until the doctor comes, and I must be sure you are feeling quite all right before I let you get up. Please, lie still for another short while and then we will see if you are really feeling better.'

'How long?' Sarah looks as though she is going to weep again.'

'One hour, OK? Then we will see.'

'Then I will go. You'll understand if you are a mother too.' Sarah thinks, I must make her understand that I have to be there with them. It's for the last time. She says, 'We spend so many years of our lives being responsible for our children, reacting to their needs and cries for help. It's not something you can switch off overnight when they think they're grown up.'

'But you have to let them go, nè?'

'Oh, I know. I'm not one of those clinging mothers, Sister. My work is too important to me. It was easy to wave Rose goodbye when she wanted to share a house with friends. I have to admit it was harder when she decided to marry Jake. Legal barriers apart, his background was so very different from hers, and they would face a hard life in exile. But we came to admire him very much. Jake could be hot-tempered, but he was also kind and clever and dedicated to an ideal. And he loved her.'

'Yes, he did.' Sister Quthing thinks, I must keep her talking. It will distract her. She dips a cloth made from a threadbare square of towelling into the bowl of cool water on the bedside table, and wrings it out. Many of the clinic bandages are rolled strips torn from old sheeting that has been well scrubbed on the rocks down by the stream and left to dry in the sun. In a poor country, people have to be resourceful about things richer countries take for granted.

'She didn't often ask for help,' Sarah goes on. 'She was a very independent child, confident about the things she was good at, and not a complainer. So when she did ask for something, we knew she really needed it.'

'I'm going to put the compress on now. Ready?'

Sarah nods, and the sister folds the damp cloth in two and lays it gently over the blue and purple swelling. Sarah winces, but says, 'That feels nice. So cool.'

'We'll leave it there for five minutes or so, then do it again. You were saying about Rose – ?'

'She hated asking for anything. She used to say that she was so privileged compared to nearly everyone else she knew, that it wasn't right to ask for more. But there were rocky patches when it was hard not to go rushing to help her. When a child stumbles and falls, you're programmed to respond.'

'I know.'

'You're a mother too?'

'A boy and a girl. Six and three.' Because Sarah has had enough sorrow to cope with today, Sister Quthing does not add that the girl was born with cerebral palsy after a difficult birth, and had to be sent to an institution in Maseru when she was two. There are no facilities in the village for handicapped children. It is one of the bitter ironies of her life that she, a trained nursing

213

sister, is not able to look after her own child. The head of nursing services has said that she is needed in the village and cannot expect a transfer to the institution until a replacement has been found.

'We lost our son early. He had cystic fibrosis.' Sarah tries to remember what David looked like and fails. He has receded into the past, a sad little sepia photograph on the mantelpiece.

'Your family has suffered much.'

'I never thought of myself as suffering.' Sarah looks back over her life, assessing. 'I've had a very easy life, really. Lovely homes. People to help me run them. A father who believed in me, and a husband who has learned to love me, as I have him. A daughter who grew into a young woman we could be proud of.'

'You have not mentioned your mother.'

Sarah gives a faint smile, the first of the day. 'She – found it hard to accept that I had a mind of my own. We had a terrible argument just after Rose was born, and things were never the same between us again.'

Sister Quthing sighs. 'That is very sad. A mother is something that cannot be replaced. Or a grandmother.'

'She was never easy with the children. She couldn't unbend, though I think she tried to. For a long time I wondered what had made her like that, if it was my fault for being so wrapped up in my own concerns that I had neglected some essential daughterly response, had not loved her as I should. But Dad said once, "You must never blame yourself, Sarah. It's nothing you've done. Your mother was damaged when I married her. I was a fool to think I could heal her." I tried to make him tell me what he meant, but he wouldn't. It was only after she died and I found the bundle of old news clippings at the back of her desk drawer that I learned how she had been damaged. Her father had been jailed for incest when she was only twelve. Her mother had lain beside her on the bed while it was happening, holding her hand. She found it hard to trust anyone after that, and when I let her down –'

Sarah falls silent. Sister Quthing lifts off the damp cloth, now warm, dips it in the water and wrings it out again. She is thinking, So much sadness. It is a wonder what people can go through and stay in one piece. She says, 'I think you were a very good mother for Rose. She cared so much for other people. Hold still, Mrs Kimber. I'm putting the cloth on again.'

'Rose.' Tears begin to well up again in Sarah's eyes. 'Oh

God, I can't believe she's gone. She's too young. It should have been me. It should have been me!'

The sister bends down and puts her arms round the sobbing woman. 'Shhhh, now, lovey. Don't cry. When our time comes, it comes. Rose was happy in her life. Now it is for you to make her baby happy too.' She goes on talking like this until Sarah's eyelids close as though they have heavy weights on them, and she sinks into an exhausted sleep.

Sister Quthing stands looking down at her. There is a little more colour now in the broad face. The worst of the dust has been brushed off the front of her vivid dress. Her hands lie on top of the sheet, rough-skinned working hands used to stretching canvases and washing brushes out in turps and mixing paints to the exact colour she wants.

But not to the daily monotony of mops and brooms and dusters. I envy her that, the sister thinks. To have somebody else to do the work that must be done day after day in a house, and nobody ever sees. Maybe that is one of the reasons why people get so mad with white South Africans, because they still have servants.

Chuckling at the thought, she bends over to check on the sleeping child, then goes across to the dispensary to fetch some aspirin tablets for when Sarah wakes up. Her brisk footsteps take her past a window through which she sees Gordon walking up the rutted track towards the death hut. There is a knot of people outside, waiting. Cloud shadows splotch the stony slopes of the valley beyond, gathering like the high-planing vultures.

The black township of Soweto lies to the south-west of Johannesburg, just far enough away to be out of sight of the nearest white suburb. Nobody knows how many people live in its eighty-five square kilometres, but estimates range from a million upwards. It is not a shanty town. The small row houses are built of brick and cement blocks and though they are often badly finished, poorly serviced and overcrowded, each stands on its own small piece of ground and rents are low. Soweto could have been considered a major achievement in sub-economic housing were it not for the fact that its inhabitants have to live there or in a similar 'black' area, even those who can afford better.

Since half the black population of South Africa is under twenty, Soweto has many schools. At the beginning of 1976 the Nationalist government, wishing to promote the use of its mother tongue among black people (who seemed unaccountably to prefer English), decreed that certain school subjects should be taught in Afrikaans. Letters were sent out by the Department of Bantu Education, and a great shout of resistance went up from teachers, parents and pupils. By May, dozens of schools were out on strike and a black Afrikaans teacher had been stabbed with a screwdriver by a pupil. By the beginning of June, when Jake and Rose were leaning together over a table in the cafeteria talking of poetry, pupils were refusing to write their exams in Afrikaans. They began to throw stones at the policemen who were sent to investigate the unrest. Soweto was buzzing like a kicked-over beehive.

People who saw how angry the pupils were becoming sent urgent telegrams to the Department, but they were not taken seriously. On 16 June there was a protest march by ten thousand pupils that converged on the Orlando West High School. It was peaceful at first. The pupils were mostly adolescents and those in their early twenties who were still trying to beat the odds and gain a Matric certificate, though a lot of little brothers and sisters tagged along. They walked in their school uniforms, calling out slogans and carrying dustbin lids and banners saying 'Away With Afrikaans!' and 'We Are Not Boers', angry but having fun at the same time. It was good to be missing school and showing the government that they weren't going to be pushed around like their parents.

There were armoured troop carriers and policemen with guns and batons and police dogs lined up in front of the school. As the crowd of taunting, jubilant, fist-waving schoolchildren approached, an order was given and teargas canisters were fired. Holding cloths over their mouths and noses, the pupils stood their ground and let fly with stones and half bricks. Warning shots were fired over their heads, but the stones kept coming. The policemen were ordered to lower their rifles. In the volley of shots that turned the crowd into a fleeing rout, a 13-year-old boy called Hector Petersen was shot dead.

The people of Soweto erupted in fury. It was the beginning of days of rioting, burning and killing. By the end of June when the worst was over, 176 were dead, well over a thousand injured, and twenty-four schools, three clinics, nine post offices,

216

eighteen bottle stores, eighteen beerhalls, fourteen business premises, three libraries, one court building, nineteen shops, two community halls, nineteen houses, forty-two Administration Board buildings and 114 vehicles had been looted and burned. The police had arrested dozens of black leaders. When the schools re-opened again on 22 July, they were mostly deserted. Neither parents nor police could make the pupils go back to school.

Jake and Rose were sitting on the library steps in the winter sun on 16 June when a young man hurrying past flung out the news of the shooting.

'Bloody murderers!' Jake's face looked as though it had been covered with a thin layer of dun latex and pulled down, hard.

'It's awful.' Rose was stunned. How could this terrible thing be happening only a few miles away from a quiet sunny campus where the major worries were mid-year exams and the soggy chips in the cafeteria?

Jake swung round at her. 'Kids are being shot dead, and all you can say is "It's awful"?'

His sudden hostile rage was like being clubbed in the face. She said, 'It was the first word that came into – '

'Awful. How terribly, utterly awful that kids should have the temerity to stand and throw stones at the police.' His mimicry of her English-accented voice was savage. 'Naturally they must be answered with bullets to teach them a good lesson so they don't do it again. I mean, they're only blacks, hey? Who cares if a few get gunned down? Plenty more where they came from. Not so, white chick?'

Rose's eyes filled with tears. 'You know I don't think that, Jake.'

The sun shining through his hair made it look as though it was on fire. 'I don't know anything any more! Except I'm wondering what I'm doing here, playing with words while kids are fighting my fights for me.'

The tears spilled down her cheeks. There was nothing she could say to this man whom she had thought was her friend, and clearly wasn't.

'Don't just sit there crying!' Her tears made him even more angry. 'Women always bloody cry, just to make us feel bad.'

'I'm not – '

He jumped up and stood in front of her. 'You can't catch me

that way. I've got sisters. I know how they operate. Whenever something happens that they don't like, they cry. They carry on bawling for half an hour sometimes, and at the end of it they blow their noses and look around with their red eyes, and say, "Ag, I feel better now. Who's making the tea?" Crying isn't going to help that Soweto kid. Or change what's been happening in this country for the past three hundred fucking years. Those students have got the right idea: we've got to stand up and fight now. We've been patient long enough.'

'Jake.' She was wiping the tears away with the back of her hand, like a child. 'Please don't be angry with me. I haven't done anything.'

'You're one of them!' His words cracked over her like a whiplash.

'I'm not!'

'You bloody are! You're part of the system, whether you like it or not! I shouldn't have tried to kid myself you were any different.' She flinched as he bent down towards her, but it was only to scoop up the files he had left lying on the step. 'I'm going to find someone who can tell me what's happening. So long.'

The injustice of what he was saying made her cry out, 'I'm not part of any system! I've never even voted, and if I had, it certainly wouldn't have been for anyone in this government.'

'Because you know they'll get in anyway! Like all the English in this country you hide behind the Nationalists, moaning about their terrible accents and singing your nice liberal songs while they do all the dirty work. You people are worse than they are.'

'That's not true! Not fair!'

'Not fair?' His slanted cheekbones were flushed with fury. 'What the hell ever was fair about this stinking place we live in? I've had enough. I'm going.' He turned his back and took the stone steps up to the roadway two at a time.

She did not see him again for four years though he managed to get a parcel to her several days later, wrapped in brown paper. It was the painting of her that Sarah had given him. The note said, 'Tell your mother she can keep her thirty pieces of silver. You can keep the poems in memory of some good coffee and a mouse that stuck its head out once too often. Jake.'

She tried to find out from other coloured students what had happened to him, but nobody seemed to know. There was a rumour that he had joined the Soweto Student's Representative Council. A few months later she heard that he had slipped across the border to Botswana, and disappeared.

For weeks after their last meeting his accusations went round and round in her head like a carousel going too fast. 'You're one of them! You're part of the system, whether you like it or not! You people are worse than they are. I've had enough. I'm going.'

Does he hate me now? she wondered. I thought we got along so well together, but I must have been imagining it. Maybe the gap between black and white in our country is too wide to be bridged in a few months. She grieved for the loss of a friend, pushing away thoughts of his being anything more.

As a memorial to their friendship she became more militant in the anti-government student movement, joining the committee that organised demonstrations. They spent a lot of time agonising over questions like: How can we best demonstrate our solidarity with black students? and, Are we condoning a system that shoots children dead in the street, just by the fact of being white and of voting age? 'No,' she stood up and argued on the second question, 'we can't help what we are. But we can make more noise about the things that are wrong.'

'Bravo, Rosie,' said the chairman, a masters student in political science called Chad Whitaker who had hardly looked at her before. He was tall and dark and haggardly handsome, and stalked about the campus in a black leather jacket and white polo-neck sweater looking like a secretary bird. But he had an unexpected, irrepressible smile, and Rose was pleased and flattered when he asked her out after the meeting. Their romance was a heady mixture of deep discussions, late-night strategy meetings, police baton-dodging and breathless sex afterwards. It took a long time for Rose to realise that Chad's passions would always be more political than personal; he was an intellectual down to his black moccasins for whom sex was a pleasant necessity rather than an act of love. Sometimes when they made love she wondered what it would have been like with Jake but then she would feel guilty, as though she were desecrating the friendship that had flowered so briefly and ended so abruptly.

During that year, 1976, the United States celebrated its 200th anniversary by electing Jimmy Carter, Mao Tse-tung died, the Montreal Olympics were held, Transkei became the first of the black homelands in South Africa to gain its dubious independence, and Rose came close to being arrested twice. After her honours exam she applied to study for a diploma in higher education the following year, and was accepted, 'On one condition, Miss Kimber. You will have to curtail your radical activities, or you will have difficulty in finding a school that will accept you for the necessary period of teaching practice.'

'What I do in my own time is surely irrelevant?'

The dean of the faculty of education gave his keen pearly smile. 'Teaching is a profession that tries to maintain the highest standards, Miss Kimber. We believe that our task in educating the adults of the future is a vital one. Therefore we do not welcome fanatics or hot-headed reformers, preferring to err on the conservative side rather than expose our charges to extremes. If you don't understand this, I don't think you would fit into our diploma year very well.'

'Oh, I understand.' Rose thought, This is how the system works, of course. White people are so comfortably parcelled up in their well-paying jobs and their lovely homes and the excellent education for their children, that there's no incentive to look beyond gift-wrapping. I'll have to keep myself well wrapped up too, if I want to get my diploma. 'I'll conform, Professor,' she said through gritted teeth.

She passed her diploma exams with an upper second, but only a lukewarm personal assessment from the dean, who was no fool. She had been a fiery speaker at the protest meetings over the death in detention of Steve Biko, the black student leader. Rose was classified by the Department of Education as 'too political' to teach in either white or black government schools, and it was too late by then to apply for a private school post. After five years at university, she couldn't find work.

'Take that trip to Europe you've been planning with Ursula,' Gordon urged her. 'Don't worry about a job. I'll foot the bills until something turns up. You've earned it, Rosie. You should have some fun before life gets too serious.'

As he walks up the stony track now towards the hut where she lies with blood matting her lovely blonde hair, dead at twenty-nine, he remembers those words and thinks, Thank God she went. At least she had a year of being young and carefree and out from under the shadow of Africa.

21

For the first time since he has come, Gordon looks around him. Now that the sun is moving closer to the western rim of the valley and no longer beats down so brutally, the closed and shuttered midday village has come to life. Women and children are walking along the well-trodden paths between the huts and sitting silently in the doorways. He nods a greeting as he passes, and is answered by a 'Dumela, Morena' with respectful eyes lowered in return.

The older girls wear lengths of cotton printed in sizzling colours knotted above their breasts and falling almost to their ankles. They have smooth brown bodies and wear their hair in intricate braids, showing a shy flash of white teeth when they walk past him. Unless they escape soon across the border to the towns and cities of South Africa, the bloom soon fades into the harsh reality of scratching crops from the thin soil and too many children. Their mothers wear sombre brown and dark blue prints from the trading store, and their barely middle-aged grandmothers sit swathed and subdued in grubby checked blankets, even in the afternoon heat. All are barefoot; shoes are too expensive to wear every day.

Most of the huts are solid structures of dressed stone with the chinks filled with clay; the Basotho are among the best builders in Africa. Wood is scarce in these harsh treeless mountains, and mud huts like the empty one where Rose and Jake are lying begin to crumble after a few years of winter frosts and heavy summer rain. All the huts are built in the traditional shape, a circle several metres in diameter with a conical thatched roof, and door and window openings picked out in mud plaster. There is a smudge of soot at the top of each opening where the smoke from the daily cooking fire seeps out. Gordon knows from his visits to the villages on his farm that it is dark and close inside, and the smoke stings your eyes. It also clings tenaciously to the people who live there, insinuating itself into their clothes and blankets and hair, the world-wide smell of the peasant.

The huts look as though they have grown into being, pushing up from the earth like squat mushrooms, part of the natural landscape. Their mud and stone walls are the colour of the surrounding soil and rock: russet, ochre, bronze, slate blue. The thatched roofs have weathered to silver grey and are shaggy at the lower edges, like grandfathers' moustaches. Next to many of the huts are pear-shaped grain storage baskets as tall as a man and flaring broadly at the base. Here the mealies and sorghum, a kind of millet, grown and tended by the women during the summer are stored against the long dry cold winter.

Where the clusters of huts peter out further up the hillside are a series of round stone kraals where the village cattle and horses and donkeys and goats are driven in at dusk. Beside each entrance is a tangle of wooden stakes and barbed wire which is drawn across to keep the livestock safe. There are jackals in these mountains, and the older people speak of leopards up in the krantzes, though nobody has seen one for years. The village children are used to keeping a wary eye out for hovering hawks and eagles when there are young chicks running after the rangy hens that are out pecking round the huts now, busy after their midday torpor.

The only buildings in the village that are not round are the government offices, the clinic, the school, and a handful of cottages for teachers and civil servants. All these are built of cement breeze blocks, cheaply plastered and whitewashed, with corrugated iron roofs that soon begin to rust around the nail-holes. The steel windows and pine doors are painted the same brilliant green as Sister Quthing's furniture family. Must have been a job lot, Gordon thinks. Viper green. God, this place is depressing. He asks himself again, I wonder how Rose stuck it?

Looking for an answer, he turns off the track on to a path that leads past the school building, behind which Cordelia has told him Rose and Jake lived. They were moved up to the empty hut as soon as the police left this morning, to be mourned in decent privacy while their home is cleaned of blood and plaster and splintered wood in time for the funeral.

He sees the answer as soon as he walks round the corner of the school. In front of a small whitewashed cottage with fresh cotton curtains at the windows are two flowerbeds edged with rows of small stones and planted with nasturtiums and bright yellow marigolds. Despite the day's heat, the well dug-over soil is still damp under a thin layer of kraal manure. A yellow bucket in which water must have been fetched every day from the nearest village tap stands on one of the steps leading up to the front door.

Gordon thinks, She did it by putting down roots. Making a home. Learning how to belong. It must have taken such guts. Oh, Rosie, I'll miss you so much.

He sits down on the step next to the bucket, puts his face down in his hands, and cries.

Rose and Ursula returned from their year working and travelling in Europe having decided to look for a house to share. They had done all the things young people do: worked as waitresses and in vineyards, travelled on trains with Eurailpasses and back-packs, stayed in youth hostels, eaten in markets and station cafés, met and talked for hours with other travellers. Europeans don't realise how lucky they are, being able to visit and explore nearby countries so easily, they had agreed. When you live in distant corners of the globe like we do, it costs a fortune in air fares to get anywhere.

Ursula registered at Wits for her masters year in sociology, and since Rose still had to look for a job, she offered to do the house-hunting. Rented accommodation was scarce, and it took her some weeks to find the rambling old bungalow in a Yeoville street that met both their families' specifications: it was well burglar-guarded and in a 'nice' area. It also had four bedrooms, which meant they would have to look for others to share with them.

'Guys would make a good change after Sunnyside,' Ursula said. 'Enlarge our social circle too.' She put up a notice on the varsity board, and they were surprised at how many answers there were.

'How are we going to choose the right ones?'

Rose was sitting on the stone balustrade of the stoep, basking in the glow of having her own home. Both mothers had helped them move in, donating odd pieces of furniture, carpets and curtains that had been retired to store rooms, old kitchen equipment, remnants of crockery. Rose was rather shocked at the predatory way she found herself walking round on her visits home, looking for things that wouldn't be missed. It seemed quiet and gloomy now that she had moved out. Sarah spent nearly all her time in her studio, and Gordon was busy with a major business takeover which involved a lot of travelling and made him short-tempered. Agnes had developed arthritis in both hands, and was sour with worry over what would happen if she had to stop working.

'How do we choose? Elementary, my dear Kimber. We ask all the possibles round for an interview, one by one.'

'But you can't tell what people are like in a few minutes. This isn't one of your sociology assignments.'

'Why not? That's exactly what sociology's all about, social interaction between people. Maybe I could do my thesis on the selection of house-mates for communal living.' Ursula drifted off in thought, deep in an old deck chair, her face shadowed by the wild bubble of black curly hair that she seldom seemed to have time to pull a comb through.

'We're getting off the point,' Rose said, 'which is how to find ourselves two guys who are easy to live with.' Ursula's current boyfriend has been excluded as a possibility because one of the rules of the house was to be No Romances, which caused too many complications, other commune residents had told them.

'OK. We'll make it a long interview, like having him over for tea. A sort of social inquisition. Then we'll draw up a list of secret tests he has to pass, such as: Does he crook his little finger when he lifts his cup? Can he talk intelligently about good movies? Is he sensitive to women's issues? Does he wear slip-slops?'

'Why slip-slops?'

'I can't stand the noise of people walking round in them, each step dragging on the floor. I'd go bananas if I had to share my house with a pair of slip-slops.'

After a series of hilarious tea parties they chose Boff Jordan, a computer science student who played rugby for the varsity first fifteen ('Brains and brawn in one package,' Ursula said), and Colin Amoils who was doing his masters in clinical psychology, and who claimed to be able to fix anything from blocked drains to broken hearts. Both had steady girlfriends, and both had solemnly sworn to do their share of the housework and cooking. 'No macho excuses,' Ursula said, fixing Boff with a beady eye. 'We're equal partners here.'

'No macho excuses,' he agreed. 'I've got three sisters, and

they licked me into shape long ago. I'd rather face a scrum any day than three furious females.'

'That's it, then,' Rose said after they had made all the arrangements. But they had not reckoned on Didymus.

The phone rang one Saturday morning about a week later and a squeaky voice said, 'Are the rooms let yet?'

'I'm afraid they are,' Rose said.

'But they can't be! I need one.'

'I'm sorry. We've already got people moving in.'

'You must have a corner for me somewhere. One end of the dining room? A pantry? A laundry cupboard? I'm used to sleeping on shelves. I'm not fussy.'

'We are. And we've already chosen our – '

'But you haven't met me yet.' Anxiety made the voice go up another octave. 'I'm the ideal companion. Clean-living, house-trained, a good cook, and thoroughly nice. When a mother meets me, she knows her daughter's going to be in good responsible hands.'

Rose laughed. 'I'm sure you're nice, but we really don't have a vacancy.'

As she started to put the phone down, the voice squeaked, 'Wait! I know you'll like me if you meet me, so I'm coming round. I'll be there in twenty minutes.' And the phone was slammed down.

'There's some weirdo coming about a room. I couldn't stop him,' Rose told Ursula, who was slumped in the deck chair on the stoep, surrounded by the debris of a late breakfast.

'Damn. I shouldn't have put the address on the notice. We'll have to go inside and lock the door and pretend we're not here.'

They were sitting on the floor behind the old chintz sofa when there was a knock at the door and a voice said, 'Hullo. It's me.' After a few minutes, it said, 'Yoo-hoo, it's me, Didymus. Anybody in there?'

'Didymus!' They collapsed into giggles.

Footsteps went along the stoep, down the steps and round the house. Rose couldn't resist peeping through the curtains as he went past. He was tall and knobbly, with hair like a white rabbit's and a long neck with a prominent Adam's apple, and he was wearing a grubby motor mechanic's overall and bicycle clips. 'He's got acne too, yuk,' she told Ursula.

The steps came back to the front door. 'I know you're in there,' the voice squeaked, 'because the stoep has an air of recent abandonment. So I'll just lay siege here until you come out. I forgot to add that I'm very patient.'

Half an hour later they were sitting round the kitchen table laughing together, and had agreed to let him the servant's room across the back yard. 'Luxury,' he sighed, leaning back and closing his watery blue eyes in contentment. 'It's even got an *en suite* bathroom, though I'll have to do something about the cockroaches. I said you'd like me, didn't I?'

Didymus Scott was a theology student whose parents were missionaries in Kuruman, and to supplement his meagre church scholarship, he serviced other students' cars. He never spoke less than the absolute truth, and his talents included the ability to make anyone laugh inside a minute. He could also whip up a sumptuous meal from a packet of beans, a few chicken pieces and some vegetables. 'Missionaries have to be resourceful,' he'd say, 'and their long-suffering children even more so.'

'It doesn't bother you to share your home with a Jew?' Ursula said on that first morning.

'Why should it? Jesus was a Jew.'

'Or an atheist?' Rose had decided after trailing through what seemed like hundreds of cathedrals and churches in Europe that the idea of a God or gods had been invented by humankind to assuage our fear of death, and comfort us in adversity.

'No sweat,' Didymus said, 'even though I know you're wrong. You needn't worry about me being a Bible-thumper. I'm not going to be muttering prayers over the pototao peelings or dishing out sermons with supper. I am exceptionally pure in heart, as it happens, so I shall simply let my example shine before you heathens.'

After fumigating and whitewashing the small, filthy rooms across the yard, Didymus moved in with his sole possessions: an old black delivery bicycle, his bedding, and what he called his travelling library, a tin trunk full of books. And he became the life and soul of the house, always funny, cheerful and obliging, though he never joked about his vocation. 'I know that the Lord intends me to be a bishop one day,' he would say, 'but His church isn't flush with money, so I have to put in a lot of extra elbow-grease to get there.' When Didymus left in the mornings, pedalling off with his books in the delivery bicycle's front basket, it seemed as though the light dimmed a little.

It was he who told Rose about the teaching job at a church-run adult education centre in Germiston. 'The pay is next to nothing and the hours are rotten, three nights a week and all day Thursday and Saturdays,' he said, 'but you'll like the students. They really want to learn, and they appreciate a teacher who cares.'

Rose remembered Gloria saying, 'I want to better myself,' and teetering up the drive in her high heels on her way to night school, homework and text books proudly cradled in the crook of her arm. How could I have been so mean to her? she thought with shame. Maybe I can make up for it now. That the job paid badly would not matter, as Sarah had recently given her control of her grandfather's trust fund, saying, 'The income will make you independent, which would have pleased him very much.'

Didymus took her to the St Aloysius Centre, a barrack-like complex of dingy brick buildings that had once been a mine compound. It stood among scraggly gum trees next to a mine dump off which the fine yellow sand blew in sheets when it was windy. Father Basil, the principal, had black curly hair threaded with silver and a deeply creased face that looked as though it had been slept in for a year. He wore a long black cassock covered with paint and plaster stains.

'Excuse the gunge,' he said, indicating the stains as he hitched a solid rump on to an old-fashioned wooden school desk. 'We're redecorating. The mine management lets us use these buildings only on condition we keep them properly maintained. You want to teach English?'

'Yes.' Rose nodded firmly. Didymus had told her that he liked people to be definite.

'You know what you're letting yourself in for?' He had shaggy eyebrows like two black caterpillars bristling at each other.

'I know. I concentrated on second-language teaching when I did my teaching diploma. That's why I did it, to help people who otherwise wouldn't have access to properly trained teachers.'

Shrewd grey eyes appraised the silk shirt she had bought in Italy and worn with a teacherly-looking skirt for the interview. 'You're not slumming by any chance? This isn't a picnic we're running down here. We're very serious.'

Jake had accused her of slumming once. Rose said, 'No, dammit! I'm serious too. Ask Didymus.'

'I think you'll find that she's the answer to a principal's prayer, Father,' the squeaky voice said on her right. 'She's bright and she likes people. She also has private means, so the money isn't important.'

Rose thought, Private means! It sounds awful.

'Coming from Didymus, that's an accolade.' The creased face crumpled into a smile. 'I'll try you out, Rose. We badly need a good English teacher. But a lot hinges on whether you can handle our students. Teaching adults who work all day isn't easy.'

Rose soon learned what he meant. Her students were labourers and domestic workers, shop assistants, till cashiers, mine workers and messengers. Working at full-time, physically demanding jobs, they often fell asleep over their books. Their English was poor, their writing slow and laboured, their understanding of the Matric set books severely limited. But they were desperately eager to pass this exam which would mean so much to their pride, and in many cases increase their wage packets. They listened to her as though she were dispensing the law, worked diligently at their assignments and often would not let her go when the buzzer sounded for the end of classes, crowding round her desk asking questions.

'Rose, what does this mean?' Father Basil had decided that surnames were redundant on both sides.

'What is the writer saying here?'

'Why do you have to say "went" and not "goes"?'

'Who is this man George Eliot?'

'I don't understand.'

'I don't understand.'

'I don't understand.'

She would get into her car afterwards feeling wrung out, wanting only to sink into one of the deck chairs on the stoep at home, and sleep. Europe could have been a million miles away from the shabby school buildings set in their wilderness of square-topped mine dumps whose sides were already eroding into jagged gullies. Looking up at the dun, dead, poisoned sand slopes where nothing grew, she would think of the miners in her classes who toiled thousands of metres under the earth to bring the precious gold-bearing ore to the surface, yet whose wages barely totalled her monthly rent. And forget them minutes later when she turned out of the gate towards home, a bath, and supper round the kitchen table with her friends. By the time she fell into bed in her pleasant room with its ornate pressed steel ceilings and an old khelim in soft pinks and browns on the floor, nothing could have been further from her mind than the people in her classes.

During the weekends the big Yeoville house buzzed with friends, and there were parties and picnics and lazy lunches on the stoep. Rose began an affair with a hyperactive electrical engineer called Vernon Davis who was always dragging her down to Vaal Dam to water-ski or on long hikes into the Magaliesberg or Drakensberg mountains. They explored odd corners of Johannesburg together, shopping for curry spices at the new Oriental Plaza, pulling faces at each other through the mouldering palms and ferns in Joubert Park's glass-house, cycling past the old mining magnates' mansions in Parktown and Westcliff, peering over their stone walls at faded elegance and once-grand gardens. Vernon had a beautiful body and a robust sense of humour but he was exhausting, and the affair petered out after a few months. Rose met Chad Whitaker again at a party not long afterwards and went out with him several times, but it was not a success. He talked about the trade union movement and foreign films she had not seen, and seemed to have lost the art of listening altogether.

Apart from Ursula, she did not ask her friends home to Houghton. The house that Gordon had bought to signal his arrival at the top was beginning to feel more and more like a well-run hotel, immaculate but impersonal. Yeoville was home now. Rose grew fond of its mixture of aging hippies and students in noisy digs, and orthodox Jews who walked in sedate black-hatted twos and threes to shul on Saturday mornings. Wedged between scruffy shops and haphazard flat buildings were little old houses with double bay windows like two cheerful bulging eyes. Schoolkids dragged their bags home along the pavements in the afternoons, often to empty flats, or if it were a Wednesday, to the Piccadilly Bioscope to swap comics and throw popcorn at each other during the matinee, infuriating the pensioners for whom it was their weekly treat.

Sometimes Rose and Ursula would spot a St Winifreds uniform, though not often, since most Yeoville residents would not have been able to afford the fees. 'I don't know how we managed to stick it out,' Ursula said one day when they saw a St Winifreds girl with an array of achievement badges pinned down the lapel of her blazer.

'We didn't have much choice. Dad was so keen for me to have the best education he could buy with his new money, and your father used to say – '

' "You are going to have all de advantages I never had,

Princess",' Ursula quoted, and they both laughed.

'At least we had each other.'

'Sisters in crime.'

'If I ever had a school to run, I'd abolish uniforms completely,' Rose said. 'Kids in comfortable clothes must be more receptive than those who are being strangled by school ties or sweltering in tight gyms and blazers. My kids would be allowed to wear whatever they felt comfortable in, within reason. And they'd always be allowed to walk on the grass.'

Walking down the sunny Yeoville street, she had no premonition of the school she would one day run in Lesotho where the children would be lucky to own a change of clothing, and the 'grass' would be bare stamped earth.

At the end of the year her first adult students wrote Matric, and just before Christmas Father Basil phoned to tell her that eighteen out of fifty-three had passed.

'It's probably my fault,' she apologised. 'I don't seem to have made very much headway with them at all.'

'What do you mean? This is the best percentage pass we've had so far,' Father Basil boomed, having spent a large part of his life on isolated mission stations where it was necessary to shout down the telephone to be heard at all. 'You're doing a marvellous job, girl!'

'But only eighteen passes. I feel I've let the others down.'

'Eighteen passes and thirty-five students who understand a damn sight more than they understood at the beginning of the year. They'll be back again in January, then watch their smoke. You're definitely coming back?'

'Wouldn't miss it, Father.'

'I'm glad. The students think the sun shines out of you. "Rose explains so nice," they always tell me, "and she smells nice too." ' There was a deafening bellow of laughter down the phone that made her snatch the earpiece away. 'Something to be said for Chanel No 5, eh?'

She thought, It's probably the only scent he knows, and said, 'I'll make sure someone puts another bottle into my stocking. Happy Christmas, Father.'

'And to you, Rose, my dear. Bless you.'

The St Aloysius Centre had received several large grants during the year. One was from the mining house which had donated the buildings, and had recently been embarrassed by a news report on how shabby and inadequate they were compared with its head offices. Others came from American companies anxious to placate shareholders at home, who had been made nervous by the Soweto riots. Since many high school children had had their education disrupted in the long school stay-away that followed, Father Basil had used the grants to buy some second-hand prefab offices from a construction company and was expanding classes to include full-time Matric students. Rose took on a full teaching load in the New Year.

Her old students greeted her joyously when she walked into her first January evening class. They crowded round her with their news, drawing her attention by touching and patting her as though she were a talisman who had brought her luck, and would do so again if touched often enough.

'Rose! Rose!'

'My marks weren't so bad! I'll pass next time.'

'I understood nearly all the questions.'

'I made this for you, to say thanks.' It was a beautifully crocheted pink tea-cosy with a darker pink rose embroidered on each side.

Rose had tears in her eyes. The warmth and friendliness was so unexpected. 'It's lovely, Tryphina, and something I'll really use. We drink a lot of tea at home.'

'Where do you live, then?' Fat, jolly Tryphina was a domestic worker who came all the way from Springs three times a week for classes, determined to get her Matric before her children did. 'I must show them their mother is not so stupid like they think she is,' she said often, shaking all over with laughter.

'I live in Yeoville, not far from Rockey Street.' It was a relief not to have to say 'Houghton' any more, specially in the spartan classroom surrounded by people whose homes would have fitted comfortably into her mother's dining room.

'My friend, she works in Yeoville. It's a nice place, I think.'

'It's a nice place,' Rose confirmed, thinking, She sounds exactly like Mum.

When the class finally settled down at the old school desks Father Basil had scrounged, which were ludicrously small for adults, Rose saw that there were many new faces. A burly young man in overalls sitting near the back looked familiar, and when she took their names she realised why. It was Ben Tsolo, one of the workers who had left Isidore's group because the discussions had become too theoretical. She remembered him saying angrily, 'I'm tired of listening to big talk, of learning, of waiting.

I want to go where I can do something for myself.'

She stopped next to him while the class was busy with a written exercise. He was still wearing steel-capped boots. 'Do you remember me, Ben?'

He looked up, unsmiling, and nodded. 'The place of much talk.'

'I'm glad to have you in my class. It was partly those meetings that decided me to become a teacher.'

He nodded again. 'Is good.'

'Do you ever see any of the others who used to come to those meetings? Pinky Bhengu? Sebenzile? Nyemzele?'

He shook his head. 'Never.'

'I tried to find out what happened to Pinky, but nobody seems to know. I'd very much like to see her again. If you ever hear anything, will you tell me?'

'OK.'

She saw his right shoulder hunch forward and his fingers clench round the pencil he was holding and thought, I'm preventing him from getting on with his work with my small talk. She said, 'Thanks,' and moved on, reminding herself how hard it was for adult black men to take instruction from a woman when their culture taught them from birth that women were secondary to men. 'Being a black woman is being at the very utmost bottom of the heap,' Pinky had said once. 'Not male, and not white. But we shall overcome, nè?'

Rose tried again to find out what had happened to her, phoning Isidore's mother who said that she had lost touch when Pinky was discharged from prison. 'But my Isidore is all right, praise God. He is lecturing at Leeds University, and married too. A nice Jewish girl. They will come to the university in Zimbabwe next year to be nearer home.'

'Izz will always fall on his feet. He knows which end of the baby is up, that one,' Rose remembered Nyemzele saying. She had a brainwave and phoned Prison Headquarters in Pretoria to ask if Nyemzele was still in service as a social worker.

'What you want her for, lady?' The official voice on the phone sounded deeply suspicious.

'I'm a friend. I'd just like to get in touch with her again.'

'Oh.' There was a long pause as the information that a white-sounding woman could be friends with a black social worker was taken in and digested. 'You better give me your name and telephone number, then.'

I wonder if they'll check me against their little black lists, Rose thought as she gave the details. I must be on quite a few of them by now. The police did not bother to hide the fact that they paid student spies to attend all the English-speaking universities to keep an eye on radical activities, saying that subversion was a natural concern of police forces all over the world. 'Students always go overboard,' one police officer was quoted as saying. 'We've got to watch out they don't pull the ship down with them.'

But few people realised the extent of the surveillance. Rose had been chilled to hear at a student meeting the testimony of a girl who had been at Rhodes University in Grahamstown. After being arrested at a demonstration, she had been left alone in an office at the police station, and had pulled out a drawer in one of the big filing cabinets ranged round the room. She had been shaken to find complete files on several students she knew who belonged to Nusas, the National Union of South African Students. 'They had photographs, dates and places of meetings, subjects being studied, known boyfriends, IQ test ratings, photostats of telephone bills, the lot,' she had whispered. 'I couldn't believe it. It was so paranoid.'

Several days later, Ursula called Rose to the phone one evening saying, 'It's Nyemzele on the line.'

The gravel voice said, 'Ja, Rose. You remember where to look for me, eh?'

They had a long conversation, catching up with each other's news. Towards the end Rose said, 'Whatever happened to Pinky and Mpho? I always wondered.'

Nyemzele's amused cackle ended in a wheezing smoker's cough. 'Don't you ever read your newspaper? She's running the best shebeen in Soweto. Very high-class stuff. Professional and businessmen only, imported Italian furniture, French champagne, the lot.'

'No! *Pinky*?'

'Why not? Her boyfriend owns it, and she's got brains, that girl. You should see the tight sequin numbers she wears, ai! Straight out of *Vogue* via her sister's sewing machine. People can go blind when she walks past.'

'I'd love to see her again.'

Nyemzele hesitated before answering. 'She may not want to see you.'

'Why not?'

'She – has problems with white people these days. It made her mad that she had to go to jail while Izz got off with a suspended sentence, and then left for good. "He's run away," she told me the day they let her out. "I'm not running. I'm a fighter. I'll get on the other side of the law where there's room to breathe, and I'll show Izz where he can stuff his little socialist prick." ' Nyemzele sighed. 'That's what I can't forgive this system. It's not evil, it's just stupid. Walking all over people's lives and dreams with big hobnail boots, like they don't exist.'

Rose said, 'And you pick up the pieces.'

She could almost hear Nyemzele's shrug. 'Somebody has to. It's not a big deal.'

They arranged to meet for lunch in town one Saturday with Sebenzile and Ursula. 'Where would you like to go?' Rose said.

There was a snort at the other end of the phone. 'You mean, out of the big choice available to us? One of the hotels might let us in, if we pretend to be foreign visitors and warn them in advance. Or there's the Palm Café in Braamfontein. They turn a blind eye to somewhat Technicolor customers.'

I've done it again, Rose thought. Maybe foot-in-mouth disease is incurable.

Nyemzele's parting words stayed in her mind for months. 'I think sometimes it will never end, this struggle to live like human beings. The laws and customs and habits that govern our lives are so very powerful.'

22

Sarah wakes to the sound of the clinic door being quietly closed, and surreptitious footsteps. There is a whispered conversation near Sister Quthing's desk. She opens her eyes to a row of high iron beds that seem to be standing on tiptoe, each chastely clothed in a white cotton bedspread and two pillows that look as smooth and soft as the breasts of white ducks. How comforting hospital beds are when you're sick, she thinks. So crisp and clean-smelling. You feel that germs don't have a chance against all that starchy virtue.

But I'm not sick. I'm – Rose. The memory of her daughter's bloodied body comes not as a hammer blow this time, but stealing into her mind like a cat burglar. Tears begin to well again, spilling out of her eyes to run warmly into the pillow. She thinks, I must go to her. She and Jake are all alone in that grim dark place, not even covered decently. I must pull myself together and go to them.

She turns her head. The sister with gentle hands is talking to a woman whose face she has seen recently. In the hut? Yes, carrying an electric fan. Talking about Rose, before Sarah got so angry and fell. She can't remember her name.

She bunches up a handful of sheet and blots away the tears. There is no time for crying now. She has to be a strong mother and go to the child who needs her. The pain in her head has gone, though it still feels tight and swollen above her right eye. She lifts her hand to feel the swelling, an abrupt puffy bulge the size of a bantam's egg. It's just a bump, she thinks. Nothing to keep me here.

She calls, 'Sister.' It comes out in a croak, so she clears her throat and calls more loudly, 'Sister!'

The two women break off their whispered conversation and come towards her. Sister Quthing, in front, is a slight brisk woman in a blue uniform with maroon epaulettes on the shoulders, and a frilly white cap anchored like a toy yacht in the dead centre of her hair. Her hands fuss automatically with the damply crumpled sheet, trying to smooth it down. 'You're awake, my dear. Would you like a cup of tea now?'

'Thank you, Sister, but no.' Sarah speaks as firmly as she can. 'I must get back to my daughter. You said I could go when I was feeling better. I'm fine now.'

'I'll believe that when I see you standing up.' Sister Quthing smiles to take the sting out of the implied threat.

'Let me out of these sheets you've got me so tightly tucked into, and I'll show you.' Sarah smiles back, willing the tears not to well up again.

'Very well,' the sister sighs. 'I don't suppose I can keep you here much longer if you are really feeling better. The mission doctor phoned to say that he has to do an emergency operation, and to use my own judgement where you are concerned. Help me get her up, Delia.'

The second woman comes closer and stands looking down. She is larger and moves more slowly than Sister Quthing; under the dark blue print headcloth that matches her dress, her face is round and strong, with the high Basotho cheekbones that are like knobs of granite worn smooth by the harsh mountain winters. The whites of her eyes have a muddy look, as though they have been stirred too often. She says, 'I'm Cordelia Motaung, Mrs Kimber. I don't know if you remember me coming to – '

'I remember. You're Rose's friend, the school inspector.' Sarah turns triumphantly to the sister. 'Total recall. Proof that I'm better.'

'Let's have you up, then.'

The two women turn down the sheet and help Sarah to sit up and swing her legs over the side of the bed. It is an effort for both of them. Sarah is heavy and in her need to show that she really is better, keeps pushing in the opposite direction. When she is upright, however, she sits without any sign of dizziness and is soon lifting a hand to her dishevelled hair. 'I must look a fright. Do you have a comb I could use?'

'There's one in my desk drawer, and some lavender scent too. I'll get them for you. There's a mirror and a toilet in the bathroom over there.'

'Thank you, Sister,' Sarah says when she brings them. 'You've been so kind.'

Sister Quthing spreads her hands in denial, scrubbed pink palms downwards. 'Kind! It's my job.'

'I've always thought that the bedrock of nursing is kindness. Without it, the profession wouldn't exist.' Sarah eases herself off the bed and on to her feet, looking down with surprise when they encounter the polished cement floor. 'Do you have my sandals?'

'Here, in the locker.' Sister Quthing bends down to get them out, then helps Sarah put them on. The broad white feet are dry and callused, with hard ridges of skin and fine dirt-ingrained cracks that show Sarah to be a habitual sandal-wearer. 'There,' she says, tightening the buckle of the second strap. 'Have a wash and fix your hair, and we'll see how you feel.'

'I told you, I feel fine.' Sarah's firm reply shows that she will brook no more well-meant bullying, and her gait is straight and steady as she walks towards the bathroom with the comb.

But Sister Quthing is not about to let her patient off scot-free. 'Will you walk up to the hut with her, Delia?' she asks in a low voice after the bathroom door closes. 'I don't think there's any serious concussion, but you never know. A head injury isn't funny at that age, she's got high blood pressure and there's probably still some shock. This thing with Rose and Jake – ai!' She shakes her head in disbelief.

'For me, the worst is not knowing who did it.' Cordelia shivers. 'Mr Kimber asked Max if it was MK, and I thought he was going to explode.'

'They should never have been allowed here in the first place.' People in the village are careful what they say about the well-hidden ANC training camp further up the valley where young men are taught the arts of furtive warfare, but Sister Quthing can allow her real feelings to show with Cordelia. 'It frightens me what happens in that camp. Kids from the townships come here with ink on their fingers and dreams of liberation in their heads, and six months later they're calling themselves freedom fighters and talking about capitalist exploitation. I see them walking down the road with their boots crashing and their eyes all over the place like they're thinking how many sticks of dynamite it would take to blow everything up, and I think, "You should still be in school, my boy, where you belong." At that age, they shoot first and think afterwards.'

'This terrible thing wasn't done by kids.' One of Cordelia's duties this morning has been to cross-question the clerk with eyes like wet drawer knobs. She lowers her voice. 'Max thinks it was a South African commando raid to put pressure on our government to get rid of the ANC presence here. They can't afford to have our little Lesotho lying like a snake in their belly, training their enemies. He also thinks they wanted to get Jake before he was moved back to Dar-es-Salaam.'

'Why Rose too? She was white like them!'

'But married to a man who was not white. A traitor to her race. Don't forget, these people are crazy in the head about staying pure and unadulterated, Sisi.' Cordelia gives a grim laugh, then with a glance at the bathroom door, drops her voice even lower. 'I could never understand why Jake stayed on with MK. He hated fighting. He would get mad if anyone even kicked a dog when he was around, and he used to hold his baby like she was the crown jewels. I wish our men would be more –' She leaves the wish dangling; they are both casualties of broken traditional marriages, as professional black women often are. To reconcile centuries-old tribal attitudes with the needs and aspirations of modern women is an almost impossible task.

'I still can't understand how anybody could do such a thing.' Sister Quthing remembers the torchlit scene that confronted her in the middle of the night: the bullet-ripped bodies, the arcs of blood spattered up the walls, the weeping clerk who ran to fetch her, the room in a shambles. 'Jake being killed, yes, that I can just understand. He was dangerous to them because he was a thinker who fought them with brains and ideas. But coming in the night to shoot a woman dancing at a party, that is the behaviour of wild animals, not men.'

They fall silent. From the bathroom comes the sound of Sarah washing her hands and face. Above the sagging ceiling overhead, the corrugated iron roof is ticking again as it cools down. Clouds have begun piling up above the peaks of the Malutis to the east, forming a mass of threatening grey cumulonimbus. A first gust of wind licks down the valley, slamming one of the clinic windows shut and blowing a rolling billow of dust down the dirt track outside, then it is still again. From higher up the hillside come the cries of herdboys bringing in the cattle before the rain starts.

Sarah comes through the door. She has washed the last of

the dust off her face and arms, put on some of Sister Quthing's lavender, and combed her hair into a thick silver plait that hangs forward over one shoulder, secured with a rubber band. In her bright floral cotton shift and sandals, smiling so the two watching women will not try to hinder her any more from her purpose, she looks ten years younger. She says, 'Is Hope still sleeping, Sister? May I leave her here with you?'

'Of course,' the sister says with some asperity. 'I have been looking after her all morning. Go now to be with her mother.'

Sarah thinks, Will Rose know I'm there with her? That I came to sit by her side through the long day that is only the beginning of her long night? She feels the tears threatening again, and blinks hard. 'Thank you, Sister, for everything. I'll be going now.'

'Delia will go with you.'

'Oh no, I couldn't put you to any more trouble.' Sarah's words almost fall over themselves. She doesn't want anyone with her but Gordon – and certainly not a strange woman, however friendly she has been with Rose.

Understanding, Cordelia says, 'I'll just walk with you to the hut door, Mrs Kimber. I won't come in.'

Sarah nods, relieved. 'Then thank you. I'd be grateful if you'd walk with me, Mrs Motaung.'

'Cordelia, please.'

'Sarah.' She accompanies it with a wan smile. 'Shall we go?'

From the door of the clinic, Sister Quthing watches them walk slowly up the rutted track in the direction of the death hut, arms linked.

There is another rumble of thunder, closer this time.

It was the end of 1980, the year in which Robert Mugabe became Prime Minister of Zimbabwe, Ronald Reagan ousted Jimmy Carter, John Lennon was shot, and President Tito, Alfred Hitchcock, Mae West and Peter Sellers died. Mount St Helens blew its head off in a terrifying eruption, Poland, Iran and Iraq were simmering, Voyager I set off for Saturn, local boxer Terror Mathebula became flyweight champion of the world, and Bjorn Borg won his fifth consecutive Wimbledon.

The black school boycotts in April, May and June had resulted in thirty deaths and an even heavier work-load for Rose. She was now teaching two shifts a day at St Aloysius as well as her night classes, with the help of a willing but very shy young Irish nun on her first teaching assignment in the baffling continent she had chosen as her life's work. 'I can't onderstand what in the world they're sayin' half the time,' she whispered behind her hand to Rose, her milky cheeks stained pink as though somebody had been dabbing on cochineal.

'They'll tell you with their eyes and their hands what they can't manage in words, Sister.' Rose bent in a tired stoop to pick up her satchel of notes and homework that would have to be marked before Saturday's classes.

'It's so different from the trainin' college. They're all so very *big*,' Sister Imelda sighed. In her abbreviated cream Trevira robe specially designed by her order for their tropical convents, she looked like a wilted lily in the giant zinnia patch of the classroom, where students were ablaze with the vivid pinks and reds and yellows and lime greens of that year's township fashion.

Remembering the misty greys and greens of the Ireland she and Ursula had travelled through, Rose thought, How can they send these timid women out here and expect them to cope with such a different world? She's overwhelmed. I'm going to have to ask Father Basil for someone else.

But he was not hopeful. 'Where do you think I'm going to conjure up another teacher who'll be prepared to work in this dump for next to nothing, girl?' he boomed. 'Treasures like you aren't easily found.'

'Flattery will get you nowhere, Father. I need better help, or I'll let my students down.' Rose enjoyed their verbal sparring, but this was serious.

'I know it. And you know there's nothing I can do except pray for a miracle.' His shoulders drooped under the stained black cassock. 'We're strained to bursting, even with the prefabs and a doubled-up teaching staff.'

He must have done a fair amount of praying, because the answer was waiting on her doorstep late one Saturday afternoon in November, when she came home with a basket of the household's clean washing after her monthly stint at the laundromat. A man was sitting with his back against the stone balustrade of the stoep and his arms wrapped round bent knees, sleeping with his head resting on one forearm. His neck between the blue sweater and the fuzz of hair was a darker tan than she remembered, but she knew it was Jake. She stopped on the bottom step with her basket resting on her hip.

240

The noise of her shoe grating where the step had not been swept woke him. He turned his head and looked up. 'Howzit, Rose. They said you'd be along soon.'

'You're back.'

'Large as life. Can I come in?'

She stood looking down at him. The skin was pulled tight over his slanted cheekbones as though he had been under strain for a long time. By his side was a travel-soiled khaki canvas rucksack. She said, 'Are you still mad with me?'

'Does it make a difference if I am?'

'Yes. You said some hard things on that last day. I don't think I deserved them.'

'And you want a nice polite little "sorry"?'

Rose felt the hot prickle of tears. It had taken her months to get over the feeling of being betrayed by someone she had thought of as a friend, and she had not been able to forget his bitter accusation as he turned away. She said, 'I don't want anything any more. Please go,' and started to walk up the steps.

He caught her arm, looking up with the swamp water eyes as still and clear as they had been when she first met him, though sunk now into grey-smudged hollows. 'I see I hurt you more than I thought. For that, I'm sorry.' His voice was hoarse, the Afrikaans accent less pronounced.

'Do you really mean it?' His hand was brown and sinewy, with hard ridges where the palm touched her skin as though he had been doing manual work with them for a long time. She found she wanted him very much to leave it there, resting on her arm.

'Ja, I mean it. It was an ugly way to say goodbye. My only excuse is extreme provocation at the time.' He gave her a ghost of the ferocious grin. 'Now will you let me come in?'

She thought, He shouts at me, breaks up our friendship, disappears for four years and then pitches up on my doorstep threatening to disrupt my life all over again. Do I really want him to come in? She could almost hear Ursula saying, 'You've got to be crazy, kiddo.' And yet –

'I know it's a cheek to ask, but I don't have a lot of alternatives right now.' Jake took his hand away to push himself up off the step so he could stand. From the slow way he straightened, she could see that he was exhausted.

The laundry basket was getting heavy, and she put her foot up on the next step so she could rest it on her knee. 'Are you in trouble, Jake?'

He shrugged. 'Only if the cops find me. You probably know that I left in a bit of a hurry over the border without a passport.'

'Where have you been all this time? I think you should tell me before I decide.' Rose looked straight at him. 'If it's where I think, you're putting me and the rest of my friends in this house in danger just by being here.'

He said in a tired voice, 'I know that. I only came because I'm so clapped that I can't be as choosy as I would be otherwise. Could you stretch a point for a night, maybe? In memory of a friendship that lived for a few months at least before it was kicked to death?'

She thought, He's not denying it. He would have gone over the border with so many of the young men from Soweto, to join the ANC and be trained as guerrillas in what they call the freedom struggle, and the police call terrorism. She felt a shiver of ice down her back. There could be plastic explosives in that dirty canvas rucksack.

Seeing her hesitation, he said, 'I'll be gone before anyone wakes up tomorrow. Just a night won't contaminate any of you, I promise. I could sleep in the servant's room.'

'It's already occupied, by a theology student.'

'White?'

She nodded. 'And poor. And not proud.'

'You don't say! They told us things were changing back here, but not that much.' This time he really smiled, and the lines on his face relaxed into the Jake she remembered talking to over cup after cup of coffee.

She said, 'Listen, I'll have to ask the others, OK? We're a democratic community and make our decisions by majority vote.'

'No hierarchical nonsense about she who signs the lease being queen?'

She ignored the sarcasm. 'I'll be back in a minute. Will you wait here?'

'I chose these steps because they can't be seen from the street, so I guess it's as good a place as any.' He sat down again, folding himself up into a small space with a weary economy born of months spent in cramped places – huts, cattle trucks, transport planes, crowded lecture rooms.

He looked like a puppet whose strings had been dropped.

After a moment she picked up the laundry basket and went on up the steps and into the house. Since they did their household chores on Saturdays, the others were in the kitchen: Ursula reading the paper, Colin under the sink trying to fix the blocked U-bend, Boff with the scientific calculator that lived permanently in his pocket, busy working out what they owed each other for groceries that week. Didymus was stirring the contents of a large saucepan and telling a story about a well-known bishop and the comely mission organist.

' – and then she said, "You can finger my keyboard any time, Your Grace," batting the mink eyelashes she had gone all the way into Kimberley to buy for the occasion. He went as scarlet as his chasuble. The funniest thing about it, of course, was that she wouldn't begin to understand the innuendo. Miss Dolores is as innocent as the ministering angels she's always talking about.'

'Sounds as though you have some wild times out there at the mission,' Colin muttered from under the sink.

Ursula looked up and saw Rose in the doorway. 'Hi. Did you find Mr Wonderful waiting on the doorstep?'

'Yes.' She put the laundry basket down on the table.

'He's got a nerve to come back after what he did. You've told him to push off, I presume?'

'Not yet. He wants to stay the night.'

Ursula collapsed the paper with an angry rustle. 'You're not going to let him? Rose, you can't! He's bad news, that guy.'

'I said I'd ask the rest of you.' She sat down on a chair, facing them. 'The position is this. He's dead tired, and he's trying to avoid the police. He says he only needs to stay the night, and he'll be gone first thing in the morning.'

'Why is he avoiding the police? Do you know?' Ursula demanded.

Rose looked down at her hands. 'He's been over the border. I think we can guess who with.'

'The ANC,' somebody said.

The name of the banned organisation seemed to make a black hole in the kitchen's warm fug. It was something you read about in newspapers and heard reviled from political podiums, an acronym to dread for the threat it posed to your white future and for its connections with the creeping red stain of communism, as apparently ambitious for conquests as the British Empire had been at its majestic pink apogee. Not an exhausted man who had once been a fellow student, and was now begging a roof for the night.

'We can't even consider it, then,' Ursula said.

'Agreed.' Boff looked up from his calculator. 'My inclination would be to call the cops.'

Rose swung on him with an angry, 'You can't!'

'Why not? He's a terrorist who must have been trained to kill people. If we have him here, we're condoning that.'

'I can't believe Jake would ever be a terrorist. He's a poet,' Rose said.

'Poets can shoot too. Stick a gun in a guy's hands and you never know how he'll react.'

'I know this one. He's not like that.' Rose remembered his long fingers wrapped round his coffee cup. 'We can't talk anyway, Boff. None of us has had to cope with even a fraction of what he and his family have been through.'

Colin had been leaning over the sink, pushing a piece of wire down the plug-hole. Now he turned and said, 'Rose is right. We can't set ourselves up in judgement when we don't have personal knowledge of the guy. I vote we let him stay, on condition he leaves tomorrow.'

'I've got personal knowledge,' Ursula said. 'He's arrogant, foul-mouthed and rude, with a chip on his shoulder the size of the Brixton Tower. He treated Rose like a real jerk. No way does he stay.'

'Don't listen to her, she's biased.' Rose turned her back on Ursula to plead with the others. 'He's not usually like that. His poetry is really good. Direct and strong and sensitive.'

'So sensitive that he's spent, what is it, four years, learning how to kill people? Tell me another!' Ursula picked up her paper again.

'That's just conjecture! We don't know what he's been learning. Anyway, what would you be doing if you were coloured like he is?' Rose was furious. They were sitting round a table in a warm kitchen, comfortable in the knowledge of well-established homes and families, secure in their good educations and the good jobs that would follow, passing judgement on a man who had nothing. 'Would you be sitting back saying, "Thanks for taking my vote and my home away, please help yourself to whatever else you want?" Or would you be protesting as long and loudly as you could?'

'I wouldn't be learning how to kill people!'

'Me neither. It's never a solution, terrorism. It just escalates the level of violence.' Buff waved his calculator. 'Much better to reason things out logically.'

'Reason! With this government?'

'It's better than killing.'

'How long are people expected to go on reasoning things out, indefinitely? Or until they shoot so many children that a little mild anger may be in order?' Rose shouted. 'You make me sick, all of you!'

'Hey, I agreed with you, Rosie,' Colin said. 'I think we should let him stay.'

'I don't,' Ursula snapped.

'I don't either, which makes it two against two.' Boff turned to Didymus, who had been silent until then. 'What do you say?'

Didymus was waving a chunk of chicken around on his wooden spoon to cool it for tasting. He said in a voice that was somehow less squeaky than usual, 'In my opinion what we have here is not the moral dilemma of who is doing the right thing in South Africa, but a man who was once Rose's friend asking for a place to sleep for the night. He's welcome to my humble abode if you want him to be physically outside the house. I can kip down on the sofa, or on Colin's extra mattress.'

Rose thought, If there is a God, he's got a good man in Didymus. He always puts things into perspective. She said, 'Thanks, D. That's really kind of you.'

'We're outvoted, Boff.' Ursula threw down the crumpled newspaper and stood up. 'If he's coming in here, I'm going to eat in my room.'

Boff said, obviously reluctant to leave the warm room and the prospect of supper round the table, 'I don't think we're necessarily condoning what the guy does by giving him a place to sleep for the night.'

'You are, and you know it!'

Rose said, 'I was the one who asked, and I'm not condoning anything. I just can't not help him, OK? You don't have to leave the kitchen. I'll take him to my room and give him something to eat there before he goes out into the yard.' She got up and went towards the stove. 'Is there enough for one more?'

'I'll chuck in an extra tin of beans.' Didymus put his spoon down to reach for the tin opener. 'When he's had a wash and brush up, as the Aged Parents always say, I'll bring a plate to your room. Have you got some clean sheets in your basket for him?'

She bent into the steam rising from the saucepan to kiss his spotty cheek. 'Help yourself. I don't know what we'd all do without you.'

'Never have to worry about our consciences, that's for sure,' Ursula muttered, sitting down again and looking up at her. 'Listen, Rose. Don't get involved again. Jake's damaged goods. You can't help him in any meaningful way.'

'I'll decide that!'

'Just so long as you accept that their struggle isn't our struggle. Remember what Steve Biko said: "The biggest mistake the black world ever made was to assume that whoever opposed apartheid was an ally." The black people I've heard talking at varsity don't want well-meaning white liberals blundering around feeling sorry for them and getting in their way. And you do rather go in for lame ducks.'

Rose, about to flare up again, saw that Ursula's dark eyes were shiny, and thought, She's right, of course. I don't want to be a well-meaning white liberal. She stuck her chin out in the Gordon-gesture that Sarah knew so well, and said, 'Point taken. Can I get on with my lame-ducking now?'

Everyone laughed, and the warm fug seemed to settle round them again like a security blanket as she went out.

Jake lifted his head as she came on to the stoep. 'What's the verdict?'

'They've agreed on a compromise. You can stay in Didymus's room across the back yard. It's a place to sleep, but not quite under our roof.' She felt herself going pink. 'It wasn't my decision.'

He shrugged. 'I never thought you'd lay out the red carpet. At least you're not turning me in.'

'Did you expect us to?'

'It was a possibility, not so?' His hard upward look made her go even pinker, and he nodded as if satisfied. 'I'd have been gone long before the cops got here; I was listening for the sound of someone using the phone. In my line of business, you learn to be very careful.'

She thought, He's changed. Been changed? What has he seen and done these past four years? She said, 'Come inside first and have a wash. Didymus will bring supper to my room.' She held out her hand to help him up.

He ignored it, pushing himself up and saying in a sarcastic voice, 'Something to eat thrown in too. What did I do to deserve the royal treatment?'

246

She thought, In that respect he hasn't changed. Bitterness still slops out every time he opens his mouth. Maybe Ursula's right. He's damaged goods, probably beyond repair.

He stooped down for the canvas rucksack and she stepped quickly back, apprehensive of its contents. He said with a faint smile, 'Moenie panic nie, it won't go off pop. I've only got a couple of heat-seeking missiles and my special fold-up AK 47 for assassinating cabinet ministers in there. I left the heavy stuff for my squad of highly trained car-bombers to bring in.'

She said, 'It's not funny!' but she was thinking, I'd forgotten his sense of humour.

He washed his hands, refused a shower, ate the plate of food Didymus brought to her room with silent concentration, then said he'd like to sleep. She walked with him across the moonlit back yard and showed him Didymus's small room, which had been made welcome with clean sheets and a candle stuck on a saucer for him to read by when the naked light bulb glaring from the middle of the ceiling was switched off. When she stopped behind him in the doorway, he turned and said in quite a different voice to the one he had used earlier, 'Thanks a lot, Rose. I'm grateful, even if I'm not very good at showing it. You've been a better friend to me than I ever was to you.'

'Oh, not really.' She felt her cheeks beginning to go pink again, and was glad she was standing in the doorway where the harsh light couldn't reach.

'I'll be gone by the morning, and I won't leave any incriminating traces, promise.' Again the ghost of the ferocious grin.

'Do you have somewhere to stay?'

'For the time being. Though I'll have to look for a job and a permanent place to live soon.'

'What sort of a job?' A picture of Sister Imelda hovering at the back of the classroom, trying to gather enough courage to venture down one of the untidy aisles to check the students' written work, flashed into her mind. Jake would make a very good teacher if he could control his impatience.

'Have you got one in mind?' He was standing very close to her.

'Possibly. I – I teach at an adult education centre that operates as a senior school during the day, and our principal, Father Basil, is always looking for good teachers because the pay's so rotten,' she said. 'I could ask him, if you like.'

'Father Basil. A pillar of the church, ja? He wouldn't want the likes of me as a teacher.' Jake turned to dump the rucksack down next to the bed. 'I go against all the holy principles, don't forget.'

'He's a very special man,' Rose said. 'I think he worships education almost as much as he worships his God. He's quite capable of turning a blind eye to things he doesn't want to see, if it means getting more of his students through Matric.'

'But do you want me hanging around your life again?' Jake had turned back and was looking down at her.

'Yes,' she whispered. 'I've missed you.'

The harsh grooves running down either side of his mouth softened. 'I missed you too, Rose.'

'I thought you'd never come back.'

'For a long time I didn't want to. Then – ' His voice broke and he said, very low, 'It was terrible in the camps. I hated myself all the time for learning all that stuff, but I had to do it. I'd gone over for a good reason, and I had no choice. Can you understand?'

She nodded, unable to speak for the lump in her throat.

They stood looking at each other until he reached out and took her hand between both of his, tightening his grip until the hard places on his palms bit into her. 'I'll phone.'

As she walked across the back yard towards the house and the warm glow of the kitchen window where her friends were still sitting over an emptying bottle of red Tassenberg, she was thinking, Does he love me? What am I getting myself into?

23

Sarah and Cordelia are walking up the stony track towards the death hut. Just after the school building, a path leads off to the teacher's cottage where Rose and Jake lived. Coming down it is Gordon, with a yellow plastic bucket in his hand.

When he sees them, he hurries towards them. 'Sarah! Are you all right? They shouldn't have let you – '

'I'm fine now. Cordelia offered to walk with me.' She summons up a smile to allay his alarm. His eyes are red and watery, and she guesses that he has been crying. 'Where are you going?'

He grasps one of her arms so he can scrutinise her face. 'Are you sure you're all right?' The lids around the pale blue eyes are very swollen but her pupils look normal, no longer dilated as they had been when she was unconscious. She has tidied herself up, plaited her hair the way he likes it, and looks calm enough standing with her other arm linked through Cordelia's.

'I told you, I'm fine.'

There is a tinge of annoyance in her voice and he thinks, That's a good sign. The old Sarah. And I'm sure Sister wouldn't have let her go if she hadn't thought she was up to it. He says, lifting the bucket, 'I thought I should water the plants outside their cottage. It's been such a hot day.'

'The closest tap is on the other side of the school building.' Cordelia points out its position. 'You may have to wait. There's usually a queue at this time, when people are starting to cook.'

'You've seen the cottage already?' Sarah feels a surge of jealous curiosity. She has never seen Rose's new home except in photographs, and has been looking forward for months to this visit. In the car next to the pram body are the house-warming presents she has been gathering: handwoven carpets and pottery from the Rorke's Drift art centre, soft mohair blankets in Scottish heather colours, a beautiful brass Coleman lamp – luxuries to make the small bare rooms Rose has described in her letters feel more like home. Now she will never see them, just as Sarah will never be able to wrap her arms round her daughter and hug her with gladness at seeing her again.

Gordon sees tears threatening and says quickly, 'It's just up here. Come, we'll – '

'No. I must get back to Rose.' Sarah thinks, I mustn't keep crying! I've got to be strong. Rose needs me. 'I can see the cottage any time.'

'I'll come up to the hut with you.'

'No. I think you should water the flowers. Rose would have liked that, and you'll feel better if you're doing something positive, darling. Cordelia will come with me.' She prises his fingers gently off her arm and bends forward to kiss his cheek, which is still sweating, though it is cooler now that the rain clouds are gathering. He looks old and anxious and sad, she thinks. We thought we were sailing so serenely into our older years, and now –

'Are you sure?' he worries.

'Quite sure. I promise I'll sit in the chair and not do anything silly.'

He looks relieved. He understands her need to be with Rose, but he can't go into the death hut without a sick rush of blood to his head. The sight of his daughter lying dead and mutilated when she is still so young, hardly beginning her life, enrages him. He fears that, with Sarah feeling better and not needing so much of his attention, he will lose control if he has to go in there again, and yell and stamp and gibber like a madman. He would much rather water the flowers that Rose planted, even though the gathering clouds mean that it will probably rain soon. At least he doesn't have to move the car now. 'I'll come up when I'm finished,' he mutters, hoping that the mortuary van will have arrived by then.

The smile she gives him this time comes from their later years together, when they had learned to heal each other's wounds with bandages of mutual concern and kindness. It is so intimate that Cordelia turns away, envying. How do people achieve these relationships? she wonders. Why can't I too? Is it a fault in myself, or is that black men are too conditioned from an early age to ever be able to accept women as equals? Until they do, we will never achieve what we should in Africa.

Gordon turns away and Sarah says, 'Shall we go on?'

There are knots of children standing along the track,

watching them. As they pass the children fall in behind them, and soon they have become another procession, a children's crusade for a dead teacher. Bare feet walk more slowly, ragged clothes are straightened, lively faces stilled to solemnity. An older girl takes it on herself to wipe the trails of snot off the upper lips of several of the little ones, using her skirt. A child comes up to Sarah with a shy smile and gives her a small handful of pale pink everlastings, the straw flowers that star the mountain grass in summer. She thanks the child and finds the little brown hand slipping itself in next to the flowers.

When they reach the hut there is a sombre group of people waiting outside. Cordelia talks to them in Sesotho then turns to Sarah. 'They have come to pay their respects, and ask me to tell you this. They don't want to come in, just to stand here for a while.'

Sarah nods, unable to speak. The children have gathered behind her in a sympathetic throng, and for the first time since coming to the village she feels as though she is among friends, buoyed by their collective concern and sorrow.

'I'll be running along now, then,' Cordelia says. 'I'll be in my office if you should need me.'

'Thank you for understanding so well.'

'How could I not? We are both mothers.' Cordelia slips her arm out and adds as she turns to go, 'These women say also that there is a white man inside, a man of God. He is sitting with Rose and Jake.'

How dare anyone intrude! Sarah gives the door an angry push and walks into the hut ready to do battle with the Archangel Gabriel himself, if he should have had the nerve to show his face here.

But it is not the Archangel Gabriel sitting on the chair with his head bent in prayer. It is Didymus who jumps up, his Adam's apple jerking up and down his throat as he speaks. 'I came as soon as I heard, Mrs Kimber.'

'Oh, Didymus,' she says, reaching out for him, and before she can help it, her eyes fill with tears again. 'Oh, Didymus, why? How could this happen?'

He folds his bony arms round her, knobbly as a stick insect. He is wearing running shoes and a black tracksuit with ROMA across the back, having been told of the shooting in the middle of coaching athletics. He is Father Didymus now, and has been seconded by his church to the National University of Lesotho at Roma as part of their outreach programme to under-developed neighbouring countries. He says in a voice that wobbles on the edge of tears, 'I can't tell you why. I'm still asking myself.'

'Ask your God!' she rages, pulling away. 'He always has all the answers.'

'I have, and He doesn't seem to have heard me.' Didymus has not stopped asking since he heard the news. He conducted the marriage here in the village just over a year ago, and has been sitting now for half an hour looking at the dead, staring faces of his friends and trying to think what God's purpose could have been in allowing them to be so brutally killed. He is beginning to suspect that there is no purpose. It is the severest test of his faith that he has ever had to face, and the strained white face he turns down to Sarah shows it.

His anguish makes her regret her outburst. He looks painfully young and brittle, as though the skinny neck and wrists and ankles sticking out of his tracksuit could snap at the slightest applied pressure. She thinks, with a mother's automatic habit of scrutiny, He looks as though he never gets enough to eat. I can't load him any more. She says, 'Maybe we should both sit down quietly and keep watch over them. We have to be brave for them now.'

He nods. 'I'll try and pray.'

She goes to the chair and sits down as she had earlier, with her roughened hands clasped in her lap and her eyes on Rose's drained grey face, rocking her body very slightly backwards and forwards. He kneels on the dung-smeared floor looking across the sheeted bodies of his friends at the mud wall of the hut, trying to erase the loop of film running through his mind of the last time he saw them, radiant with joy in the Queen Elizabeth Hospital in Maseru just after Hope was born.

There are two fans turning their whirring faces from side to side over Rose and Jake now, and the stained sheet lifts and stirs in a parody of life with each mechanical gust. The pooled blood on the grass mat has dried to dark brown. Up near the apex of the conical thatched roof, the bluebottle fly buzzes round and round without settling.

*   *   *

252

Jake began teaching at St Aloysius at the beginning of 1981, and he was a natural. Rose had said to Father Basil when she first spoke to him about Jake, 'I think he'll be a good teacher, though you may have some difficulty with his personal circumstances.'

'Delicately put.' When Father Basil smiled, his eyebrows reared their caterpillar backs into twin shaggy arches. 'I presume he is shy of the police, which is why he needs an out-of-the-way job in a place like this. Judging by his age and the convictions you have thought fit to tell me about, he has probably spent some years over the border learning a number of illegal and dangerous skills.'

Rose thought, Whoever called priests unworldly? The ones I've met seem to have very efficient tentacles stretching in all directions. She said, 'You'll have to talk to him about that.'

'But I'm not wrong, am I?' The shrewd grey eyes bored down at her in the look she privately called Father Basil's brain scan; he could see the shapes of your thoughts before you'd even recognised them yourself. 'What's your interest here, Rose?'

'He's a friend, and he needs help.' She willed herself not to look evasive. 'I met him at varsity when I was in third year, at a socialist discussion group.'

Father Basil nodded. 'And were attracted to him, yes? A meeting of true minds? No doubt marred by the problems of getting together without causing heart failure among the more conservative onlookers. What a country this is.'

'You're not far wrong,' she admitted, 'though we lost touch for four years. Now he's come back, all I know is that I must help him. I don't like what he's been doing, but I don't think he does either.'

'If he's someone you admire, I'm sure he doesn't. Though there's no possible excuse for initiating violence; the church is very clear on that. To defend yourself is allowed, naturally, but to set out with the deliberate intent to hurt or kill is to deny humanity.'

'Jake isn't a killer, Father,' she said. She knew it in her bones. 'He's been sent here to print and distribute underground pamphlets. He says that the ANC didn't start the violence anyway, they're just responding to the violence that has been practised on black people here for the past three hundred years. They tried every other avenue first, without success, so in the early 'sixties they established a militant armed wing called Umkhonto we Sizwe to – '

253

'Yes, yes, I've heard the justifications.' Father Basil cuts her off with an impatient gesture. 'None of them are valid, and do you know why? Innocent people keep getting hurt. Violence is evil incarnate.'

Defensive of Jake, she said, 'The Church doesn't have a great record on that score, Father, even you have to admit.'

'No, it doesn't,' he sighed. 'Certainly not in the past. I've often wondered what sort of world it would be if we had followed Jesus's admonition to "Love Thy Neighbour" more faithfully, and not got sidetracked into crusading and holding inquisitions and burning people whose ideas we didn't approve of. Religious fanaticism has set some terrifying precedents.'

He sat in the sagging armchair on which he took catnaps between the day and the evening sessions, looking out of his office window. The view was of mine dumps and yet more mine dumps, the appropriately yellow detritus of the precious metal that has made South Africa rich. Closer by, the headgear of an old mine shaft reared up against the blue watered silk of the sky like a pair of giant compasses with points stuck down into the earth and abandoned, the great spoked wheel at the top that used to raise and lower the cages of miners rusted still at last.

'He's a poet, Father, not a violent man at all,' she blurted, wanting him to know that Jake was special.

He turned back to her. 'I'll see him, of course; have a straight talk with him, and make up my mind based on what he says. God knows we need teachers.'

She never knew what they said to each other but when Jake came out of the meeting, he gave her his most ferocious grin. 'He's quite a guy, that Holy Joe of yours. Offered me a job so long as I swear I won't bring any aspect of my other life into the school – no talk of politics or violence, not a whisper. He almost had me promising not to think impure thoughts here.'

Rose laughed. 'I never have time. You won't either, with the teaching load we have. Fifty more students are being squeezed in next term. The black schools are still in chaos, even though the government keeps saying that everything's under control.'

Jake went on, 'He didn't pull his punches. He said, "Because I need your skills badly, I'll overlook the aspects of your life that I don't like. But don't make the mistake of thinking that I condone what you're up to. I don't. In the strongest terms I don't, young man." Nobody's called me young man since high school.'

'He always calls me "girl", specially when he's shouting down the phone.' She started the car and backed out of her parking place in the sparse shade of the gum trees. 'Have you found somewhere safe to live, Jake?'

'Ja. I won't tell you where, in case anybody asks you. It's better you don't know.' When they had swung out on to the road and she had changed into top gear, dropping her hand on to the seat between them, he covered it with his. 'When am I going to see you again?'

'When term begins, I suppose.' She could feel her heart beating heavily.

'Not before?'

'Where would we go?'

They drove in silence, each trying to think of a place where they could meet without arousing attention. Rose could only think of the Wits cafeteria where they used to have coffee together, but neither of them was a student now. There was the Yeoville house, but except for Didymus the others had made it plain that they did not like the idea of Jake visiting.

'He puts us all at risk,' Ursula said. 'I've got no wish to be banned or to go to jail for someone else's convictions.'

'You used to be so different!' Rose flared. 'At school, you were the ultimate rebel. Now all you're interested in is your damn masters thesis.'

'That's bull, and you know it.' The accusation had hurt; Ursula was concentrating too hard on stirring her coffee. 'I'm as concerned with what's happening in our country as you are, but this is Jake's fight. Not ours.'

'If we don't help those who are fighting the injustices, we're as guilty of them as the government is!'

'Not this way. Not by stealth and hate and violence.' Ursula's voice wavered. 'I've seen what they did to my grandmother.'

'But Jake's not like that.'

'It doesn't matter what he's like, or even what he's doing. It's the principle that's wrong, Rosie. You've got to respect our feelings in this matter, as we respect yours. I've got nothing personal against Jake.'

'He's only arrogant, foul-mouthed and rude.' Rose had not forgotten the night round the kitchen table.

'Even you could hardly call him a little ray of sunshine.' Ursula's dark eyes invited Rose to smile.

'He hasn't got a hell of a lot to be sunny about, in case you hadn't noticed.' She would not smile back.

'None of us can help but notice. You've been talking about nothing else but Jake's problems since he got back.'

'It's hard not to. The comparison with our lives is so odious.'

'Listen.' Ursula was thinking, How can I get her to see reason? 'How you feel about him is strictly your business. But if he threatens to bring danger into our small community, it's our right to say no to him. You've got to agree.'

'I suppose I have.' Rose sighed. 'I don't like what he's been doing either. But none of you know him like I do. He's got such depth to him, and he cares about real things, not just where the next beer's coming from or who's going to win the next rugby test.'

Ursula murmured, 'Rare for a South African male, I admit. How hard have you fallen for him?'

Rose looked down at her hands. 'I don't know. I hadn't thought about him for months, but when he turned up again it was like I'd been, somehow, waiting for him all along.'

'I sincerely hope it's not true love. Your life would be nothing but hassles.' Ursula leaned forward. 'Fight it, kiddo. The percentages are just too low.'

Boff had said much the same as Ursula, and so had Colin. 'A room for the night's one thing; having him around more often is another. I don't want to end up in jail either, with my internship and my thesis looming.'

Only Didymus, the committed pacifist, said, 'I don't mind him coming, as long as he leaves his bags of tricks outside. He doesn't strike me as a bad man.'

'He's not. And he doesn't have bags of tricks. His job is to handle publicity, getting underground pamphlets printed and distributed.' He had not told Rose that the distribution would sometimes be done by pamphlet bomb, or that he had received intensive training in the use of the explosives that would be following him over the border by courier.

'They're all thugs, trained to kill,' Ursula said.

'Jake wouldn't,' Rose said with conviction. 'Anyway, he says the ANC policy is to bomb buildings that support the apartheid regime, like military installations and electricity sub-stations and Bantu Affairs offices, not civilians. People must be made continually aware of the struggle.'

'You sound like a Marxist textbook already,' Ursula said with disgust. 'We're talking bombs here, not firecrackers. What if someone nearby gets hurt, like that poor little girl and her granny on Park Station who just happened to be sitting next to a suitcase packed with explosives?'

'But that was years ago.'

'It's the same principle.'

'It's not! Anyway, I know that Jake would never knowingly endanger an innocent life,' she insisted, but it did not change any minds. She was outvoted.

Now, sitting in the car with his hand warm on hers, she was thinking, Where can we go to be alone, besides in this car? And it was dangerous to drive together, a coloured man sitting next to a white woman in the front seat and not at the back where employees usually sit. Any alert security policeman who saw them would be bound to check up on her number plate, which would lead him back to her student file and, more than likely, a cross-reference to Jake's.

'I could always disguise myself with a blond wig, if I cut this bush back a bit.' He spurted corrosive laughter and ran his other hand over his hair. 'I could play-play I was a beach boy, complete with surfboard and dark shades. Most of them are much more tanned than me.'

'Don't joke about it. It's not funny.'

'What else can I do? Spend my life crying?'

'At least don't joke.'

'Ag, all life's a joke. And this country's the biggest joke of all. So funny it makes you want to cry.'

She felt his hand beginning to sweat on top of hers, and said, 'We could turn in here, if you like.'

They were driving past a narrow track that led into a gum plantation; there was a glitter of water through the trees. He shrugged. 'It looks as good as any.'

The track had a high grassy middelmannetjie, and Rose had to drive the car along the sides of the sandy wheel ruts to avoid scraping the bottom. It was a service road for clearing underbrush and timber-felling, and led to a disused mine dam. They were not the only ones it had beckoned that day. From where Rose parked the car in the shelter of some bushes, they could just see two fishermen in folding tubular chairs, a radio blaring between them, cool-bags next to them, and a pile of beer cans glinting in the long grass. Each had two rods propped up on a dual-armed metal holder stuck in the ground in front of him, and the lines ran down to red floats on the dam's scummy green surface. Both were asleep.

'The joys of being a miner on his off day,' Jake said in the awkward silence after Rose switched off.

'If they're asleep, they won't bother us.' She wasn't sure what to do next. She had never been completely alone with Jake, and didn't want to turn to him looking expectant only to have him make another joke.

He sat unmoving, thinking, It's so quiet and peaceful here, though it's only a few hundred metres away from the main road. All his life he had been surrounded by people closely packed together in tiny houses out of which they exploded when the pressures became too much. The last four years had been no different: crowded huts in bush camps, crowded prefab dormitories, crowded eating halls and lecture rooms and parade grounds where he had had to learn to march and drill in the choking dust along with the young men he was assigned to teach. 'We are all equals here, comrades!' the instructors had shouted over and over again until the words rang like cracked bells, strident with repetition. 'We have to be good soldiers for the struggle!'

He said, turning to her, 'It's what I envy you whites most, the privacy and quiet of your big homes.'

His eyes were the same green as the dam water, oases in the desert landscape of his face which was more deeply scored now than she remembered. She felt herself leaning towards him, drawn by a longing that had been growing between them, fuelled by touches and looks that they could not seem to break off. He breathed, 'Can I kiss you, Rose?' but gave her no time to answer.

His mouth was soft and warm, as tentative at first as his question. Her eyes closed. She had imagined this so often at the edge of her thoughts, and pushed it away. He was coloured, out of bounds, the untouchable. But with her eyes closed he was a man like other men who had kissed her; cud-sweet breath, a rasp of stubble, searching lips that grew more demanding as he moved closer and put his arms round her. She felt a hot surge of joy that seemed to melt her bones against his body and open her mouth like a flower to rain. This wasn't other men but Jake, her angry poet. The man who had scorned her whiteness and was now besieging her with an urgent need that gave his tongue a live, probing, dizzying sweetness. His hand moved to her breast, and its warmth burned through the thin fabric of her shirt like fire, quickening her body so that every nerve seemed to be crying out for him.

Jake. Jake. Her mind reeled and spun, a humming top singing a deep note of gladness. She had been kissed before, but never like this. It was like coming alive and drowning at once. She was afraid she would stop breathing if he didn't –

He turned his head and nuzzled her cheek, murmuring, 'How long I've wanted to do that. You're so lovely, Rose. Like your namesake.'

She caressed his face, tracing with her fingers the fine crow's feet at the corners of his eyes and the harsh lines on either side of his mouth. 'I've wanted it too. I used to dream about you kissing me, then tell myself you'd never try to because I'm, well, on the other side.'

'Beyond the pale?' He kissed her again for a long time, one hand a warm live weight on the nape of her neck, the other gently stroking her breast until her nipple hardened, sending little juddering thrills through her like electric shocks.

When he pulled back she begged, 'Don't stop.'

'I must. It'll be torture if – '

'I don't want you to! We don't have to stop. We can get in the back.' She pulled him closer, feeling her body turning into a magnet that wanted to suck him in, all of him, now. 'You can't kiss me like that, then just stop.'

'The fishermen – '

'They're too far away to see us. Jake, please. Hold me. It's been so long.'

He felt the power of her need pulling him towards her with a force that gained strength from her white will, unused to being denied. She can't have everything she wants! flashed through his mind. Not me, anyway. And he slid his hands out and turned away and said in a thick voice, 'We can't. You know we can't.'

'Why not? There's nothing to stop us.'

'There's everything to stop us. Everything! I'm mad at myself for even liking you.'

'Pity. A few more kisses like that,' she tried to move close to him again, 'and I think I could – '

'Don't talk of love,' he said quickly. 'It's not possible.'

'Ag, what are a few lousy laws between friends?'

The way she said it, flippantly, mocking his accent, made him mad. 'Be reasonable, Rose, man! I'm not only the wrong colour, I'm also hiding from the police. If they catch me, it's tickets. You can't think about me in that way.'

'I'll think about you however I choose.'

She stuck out her chin in the stubborn gesture he soon grew to know well. He had the helpless, guilty feeling he used to have as a child when he had done something naughty, knowing that retribution would come, and shouted, 'You're being completely unrealistic! This is real life, not *Romeo and Juliet*. Shit, you hardly even know me.'

'Shhh. You might wake them up.' She indicated the fishermen with her head, looking blonde and sure of herself, infuriating. 'Your language needs cleaning up, it's true, but I like most of the other things I know about you.'

'It's just asking for trouble,' he groaned. 'You're white, I'm black – '

She pursed her lips and said, 'More brown, I'd say. An elegant tan that most white South Africans have to pay through the nose to acquire on beach holidays.'

'Don't bloody make fun of the situation!'

'I'm trying to say it doesn't matter to me what colour you are.'

'Then you're kidding yourself.'

'Maybe.' She turned her head away from the pain in his eyes. 'But since we're here, shouldn't we make the best of it?'

He kissed her again but it was angry and bruising, and they drove away in silence. For months after that he held back from committing himself to anything more than occasional visits to the dam, because as he fell more and more in love with her despite the voices yelling warnings in his head, he became increasingly afraid for her.

There were few enough opportunities for them to be alone together, though they saw each other every day in school. To his surprise, Jake found he enjoyed his new job. He had spent dreary months in bush camps where discussions and lectures inevitably became political arguments during which everybody talked passionately and nobody listened, and two grinding years teaching communication and code skills to furious young men who would rather have been ripping targets to shreds at rifle practice. Now he found himself plunging into each lesson with an enthusiasm fed by kids who drank in everything he had to say as though it were a golden elixir that would magically conjure up a Matric pass for them, opening doors to the wonderful world of adulthood and employment. He had to teach them patiently to question him, to argue, to think out their own ways of saying things, rather than trying to remember by rote as they had been taught to do by their poorly trained and even worse paid government school teachers. Sometimes he and Rose and Father Basil would stage a short debate so they could understand that it was permissible to hold a dissenting opinion, as long as you could supply your reasons for doing so.

The adults were different, wary of the fact that he was coloured and not black or white like the other teachers, and slower to respond to new ideas. They were conscientious about their assignments, however, and when he began to introduce them to the African poetry that was his passion, they were amazed and pleased that black people should be writing and having published the thoughts they often had themselves.

'Is that written down in a book for all to see?' Tryphina asked one evening after he had ended a lesson with Mongane Wally Serote's *City Johannesburg*: 'Where death lurks in the dark like a blade in the flesh . . .'

'Yes, and more. There's a lot of good stuff being written now in the townships. Would you like me to get a class copy of this poetry book for you?'

Heads nodded all over the room, and poems by black African writers were demanded daily after that. 'Just to send us home with a good taste in our mouth,' Tryphina would say, her several chins wobbling as she chuckled.

Jake had moved into his cousin Ivan Rabie's small cottage on a Portuguese market gardener's farm on the outskirts of Johannesburg's southern suburbs. Since Ivan worked nights as a reporter on the *Rand Daily Mail* and Jake worked mostly days, the arrangement suited them both. The cottage was some way away from the farmhouse, in a clump of trees with a good view of the little-used road that went past it, which made it an ideal place to hide.

He bought a second-hand Honda motorbike with capacious panniers for the parcels he would have to carry. Its other virtue was that he could be safely anonymous in the crash helmet that he was required to wear by law, which had a smoked glass visor, and the black leather lumber jacket, boots and gloves that made him look like any other serious biker. The ANC couriers who came one by one over the border after him with their freight of plastic explosives and TNT and detonators were met in back-yards and deserted alleys so he could take transfer without their knowing where he was based. He wrapped the explosives in thick plastic sheeting and buried them between the roots of an old willow tree, ready for assembly into pamphlet bombs.

261

It was an unexpected shock when three months later one of the couriers handed him two heavier parcels, with instructions to bury them in the same spot.

'What's in them?'

'Dismantled AK 47s. You should assemble them before caching so they're completely ready for use,' the courier said.

'But the unit commander didn't say anything about this at my briefing!' Jake protested. 'I asked specifically not to be sent on missions that involved the use of arms. I'm a teacher, man.'

The courier gave him a conspiratorial wink and said, 'They never tell you the whole story till they get you in position. These AKs are all yours now.'

'But they promised me – '

The other man's face grew still and he said, 'Take a tip from me, bra. Forget the promises. Just concentrate your mind on doing what needs to be done, and on staying alive to do it. The struggle goes on.'

Later couriers handed over consignments of Makarov and Kalashnikov pistols and ammunition, grey-painted limpet mines and F 1 hand grenades, which Jake wrapped and buried with a churning stomach. Several times he was sick afterwards into the willow tree roots. The arms cache grew larger every month.

Ivan knew nothing of what he was doing. Nor, dreaming of him every night in her high-ceilinged Yeoville bedroom, did Rose.

24

Gordon walks slowly, feeling the pulse of the village. Outside each hut there is some activity: a woman sitting on a sack tearing wild spinach into a chipped enamel bowl, a dreaming girl sorting through dried beans, an older woman bent over a large gourd stirring the fermented sorghum beer that everyone will drink with the evening meal. Another kneels next to a hollow stone, stamping a handful of yellow mealie kernels with a tall wooden pestle. Next to her is a shallow round basket into which she tips the coarse mealie meal ready for cooking. Mealie meal is the staple food of Southern Africa, cooked with water in a three-legged black iron pot over an open fire to make the stiff crumbly porridge called phuthu. It is eaten with the fingers, unaccompanied if the family is poor, but preferably with a spicy meat and vegetable sauce.

Other women are collecting sun-dried washing and sleeping blankets hung up to air off the thatched stockades that surround the huts; the sky is clouding rapidly now. A small girl sings to herself as she scrubs out a tin bath. Another feeds chunks of coal into a fire made in a small round drum that once held lubricating oil; holes punched in the sides have turned it into a brazier. When there is a good bed of red coals, it will be carried inside for extra warmth during the night, which can be cold even in summer in these mountains. It is just as well that the huts have ill-fitting doors and windows and many chinks through which the invisible and deadly carbon monoxide emitted by coals can escape. Every year there are deaths in the cities and towns in back-yard rooms that have been too well sealed with newspaper and rags before the brazier is brought in.

Clustered round the community tap and its concrete trough on the edge of the school yard is a group of women and girls whose chattering fades as Gordon comes towards them with his yellow bucket. Three almost-naked toddlers who are playing in the wet patch where the trough overflows look up at the sudden silence, see the faces turned to Gordon, and run to their mothers to bury their heads in their skirts, making star-marks with muddy little hands.

'Dumela,' Gordon says. He is not sure whether to raise his free hand in greeting or not, and awkwardly dips his head instead.

He has left the green hat resting on the windowsill of Rose's cottage, partly because the punishing sun is about to disappear altogether behind rain clouds, but also because he wants to leave something of himself there in case Rose comes. It is a gesture that would be out of keeping with his blunt, practical nature in other circumstances, specially as he does not believe, has never believed, in reincarnation or restless spirits or what he thinks of as all that Christian claptrap about life after death. Sitting on the cottage steps, however, has given him a strong feeling that Rose has not quite gone yet, that she has lingered somewhere in a corner of this dusty village straggling down its mountain valley to make sure Hope is going to be properly cared for, and to say goodbye.

Several of the women mutter, 'Dumela, Morena,' looking down to show respect. The girls are bolder; though they lower their heads, he sees them peeping up at him bright-eyed under smooth brown eyelids, most of which have been discreetly edged with a darker line. These teenagers may not be able to afford the lavish makeup their city sisters wear, but they know how to use charcoal and plant pigments and sweet herbs to good effect. Their bodies under the jazzy knotted cotton squares are glossy with daily rubbings of glycerine and, when they can afford it, scented pink hand lotion from the trading store.

Gordon remembers Rose hunched over her mirror with her first lipstick trying out different lip shapes, and thinks, Girls are the same everywhere. Indispensable. Rose has always been the apple of his eye, even when David was alive, and he has not felt the lack of a son like so many men do, lamenting the fact that their names and patriarchal bloodlines will die out. Because of Rose and his relationship with Sarah that has deepened and strengthened over the years, he likes women and enjoys their company. He watches girls now with an appreciative but not lustful eye, taking pleasure from their young-animal beauty without wanting to use it. Focused for most of his adult life on succeeding in business, he has been briefly unfaithful to Sarah only twice, both times on long trips away from home with much younger women who reminded him so much of her when she was young that he found them impossible to resist. Both encounters are long in the past.

He says, 'I've come for some water. Is there a queue? Where shall I stand?' He holds up the bucket in explanation.

Though most people in the village understand English and can speak the words they need to communicate with non-Sotho strangers when necessary, they are too shy to say anything to this important white man who has arrived in their midst in a big cream Mercedes, even if he is Rose's father. A woman with a face like a walnut, deep brown and intricately wrinkled, turns to the one who is busy filling a paraffin tin at the tap and says something sharp in Sesotho. The woman at the tap snatches her tin away as though the water has suddenly turned scalding hot, and shrinks back among the waiting women. The wrinkled one gestures at Gordon and then the running tap, inviting him to fill up next.

He makes a sign of denial with his free hand and says, 'Oh no, I'll wait my turn. I'm not in a hurry.'

The older woman insists in sign language. He is a visitor, a guest, and therefore must take precedence.

He looks round the silent semicircle, seeing on their faces a matter-of-fact acceptance of his authority that comes from years of submission to men and pompous officials and white people who stride the earth knowing they own it. And these are the ones who till the stony fields and bear the children and look after the animals and hold their families together on miserable remittances while their men are away all year on the gold mines, he thinks. I don't know how they do it.

He says, 'I'd rather wait my turn. I'll sit over there until it comes,' and goes to sit on the low cement-block wall of the school yard.

They don't move at first, and stand watching him as though he is a magician who is about to pull a dubious trick out of his sleeve. Then one of the girls claps her hand over her mouth to stifle a nervous giggle, and the sound brings the group to life. The wrinkled woman jerks her chin at the woman with the half full paraffin tin, who ventures forward and holds it timidly under the running tap. They begin to talk to each other in low voices, glancing at him every now and again. The little ones go back to playing in the mud.

Gordon thinks, If you ignore the brass tap and the water

containers they're using, this could be a scene out of the Bible. Most of the women are carrying plastic bottles and tin cans that once held cooking oil and petrol, but coming towards them is a young mother with a baby tied to her back and a round clay pot balanced on her head, walking like a queen.

He watches her approach the group round the tap, reach up for her pot and swing it down in a graceful arc to rest on the edge of the water trough. The baby is fast asleep, its head tilted to one side, its chubby arms and legs spreadeagled against its mother's back, held firmly in place by a cotton baby blanket that she has knotted above and below her breasts. The blanket has a repeating pattern of pink and blue fluffy rabbits with silly grinning faces, and he thinks, Why do people who design for babies use such inane symbols and insipid pastels? Sarah's delight in strong colour has meant that her babies wore cheerful reds and blues and bright yellows. They weren't carried on her back in this child's blissful security, however, hugged to its mother's body and moving with her all day.

Rose's last letter was full of her first few days in the classroom after her three months off for Hope's birth, when she tried to keep her tied to her back and failed. 'The knots in front hurt and my back hurt and I couldn't sit down comfortably,' she had written. 'Jake says I'm a very bad African mother. But I make up for it in other ways.'

He looks away from the mother at the tap to dispel the thought. Coming down the track is a gaggle of goats and cattle driven by several herdboys in ragged shorts, and a yapping dog. Each wears a loop of limp brown cloth knotted over the shoulder and carries a pair of sticks in one hand with which he chivvies the animals along, tapping dusty matted flanks and calling out commands in a bossy voice for the benefit of the late afternoon female audience.

In Africa, herdboys carry a special responsibility, since the traditional wealth of a village resides in its livestock. It is permissible to squeeze a few mouthfuls of milk from a cow or to play a musical instrument or games with small stones and lines drawn in the dust to while away the long days on lonely hillsides, but not to engage in serious pastimes like stick-fighting, which might divert too much attention from their charges. Basotho herdboys have to be particularly tough. The Maluti mountains soar to over three thousand metres above sea level, and a sudden winter snowstorm can keep a boy huddled under a freezing overhang for days without food before he can struggle back to the village to summon help, if he has not already succumbed to exposure.

One of the herdboys carries a bow made from a slender flexible stick with its bark stripped off and a sinew stretched across the mouth of a gourd, which will resonate when it is plucked with the fingers or stroked with a twig. The short tune he will make up for himself will be repeated over and over again when he plays, and he will take it to the city with him when he goes to work there, to play on a cheap guitar as he walks down the street.

Gordon thinks, That's what I missed most about home when I was away in Europe and America, the repetitive African music of a guitar coming closer and receding down suburban streets during summer afternoons, and sung from deep in the chest by a row of labourers as they bring down their picks in unison. Does that make me an African in my bones, as Rose always claimed she was, or will my whiteness always exclude me in some essential way? We are going to have a hell of a time bringing Hope up if things go on like they are.

The sun has disappeared completely behind the clouds now. Coming down a long red scribble of path on the hillside are some girls with small bundles of sticks on their heads tied round the middle with rough grass plaits; since there are few trees in the valley, they have had to be diligently garnered from the scrubby bushes that grow in the nearby kloof. As the girls pass the stone wall of the empty kraal to which the cattle and goats are being driven, several children appear dragging a plastic fertiliser bag full of dung cakes which they shaped that morning and left to dry all day on the stones in the sun.

Another gust of wind blows down the valley, flattening the flames of the cooking fires outside the huts, hissing through cracks, swirling down the sandy track and along the road to Maseru. From the middle of the cloud of dust it raises, Gordon sees a square grey police van hurtling towards the village as though chased by the hounds of hell. Doesn't anyone drive at a normal speed here? he thinks with irritation. What if a child runs out in front of it? He watches it pull up outside the government offices next to the metallic blue BMW, sending the horses tied to the hitching rail into another nervous sideways jostle, and a policeman in a black uniform get out.

'Ntate wa Rose.'

He turns to find the woman with the face like a walnut standing next to him with her plastic water bottle, now full, balanced on her hip. 'Metsi,' she says, gesturing at the tap, which is now free.

He stands up and says, 'Thank you,' regretting that he doesn't know what to call her. He must ask Cordelia to teach him the words that will show his gratitude towards the people of this village where Rose lived. Even though they were not able to protect her, they were all obviously fond of her, and it means a lot to him.

It takes two trips with the yellow bucket to water both flower beds. He is tipping the last drops out over the second when Tshabalala comes round the corner of the school building with the policeman.

It was months before Rose managed to persuade Jake that she was serious about loving him. He threw up barricade after barricade to try and stop her persistent storming of his defences, already weakened by four years of longing for her. He had given her a censored account of his training in hand-to-hand combat, light arms and the use of explosives, hoping to make her afraid of the guerrilla he had become (and had terrible dreams about nearly every night, waking in a cold sweat of dread and disgust).

But all she said was, 'I know you're not like that, Jake. You can't scare me.'

'How do you know? Your life has been so different from mine that you can't even begin to imagine what I'm like, who I really am!'

'I just know,' she said, giving him her Bette Davis inscrutable-woman look.

'Christ, but you can be irritating!' he had shouted. 'Do all white chicks carry on like this, acting as though they know everything?'

'I told you, I'm not a chick and insults won't work.' She summoned up a teasing smile that made his heart thump like a drum. 'You won't put me off by shouting and swearing either. I know what I want, and I'm used to getting it. You should know better than to cross swords with an only child.'

'Spoilt only child!'

She shrugged. 'Maybe. But iron-willed too.'

'You don't know what you're asking.'

'I do! Make love to me, Jake. Forget the stupid laws that forbid us to fall in love with each other. They don't matter.'

'You know they matter! And they're not the only consideration. There's my mission too. I can't endanger that any more than I can endanger you.'

The deadly chill of his words lay between them for another month, until an afternoon in the car by the deserted mine dam when their kissing had reached such an intensity that his body ached all over with his need for her. She moved against him, warm belly and breasts, soft open mouth, hair like winter grass getting in his eyes, murmuring, 'Please, Jake. I love you. Please?'

He had never had a woman beg him to make love to her. Were all white women like this, so shameless? He groaned, 'We can't, Rose. You know we can't.'

'We must. You know we must now.'

They got into the back, fumbling at the handles and each other in their haste, but despite the pillows Rose had brought it was uncomfortable and cramped. Jake had to fold himself almost in two just to get his feet inside the door, and they had to tangle like snakes to get close to each other. They could not take too many clothes off for fear of others who might come down the grassy track – the fishermen again, or labourers seeking a quiet place after work to smoke illegal dagga.

'It wasn't much of a success, was it?' Rose said afterwards, buttoning up the front of her shirt.

'I wasn't.' Jake's cheeks had a dull blush. 'Sorry, Rose. I just can't seem to – ag, I just don't know what you – '

She leaned forward to kiss him. 'I love you, Jake. We'll get it right.'

He murmured against her lips, 'Maybe I ought to try and find a copy of the *Kama Sutra*. That might give us some useful ideas.'

She laughed, feeling bubbles of happiness rising through her body despite the restless need that he had not been able to satisfy. She was thinking, I've got to talk the others into letting us use my bedroom. We can't go on like this. It'll destroy what's happening between us.

That night she called a meeting and asked them to reconsider their decision regarding Jake. 'Look, I know how you feel about him and what he represents, and I respect it,' she said, 'but try to see things from my point of view too. I love him and he loves me.

We need a place where we can be alone together to work things out without looking over our shoulders all the time. I'm asking you to let him visit sometimes.'

'You're asking a hell of a lot,' Boff said. 'I also think you're crazy to get involved with this guy. He can only bring you grief.'

'Have you really thought out the consequences of the relationship?' Colin said. 'I mean, culture differences between white people of different nationalities are bad enough; stir in a different skin colour and the historical hatreds in South Africa, and the gaps become chasms. I know what I'm talking about.'

'I didn't ask for the psychological justification of racism, Colin. Just a simple yes or no will do.'

'Hey, don't bite my head off.' Colin reached into his shirt pocket for the pipe he used as a prop when talking to patients, and began to fill it from a bag of cheap Magaliesberg tobacco. 'Ursula and I are Jews, remember? We're a people who have survived by marrying within the faith, and the weeping and gnashing of teeth when someone in the family decides to marry a gentile, even now, has to be seen to be believed. Differences between Israeli Jews and South African Jews are also enormous, and you could hardly call that racism. All I'm saying is what I'd say to anyone who's thinking of forming a permanent relationship with someone who comes from a very different background: you owe it to yourself to take a very hard look at the possible conflicts you'll be facing.'

'We couldn't even begin to dream of a permanent relationship.' Rose's voice was bitter. 'The furthest ahead we ever talk about is next week.'

There was silence round the table. Ursula, who had not yet said anything, was thinking, No matter what your circumstances in South Africa, the threat of the unpredictable future is always there hanging over you. She remembered her mother saying only a few weeks before, 'The worst is, I can't plant a tree in the garden and know that my grandchildren will be able to swing from it one day.' She recalled the noisy protest marches that were shown on TV during the school boycotts, students her own age waving fists in the air and shouting slogans as they marched towards the grim khaki armoured cars crouching behind lines of riot-helmeted policemen with rifles. Their future is as unforeseeable as ours, she thought. I guess we must all take our happiness where we can, and be grateful for it.

She said, 'I've changed my mind. I don't mind if he comes, as long as he does it discreetly. I'm glad you're happy with him, Rosie.'

'Seconded,' Didymus said. Rose had tears in her eyes when she got up to embrace them. Colin said, 'Do I get a hug too if I agree?' and she braved a cloud of newly-lit tobacco smoke to do so. Only Boff held out, saying, 'I'm still against it, but of course I'm outvoted. Just make sure he doesn't bring anything here with him that could incriminate the rest of us. No way am I going to languish in Pretoria Central for something I haven't done.'

Their first night together was more than a celebration. By some lovers' magic it became a ceremony of commitment to each other that was to sustain them through all the separations and disappointments before they were at last able to marry.

The others were going out to a party, and Jake was to come at eight. Rose bought six fat red candles and flowers and champagne, and food for a midnight feast. She tidied her room and drew the curtains, pushing the bed against the wall and piling it with cushions to make it look like an exotic eastern divan. She put the Mozart clarinet concerto on the turntable and stood the candles on the bedside table, next to a plate of cold meats in glistening pinks and browns and a small salad. Then she put some crusty rolls into the warming oven while she had a scented oil bath. When she heard Jake's motorbike throbbing up the street and the scrape of his boots on the driveway outside, she just had time to dry herself and light the candles and pull on her white towelling dressing gown before letting him in.

'Oh God,' he breathed when he saw her standing in the door with her damp hair and her skin scented and glowing from the bath, 'you're so beautiful, Rose. I don't deserve you.'

They drank the champagne sitting naked on the bed looking into each other's eyes, saying nothing until Jake began to quote.

'How do I love thee? Let me count the ways.
I love thee to the depth and breadth and height
My soul can reach . . .
I love thee to the level of every day's
Most quiet need, by sun and candle light.'

'Browning,' she murmured, and the poetry and the champagne and the look on Jake's face were like the slow drip of a transfusion, suffusing her bloodstream with love. He reached out his hand to stroke her breasts and her long smooth back and the womanly swell of her hips, and presently they lay down together to explore each other's bodies in comfort at last. Hers was so translucent where it had not tanned that he could trace the blue veins like rivers under her skin, making her shiver with pleasure. His was lean and hard and scarred by his years of bush training, each muscle separate and distinct like an idealised anatomy drawing. In the candlelight he looked as though he had been carved from polished yellowwood, deepened to a rich secret brown in the shadowed places. She thought, looking down in the flickering light at the length of their joining, How can anyone believe pallid white is superior? and whispered, 'Jake, I don't deserve you either.'

He would not let her say any more. Words that were not poetry were unnecessary that night and the nights that followed. He came by arrangement when the others were out, always with a poem learned or written for her, often with a handful of flowers or veld grasses, and though he would sometimes stay into the early morning hours, he was always gone before anyone else stirred. Rose would lie among the cushions on her bed, drowsy with loving, and listen to the sound of his motorbike fading down the dark Yeoville street wishing he didn't have to go, knowing he was going to the dark, dangerous side of his life that ate into him like acid. Under the willow tree on the market gardener's farm, the plastic bags of arms, ammunition and explosives were accumulating.

A weekend came when his cousin Ivan said, 'Listen, bra, I've got my Ma coming for a few days and I'll need your bedroom. Can you stay over with your girlfriend just for two nights?'

Jake had told him the bare facts about Rose, that she was white and they worked together as teachers, but not that her house-mates had made conditions about his staying with her. He could not, of course, go home to Bosmont in case the security police had watchers on the house. He met occasionally with one or the other sister, always in crowds, to get news of the family and specially of his father, who was suffering from increasingly severe asthma attacks. The family knew he was doing something illegal but, apart from Yasmin, nobody mentioned it or tried to find out what it was. Yasmin had said, her knowing teenage eyes sharpened to pinpoints by the Mandrax and tranquilliser tablets that were to kill her when she began to inject them, 'I know what you're doing, Jakie, but I won't tell, OK?' and gone into a fit of giggles. The fact that he could do nothing to help her, on top of the strain of repeated clandestine meetings and living on continual alert, was giving his face the gaunt look of a man on a hunger fast.

When he told Rose that he would not be able to come to her at the weekend because he was going away, she soon wangled the reason out of him and insisted that he stay with her. 'I'll square it with the others, don't worry,' she said. 'They're sympathetic except for Boff, just concerned with not getting involved with – what you're doing.'

'I won't stay if I'm not wanted. I wouldn't want to contaminate the place.' He turned away from her to glower at the view from the classroom window, a depressing sight now towards the end of the winter drought.

'Jake, don't start that again,' she pleaded. 'You've been so much less bitter recently.'

'What I feel inside hasn't changed.' He turned back to take her hand and lift it to his lips, caressing her fingers with his thumb. 'I just try not to let the bad stuff pour out all over you. We've got to keep this part of ourselves separate so it doesn't get polluted.'

'Nothing could pollute it.' She looked up at him with the blue eyes in which he no longer saw icebergs, only plumbago flowers. 'You make me so happy.'

Coming earlier than usual through the classroom door, Tryphina saw them and crept away, envying. Both her husbands had left her for younger, faster women, disappearing so thoroughly that she could not find them to demand support payments for the children. The wage she earned as a domestic worker did not go very far towards feeding, clothing and educating five.

It was agreed that Jake could stay for the weekend in Yeoville; they had got used to the idea of his being there on occasional nights. He came on his motorbike late on Friday night, but stayed in Rose's room saying, 'I know I'm here under protest. Better if I keep out of sight.'

'They won't bite you.'

He gave her a shadow of his ferocious grin. 'It's not their feelings I'm worried about so much, it's their being able to recognise me. Ursula's the only one who knows my face, and I'd like it to stay that way.'

On Saturday morning Jake was reading in her room while the others did their household chores. Didymus had begun to paint the outside of the house in stages as his contribution, saying, 'I am the Picasso of the paint roller. Genuine. Cracks positively quiver when they see me coming.' He was halfway up the ladder in his most disreputable overall, working on the kitchen wall that faced across the back yard, when he heard voices next door and saw several policemen, one with an eager-looking Alsatian straining at the leash in his hand, talking to the owner of the house.

'This is a routine inspection, lady,' one of them was saying. 'We're just checking all the houses on this street for illegals.'

'You won't find any in my khaya.' The woman was wearing a floral doek over a headful of hair curlers. On Saturday nights she always had what she called a spot or three with her other widowed friends in the Ladies' Lounge of a Hillbrow hotel and went on to the bioscope afterwards, all of them covertly scanning the single men in view. 'I sacked my girl for drinking last year already. They nothing but trouble, these kaffir girls. I'd rather do the work myself. You'll find just the lawnmower in there, and some spades.'

Didymus put down his roller, climbed down the ladder and went into the house to look through the lounge window into the street. Then he ran to knock on Rose's door. 'Rose, quick!'

'What is it?' Her hair was messy and her face looked flushed when she opened the door. She had done her chores early to be able to enjoy the luxury of a whole day alone with Jake.

'There are cops next door, checking for illegals. They'll be coming here next. What about Jake?'

He was behind her in seconds. 'I'll go out the back way. Show me where, priest.'

'You can't. That's where they are now, and they've got a dog with them.'

'Out the front way, then.'

'There's a police van in the street, and more cops with dogs doing the houses on the other side.'

'I'll have to hide.'

'The dogs will find you. They're trained to sniff out – ' He stopped.

'Blacks? We have this characteristic smell, of course. *Eau d'Afrique*. Unmistakable.' Jake bared his teeth, but it wasn't a smile.

Rose's face had gone dead white. 'What are we going to do?'

'There's the trapdoor in the pantry,' Didymus said. 'It opens into the space under the house.'

'Piece of cake for a dog. Ceiling too. I've seen them in action. They're damn well trained.' Jake spoke in staccato bursts.

'There's my car,' Rose said.

'No good. It's out in front, full view. I'll just have to take my chances that they don't come inside.'

'They have to come through the house to get into the back yard.' After a spate of burglaries in the street, the landlord had recently closed off the alleys on either side of the house with barbed wire fences.

'Then I've had it.'

'No, Jake! We've got to think of something.' Rose clutched at him.

He pushed her away. 'Best I get out into the back yard. Pretend I've jumped over from somewhere else to hide there. Can't incriminate you. Stay here.' He was through the door before she could cry out in protest.

Didymus gestured. 'The back yard's that way.'

They ran through the kitchen, where Ursula was standing ironing. She said, 'What's the rush?'

'Cops coming. He's getting out of the house.'

At the open back door Didymus put his arm across Jake's chest to stop him from going out, and leaned round to see what was happening next door. One of the policemen had gone inside the disused maid's room with the owner; policemen are lied to so often that they don't set much store by people's assurances. The one with the dog was going up the steps to the back stoep.

Didymus hissed, 'Wait until they've both gone inside, then you can hide in my room.'

'I wouldn't do that.'

'The so-called servant's quarters would be more appropriate under the circumstances than Rose's bedroom.' Didymus flashed his white rabbit's smile, exposing two large top teeth. 'I've got tins of paint stored in there, so you could – hey, that's it!'

'What?'

'Change clothes with me. You could be the painter we've hired to do the outside of the house. I presume you've got a valid ID?'

'Ja, I'm supposed to be a welder by trade. Good occupation for a skilled coloured, welding.'

Didymus grinned. 'That's fine, then. Put on my overall and

get up the ladder outside, and you're a welder making a bit of extra cash by painting at the weekend. Quick, man!'

He was unbuttoning his overall as he spoke, exposing a white vest and a pair of purple and green underpants in a violent paisley that his mother had sent him for his birthday. In seconds, Jake had his sweater and jeans off and was pulling on the paint-spattered overall.

'Just what are you guys doing?' Ursula stood with the iron poised over a pillowcase.

'Can't you see? Jake's going to be our painter. Tell the others, will you? They must back up the story.' Didymus was threading his long skinny legs into Jake's jeans; when he pulled them up, the hems came above his ankles. He said to Jake, 'There's a paint tray half full of PVA on top of the ladder. Flick the roller so it sprays across your face and arms. Got to look as though you've been at it all morning. It'll come off with water later.'

Jake buttoned the overall with shaking fingers. He said, 'Ta, priest.'

Didymus went red. 'Listen, I'm not a priest yet.'

'Ta anyway.'

Jake was on the ladder swishing the roller up and down the dingy wall in broad white strokes when two policemen came through the kitchen and out into the yard, talking to Ursula. 'You say a white person lives in the servant's room?' one of them was saying.

'Yes. He's quite poor so he can't afford to pay much rent, but he's fixed it up very nicely,' Ursula gushed. 'He's a theology student, actually.'

'A dominee? In *there*?' The policeman was incredulous.

Ursula turned to look at him. 'Blessed are the meek, Sergeant, for they shall inherit the earth,' she said in a grave voice.

'Ag, ja, of course.' The policeman looked embarrassed, partly because he had heard his own dominee say the very same thing in Afrikaans from the pulpit last Sunday, and partly because he was only a constable who was still aspiring to the rank of sergeant. He stuck his head into Didymus's room and gave it a cursory look. 'Is this the only one?'

'Yes.'

'You haven't got a girl, then?'

'We have a woman who comes in once a week to do some of the heavy work. She lives in Alexandra.'

'And the klonkie up the ladder?' He jerked his head at Jake.

'He's just a painter who was recommended to us. We're paying him by the hour. I don't know where he lives.'

'Hey, you!' the policeman called.

Jake went on sweeping the roller up and down with the air of someone who knows he is being watched, and wants to impress the onlooker with his diligence. There was a slash of paint across the top of his hair.

'Hey, you up there!' The policeman with the dog went across to the ladder, tugging at the leash to make the dog follow him, and shook it. 'Klim af, man. Show me your identity document.'

Jake feigned surprise at the sudden movement, dropping his roller clumsily into the paint tray and clutching at the top of the ladder. 'What you doing that for, Master?'

Didymus, listening from inside the kitchen, could not believe the change in his voice. It had slid up the register into an exaggerated Cape coloured accent.

'Get down, man! Show me your ID.'

'I'm coming, Master. Don't make me fall, Master. Please, Master, I'm coming.' Jake began to come down the ladder backwards, very slowly, feeling for each rung with his right shoe, which was also spattered with paint.

'Maak gou, skepsel,' the policeman at the bottom said. The dog, suddenly seeing the descending feet, growled and strained at the leash.

'He's perfectly legal. I checked his ID and his references,' Ursula said. 'We wouldn't take just anybody off the street, Sergeant.'

'Very wise, lady. You never know what they might do,' the first policemen said. 'Just the other day, a garden boy robbed a old lady who gave him work off the street of four hundred rand! Raped her too. Shame.'

'Shame,' Ursula said faintly.

'Jou ID,' the other policeman demanded, holding out his empty hand and loosening the leash slightly with the other so the dog's bared teeth were only inches from Jake's feet as they touched the ground.

'Yes, Master. Just give us a chance, Master. It's in my inside pocket.' Jake gave him an ingratiating smile and reached inside the overall for the coloured identity document that had been forged six months ago in Lusaka; its plastic cover had been repeatedly put through an old mangle with cloth-covered rollers

277

to make it look as though it had been inhabiting inside pockets for years. Jake said, handing it over, 'Here you are, Master. All present and correct. I'm a welder by trade, Kosie Abrahams from Riverlea Extension.' It was a township close to his Bosmont home which he knew well.

The policeman with the dog took it between two fingers and passed it to the first policeman. 'Looks OK, hey?'

The first policeman was trying to work out why Ursula, not a bad-looking girl in spite of the funny skirt she was wearing that went right down to her ankles, had such tightly curled dark hair. Is she a Jew, he was thinking, or was there an ouma somewhere who lived in the back yard? He glanced at Jake's identity document. 'Looks OK to me. Ask him where he lives.'

'He already said. Riverlea Extension. You want me to check his registration number through with John Vorster Square?'

'Wat dink jy?'

Ursula said, 'Can I make you some coffee or tea, Sergeant, while you make up your minds?'

The first policeman turned to her. 'Ag, that's nice of you, lady, but we can't whilst we on duty. We've got this whole street to do before we come off shift.'

The second policeman said doggedly, 'Must I check or what?'

Keeping his face turned to Ursula, the first one said, 'We haven't got time to check them all, Kerneels. If it looks OK, I'd say leave it. We should be moving on.' He said it with reluctance. Ursula was smiling at him in a way the girls in their prim lace collars and white hats outside church never did.

Jake took his ID back with a touching display of gratitude, cupping one hand under the other to receive it as though it were a communion wafer. 'Dankie, Master. Thank you, my Master. Can I carry on now?'

'I reckon you better, or the Madam will be complaining, hey?' the first policeman said with a heavy wink at Ursula, who smiled her appreciation. He thought, Shame about that hair. She's not bad.

'Thank you, Master,' Jake said, and turning to the ladder began to climb it as he had come down, moving his right foot up to each rung and pulling the left after it.

'Jislaaik, you get some chancers,' the policeman with the dog muttered, tugging it towards the kitchen steps, annoyed that he had not been able to let him off the leash even once this afternoon. They hadn't found a hint of any illegals yet, let alone

one trying to escape. He and his dog made a good team, but they had too few opportunities to show it.

From the top of the ladder, Jake heard Ursula call out, 'Totsiens, Sergeant, and thanks very much. It's good to know you people are keeping an eye on the situation round here.'

'You wouldn't believe what we find sometimes, lady.' He lifted a large freckled hand in reply to her farewell wave. 'Thanks for your co-operation, you hear?'

Only when the police vans had disappeared round the corner did Ursula come out of the kitchen door and call up to Jake, 'It's all right now, Kosie, you can come down. Work's finished for the day.'

He was about to make a joking reply when he saw the look on her face, and realised that she was saying it for the benefit of the neighbour, who was sweeping her back stoep. He said in a subdued voice, 'OK, Miesies,' and came down the ladder carrying the roller and the now-empty paint tray, which he washed carefully under the tap and propped against the wall to dry. Then he went up the back steps and knocked on the door. 'Can I have my pay now, Miesies?'

'You want some coffee before you go?' Ursula's face was bright pink with suppressed laughter. 'Come into the kitchen, and I'll give you some.'

'Dankie, Miesies.'

Rose threw herself at him the moment the door closed. 'Oh, Jake, I was so frightened!'

But he was laughing with relief, laughing with Ursula until they could hardly stand and had to sit down weakly at the table. 'You were brilliant!' she choked out. 'I nearly wet myself, it was so funny.'

'You were brilliant too,' he said, wiping tears away with knuckles still spattered with white paint. 'I'd recommend you as a Miesies any day.'

'We could go on the stage as a comic duo, maybe. Ginsberg and Van Vuuren – sorry, Abrahams. Painter in Peril or, How to Fool the Force.' She dissolved into laughter again.

Rose said, 'How can you laugh? I was petrified.' She had pulled up a chair close to Jake's and was sitting holding his hand as though she would never let go.

'Me too.' Didymus was boiling the kettle and getting out the coffee mugs. 'If they'd thought to look at me closer, they'd have found paint everywhere.'

Colin said from the doorway, 'Is there some coffee for us? We were manning the front windows.' He and Boff came in and sat down, Boff on the far side of the table from Jake.

'I can't stay too long in case the lady next door wonders why Kosie is being so pally with the Miesies all of a sudden,' Jake said. 'I'd better go out the door in these overalls and away down the street, just on the off-chance that she's watching. She won't connect me with the guy who comes on the motorbike if someone else rides it out wearing my helmet and leathers. And listen, I'd like to say a big thanks to you all.'

'Me too,' Rose said, with feeling.

'I know you're not crazy about having me here. I know you think I'm some sort of devil with horns, leading Rose into the firepit.' He looked round at them, young faces gone serious in the orange afternoon sunlight that was coming through the window, and went on, 'You're entitled to believe what you like, but just remember one thing. I was a Wits student like you, but I couldn't go on sitting in that fancy ivory tower while my people were suffering. I had to do what I did, what I'm doing. Maybe you would be doing the same if you were on my side of the line. Think about it.'

After that day, even Boff grew more friendly and Jake was asked to join them at meals on the nights he spent with Rose, though they were never very comfortable. 'They understand how things are for you, but they don't like what the other people in your organisation are doing,' Rose reported.

He turned his head away so she wouldn't see his face. He had not told her about the arms cache buried under the willow tree, hoping that there would be no need. And then a week ago he had received a phone call in a public phone box on the Park Station concourse at a pre-arranged time.

'There's going to be a major offensive in December, just before Christmas,' a voice had said. 'We're going to need most of that stuff. Make sure it's ready.'

'But I asked not to have to handle weapons,' he protested.

'No arguments!' the voice had rapped. 'By joining us, you accepted the necessity for the armed struggle. Now we need your full co-operation, no ifs or buts. Be ready.' He lived in increasing dread of another phone call.

At the Yeoville house, Ursula was more friendly than she had been before and often called him 'Kosie' with a grin, but only Didymus made any real attempt to get to know him better. One evening when Jake was sitting reading in Rose's room, waiting for her to come home after a late class, Didymus put his head round the door and said, 'Will you come and have some coffee in my humble abode? I want to ask you a few things.'

In the small servant's room, he switched off the glaring electric light bulb as soon as he had lit the paraffin lamp that stood on the tin trunk by his mattress. 'That's better. I'm more used to paraffin. We had it for years at the mission.'

The warm oily smell reminded Jake of the Sophiatown kitchen where his ouma had cooked on a paraffin stove. He said, 'You're a surprising whitey, you know? I mean, this room isn't exactly – '

'The usual perquisite of privilege. I know,' Didymus sighed, 'but it's all I can afford. Please make yourself comfortable.'

Jake sat down on the mattress with his back against the wall, cradling his coffee mug between both hands. 'What did you want to ask me?'

'It's sort of difficult.' Didymus sat down next to him and stretched out his long legs.

'Try me.'

'I want to talk to you about what you're doing, and why. I need to understand, you see.' Jake watched his Adam's apple jerking up and down his throat as he spoke. 'The reason is that if I'm going to be a good priest, I must know what makes people tick. Why they do things against – well, against their better natures.'

'What do you mean by that exactly?'

Didymus blurted, 'I don't think you've told Rose the whole truth. It's in your eyes all the time.'

Jake shrugged. 'I do what I have to do. When there's a war on, soldiers have no choice.'

'So you see your cause as a just war?'

'Sure. How else?'

'But violence inevitably leads to more violence. It's a vicious circle. And it's often the innocent who get hurt, whether it's a bombing or a police raid. Wouldn't compromise and negotiation be better, even if they take longer?'

'How long? Ten years? Fifty? A hundred? Don't be naïve, priest. This government's never going to give up power unless they're forced to; no goverment in history has ever given it up voluntarily. And they're so used to ruling by violence that it's the only threat they really understand. Whether we like it or not, it's our most effective weapon.'

Didymus said, 'I find it hard to accept a line of reasoning that answers one evil with another.'

'But your God understood it. "Eye for eye, tooth for tooth, hand for hand, foot for foot, burning for burning, wound for wound, stripe for stripe." It's in the book of Exodus.'

'One of the Old Testament sentiments I could never agree with. You know your Bible, then?'

Jake nodded and said, 'Ironic, hey? We had plenty of time to read in the camps, and the King James English was soothing after having orders barked at me all day.'

The Adam's apple jerked up and down again. 'I'm surprised your – the people who trained you allowed you to read Bibles. From what I've heard – '

Jake laughed. 'They aren't all raving communists, if that's what you mean.'

Didymus's voice was very serious as he answered. 'I need to know the strength of the forces we're fighting against.'

Jake sat silent for a long while before saying, 'I'll tell you what it's like up there and what happened to me on one condition: you swear on your Bible not to repeat it to anyone. I haven't told Rose most of this, and I'm not going to. It just makes her worry more. But I'll tell you for one reason. I think we're both fighting for the same things, even if our methods and the gods we pray to are poles apart.'

Didymus reached towards the worn black Bible that lay on the trunk and held it in his right hand. 'I swear I won't repeat anything you say. So help me God.'

'Rules of the confessional?'

Didymus nodded.

For half an hour Jake spoke in a detached monotone about his recruitment, his flight over the border, his long journey in a dusty Kombi to a safe house in Maputo and his months in Dar-es-Salaam, where he was taught ANC history and security procedures. 'I asked to be used as a teacher at Solomon Mahlangu College or even one of the bush schools, but they said I had to go through the full training first,' he said. From Tanzania he was sent to Luanda in Angola, where he was given his *nom de guerre*, Kosie Abrahams, by the security department. At Quibaxe camp and later Caxito he was endlessly marched and drilled, given firearms training, and instructed in sabotage and survival techniques, explosives handling, map reading, field work and communications. He also did his stint of farm work, living in muddy dugouts roofed with corrugated iron, drinking boiled river water that tasted of dead leaves, eating donated Chinese rice with monotonous stews made of tinned food.

'Believe me, priest, the training is thorough. If whites knew how thorough, they wouldn't sleep too easily at night. I'm a hell of a lot fitter now than I'd ever have been teaching. The boring part was the political stuff the commissars fed us every damn evening, rambling on forever when all we wanted to do was fall on to our bunks and sleep.'

'Didn't you ever want to give up?'

'Often. But of course I couldn't. When you're stuck in the bush a thousand miles from nowhere, you don't have a lot of options. Then I began to realise that they had recognised my superior intelligence and were grooming me for stardom.'

'What does that mean?'

'Russia.' The soft word fell between them like a shot bird, its body full of lead. He was sent in a transport plane with a group of taciturn engineers who were returning thankfully home after a year of battling encroaching bush, tropical diseases, heat and apathy on the Zambian railway system. For Jake there were courses in guerrilla tactics, more sophisticated explosives, command skills, infantry and artillery warfare, communications, economics, international politics, Marxist-Leninist theory and historical materialism.

'What's that?'

Jake laughed again. 'History with a red tinge, and very interesting too. I'd never realised how subjective history is. Seeing it from a socialist point of view after all the ra-ra-for-capitalism stuff I was taught in school gave me a very different perspective.'

'Where did you go in Russia?'

'I was sent around quite a bit, to Simferopol in the Ukraine, then to Odessa, then to the cherry on the top, Centre 26 near Moscow. The climate is terrible, and so are the girls; they seem to think that anyone with a skin darker than birch bark is a primitive form of life, and call you "Monkey" behind their hands. But I did well at my courses, specially communications, and they made me an instructor when I got back to Angola. That was two years ago.'

'I'm surprised you didn't stay there. Coming into South Africa like this must be very dangerous for you.'

'It is. But I was homesick. Magtig, I was so homesick!' Jake shook his head with remembered loss. 'I missed my people and the smells of home and the food I grew up with and even – maybe you won't believe this – the sound of Afrikaans. And I got to thinking about Rose more and more. So I volunteered for active service, on condition I didn't have to use weapons.'

'And they agreed?'

'The deal is three missions, handling internal publicity and communications.' Jake pushed the thought of the arms cache away as not for priestly consumption.

Didymus cleared his throat. 'What I really want to know is, did the weapons training and the political indoctrination change you, the real you?'

'Ja, of course. What do you expect? Those commissar guys may go on and on, but a lot of what they say makes sense. They made me think harder about who I really am, what I want from society, what society wants from me. And the training made me tougher and more determined not to let the white man get his way forever here. I'm well motivated, if that's what you're asking.'

'A communist?'

'Does it matter?'

'As a Christian, I have to answer yes,' Didymus said. 'Not only because Marxism is intolerant of religion, but because it's so dogmatic. I mean, have you thought that you may be helping to exchange one bad system for another?'

Jake gave a laugh as sharp and final as a knife under the ribs and said sarcastically, 'Systems! Shit, intellectuals carry on about capitalism and socialism and communism as though people can be channelled into them like dumb oxen into a cattle-dip. I don't think people are dumb. You can impose a system on them for just so long, but eventually they'll start to lean on the fences, and the ropes round their necks will fray with rubbing, and they'll break out to find the pastures they want. I'm just trying to hurry the process along, to hell with the isms.'

'You haven't mentioned colonialism.'

'Case in point. Most of Africa got rid of that one some time ago; it's only down here that we're still having problems. But Africans aren't going to allow another yoke to be put over their necks in a hurry. We're sick and tired of being led by the nose and told what to do. We want to go our own way now, to live like free oxen again, choosing our own directions. Does that answer your question?'

284

'Yes,' Didymus said, 'thank you, Jake. You're a surprising guy yourself, you know?'

Jake's voice when it finally came was low and sad. 'Ag, all I really want to do is write poems good enough to reach into people's hearts and shake them up a bit, but I never seem to have the time.'

'Maybe when you go back to being an instructor?'

'Maybe.'

But the doubt on his face was the expression that Didymus would remember, specially five years later as he sits in the mud-walled death hut trying to reach his God for an explanation, and failing.

25

'The coffins have come,' Tshabalala says with the satisfaction of a man who has made something happen against insuperable odds. He stands as though rooted in the hard dry ground, feet apart, massive hands on hips, muscular shoulders straining the sleeve seams of his khaki shirt. 'It appears that there was a serious bus accident on the Mafeteng road early this morning, and both mortuary vans were sent down there. I asked the police to make alternative arrangements, and they sent Constable Tsepo.'

Gordon puts the bucket down on the step and straightens up to shake the policeman's hand. 'Thank you, Constable. I saw your van coming down the road like a bat out of hell a few minutes ago.' He turns to Tshabalala. 'Does everyone here drive like a maniac?'

The granite face cracks a little. 'Settlements are so far apart in Lesotho that if you don't step on it, you never get anywhere. Besides, it's the only thing to do on gravel roads; the wheels go over the top of the ruts instead of dropping in each time. Much easier on the shock absorbers.'

Gordon nods in sympathy. 'I thought we had some bone-rattlers at home, but I've got to admit that yours are more spectacular. How does the BMW handle on gravel?'

'Hugs it like a whore trying to earn double time.' The crack grows wider. 'As unit commander here, I get my pick of the ones that come over the border.'

'You mean it's stolen?'

'Liberated, we prefer to say.' Tshabalala is still sweating, despite the rising breeze ahead of the storm. He takes out his handkerchief and mops his face and neck. 'We have teams who concentrate on the parking lots of Johannesburg shopping centres, and others who specialise in garage removals. My best operative can get into any car in thirty seconds, and have it

286

round the corner into a pantechnicon in another thirty. By the time it reaches the border, it will have been given a new paint job, engine and chassis numbers and number plates in transit, and there'll be a driver with impeccable credentials to take it through. Bingo! More cash for the struggle.'

Gordon can almost feel the tumblers falling into place in his head. Car theft is a rapidly escalating crime in South Africa: nearly 60,000 a year are stolen, fifty a day in Johannesburg's city centre alone. So is housebreaking. He says sarcastically, 'I suppose you have sidelines in stolen TVs and videos too?'

The bullet head shakes a denial. 'That's petty theft. Not worth the risk and doesn't pay as well as cars. We got the idea from your folk hero, Robin Hood, of course. The concept of robbing the rich to give to the poor greatly appeals to me. We don't even have to feel guilty because the rich are all heavily insured.'

Gordon thinks, Another justification. The idea makes him angry; his emotions have been very close to the surface all day. He bursts out, 'But you're not giving to the poor, you're spending it on guns and bombs and training killers.'

The crack in the granite face slams shut. 'It's none of your business what we do, white man.'

'I think it is, after today.' Gordon is not going to allow Tshabalala to fob him off as just another uncaring white. 'I want justice and peace in this country as much as you do, but the cost you're forcing everyone to pay is too high.'

'Who are you to say?' The massive fists are balling again.

'I'm a father who has lost both his children. How many more are there like me? How many more women will be gunned down this month, this year, next year in the name of a mythical freedom that may never come if neither side will make concessions?'

Tshabalala shouts, 'May I remind you that it was not us who killed your daughter, Mr Bloody Kimber!'

'You led the killers to her just as surely as if you'd tethered a goat under a hide to attract lions. You should have known she was in danger, and sent her and the child away.'

'We did not know. We would have sent them all three away if we had! We are heartbroken about it too.' Tshabalala's voice breaks. 'It is a terrible tragedy for us to lose them.'

Gordon sees his own pain and loss reflected on the sweating face of the unit commander, and feels his anger subside. He is aiming at the wrong target here. To change the subject, he says, 'Why are you telling me about the car scheme? I could blow the whistle on it when I get back home.'

'Under the circumstances, I hardly think so. You are depending on me for certain information, yes?' Tshabalala stabs a thick forefinger at the cottage door. 'But I have come to talk about the funeral arrangements, not the relative merits of car theft. Can we go inside?'

Gordon gives a curt nod. All three of them go up the steps and into the small living room. It has an air of parlour tidiness, having been set straight and scoured of bloodstains by the women of the village. Even the hideous red arcs spattered on the wall against which Rose was flung by the hail of bullets have been whitewashed over. They have not been able to hide the grey pockmarks in the plaster or the stitch-lines of small holes in the ceiling, however, or the splintered gashes of fresh wood on the coffee table. Gordon's heart gives a heavy double thump when he sees them, and a wave of dizziness makes him stumble. He had decided not to come inside again after his brief look round before watering the plants.

Tshabalala says at his shoulder, steadying his arm, 'Should we go down to my office?'

'No. Thanks. I'm all right.' Real men don't admit weaknesses. 'Sit down, won't you? Can I get either of you something to drink? Tea, or cold water?' One of their wedding presents to Rose and Jake was a small paraffin fridge. He made the mistake of opening it when he first came in, and the simplicity of the domestic still-life inside – a jug of milk, a glass water bottle, cheese and butter and apples and a small bottle of mashed vegetables already prepared for Hope's lunch – is etched on his mind. Healthy food for healthy young bodies, he thinks. Dead bodies now. They'll never eat those apples.

'A glass of cold water, maybe,' Tshabalala says, and the silent policeman nods. Outside, there is a flash of lightning and a rumble of thunder that echoes from cliff to cliff down the valley.

'I'll get you some.' Gordon goes into the tiny kitchen and comes back with three glasses of cold water on a tray that he has recognised; it is the one Agnes used to bring his morning tea on, in the Johannesburg life that receded like a fading bad dream after they moved to the farm.

Sitting side by side on the low divan covered with a handwoven bedspread and cushions that served as a sofa, the two men mumble their thanks. After he has taken a long gulping drink, Tshabalala sets the glass down on a side table and says, 'The police van will take the coffins up the track as far as it can go, and my men will carry them from there. Sister Quthing will do the laying out. Maybe Mrs Kimber would like to come down here while she attends to it?'

'No.' Sitting on the edge of the armchair that was Jake's, Gordon looks round the small room. He sees the first photographs of Hope stuck under the frame of the mirror, a sweater lying across the back of a chair, a bundle of baby knitting, books and papers shoved higgledy piggledy into a cheap pine bookcase – the trivial artefacts of daily living that are like mental fish-hooks when the people who have used them are gone. 'No,' he says again, speaking with lips that have gone stiff, 'I don't think she should come here, not today.'

'Cordelia has offered you both the use of her home. It's the same as this one, but on the other side of the clinic.'

'Very kind of her. Maybe that would be the best place to take my wife.' There is another flash of lightning, followed immediately by a crack of thunder. It is getting darker outside.

'Our custom is for the funeral to take place as soon as possible.' Tshabalala is looking down at the damp handkerchief in his hand. 'Under the circumstances, the district surgeon who examined Rose and Jake this morning has agreed to waive a post mortem. I have the signed death certificate on my desk. We could hold the ceremony tomorrow, if you and Mrs Kimber and Mrs Van Vuuren are agreeable.'

'Mrs Van Vuuren?' Gordon has not given a thought to Jake's mother, whom he has not met. Sarah has visited her in Bosmont several times, the last being when Jake's father died during a severe asthma attack during one of her infrequent trips to Johannesburg. 'Is she here?'

'She'll be here early tomorrow morning. Someone is bringing her down by car. I must also tell you that some of our DIP officials are flying in from Lusaka this evening. We want to make it clear to the world that we honour Jake and Rose, and will not let their murder go unrevenged.'

'DIP?'

'Department of Information and Publicity. A very necessary aspect of the struggle.'

Gordon says sharply, 'You're not going to let the press turn this funeral into a public circus, I hope? We'd like it to be as private as possible. I'm sure I speak for Mrs Van Vuuren too.'

Tshabalala looks apologetic. 'I'm afraid it will not be possible to keep the press away. My office has been besieged all day with phone calls from news agencies and overseas TV teams who –'

'No!' Gordon shouts, jumping up. 'For God's sake, no. She'll be pilloried as a kaffirboetie in most of the local papers, and the foreign ones will try to turn her into a symbol of everything that's wrong about South Africa, which she would have hated. You've got to stop them.'

'I can't, and you know it. What happened this morning entered the public domain the moment the news went out on the telexes.' Tshabalala gets up too, putting the empty glass down on the table with a thunk. 'What I can do, since there is only one road into this valley, is limit the numbers attending the funeral. My office will issue a directive to the press that only, say, twenty journalists and photographers will be allowed in, and my men will set up a road block with police assistance at the valley entrance. Will that satisfy you, Mr Kimber?'

'Under the circumstances, I have to say yes. Thank you.' Gordon has to force out the thanks. 'I hope your people can keep the press in order too.'

'I'll see to it personally. We want this ceremony to be as dignified as you do. It's important when the eyes of the world are upon us that they see us as a well-disciplined organisation with – '

'Goddammit, this is my daughter's funeral, not a propaganda exercise!' Gordon is furious again. He has begun to think that Tshabalala understands, but now he seems more concerned with how the funeral looks than whose it is.

The big man moves closer to him and puts one large damp hand on Gordon's shoulder. 'Please,' he says, 'please, Mr Kimber, understand that every incident between white and black will be used for propaganda by one side or the other. These are small fights in a war that started three hundred years ago, but is only now beginning to run away like a veld fire through dry grass in a high wind. You are trying to put it out by smacking the edges with wet sacks, and we are setting more fires to make it burn faster. If we are to survive this holocaust, we have to be able to see each other's signals through the smoke. I am signalling you that I will do my utmost best to make sure your daughter is buried decently and with honour, but I can't control the movement of the wind too, OK?'

The black eyes are round and shiny like the water-smoothed pebbles in Lesotho's mountain streams. After a long moment, Gordon nods and says, 'Thank you. I – we appreciate it.' This time the thanks are not forced.

Tshabalala drops his hand. 'I must get back to camp before the rain starts. Just two things more. There will be a funeral feast afterwards, for which we have chosen two black bulls. Will you cover the cost?' Gordon nods. 'It is also customary to dig the grave in the morning, and for the closest male relative to start first. Do you think you can do this?'

'Of course. Of *course*,' Gordon emphasises. 'But don't you mean graves? Would I qualify as one of Jake's male relatives too?'

'There will be only one grave. The Basotho people bury their dead in a niche cut into the side of a grave and closed off with stones before it is filled in. For Jake and Rose there will be a niche on either side.'

'Very fitting.' Gordon's voice is gruff. 'Thank you,' he says again.

Tshabalala nods his acceptance. 'Maybe you should go and fetch Mrs Kimber now, before we bring the coffins up. There should be – ' he goes towards the window and leans down to peer up at the sky, ' – ten minutes or so before it starts to rain.'

'I'll go straight away.'

As the men hurry down the path, he puts the yellow bucket inside the door before closing it. Looking up, he sees black clouds boiling over the valley's rim, and behind them a towering crystal palace of cumulonimbus formed in the hot summer updraught of the Maluti mountain mass. The sunlight slanting under the encroaching clouds blazes orange on the sandstone cliff above the village, where Rose has told them are the caves and overhangs of the long-gone San people, the Bushmen, with their lively rock paintings of men and animals. At the foot of the cliff the sun glitters on the weeping stones of the granite layer, turning them to black diamonds.

He thinks as he walks up the rutted track how much Sarah would have enjoyed painting this dramatically lit afternoon in the valley, if things had gone according to plan. If. If. The vicious little word taunts him all the way up to the death hut.

*   *   *

Jake became more and more tense as the end of the year came and the Matric exam loomed. Rose put it down to exam nerves. The teachers at St Aloysius were cramming in as many extra lessons as their students could manage to attend, in a last-ditch struggle to make up the deficit of years of inadequate schooling. Jake and Rose had started a system of small tutorial groups for their English students, who were often too shy to speak in front of a whole class but would give hesitant opinions in a familiar small group. There were two students who showed a special aptitude for creative writing: a lanky boy of nineteen who began to write poetry under Jake's encouragement, and a friend of Tryphina's who confessed shyly one day that she had written a novel.

Rose had been so struck by her hand-written story, which moved from an idyllic childhood home in a Zulu kraal to a brutal gang rape in a city alley, that she had taken a photocopy and sent it to a publisher who specialised in African writers. He had written back, 'I'm impressed, but alas I couldn't sell enough copies now to cover my printing costs. Ask her to finish it and bring it back to me in two or three years' time. We may have managed to persuade the black reading public that there are better authors than James Hadley Chase by then, and the white reading public that blacks are also capable of writing English. Though that won't be easy.'

'Why are South Africans so cynical?' Rose had asked Jake when he read the letter. 'It's almost as though we enjoy our increasing notoriety.'

'It's the backs-to-the-wall-but-all-flags-flying syndrome,' Jake said. 'You can see it in ex-Rhodesians.'

'I think it's a self-defeating attitude. We'll never get anywhere if we start off thinking the whole situation's hopeless.'

'Isn't it?'

'No. And you don't think so either, or you wouldn't be doing – what you're doing.'

She tried not to comment on his occasional disappearances during school holidays, on the mornings when he came to work with dark pouches under his eyes from lack of sleep, and his reticence about where he lived. She didn't tell him that she had seen him once in the centre of town being driven in an old cream Valiant by a man in dark glasses. She didn't want to know who the man was, or why Jake's expression had been so grim.

His tension came from the increasingly urgent tone of the

instructions he was receiving to prepare for the December offensive. 'We must show our contempt for the white election results, even if the Nationalists did lose six seats,' the voice on the telephone said. 'We will be targeting certain police stations. Check all the hardware.'

'But I've done my job already, hiding it!'

'You've done your job when you finish what is required of you.' The voice on the phone was peremptory. 'We won't ask you to place the limpet mines, but you must find someone who will.'

'Where?'

'We'll get the information to you. When it comes, plan carefully. Think twice and act once. We want results, not dead heroes.'

Getting into police stations with explosives, even mini limpet mines, would be almost impossible for a coloured or black member of the public. Jake was sent a list of white radical sympathisers who had received training in underground activities. He was to steer clear of university students, who were often startled when asked to act on their loudly proclaimed principles. He settled on a social worker whose skills included a brief training in sabotage during a holiday trip to Kenya, Selma was tall and bony with prominent freckled features and the curly ginger hair of the pure Scot, cropped short. In earlier times she could have been the chieftainess of a warrior tribe, used to riding into battle at their head, but twentieth-century men were less admiring of brute force in a woman and she had channelled her aggression into political and feminist activism.

He did not tell Rose that the job he was doing night after night in the October school holiday was planning the December offensive with Selma over endless cups of herb tea in her flat. He kept what he thought of as his mission completely separate from his lives as teacher and lover. Going from one to the other was like stepping in and out of three different stage plays separated by short intervals filled with the throbbing roar of his motorbike. Sometimes he felt like an anonymous knight errant in the dark-visored crash helmet, swooping to the rescue of his chained people, but more often he worried about whether the work he was doing was justified by its ultimate goal. Having to ask a woman to carry limpet mines into police stations sickened him, and the possibility of the explosions killing anyone but policemen gave him nightmares. Policemen who helped to prop up the apartheid regime could be regarded as soldiers, fair game in war, but a passing child hit by exploding debris was too terrible to think about.

Four Johannesburg police stations were to be hit on the same day, as close in time to each other as possible to create maximum publicity and panic. Selma was to play the part of a woman coming into the charge office to report a motor accident, then asking to use the lavatory. She would put a mini limpet mine wrapped in a plastic bag into a sanitary bucket in one of the cubicles and set the timer before leaving. The mines were planned to go off an hour after being placed, at five-minute intervals. She would wear a wig to conceal her distinctive hair and use a hired car to get from one police station to the next; the only real problem they could foresee was the provision of a convincing bag or container for concealing the mine in.

The operation was planned for the week after school broke up for the long summer holidays, when police numbers would be diminished by men on leave and their attention distracted by requests for supervision of empty houses while their owners were away. The burglary season gets into full swing in Johannesburg in December, shortly after the lemming rush of thousands of families to crammed seaside resorts where they slowly spit-roast on the hot beaches, acquiring hefty doses of sun damage and skin cancer with their summer tans.

Jake had urged Rose to go with her parents to the cottage they had rented on the South Coast for Christmas. 'I have to go away, and I'd like to know you're with your family.'

'You haven't been recalled?' Rose was alarmed. Her life had been so full and satisfying for the past few months that she sometimes forgot Jake's real purpose for being there.

'No.' He would not discuss it, saying only that he'd be back in January for the opening of school.

'I'll miss you so much.' Rose put her arms round his neck and leaned her face against his springy hair, savouring its aroma of nutmeg. Sometimes she thought that the spicy scent of him was what attracted her to him the most: his smooth tan body smelled of apples dusted with cloves, his hands with their slender callused fingers of the coal-tar soap he liked to use, his neck and his secret places of sandalwood, musk and cinnamon.

Gone was the smell of the crumpled Texans he had chainsmoked at university. 'The tobacco they dish out in the camps is terrible stuff, so it wasn't hard to give up,' he'd said.

Now he was smiling down at her, all the new lines on his face relaxed. 'I'll miss you too, poppie. You know that. We're good together.'

He made sure that she and her parents had left Johannesburg in Gordon's new black Mercedes before giving the final signal for the police station bombings. Selma managed to secrete her limpet mines successfully in three of the women's lavatories, but was detained by a suspicious desk sergeant while she was on her way into the fourth. When they found the mine on her, a highly trained emergency bomb squad was rushed into action. Two of the mines were found and defused in time. Only one went off, slightly injuring three young policemen who were protected by a jutting wall. Jake was telephoned at a callbox with the news, as agreed, and told where to meet the driver of the furniture removal van with false compartments that would take him north over the border.

'But what about Selma?' he protested. 'I can't just leave her.'

'You have to. She'll tell them everything.'

'Not Selma. She's strong, man.'

The voice said, 'Believe me, she'll tell them everything. You must go. Now.'

'I didn't expect – '

'None of us ever expected!' the voice shouted. 'We just do what we must.'

By nightfall, he was safely over the border and on his way to Lusaka. Next day the newspapers were full of 'The Red-headed Bomber' and Selma's glum passport photograph, along with the information that she was an ex-Wits student. The Minister of Education's office received the usual flood of phone calls, telegrams and letters demanding that the government withdraw its subsidies to the liberal English-speaking universities, which were clearly producing a breed of anarchists and commie sympathisers who were a danger to the state. Security was tightened up at all police stations and government buildings.

On the South Coast, Rose heard the news flashes with dread. However hard she tried to close her mind to what Jake could be doing when he was away on his mysterious missions, she knew it must be more than distributing subversive pamphlets. She scanned the news reports under screaming headlines in the *Natal Mercury*, and was relieved to read that 'the person detained in connection with the limpet mine explosion' was a young woman. When several days passed without any more arrests, she allowed herself to think that it could not have been anything to do with Jake.

She spent the holiday in a preoccupied dream, which Sarah put down to exhaustion from overwork at school and Gordon said was just her age. 'Don't you remember spending days on holiday at that age in a state of complete sloth?' he said when Sarah worried out loud over lunch that Rose was still sleeping.

'I was married with two children at that age, if you remember,' Sarah said in a tart voice. 'There wasn't much time for sloth.'

'I remember,' he said, smiling.

She thought, He looks a different person out of his business suits, though he's put on more weight this year. I wish he'd do something about the paunch and the smoking and those dizzy spells he keeps having and thinks I don't notice. She had given up trying to get him to go to the doctor for a general check-up. 'I'm fine,' he'd say in the dismissive voice he used to skim over problem areas in board meetings. 'Nothing that a few days down at the coast won't fix.'

But he would be panting at the top of the first rise on the path up from the beach, and there was a dull pain that came and went in his chest more often than it did at home, where his exercise was confined to a slow walk round the garden in the evenings. Sarah worried about the blue gouges under his eyes and the dreamy daze Rose seemed to be in all the time, irritated that they should take her attention away from her painting.

Rose lay thinking of Jake night after stifling night when the thin, high whine of mosquitoes kept her awake, and the sea pounding on the beach made her think of his heart beating under her ear as she lay on his chest.

On New Year's Eve she and Gordon and Sarah made a bonfire on the beach and sat reminiscing about the old year over gin and tonic out of a thermos, each of them wrapped in the melancholy of remembered wrongs and things left undone. Far away on a farm outside Lusaka, Jake was sitting next to another fire on which game birds were being roasted, listening to the fervent singing of young men who have just completed their training in the fight for their cause, never believing for a minute that they will probably die for it.

26

The thunder and lightning are almost continuous. No sooner do the reverberating echoes from one thunderbolt die away down the valley than another flash of lightning cracks down. As Gordon hurries up the track, the gusting wind throws up eddies of dust that make him hold the green hat over his mouth and close his eyes to slits.

Everyone is hurrying now. Women are scooping up babies and cooking pots and dragging smoking braziers in through hut doors. One of the girls from the hillside runs past with her bare feet slapping the earth and her hand steadying the bundle of sticks on her head. The three horsemen have unhitched and mounted their ponies and pass Gordon riding at a fast triple, conical hats pulled low over their faces, blankets flapping over their saddles.

Penny-sized dark splats of rain appear on the red earth yard round the death hut as Gordon crosses it. The mourning group has dwindled to a middle-aged woman under a black umbrella. Tears are running down her cheeks and she begins to sob as he comes closer, looking at him with tragic swimming eyes. He stops and reaches out to touch the sleeve of her print overall. 'The rain is coming, mama. Go home now.'

'Rose – ' Her sobbing rises to a wail, and she grasps his hand tightly in both of hers, kneading it with strong gnarled fingers. 'Ai – ai – ai – '

He is at a loss, not knowing how to disengage his hand without giving offence. He had hoped to get Sarah away down the path before the rain started, but now all he wants is to get inside to be with her until the storm passes. It will be very dark in there, and she must not be alone. He says, 'Please, go home.'

But the woman does not seem to hear him, moaning 'Ai – ai – ai – ' with her eyes closed and her fingers savaging his hand and the tears pouring down her face.

297

A voice behind him says something in Sesotho, and the moaning stops as though it has been cut off with a knife. He turns to find Sister Quthing in a blue raincoat splashed with rain, her cap skew on her hair from running, a paraffin lamp swinging from her hand. She says, breathlessly, 'Mrs Mofufi is one of the women Rose was teaching to sew.'

'She'll get wet. And holding an umbrella with this lightning around – '

'I've told her to go next door to her friend.' Sister Quthing reaches out and gently prises the woman's fingers away, talking in quiet Sesotho and turning her, still shaking with sobs, towards the gate.

'Thanks. I didn't know what to do,' Gordon says. 'Crying women make me feel completely helpless.'

Standing as they are under the low tongue of thatch jutting out over the door, Sister Quthing's face is very close. It is round and kind, with small neat features like a doll's house mother: shrewd black eyes, a putty-dab of a nose, a mouth with a prim smile. She is saying, patting her cap back into place, 'You should be used to women's ways, with a wife and a daughter.'

'They've taught me a lot,' he admits. 'Growing older makes a man respect women's strength. I'll be a better grandfather to Hope than I was a father to Rose. But when they cry, I turn to jelly.'

'No time for jelly today,' she says, 'or tomorrow. We'd better go in before the lightning gets too close.'

As though on cue, there is a sizzling flash followed immediately by a sharp crack that seems to tug at the sparse hair on his head, and an avalanche of thunder.

'In, quick!' she shouts.

A wind-blown flurry of rain pelts the door as they open and close it behind them. The hut is very dark and curiously quiet inside after the noise of the storm. It takes Gordon the full minute while his eyes adjust to the dark and the terrible stillness of the sheeted bodies to remember that heavy rain makes little noise on thatch. At the farm it sounds like machine-gun fire on the corrugated iron roof, and hailstones sound like a cannon barrage.

'You've come.' Sarah's voice. He goes towards her thinking, But who is this other kneeling person?

Sister Quthing puts down the paraffin lamp and bends to light it, saying, 'I thought you would like some light, Mrs

Kimber.' She lifts up the glass funnel and holds a lit match to the wick, then lowers the funnel again and adjusts a small notched wheel with her fingers to make the flame burn clear and steady.

'That was kind of you, Sister.' Sarah would rather have gone on sitting in the sympathetic dark, but she cannot say so. She turns and looks up at Gordon. 'Do you remember Didymus, Rose's priest friend? He came to be with us.'

The kneeling figure unfolds like a carpenter's rule, awkward and angular, his white rabbit's hair shining like fibreglass against the sombre thatch. 'Hullo, sir.'

Gordon shakes the diffident young hand. 'It was good of you to come.' Formula words which he knows will have to be repeated over and over during the next days and weeks, but which carry real thanks for the comfort given. He thinks, I had not realised there was such solidarity in grief.

Didymus blurts, 'Would you and Mrs Kimber allow me to help conduct the funeral service?' His Adam's apple bobs up and down. 'I married them, and it would mean a lot if I could – well, help to bury them.'

'You know neither was religious?'

Didymus nods. 'Rose and I used to talk about it in the Yeoville house. She didn't like the established churches, but she'd always say, "I believe in a life force, call it God or goddess or a universal spirit that is the sum total of all living creatures, and I know it's good. I don't believe in evil." ' The thought has been crouching like a black beast in his head ever since he heard the news of her death. 'She said, "I don't believe in evil," but she had to die like this.'

As his voice fades in horror, Sarah says flatly, 'She was wrong.'

Her words could be part of the storm howling and battering at the hut. As if drawn by magnets, their heads turn to the sheeted bodies lying on the grass mat. In silence they stand like the shadow-cowled shepherds in renaissance nativity paintings, their faces grave in the flickering lamplight as they look down, not on the miracle of life, but on its destruction.

Rose did not tell her parents she was seeing Jake again, knowing it would alarm them. When they asked her about boyfriends, she mentioned several names in a casual way, adding, 'But there's no one special. I'm having too much fun to want to settle down with one guy at this stage in my life.'

'You're being a lot more sensible than I was,' Sarah said wistfully.

You wouldn't call it sensible if you knew, Rose thought. She had been angry with her mother ever since Jake had told her of Sarah's warning during his visit to her home four years ago.

'I don't know why you're so mad with her,' he said. 'It's quite an understandable reaction.'

'It's none of her damn business who my friends are! Parents have no right to interfere.'

Jake shrugged. 'She was trying to protect you.'

'How can she know what's best for me? I'm somebody completely different, not at all like either of them!'

'Rose, they're just normal parents.' He remembered the mansion they lived in and thought, Can anyone live like that and stay normal?'

'Racists!'

He laughed. 'Face it, poppie, would you like your sister to marry a black man?'

'It would depend on the man, for God's sake!'

She was stiff with rage, her cheeks a furiously mottled pink. He went and put his arms round her and rocked her from side to side, saying nothing until she relaxed. Then he said, 'If you want to get mixed up with coloureds, you're going to have to learn how to handle stuff like that.'

She thought, Mixed up. Is he beginning to take me seriously at last? She said, feeling her anger subside at the thought, 'You and I are quite alike, considering.'

'Considering our different degrees of tan?'

'No, mompara! Our different backgrounds. I mean, we grew up at nearly opposite ends of the – '

' – tracks,' he put in, caressing her silky hair with his mouth.

'I was going to say, social spectrum. Yet we think a lot alike. Do you think we could be destined for each other?' She turned in his arms to face him, nose to nose.

'Don't count on it,' he said. 'Don't count on anything, Rose. Life's too damn complicated as it is without stirring in a whole lot of wishful thinking.'

She was mulling over what he could have meant during the silences of a long drive with Agnes. On her return from the beach, at a loose end with Jake still away and school not yet open, Rose had volunteered to take Agnes to see the plot of land her husband Harrison had secured for a retirement home.

She had not seen Agnes for some months, and was saddened by the changes that the onset of arthritis had made. She remembered her as a big bossy woman who had dominated a large part of her childhood; the picture she had kept in her mind was of the two of them sitting on the back stoep steps at Buckingham Circle, with the tea tray between them and Agnes's friendly potato face bent over a piece of embroidery. Now she had grown thin and old and sour, with varicose veins like grape clusters on her legs, and her eyes sunk deep in peevish wrinkles.

With only two people to care for and a younger woman to help her with the heavy work, Agnes's duties were not onerous. To Sarah's increasing irritation, however, she spent a lot of time sitting and sighing in the kitchen.

'No matter what I do to try and help her, she has a long face,' Sarah had said to Rose that morning before they left. 'We've offered to retire her on pension, but she says she isn't old enough to be useless yet, and she'd rather wait for Harrison to retire too. I take her to the arthritis clinic once a month, but she says the pills give her a headache and she'd rather have the pains. Then she sits moaning about how her joints ache when she has to go up and down the stairs. This is the trouble with servants who stay with you for a long time. They're like old dogs that you feel too guilty to give away or put down, because they've been part of the family for so long.'

Rose had been shocked. 'Mum, how can you talk about Agnes as though she's a dog? That's disgusting.'

Sarah sighed, unaware how like Agnes's sighs it was. 'It was only an analogy. And don't attack me like that. You know I'm a much better employer than most.'

'The whole idea of having servants is obscene.' Rose was thinking about the indignities related to her over the past two years by the domestic workers in her class: wages docked for accidentally dropping a glass, beatings by the master of the house for alleged stealing, dismissals for 'being cheeky'.

'It's part of the system in this country and I can't deny that I've benefited from it,' Sarah said. 'But you must also remember that domestic work offers employment to thousands of women who have no qualifications, and no hope of ever getting any. Did you know that Agnes is illiterate?'

'No. Why haven't you done something about it, then? You

could have. You could really have helped Agnes in a positive way by sending her to literacy classes.'

Sarah said crossly, 'I'm not supposed to know about it, that's why. Like I'm not supposed to know she smokes in her room and Harrison stays with her most nights and she helps herself to butter whenever she feels like it. That's how it is between employer and employed. There's a point past which you don't go because it would be an invasion of each other's privacy.'

'You should buy her butter.'

'I buy her margarine because that's what she asks for when we discuss her food. What *she* asks for.'

Goaded by the defensive look on Sarah's face, Rose said, 'Snappy today, aren't you, Mum?'

'Oh, shut up! I'm going to my studio.' And Sarah had gone off in a huff, leaving Rose wondering why she was so uncharacter-istically waspish. The holiday at the beach cottage didn't seem to have done her or Gordon any good at all. Are all parents like mine? Rose was thinking as she slowed the car to take the left turn Agnes had indicated. Our lives are light years apart.

The gravel road had been recently widened and graded. Rose said, 'Are you sure this is the right way?'

'Sure.' Agnes gave an emphatic nod. 'The gov'ment is fixing it up now-now for all the peoples coming to be living here.'

'What do you mean?'

'All the peoples from – ' and she named a squatter settlement near Pretoria whose demolition had been making headlines in the newspapers for some days.

Rose recalled the photograph on the front page of that morning's *Rand Daily Mail*, of a giant bulldozer crunching into a wood and iron shanty as though it were a tin can, while a family of eight stood helplessly watching next to their small pile of possessions. 'Is this where they're being moved to?' she asked, appalled.

Since they had turned off the main road they had been driving through Bophutatswana, one of the black areas promoted to 'independent' homelands that began to spread like patches of fungus on the map of South Africa after 1976. The veld on both sides of the road was overgrazed to the point of semi-desert. Every few hundred metres, clustered like ticks round borehole windmills, were settlements of mud-brick houses and corrugated iron lean-tos, each with its bare earth yard, its pumpkins and stones on the roof, its washing line propped up on forked branches and its scrawny dogs tied with ropes round their necks to running wires. Kaffir dogs.

Shamed that she could even think the ugly word, Rose said, 'I don't see any new houses.'

'They on a bit more. You can see just now.' Agnes indicated the road ahead.

'Will they be near your piece of land? Mum tells me that you and Harrison are hoping to start building soon.'

'Not so near, thanks be to God. I don't want such poor peoples living next to me. Is bad enough I have to live here.' She almost spat out the last word.

'But – '

'But nothing, my girl. Harrison, he's my husband. I must live where he says, but I don't like this far-out place! Why you think I keep on to work when my pains are so bad, eh? Because I don't want to come and live here, that's why.'

Rose thought, And none of us took the trouble to find out why she looks so unhappy all the time. She said, 'Does Harrison know?'

'He knows.' The head in the black doek nodded with bitter emphasis. 'He says if I don't like, is too bad. Here, he can have he's land and he's house and the white man can't take it away, not ever any more.'

'Your house too, surely?'

Agnes gave a grim laugh. 'You don't know the black mans, my girl. He's land, he's house.'

'What if you've helped pay for the house?' Rose knew that Agnes had been putting part of her wages into a building society account for years.

'Still it's he's house.' Agnes turned an accusing face to her. 'You know there's one law for white peoples, one law for black peoples in this country. And the law for black peoples says that a married woman is the same like a child.'

'Surely not?'

'Is true! The chief here by this place is telling me when I go to pay him for the land. Tribal custom, he says. Mans must look after the money for the womans.'

'But I thought the land was granted free?'

Agnes gave the grim laugh again, like a door slamming. 'Nothing is free in this place, my girl. Everything you want to do, you must pay the chief. You must pay if you want the permission to go and work in town. You must pay if you want land, if you want more cows, even if you want to put up a fowl hok. Why else you think the chief is so rich, eh?'

Rose remembered a young black student bursting out one night at Isidore's discussion group, 'The worst of this system is that it makes us prey on each other! If you know how to say "Yes, Baas" nicely, they make you a chief so you can wave a big stick and charge people what you like for the privileges you grant them. You should see how some of the chiefs live, even in the poorest areas.'

She said, 'How much did you have to pay, Agnes?'

'Two hundred.' Agnes spoke in a flat voice.

Rose thought, More than she earns in a month. It's daylight robbery. She was about to ask another question when Agnes said, pointing, 'See, that's where the poor peoples are being moved.'

It was a scene from a Kafka nightmare. On the right side of the road, stretching away as far as the eye could see, was row after row of shiny new corrugated iron lavatory huts, each with a concrete skirting and a nearby tap. 'Long drops.' Rose felt a laugh bubbling up. It was so incongruous, a forest of lavatories sprung up like tin mushrooms in this flat plain where little else grew. I must bring Jake to see this, she thought.

But next minute the laughter had died in her throat. 'Those ones are the first,' Agnes was saying.

Rising next to the row of lavatories closest to the road were the concrete-block beginnings of several houses. Their future occupants were living under an assortment of tarpaulins and sheets of plastic that wouldn't shelter anyone from a light shower, let alone a highveld thunderstorm. Cheap furniture stood about in rickety piles, its plastic veneer cracking and peeling in the sun. There were half-naked children and fowls and goats and dogs everywhere, either running about with drooling noses or sitting scratching themselves. Some government trucks were parked next to the second row of lavatories, and the possessions of the squatters who had been moved that morning were being unloaded while their owners stood by looking dazed.

'Shame, eh?' Agnes said.

Rose stopped the car so she could have a proper look. After a long minute, she said, 'Do they just drop people's belongings on the ground and leave them to get on with it? I thought the authorities provided houses.'

'Houses? You make a joke, my girl. If peoples want houses, they have to build theyselfs.'

'Even if they've been moved out of existing houses?'

'Sure.' The black doek nodded again. 'The gov'ment says, "We give you the cement, we give you the bricks, we give you the iron roof, you must build." But they lucky, those ones. Me and Harrison, we must buy everything to building our house. The gov'ment gives us nothing.'

'What if people can't build? If they're old, or the husband is away working?'

'Then they must live under the plastic or pay somebody else to build.' Agnes shook her head. 'They will be under the plastic long time, I think. In winter it will be too cold for the babies, and they will die. Is hard for black peoples.'

Her last words echoed in Rose's head all the way to the bare plot and home again, after Agnes had given it a single scornful glance. She did not seem to want to talk during the rest of the journey, sitting hunched and brooding in her seat, looking out the side window. Rose thought, People can't know what's happening out there, or there'd be more protests. But when she telephoned a friend who worked as a news reporter and told her, the friend laughed. 'Don't you read the papers? We carry reports about forced removals nearly every week.'

'Of course I read them,' Rose said.

'Then your eye probably skips over the things you don't want to know, like everyone else's does.' The friend's voice was ragged with too many cups of coffee and cigarettes, the journalist's tranquillisers. 'It never ceases to amaze me how little white South Africans know about what's happening under their complacent noses. It's not for lack of being told.'

'Haven't you tried to do something about the way these people are just dumped in the veld? Spoken to the officials concerned? Made a fuss?'

The noise that came over the telephone could have been a strangled scream. 'Made a fuss? Have you spoken to any officials recently? All they give you is the government line: we're pulling down the slums for the people's own good, and moving them to places where they can build decent, subsidised, properly serviced houses on their own land. You can't knock the reasoning. You just begin to get a bit cynical when you actually visit these little pieces of paradise and find they're in the middle of nowhere, and it takes hours by bus to get to any sort of employment, let alone a shop. Take my advice, Rose, and stay clear of journalism. You don't sleep too well at night.'

'I teach at an adult education centre,' Rose said, wanting her to know that she wasn't the only one who cared.

'Then I'm not telling you anything you don't already know. So do yourself a favour and emigrate before the insomnia gets too bad, like I'm planning to.'

'You're leaving?'

'Let's put it another way: I'm not staying to have my young life blighted by terminal guilt. They're advertising for journalists in Australia, so I'm off next month. They've been canny enough to give their miserably decimated blacks the vote, while keeping them well tucked away and supplied with plenty of booze in the outback. I don't expect a drop in the hypocrisy level there, but I hope to sleep better.'

The conversation depressed Rose for days. Most people don't concern themselves with things that happen outside the normal orbits of their lives, she thought. We live with blinkers on. Why?

Jake had an answer when she told him about the bleak resettlement scheme on the first night of his return. 'It's a squiff defence mechanism,' he said, lying with his head on her bare stomach and his eyes closed, 'like sticking your head in the sand so no one will see you. Th ostrich is so typically South African that we would have had to invent it, if it wasn't already there.'

'Oh, Jake,' she laughed with the joy of having him back again, making his head bounce up and down.

'S'true's bob,' he said, turning to look up at her with his eyes a darker, deeper green than she had ever seen them. 'The ostrich should be our national bird. It's stupid, and the males flaunt their feathers as though they're God's gift to humanity. It also comes in black and white and all shades of brown in between.'

'And it lays the biggest eggs in the world.' Rose could not stop laughing. 'What a yolk.'

But 1982 was to be no yolk. It brought the Falklands War, recession, chaos to Beirut, the ubiquitous video game, and the deaths of the enduring screen queens Ingrid Bergman and Grace Kelly. Closer to home, the government passed the Internal Security Act which sanctioned detention without trial, and for the first time in thirty-four years of increasingly authoritarian rule, the Nationalist Party monolith trembled and its right wing cracked off to form the Conservative Party.

'They'll be running the show in ten years' time,' Jake

predicted, 'and then there'll be hell to pop unless we can frighten the whites to their senses.'

'What do you mean by "frighten"?' Rose sat up so quickly from the cushions against which she was leaning drinking coffee that she spilt some of it on her blouse.

'Ag, you know, spell out the odds so you people know what you're up against.' Jake cursed himself for his slip of the tongue. To cover what would be frequent disappearances, he had told Rose that he had been put in charge of the distribution of underground political pamphlets all over the country. In fact, his second mission was to assemble and hide arms and explosives caches within easy reach of key townships in the Vaal Triangle, in preparation for what the Umkhonto we Sizwe leadership was calling with increasing confidence 'the forthcoming revolution'. When he had protested even more vehemently than last time, pointing out his failure in the matter of the police station bombings, his unit commander had said, 'The deal was three missions, Van Vuuren.'

'But I'm a teacher, not a munitions expert. I'm supposed to be handling communications and publicity.'

'Have you forgotten that we're fighting a war here? What did you think we were training you for, the boy scouts?'

'I said from the very beginning that I didn't want to use weapons,' Jake had insisted. 'It's not right to ask me.'

'Right? What's right about this situation, eh?' The commander had glared at him with the contempt of all military men for conscripts who blanch at the reek of cordite. 'You'll do what you have to, like the rest of us. Get those caches established chop chop, you hear?'

Now Rose's pale face was begging for reassurance. 'You promise that what you're doing isn't dangerous, Jake? I couldn't bear it if you were involved in anything that could hurt people, or if you lied to me.'

'I promise,' he said, and though his gaze was steady, he felt his heart give a sick thump at the betrayal. The poison in our society gets into every damn crack, he thought. It could kill me and Rose.

27

It is early evening. The thunderstorm has moved on, dragging the last of its black clouds behind like gun carriages. Overhead the sky is deepening to indigo, while the hectic flush of sunset fades to pale apricot above the valley's western rim. The wet earth is a rich, deep, dark red and there are trickles of rainwater running everywhere, down scoured paths, over steps, past hut doors, lacing the dirt road that runs through the village with a network of runnels that glint silver in the last light, but will be gone by morning. Children splash in and out of puddles, giddy with the exhilaration that rain brings after days of dryness and dust.

Sarah is walking down to the clinic with Gordon on one side and Didymus on the other. Both men keep a hand hovering near her elbow in case she slips and falls again; her thin leather sandals are already squelching with red mud that bubbles up between her toes. Though her head is beginning to ache and her limbs feel as though they are made of some heavy wood, numb all the way through, she looks around at the village preparing for the night.

From the hut doors come wedges of soft orange light thrown by fires and paraffin lamps, and the smell of cooking phuthu overlaid by the spicier smells of the meat and vegetable stews that will be spooned over each supper portion. The more fortunate families whose remittances from absent breadwinners come by postal order every month will sit down on their grass mats to stews enriched with sheep's knuckles or chicken gizzards or shreds of goat meat. The families whose breadwinners are out of work, or have spent their money on the easy women and mirror-laden bicycles and two-tone shoes that so easily tempt men new to the city, may have to eat their putu with wild spinach, or even dry. For some reason, rock-rabbits have been very scarce this year and the herdboys come home empty-handed nearly every afternoon.

The sounds of people moving and talking inside the huts they pass, the intermittent flicker of their cooking fires and occasional bursts of laughter, comfort Sarah like a warm poultice laid on the gaping, aching wound of the day. She thinks, Life goes on, as it must.

Gordon is thinking of Sister Quthing, whom they have left with two women helpers in the makeshift mortuary. During the next hour they will lay out and prepare the bodies of Rose and Jake for the rain-splashed wooden coffins that have been carried in and set down against the curved mud wall. Their wedding clothes have been brought from the cottage and lie across a chair: two fine cream wool caftans, Jake's hip-length with cream trousers, Rose's long. The circle of pink everlastings she wore in her hair lies on top of them; neither Gordon nor Sarah can bear to look at it after the first glance.

'You cannot stay,' Sister Quthing had said when both of them had protested about being sent away, 'you cannot. This is work I have been trained to do, and these women are used to helping me. I will call you when all is ready for the vigil.'

'But I want to help,' Sarah had insisted. 'She's my daughter. I have the right.'

The sister says gently, 'Please, you must not stay. It will not be nice to watch. Rather you should go down to the clinic and give Hope her supper. She is the one who needs you now. I promise to call you when they are lying peacefully again.'

Sarah had nodded and turned to go without another word, and now Gordon thinks, Quite a psychologist, that Sister. Not many people get the better of Sarah in this mood. I'm glad she made us leave. I don't want to see what else those murdering bastards did to Rose. I must concentrate on finding out who they were.

On the other side of Sarah, Didymus stumbles down the road in a daze of misery. For the past two hours he has been trying to talk to his God, who has not answered. Now it seems to him that his faith is fading with the last of the light, and that it may never return.

Not once in all his twenty-six years has even the smallest doubt entered his mind as to the existence of God, or His essential benevolence. Didymus's earliest memory is being held on his father's lap and read the story of Noah. His father peopled the Ark with the semi-desert creatures that lived in and around their Kuruman home – lizards and geometric-shelled tortoises, cobras like the one that had reared up at him near the kitchen steps before his nanny snatched him away to safety, pale bug-eyed geckos like those that skittered about the high ceilings at night, even a pair of diligent termites. As he grew older, his father had skilfully enriched God's kingdom with a panoply of spirited archangels and practical saints who went about His business with singleminded determination, and the marvelling child had grown into a young man who had never questioned the path his life had been expected to take.

Now his friends lie brutally dead and he stumbles in a nightmare, his crystal certainty shattered by a single hammer blow of logic. If God is absent in the face of such evil, maybe He isn't there at all?

Rose and Jake were sitting in the car by the dam on an afternoon in late August. After a day of furious wind that blew clouds of dust off the bone-dry highveld until the sky over the city was a murky beige and throats itched and tempers flared, the gale had subsided to the icy-keen stillness that follows a cold front moving in from the Antarctic. The low sun had no warmth, and their clasped hands were cold.

'You haven't shown me a poem for months,' Rose said.

'No time. You know that.'

'You mustn't stop writing. I know how important it is to you. It should take precedence over everything else.'

'Even over you?' He turned to her. His face looked drawn and yellow, the lines bracketing his mouth more deeply etched than ever.

'Even over me. I don't mind not seeing so much of you, honestly, if it gives you more time to write.'

He thought, What luxury, time to write. Sometimes he felt as though he was being stretched so thin between his separate lives that he would just snap one day like a rubber band. Chronic exhaustion had dulled the touchy aggression that had been his trademark at university; he felt a hundred years older than the angry student who had cursed every white person he met for the tan skin he had been born with. Four years of exile, and the year of teaching with Rose in a school where aspirations to succeed in a white world were part of the air everyone breathed, had taught him that the problem was infinitely more complex than a matter of skin colour.

Looking down at Rose's soft white hand clasped in his, a hand that could calm and soothe him on his worst days, he thought, And I am beginning to believe that the solution does not lie in violence at all, but in faith and reason.

To dispel the strained look on his face, Rose said, 'I came across that lovely poem of Spender's today in an anthology I was using in class:
"I think continually of those . . .
. . . who in their lives fought for life,
Who wore at their hearts the fire's centre."
It made me think of you when we first met, when you wore the fire's centre at your heart and tried to burn everyone who came too close.'

'Ja, I was a bugger in those days.' His smile was slow and tired. 'I don't know why you stuck with me.'

'I was a moth to your flame,' she said, joking.

'More like an egret to my veld fire. You could have got burned – could still get burned.' His face had gone serious again. 'I sometimes wish we hadn't started this, Rose. It would have been easier for both of us.'

'Meaning I'm just a complication in your life?'

'You know you are. I feel answerable to you now, where before I just had to worry about doing the right thing for myself.'

She said, 'Thanks very much for the compliment,' and tried to pull her hand away, but he held it fast.

'Don't take a huff now, Rose, man. We haven't got time for a fight. I've got to go out again tonight.' He was to meet a courier with a bigger than usual consignment, and had felt as though he was walking on razor blades all day.

Answerable. The word had hurt. She said with unusual sarcasm, 'I'd hate to stand in the way of your precious pamphlets.'

He felt himself wincing. The half-truths he had told her in the beginning had grown into lies he found harder and harder to sustain as he fell more deeply in love with her. Now the thought of her inevitable disgust and rejection when she learned what he was doing made him cling to the time they had together like a dwindling stock of gold dust, knowing it would soon be gone.

Terse orders transmitted via the couriers had commanded him to step up the random bombings that were making the country more and more jittery, and to leave the pamphlet printing on a clacking second-hand duplicator hidden in a city basement to eager local volunteers. Protesting again that he had not volunteered for sabotage, and questioned its morality, had been useless. The message back had said, 'We note your objections to the use of violence, comrade, but must repeat that the armed struggle is not aimed at civilians but at the agents and functionaries of the apartheid regime. Be strong and resolute in your work for peace and justice for our people.' His work. The man who fancied himself a poet caching guns and explosives like a killer squirrel. The Russian instructions on the limpet mines made him want to puke every time he saw them. He had nightmares every night about blowing his hands off, and Rose's face when he came to her holding out the bloody stumps.

She was saying, still in the same sarcastic voice, 'We can't allow our personal feelings to get in the way of the struggle, can we?'

'Ag, come on, poppie. We should be making love, not war.' He gave her hand a placating squeeze.

Wanting to hurt him too, she said, 'What's happened to the fire, anyway? It seems to be damped down now, and I don't know whether it's a good thing or not.'

'The fact is I haven't got either the time or the inclination to feed it.' He didn't appear to be hurt at all. 'Maybe it's just maturity creeping on.'

She thought, Now's the time to tackle him, and said, 'We've got to talk about our future, then.'

'What future?' He moved irritably in his seat. 'Don't start with that stuff now, Rose. You know how it's got to be between us, I've said it often enough. We take things day by day, and that's all.'

She looked down at their clasped hands, feeling a prickle of apprehension, and said, 'You always say that, but don't you see that I've got to have something to hold on to? I can't go on living in a vacuum, not allowing myself to dream in case the things I dream about don't ever happen. I'm twenty-six this year. I want to have babies before I'm too old to enjoy them.'

'You can't have babies with me, for God's sake! Don't even think of it.'

His panicky lick of anger made her think, The fire isn't so damped down after all. 'Why not?'

What could he say? Because I've been lying to you. I'm a dangerous man. I order bombs to be set that can kill people. If you really knew me, you wouldn't want to have kids with me. And how can I think of bringing kids into this stinking mess of a country we live in? He burst out, squeezing her hand until it hurt, 'Because they'll be coloured, dammit! Bushies. Do you really want babies with dark skins and black krissy hair?'

She felt her heart begin to thump with dread at what was coming. 'I wouldn't care what colour my kids were, as long as they were healthy. You should know that by now, Jake.'

'Shit, woman, haven't you heard anything I've said in all the time we've been together?' He was as angry as she had ever seen him, with a dull flush on both cheekbones. 'Being coloured in this country is being kicked in the teeth every day of your fucking life, and then some. I'm not going to bring my kids into a world where they're automatically inferior. I took that decision a long time ago.'

Cop-out! she thought, feeling her own anger stirring. He's beginning to use his colour as a scapegoat for every bad thing that's happened in his life. And if he goes on like this, there won't be room for any good things. She said, 'You make it sound as though you're ashamed of what you are.'

'You know damn well I'm not.'

'Then how can you object to my wanting children who look like you?' Fight him with logic, she was thinking. I've got to settle things between us. I can't go on the way we are. She turned to him and played her trump card. 'We don't have to live in this country to have them. We could go to a place where it wouldn't matter.'

'You'd leave – for me?' He looked as though she had hit him with an unexpected straight right.

But she lifted his hand to her lips, looking at him with the blue eyes that could stab his heart like blades. 'Haven't you heard what I've been saying in this year we've been together? I love you, Jake. I want to be with you all the time. And since we can't get married or even live together here without breaking the law, we'll just have to go somewhere else, won't we?'

'You make it sound so simple, but it isn't.' He closed his eyes and leaned his head back on the car seat, feeling the tiredness deep in his bones. How could she possibly know what she would be letting herself in for? She of the winter-blonde hair and skin like pale early peaches, who was used to getting her own way.

She was saying, 'To me it's simple. We love each other, so we go to a place where we can get married and get on with our lives,

313

working and having babies. Isn't that what most couples do?'

Babies. Couples. God, she was persistent. Were all white women like this?' He said, 'You seem to forget that I'm committed to doing a job here – '

'We can wait till it's finished, of course.'

' – and that other countries may not want us.'

'Oh, rubbish, Jake! I can't think of many African countries that would turn away two skilled, qualified teachers. And we could buy a home with some of my trust fund,' she slipped in, having waited months for an opportunity to mention it.

'What do you mean, trust fund?' He sat up to glare at her. 'I know your folks are well off, but you never mentioned anything like that.'

'I thought I might lose you if I did. You're so touchy about money.' She thought, Careful, Rosie. Don't blow it. 'My grandfather left Mum some money when he died, and she put it into a trust fund for me. I've hardly touched it. We could use it to buy a house if we needed to.'

'That will be the day I live off my wife!' He twisted towards her, making the car seat shudder. 'Who do you think I am, a bleddy gigolo?'

Trying to hide her triumph at his use of the word 'wife', she said, 'That's not what I said. I said we could buy a house if we needed to. The money's intended to ensure my future security, and a house would be exactly that. I don't know what you're making such a fuss about.'

'You've got the wrong man if you think I'd ever be bought.' He was furious. 'It's for the man to provide the house in a marriage, anyway.'

'Don't be so old-fashioned, Jake. It doesn't matter one little bit who provides the house.'

'It matters to me.'

'But that's ridiculous.'

'Is it?' She had never seen his eyes such a deep, dark, serious green. 'Are my feelings ridiculous, compared with your need to spread your money around to make yourself feel better about it? You talk about marriage, but the differences between us are like huge dongas with crumbling edges that aren't strong enough to take bridges. You know so little about me that it frightens me.'

'I know more than you think.' It was now or never. Her voice trembled, then steadied again. 'I know that you're involved with more than just spreading pamphlets around, for one thing.'

'What – '

'Don't deny it, Jake. I'm not a fool. I read the papers. I've watched you for months, coming and going. I see your eyes sliding away when you tell me lies about what you've been doing. You're connected with the bombings, aren't you?' Her face was as white as milk.

'What if I am?' He spoke in dread, but relief was flooding through his body. She knew. It would be over now. He could make a clean break, stop living this Yo-Yo life.

'So it is true.' She had been trying so hard to persuade herself that it wasn't. That she had been imagining things. That they could go away and make a life together like other young couples did – young couples who lived in countries where colour didn't dominate their lives, where angry men didn't set bombs and shoot children and fight each other to the death in the name of peace. If there were any such countries. She sagged back in her seat, pulling her cold hand away from him. 'I've been dreaming dreams like an idiot with you and me in the starring roles, when all the time you were just using me.'

'That's not true.' His voice was as full of pain now as hers was. 'You know I love you, Rose.'

It was the first time he had admitted it, and if he had said it ten minutes earlier she would have been filled with joy. Now she said with tears seeping from her eyes, 'What hurts most is that you didn't think you could tell me the truth.'

'How could I, when I'd just found you again? You'd have told me to get out, and I wanted more than anything to stay.'

'To use me, you mean.' She put her head down on the steering wheel with the blonde hair falling over her face, her muffled words spilling out as fast as her tears. 'You came to the house in the first place because you remembered that I was a gullible white lefty with more money than sense, and you thought I'd be useful. And I was, wasn't I? I was bloody perfect. I provided a job, a car to get around in, a place to sleep, a body to use.' She remembered the bombing that had happened during the Christmas holidays when she'd been down at the coast. 'Did you get that woman to mine the police stations by sleeping with her too?'

'No! I don't do things that way.'

Her voice grew even more bitter. 'No wonder you've never wanted to talk about the future. "We live from day to day,"

315

you've always said. And I swallowed it because I wanted to believe you.'

'But you're wrong.' He put his arm over her hunched shoulders and tried to turn her wet face towards him, begging her to understand. 'I didn't come to use you, cross my heart. I came in the first place just to say sorry – '

'Sorry! Oh God, I wish I'd never seen you again.'

'To say sorry for the way I left four years ago. I had a lot of time to think in the camps; there wasn't much else to do in our free time, besides sleep. Every time I thought about you, I remembered what I'd said and how I'd acted like a real arsehole, blaming you for what was happening in Soweto. So when they finally sent me back, I reckoned I'd come and say sorry. That was all.' She felt the arm round her shoulders tighten as his voice became indignant. 'Hell, I never meant to fall for you. You were a complication I never asked for.'

She sobbed, 'You keep calling me a complication. Is that really how you see me?'

He dropped his head against hers, feeling his insides tearing like silk, and said in a hoarse voice she had never heard before, 'I wish it was. I wish you'd never let me come into your house that first night, or into your bed to wrap your white soul and your white body round me so they'll never let go, no matter how hard I try. You'll haunt me for the rest of my life.'

They sat like that until her crying subsided and she sat up with her head turned away from him, wiping her wet face with the back of her hand. It was late afternoon now, with the winter sunlight slanting through the gum trees on the far side of the dam like swords. The cold air outside was beginning to invade the temporary warmth they had created inside the car, creeping up from her feet, even in their woollen socks, like the onset of death. She shivered and reached down for the boots that she had kicked off earlier.

He broke the silence first. 'I'll have to leave the teaching. I'm sorry about that.'

'But you've got much more important things to do, haven't you?' Her tone was low and vicious. 'Like getting your next lot of bombs ready.'

He did not answer.

'I only hope,' Rose went on, 'that you stick to buildings and don't start on people. If anybody, and I mean *anybody*, gets hurt, I'm going to the police to tell them everything I know about you.'

He nodded, almost welcoming the pain of her words. He had been dreading this for so long.

'The only thing that stops me from going now is that they'll stick me in jail for harbouring a terrorist, and we couldn't both let Father Basil down.' She gave the window a grim smile. 'Not to mention my poor unsuspecting parents.'

The mention of her lanie parents made him burst out, 'Ag, never mind, poppie, you've got your trust fund to keep you warm. You'll easily be able to buy a better husband than I would have been. And if he's white, you can stay right here in good old sunny South Africa without making any noble sacrifices.'

Maybe if she concentrated on other things, she could pretend he hadn't said it. She turned the key in the starter and reversed, saying through lips that moved with difficulty, 'Where would you like me to drop you?'

'Over a cliff, preferably.' His laugh was like a rusty tin can being kicked. 'Failing that, the nearest bus stop. My bike's in town being serviced.'

'What about your things?' He had kept a change of clothing and a cardboard box of books and notes in her room.

'I'll come and fetch them sometime.'

'Make it soon.' She drove too fast along the grassy road that ran through the trees, not caring that the car was scraping on the middelmannetjie.

'Want me out of your life double quick now, hey?' He gave the unpleasant laugh again.

She felt the traitor tears come sliding out again, blurring the road, and cried, 'What did you expect me to do, cheer you on? Hold the detonators while you fixed the charges? Bombs are disgusting, terrible things! They kill and maim and frighten.'

'These ones are only meant to frighten.'

'If you think that, you're more of a fool than I am! And that's saying something.'

The silence between them lasted all the way to the bus stop where she stopped the car and said, 'This is as far as the free taxi service goes.'

'Dankie, Miesies.' The mockery was savage.

She watched him out of the watery corner of her eye as he turned to open the door. His back looked thin under the red sweater she had knitted him at the beginning of the winter, and given him with a joke about it being a commie sweater.

'That's not even funny,' he had said into her hair as he

317

hugged her in gratitude. 'You know why I joined the ANC.'

She had thought she had known. How could she have been so wrong?

After he had got out, he bent down and said through the open door, 'I'll say it once again before you go. I'm sorry, and I didn't mean to hurt you. Just one thing I ask: try to understand why people like me are doing what you call these disgusting, terrible things, OK?'

The word rang in her head night after lonely night for months as she cried into her pillow. 'Understand. Understand.' She didn't think she would ever understand how anyone could put a cause before a person they loved. But then I'm white. I don't have to, she thought sadly. And the word kept ringing through her head in his voice, 'Understand. Understand. Understand.'

28

Gordon stands by the door of the small room off the clinic ward, watching the lamplight on Sarah's face as she cradles and feeds their granddaughter. She is frowning with concentration, not having fed a baby for over twenty-five years. 'I'd forgotten how small they were,' she says in a quiet voice, not wanting to disturb the contented rhythm of the child's sucking.

Gordon thinks, It's not going to be easy for her, starting all over again with a baby. He says, 'Do you think we'll be able to do it? Bring her up as she should be, I mean. The prospect of going through all that again is a bit daunting.'

'We'll do it.' There is no doubt in Sarah's voice.

'Your painting will suffer.'

The blue eyes lance up at him, though she keeps her voice quiet. 'My painting will have to take second place. What matters now is making Hope happy.'

'I agree, of course, but you forget how – '

'I haven't forgotten. It won't be easy.' Sarah sighs, remembering Rose as a determined small girl who always wanted to do everything herself. 'But we can afford to pay for help now. The first thing I'm going to do is look for a nursing sister experienced with babies. I'm sure Sister Quthing will know someone she can recommend.'

'Good idea.' Gordon thinks, The older I get, the more I appreciate having enough money to pay for the best. They were worth it, those years of slogging.

'She'll need to have others of her own age to play with, too. I could start a small play group on the farm for her and the labourers' children, and get in a qualified nursery school teacher.' Sarah's voice is picking up enthusiasm as the idea expands in her head. 'Children from neighbouring farms could come too. I know at least two nearby farmers' wives with babies about this age.'

'Hold on.' Gordon goes to her, putting his hand on her shoulder. 'We've got to be realistic. White parents may not be entirely amenable to – '

'If they aren't, we don't need their kids!' Sarah flares, protectively tightening her arm.

Startled, the child stops sucking and two wondering eyes gaze up at her face as if to say, Who are you, then?

Sarah relaxes her arm at once and jiggles the teat in the child's still mouth. 'Don't stop now, Hope. I'm sorry I distracted you. Keep going, lovey.'

But the child's mouth remains still and a pucker appears between the tiny arched eyebrows. These are not the arms or the voice she is used to, and the bottle's plastic teat is hard and foreign-feeling. She opens her mouth to reject it, and the suction is released with an implosion of air that cuts off the comforting trickle of warm milk. Her little body arches back, face crumpled, mouth in an O as she draws in her breath for a wail of loss and strangeness.

Sarah puts the bottle down on the table next to the easy chair she is sitting on and lifts the child to cuddle her, patting the small blanket-swaddled back and crooning, 'Don't cry, sweetheart, don't cry. Your granny's just a bit clumsy, that's all. Don't cry. I'll get it right.' The recesses of the little warm neck smell of baby powder and milk, the soft sweet smells of babyhood that give Sarah a cruel jolt of memory: David, held like this, his bony chest struggling to breathe. David and Rose, both dead.

Gordon sees the tears coming again and tightens his hand on her shoulder, not knowing what else to do. Thank God she has the child, he is thinking. Someone to hold on to when the pain comes. They are both crying, the silver head and the small dark curly head nestled into each other in an ecstasy of shared grief. He has cried too today, but it doesn't seem to have dissipated the rage he still feels whenever he thinks of Rose.

It is a relief when there is a knock at the door, and Cordelia Motaung's voice says, 'Mr Kimber?'

He goes to the door and opens it a crack. Sarah needs her privacy more than ever now. 'I'm here.'

Cordelia says, 'The ANC delegates from Lusaka have arrived. They're in the government offices. Max sent me to tell you.'

A surge of adrenalin makes his heart give another strong

double thump. These men may know who killed Rose. 'Shall I come now?'

Cordelia's kind muddy eyes move to the sobbing woman and child. 'Not if you're needed here, of course.'

He gives her a brief, sad smile. 'I'm not really needed. They need time to heal, not a helpless hovering male. I'd like to come.' He goes back to Sarah and bends down. 'Mrs Motaung wants me to go and meet someone. Will you be all right on your own?'

Sarah nods and holds the baby closer.

'You don't mind?'

Sarah shakes her head, as much to try and stop the racking sobs that seem to be tearing the fabric of her body apart, as in denial. 'Go. We'll be all right.'

He closes the door as quietly as he can and follows Cordelia past the row of stilt-legged hospital beds, their white cotton counterpanes gleaming in the blare of light thrown by a row of naked light bulbs dangling from the ceiling. Noticing his upward glance, Cordelia says, 'Even tin lampshades cost, these days.'

Outside the clinic door is another light, but the track stretches away between the huts in darkness, broken only by the lozenges of firelight spilling from their doorways. Cordelia goes ahead of him, shining a torch on the ground so he can see where he is going. The only other electric lights in the village are blazing from the government offices, outside which several cars are parked. As they get closer, he sees that the newcomers are taxis from Maseru: two old brown Valiants and a black Chev with sagging back springs. Tshabalala's metallic blue BMW looks like a scarab at a gathering of dung beetles.

Cordelia stops at the bottom of the steps up to the public entrance. 'Do you know who you have come to meet?'

'No. Tshabalala just said that one of your DIP officials would be coming.'

'Not mine,' Cordelia says quickly. 'I'm not ANC. I firmly believe teachers shouldn't get mixed up in politics.'

'Or violence?'

'That goes without saying.' Cordelia's short answer shows her annoyance. 'You should know that by now.'

Gordon turns to look at her strong round face, which despite the coolness after the thunderstorm is covered in a fine sweat that gleams in the lamplight. He says, 'I thought I knew a lot of things that have been turned upside down today. I'm sorry.'

She nods her acceptance of his apology. 'I think you don't understand the position of the ANC here in Lesotho. We already have our independence so we don't need a liberation movement, but of course we are sympathetic. Our Prime Minister, Chief Jonathan, is another matter. He will tolerate the ANC and its training camps only as long as it suits him to stick his thumbs in his ears and waggle his fingers at the South Africans.'

'And when they get angry and crack the whip?'

She shrugs. 'We're completely surrounded by them, and more than half Lesotho's income comes from the wages of our men who go over the border to work, mostly on the mines. Our sympathy cannot stretch too far.'

'You seem on friendly enough terms with Maxwell Tshabalala.'

'He is a very old friend.'

A silence falls between them. Both are holding back from going inside: Cordelia because she knows that the coming meeting will be a difficult one, and Gordon because he wants to go on talking to her. The only black women he has had any real contact with have been the domestics who have worked in his homes over the years: quiet Doris, prim bespectacled Albertina, bossy Agnes – and Gloria, who made enemies because she tried so hard. Now that he is taking into his home a granddaughter who carries the blood of black women in her veins, he wants to know more about them so he can be ready to defend her when the time comes. As it inevitably will. Farming communities are always conservative, and the one he and Sarah live in is no exception. A coloured child living in the main house with its white grandparents, as opposed to one of the labourers' huts with its black mother, will not easily find acceptance among its peers.

There is a burst of voices from one of the office windows. Cordelia says, 'Come, we should go in. The man you have come to meet is Ndlondlo, and he is not one to wait patiently.'

Ndlondlo. The Zulu word for the venomous horned adder, which buries itself by shimmying down into soft sand until its buff and grey and brown markings are invisible and only the twin eye-knobs and its tail are showing. Then it lies dead still, twitching the tip of its tail to attract its lizard prey. Gordon feels a crawling between his shoulder blades. The South African news media are not yet terminally censored, and the man they call Ndlondlo is spoken of as dedicated and ruthless. He is also a

322

gifted public speaker who recently aroused a great deal of sympathy for the ANC during a tour of Western capitals.

Gordon says, 'Why has he come? Rose always said that Jake wasn't anyone important in the organisation.'

'Of course, for the publicity value of this funeral.' Cordelia is surprised that he should ask. 'Two good young people murdered by the racists, with their baby at the graveside. The photographs and news reports will go all over the world showing a huge crowd mourning, with the ANC flag in the background.'

'I won't allow it! Tshabalala promised me – '

Cordelia says quietly, 'We of the village don't like it either. Ndlondlo coming here turns our community into a target, as if the camp up the valley wasn't bad enough. But we can't stop him coming.'

'Surely you can? An appeal to your government?'

She shakes her head and says, 'We can do nothing. You will see now why.' Her face has taken on the sullen look of people who know they can't change their circumstances, no matter how hard they try. He has not thought to see it on this capable woman's face.

'Take me to him.' Gordon starts up the steps, his stocky body recharged with the energy of rage. The crisp checked shirt and khaki shorts he put on in the grey of early morning are now dusty and limp with sweat. He is on the wrong side of middle age, his body runs to fat round the middle, his face is too florid and his scarred heart thumps when he gets excited, yet he can still move almost as fast and purposefully as the young surfer he was once, specially when he is angry. Cordelia has to run to keep up with him.

As he storms into the main office, two men in camouflage uniforms converge from either side of the door to bar his way with the AK 47 rifles they are holding. He lifts an arm to push them away. 'Let me through.'

'You must stop.' It is spoken from an unsmiling face shadowed by the peak of a camouflage cap. The rifles are held rock-steady.

Gordon turns to Cordelia. 'What the hell is this?'

'Precautions. Ndlondlo is a much wanted man. He never moves without his bodyguard.' She turns to the man who has spoken and says something in Sesotho.

He stares at Gordon without moving, still black eyes in an impassive face. There is something in him of the way a large buck lifts its head and stands motionless in the bush when it has heard an unfamiliar noise. Gordon is left in no doubt that he is the intruder here. Then the rifle moves back, followed by the second rifle, and the two men resume their posts on either side of the door, their eyes fixed on a point above his head.

'Am I permitted to go through?' he says sarcastically. 'I would have thought my credentials in this place were above suspicion by now.'

Cordelia motions him forward with her hand. 'Ndlondlo's men make no exceptions. Understandably.'

He stands at the entrance to the corridor. 'Which office?'

'That one – at the end.'

There are more armed men in camouflage uniforms in the corridor, two standing outside the office Cordelia has indicated. He strides towards it, swings into the doorway and stops.

Three men are standing in front of a desk, one of them Tshabalala. The man on his left has untidy grey hair that looks as though it was cut some time ago with gardening shears; he wears a rumpled tweed jacket and thick glasses that have slipped down his large pink nose. He has the look of a professor doing his best to project absentmindedness, though the sharp grey eyes behind the glasses belie it. The man on his right is the angry official Gordon argued with at lunchtime when he came to fetch water for Sarah. Both regard him with annoyance, as though he has interrupted something. Cordelia, having taken one look into the office, melts back into the corridor.

A fourth man is seated behind the desk in a swivel chair as large as a throne with a black leather seat and wooden arms, another relic of the colonial past. It is his frowning upward look that temporarily stops Gordon: if it were not black, the lean, severe face with its knobbed eyebrows could have been that of his prep school headmaster forty years ago, when headmasters still carried canes and could freeze little boys in their tracks with a disapproving look. But instead of a shiny navy suit he wears a beige sports coat, an open-neck white shirt and a fashionably styled Afro haircut. His long thin fingers are laced together on the desk in front of him like a tangle of baby snakes. His skin is very dark, almost the colour of black grapes with the bloom rubbed off.

Tshabalala turns round and says, 'Ah, you've come. These are my colleagues from Lusaka: Ndlondlo from the Department

324

of Information and Publicity,' he indicates the man in the swivel chair, 'and Aubrey Stimson of the Political-Military Council. Mr Phetla I think you have already met.'

'Yes.' Gordon gives the angry official a nod, which is not returned.

The man in the chair says, 'Mr Kimber, is it?' He unlaces the tangle of serpents to hold a hand out over the desk.

Gordon moves forward to shake it in the spirit of a boxer touching gloves with his opponent, then says without preamble, 'One thing I must know first. Have your people any idea who killed my girl?'

Ndlondlo does not invite him to sit down. 'The so-called Lesotho Liberation Army has claimed responsibility, but that's just whitewash. According to our intelligence, the signs point only one possible way.'

'Over the border?'

'Yes. But I must warn you not to try and take action on your own, Mr Kimber. We suspect that this may be the work of a group operating independently of the South African army and unknown to most members of your government. We don't want it disturbed or threatened in any way until we know more about it.'

Gordon is appalled. 'Do you mean to tell me – ?'

Ndlondlo says, with the pedantic air of an English lecturer who will not use one word where five will do, 'The South Africans cannot be seen to be wiping out their opponents in the freedom struggle too blatantly. Certain incidents have led us to believe that a secret service of mercenaries, many of them ex-Rhodesians, has been established to do their dirty work for them. These killers are a law unto themselves. Once they get the go-ahead to achieve a certain objective, they plan their own operation and carry it out without telling anybody. This way, the South Africans can truly say they know nothing.'

'Are you sure about this?'

'We have no hard evidence as yet but we have heard very strong rumours. However, I must repeat my warning to you: don't try to go after these people personally. They are extremely dangerous, and it would jeopardise our chances of neutralising them.'

Neutralising. Gordon thinks, Is that what Rose's killers thought they were doing when they pumped bullets into her? Just neutralising her? What sort of mindless, cold-blooded war are we fighting here? To blot out the thought, he goes on in a belligerent voice, 'I also want to know exactly what arrangements have been decided on for the funeral. I've told Tshabalala already that we want it to be as private as possible, and he –'

'It is not a question of what you want, Mr Kimber. Surely you understand that?' Ndlondlo's voice is as cold and smooth as snake scales.

'What do you mean?'

'It is a question of how best to bring this atrocity to the attention of the outside world. That is the reason I have come.'

'It's my daughter's funeral, man!'

'Your daughter for whom we all grieve very much. I would like you to remember that. She was a loyal and supportive worker, a great loss to us all.' The words sound like the eulogy he expects to be making tomorrow in front of the world's TV cameras. 'I don't have to remind you that it is also the funeral of one of our most valued members, a man who has given his life for the freedom struggle.'

'You're trying to make political capital out of a tragedy. I won't have it!'

'You have no say at all in the matter, Mr Kimber.' The dark face across the desk relaxes its severity to give a thin smile. 'We have taken charge here, and we will decide what is to be done.'

'Over my dead body!'

Ndlondlo leans back in the chair, lacing the serpent fingers over his belt, still smiling. 'Pardon me, sir, but don't you think there have been enough dead bodies here today? I advise you to accept our arrangements, or the situation will become even more unpleasant than it already is.' The 'sir' is not intended as a politeness.

Gordon bursts out, 'Why the hell should I? Who are you to tell me how to bury my daughter?'

'Who am I?' The smile is instantly switched off. 'I am one of the men who conceived the strategy of making the township ghettoes ungovernable so as to hasten the downfall of the apartheid regime. I am somebody to reckon with in Southern Africa, Mr Kimber.'

'You're a bloody Marxist, that I do know!'

Ndlondlo shrugs. 'I believe the struggle against national oppression and the struggle against capitalist exploitation are complementary to each other, if that is what you mean by Marxist.'

326

'That's just jargon,' Gordon says with scorn. 'What I mean by Marxist is someone who wants to destroy our society because of some loony ideal formulated at the time of Queen Victoria which has never been proved to work. And who wants to force his system on everyone else, whether they want it or not.'

'But forcing your system on us is acceptable?'

'That's not what I'm saying. I believe the only way out of the quicksand we're all in is to get together and hammer out a life raft that floats, however inadequate it may be at first.'

'Impossible.' Ndlondlo's right hand signals an emphatic negative. 'We are class enemies, and always will be. Your British writer, Joyce Cary, got it right when he said, "The only good government is a bad one in the hell of a fright." It is our intention to give your government such a fright that it gives up the ghost.'

'I am not British, and it is not my government since I've never voted for it!' Gordon shouts.

The men on either side of him move uneasily. Nobody speaks to Ndlondlo like this. He leans forward over the desk and hisses, 'The hell it isn't!'

'You keep forgetting that I'm an African too.' Gordon says this without irony. In his struggle to accept Jake as Rose's husband, and his often difficult adjustment to his new life as a farmer working with peasant labourers, he has begun to see himself in the physical context of Africa rather than as the world citizen he had thought himself on his business travels. He and Sarah find it hard to leave the farm now; coming to see Rose has been a major expedition. And a wild goose chase, he thinks with weary grief. It has been a long day and he is very tired.

The swivel chair squeals on the other side of the desk. Ndlondlo is rearing up, forefinger jabbing. 'You are no African! You are a foreigner here.'

Gordon looks at him and says nothing. It is hard for a white African to argue against those his forefathers have exploited and patronised as inferior beings, however strongly he may feel he belongs there by right of birth and a tenure longer than most Americans. He has to endure their righteous anger as partial atonement before trying to plead his case. Gordon has learned this from Jake. He thinks now, with surprise, I'll miss them both. Jake and I were just beginning to appreciate each other.

'You know nothing of being an African!' The thin face across the desk looks as though it has been scored in anger patterns by

327

a hot poker. 'You say Marxists want to force their system on everyone else? You can talk! Africa has been repeatedly raped since the first white man set foot here. You forced your cold foreign culture on us while you drew lines on the map to divide us up into nice neat chunks and make the job of raping us easier.

'But that was only the beginning of the pillage. Next you looted our diamonds and precious minerals, and after that you took our land to plant useless crops like tobacco and coffee and cocoa and sisal and palm oil – things you wanted to make your cosy white lives more luxurious, not the food we needed to stay alive. The result when you left? Creeping desert, famine and starvation. Pathetic photographs in the world press of kids with big eyes and sticks for legs and flies around their mouths. Isn't it terrible how Africans can't even look after themselves?

'So then we get condescending offers of foreign aid from the very whites who did the raping in the first place, three-quarters of which sticks to the fingers of the black puppets they left behind them to keep up the good work. WaBenzi, we call these so civilised black gentlemen, because of their Mercedes Benz limousines. When they are not busy moving the stolen money into Swiss bank accounts, they open new conference centres and stadiums and airports with their names on them.

'And meantime the people starve. Are you starving, Mr Kimber? Are you so poor that you have to live in a tin shack with the rain coming in? Do you have too many kids, too little work, and no say in the way your country is run, even though you pay your taxes? If the answer to these questions is No, then you are not an African.'

'I bloody am, and you know it!' Gordon can blaze too. 'I'm an African and my tribe is in power, with such a strong army that it is likely to remain in power for years to come. Those are the facts. The trouble with you people is that you refuse to recognise them. You're applying outmoded theories of revolution to a situation Marx never dreamed of. When you send impatient young men like Jake to set bombs that are about as effective as fireworks, you're farting against thunder.'

'I don't use such language!'

'That's just the trouble! We need to use plain language with each other. To reason together.'

'We tried reason, and where did it get us? Nowhere. Our leaders in jail, our people divided, our kids deprived even of decent schools. Reason, suka!'

They are shouting at each other from either side of the desk, but it could be across the Zambezi. Each is furious that the other is not responding to what seem like powerful arguments.

'Please.' Tshabalala puts a heavy arm across Gordon's shoulders and tries to turn him away from the desk. 'This sort of thing is no good. We have agreed already, you and I, on the details.'

Resisting the pressure, Gordon insists, 'I want to hear them from him.'

'I have neither the time nor the inclination.' The man across the desk stands up, smoothing the lapels of his sports jacket. 'We have more important things to discuss. You will be told tomorrow.'

'I want to know now! It's my right.'

Again the thin smile. 'You talk of right? Don't make me laugh. We will give you our decision about the funeral arrangements tomorrow. Good night, Mr Kimber.'

He is dismissed. Ndlondlo's mouth is clamped in the hard line Gordon remembers well on his headmaster's face when there was no more to be said on a matter. He turns and says to Tshabalala, 'I'll be on the steps of these offices first thing in the morning.'

The big man says, 'We have the grave to dig first, remember.'

'I'll be ready whenever you want me.'

'Maybe it would be better if I came for you at the place where you are holding the vigil. I'll be there soon after first light.'

'See you then. Thanks.' Gordon turns his back on Ndlondlo and the two other men, and walks out into the corridor to join Cordelia.

With Jake gone, Rose found herself with a lot of empty time. Ursula was heavily involved with a surgeon and the research for her doctorate, which left little time for socialising. Boff was working long hours for a computer company and playing provincial rugby, so they hardly ever saw him. Colin had emigrated to Australia to practise his skills on outback children suffering from isolation problems, and wrote occasional funny letters about his tribulations as a flying psychologist. Didymus had taken over Colin's room for his last year at university before going on to theological college and ordination. To earn the extra rent money, he had found himself a job in a Hillbrow fast-food restaurant. Often Rose was the only one sitting at the kitchen table in the evenings.

There were fewer parties, and even at the ones she went to, everyone seemed to be paired off. She began to go home for weekends, where she would lie by the pool for hours listlessly reading or sleeping. Sarah and Gordon were pleased to see more of her, but puzzled; when they asked why she was depressed, Rose said that a love affair had gone sour. She had not told them about Jake's return and she would not tell them about his leaving. The reason would have made them voluble with condemnation and gratitude, which she could not have borne. Being an only child grew no easier as she grew older. When they heard her car wheels on the gravel drive, Sarah and Gordon would drop what they were doing and insist on sitting down over tea or a drink to hear what she had been doing that week, who she had been seeing, where she had been partying, pouring their concern and love over her until she felt suffocated and had to escape to the pool. Why did David have to go and die? she found herself thinking crossly sometimes.

Sarah was enjoying her mid-forties, with a growing reputation that made even the men at business dinners speak to her with deference, which made her smile. She had once longed to be as slim and assured and *soignée* as their pampered wives. Now the same women sought her opinions and envied her bright, comfortable caftans and casually tied-back hair and blunt fingernails as symbols of an exotic artiness which gave her a standing that eluded them. A woman with turquoise eyelids and rings like knuckle-dusters on all her fingers said to her at a cocktail party, gushing sincerity, 'You're so lucky to have such a wonderful gift!' Thinking of the years of solitary work behind her, Sarah had to bite the insides of her cheeks not to burst out laughing. She was a long way from the resentful girl in jeans who had walked into the Durban church hall for art lessons.

Gordon was busier than ever, rushing off between board meetings on punishing business trips that often took him overseas. He made a concession to Sarah's worries about his health by travelling first class so he could sleep on long flights, though indigestion from the bounteous meals he was served meant that his sleep was fitful. At least, he called it indigestion. He did not tell her that the company doctor had stopped him in the passage one morning and said, 'If you don't have a check-up soon, sir, I'll not be responsible for the consequences.'

330

'No time,' Gordon had barked.

'You'll have time enough one day,' the doctor had said cryptically as he walked on.

Gordon paid lip-service to his warning by ordering grilled fish instead of steak at his business lunches, and single instead of double whiskies. His neck bulged over his tailor-made collars. When the company of which he was now executive chairman achieved a record turnover for the third year running, the board offered him and Sarah a month's cruise but he turned it down, saying that he didn't want to miss out on an upcoming merger. The real reason was that he didn't know what he would do with himself, cooped up on a ship for a month. When he told Sarah about it, she agreed.

Rose was too miserable to notice either the state of her father's health or the fact that Sarah sometimes stood in the studio window making sketches of her as she drooped or lay by the pool. The five paintings that grew out of the sketches, titled collectively *Dejected Naiad*, were said by critics to be some of Sarah's finest work. Two were bought by the Johannesburg Art Gallery. Rose went to see them to please her mother, but did not stay long. It was uncomfortable seeing herself sprawled larger than life on a public wall, and Sarah had so exactly caught her mood of gnawing sadness that she could not bear to look at it for too long.

Father Basil felt the loss of Jake nearly as badly as she did. 'That young man was one of the best teachers I've ever had. What happened, Rose?'

'I finally made myself face the truth.' She was sitting in his office. 'He's been more involved than I thought with things I can't accept.'

Father Basil nodded his understanding of what she had left unsaid. 'The loss of trust is like a small death. I'm sorry, girl.'

The sympathy in the grey eyes watching her like wise rabbits from under the shaggy hedges of his eyebrows brought a rush of tears. She said, 'If only he hadn't lied to me.'

'Would you have rejected him if he had told you the truth from the beginning?'

'I don't know.' She looked away out the window at the dreary view of mine dumps. 'It's so hard to know in our situation. I understand why Jake is doing these things and that he feels he has no choice. I'd probably be doing exactly the same if I were coloured, and brave enough. But I can't get out of my mind the idea of a bomb going off and people getting hurt.' She shivered.

'Is that what he's up to? Bombs?' The eyebrows drew together in a black frown.

'Not big ones,' she said quickly, then thought, What has size got to do with it, stupid? A bomb's a bomb. Designed to destroy and kill. She went on, 'From what I could get out of him when he came to fetch his stuff from my room, he thought that his mission was just to handle publicity. Part of the job was to stockpile the components of pamphlet bombs – you know, the ones that have been going off in shopping centres, scattering handbills printed by the underground press. Then they started sending him other things.'

'Guns?'

She was unable to look at him. 'Limpet mines too, and hand grenades and more explosives. He protested, he says, but they told him to shut up and obey orders. That I believe, Father. Jake is an angry man, not violent.'

'He's probably the co-ordinator. And you are torn between your feeling for him and your certain knowledge that if you don't report them, people may get hurt.'

She nodded, and more tears slid off her face. 'I'm being a coward. I know what I should do.'

'Do you know where he lives, then?'

'No. From the beginning he wouldn't tell me. It's somewhere south, I think. Probably on a farm or smallholding, judging by the mud on his motorbike tyres.'

'So you don't know where these – things are stored?'

'No. I wouldn't have much to tell if I did decide to go to the police, but at least they'd be warned.'

'And you would be in detention, and St Aloysius would be without two English teachers instead of one.'

Her spike-lashed upward glance told him that he had it right. He leaned back in his chair and put his hand over his face to think. She watched him tease the problem out, a large man in a black cassock frayed at the cuffs and elbows with hard use, his feet with their black-tufted toes resting on top of the health clogs that made it possible for him to stand in front of blackboards for long hours. The students called him Umfundisi, a beautiful Zulu word which combines the vocations of priest and teacher with the sound of wind in the trees.

He was thinking, Moral dilemmas don't get any easier to resolve as one grows older. Finally he said, 'Well, we have to be pragmatic, my dear. I can't afford to lose you too with Matric so close, and you haven't done anything to be ashamed of in my book.'

'I've been harbouring a terrorist.'

'More of an idealist, I'd say.'

Rose said sharply, 'Don't try and romanticise for me what he's doing, Father. He took a conscious decision to join an organisation committed to using violence as a strategy, and he must have known when he was going through the training camps that he couldn't keep his poet's hands clean indefinitely. He just wanted it both ways, like any man: a good fight to get involved in, and a willing woman to come home to afterwards.'

'That's not like you, Rose.'

'It's true.'

Father Basil shook his head. 'You mustn't allow your feeling of betrayal to overcome your natural good sense. Though I grant it's not easy.'

'It's like being in a labyrinth!' she burst out. 'If I look one way, I know I love him and that I could never do anything to harm him. If I look the other, I see a pile of guns that keeps getting higher as more are thrown on, until it looks like a huge spiky metal spider squatting there, the essence of evil. Behind me is my easy swansdown life, but in front of me there's a yawning hole out of which the sounds of nightmare are coming, bombs going off and people screaming and police dogs snarling –' She trailed off.

'Mother of God,' he muttered into the silence that followed. 'What strength we need to face these inhuman choices.'

They sat listening to the busy school hum that came through the prefab partition: voices reciting in unison, feet shuffling past in the passage, a teacher saying something in the carrying voice of all teachers which can penetrate the innermost ear. St Aloysius was noisy, ill-equipped, draughty and severely over-crowded, but there was a feeling in the air of things getting learnt and people going places, a purposeful oxygen that too few schools are ever able to generate.

Father Basil said at last, 'This is what we'll do. I will get word to the police that there is at least one arms cache being assembled somewhere to the south of Johannesburg, and possibly more. You needn't worry how it's done, but you can be sure they'll go into action fast. Your young man had better be on his toes.'

'I wouldn't know how to find him to warn him, even if I wanted to. He knows the score anyway, Father.' Bitterness

333

seeped into her voice. 'He's had long enough to prepare a bolt-hole, thanks to me.'

'Don't flagellate yourself, Rose. It serves no purpose. What's important now is that you look for a new direction. Lean on your friends and family.'

She gave a sarcastic laugh. 'I've tried. They're all as sympathetic as hell, but they're preoccupied with their own lives. I must fill the hole Jake's left by myself. Have you any good suggestions?'

'Any number, but they're probably not what you want to hear.' His answering smile was austere. 'Good works are a solace.'

'Good works won't keep me warm at night, Father.'

After thirty years in schools, he was not easily shocked. 'Ah, but they'll ease the pain. Have you talked to Tryphina lately?'

'No.' She had not wanted to talk to anyone.

'Bring her in here for a cup of tea after class this evening, and ask her about the self-help group she's started. I think you'll find the concept interesting.'

She said in a listless voice, 'I can't see a concept taking Jake's place, exactly.'

'You'd be surprised, girl. You'd be surprised.'

And she had been. Tryphina had persuaded her to go home after Saturday classes, armed with a township pass, to the two-roomed house where her children lived with their grandmother while she was away at work during the week. After a meal of samp and meat stew cooked and served by two shy daughters, they had gone on to a meeting of the self-help group in a nearby church hall.

Rose was assailed by a buzz of busy women bent in groups over sewing and knitting machines, cutting scraps of material into patches, drawing patterns on brown paper, embroidering, crocheting, knitting, and chatting over rows of teacups that were being filled from the biggest cream enamel teapot she had ever seen.

'Nearly all here,' Tryphina said with satisfaction, giving the wheezing chuckle that made teaching her such a pleasure. 'You like what you see?'

'I'm overwhelmed.'

And she was, until Tryphina took her round to introduce her and the buzz revolved itself into fifty or more women earnestly learning from each other the skills they had to pass on.

Welcomed by smiles and pats on the hand and eyes beaming through glasses, Rose felt as though she was being plunged back into her childhood when Doris and Albertina and Agnes had been her constant companions. Within minutes she was herself bent over the table where two women were struggling to make pencil loops across the pages of their literacy manuals, and by the end of the afternoon she had been swamped with invitations to visit township homes and to, 'Come again, Rose, OK? We like to have you here. Tryphina, she talks all the time about what you do for her by the school.'

After a few more Saturday afternoons, she had to acknowledge Father Basil's wisdom, because she gained so much more than she gave. First was a renewed sense of perspective: how could she, so privileged, sit moping over a doomed love affair when these women went so cheerfully about their difficult lives? Second was new friends who opened doors that were otherwise closed to her as a white woman, and that she had always wondered about. Third was a set of new skills that gave her a great deal of pleasure. Always hamfisted when it came to sewing (a legacy of Sarah's loathing of all handwork except painting), she learned how to crochet and do patchwork in return for teaching reading, and made her first-ever garment, a loose cotton top, with the help of a woman who asked only that she would explain the legal language on a hire purchase agreement.

'You see how much we can give each other,' Tryphina beamed. 'If one teaches the other one like this, we can spread our knowledge and our skills right through the township and help all womans.'

'Women,' Rose corrected automatically, then found herself blushing. She was a guest here, not a teacher. She said, 'Sorry.'

Tryphina erupted into a paroxysm of chuckles that made all her chins wobble. 'Not to be sorry, Rose! You are the teacher. Me, I'm just the learner.'

'I would never, ever call you just a learner, Tryphina.' Rose smiled at her. 'You're an amazing person. I don't know how you do it.'

'Aikona.' Tryphina made a deprecating cluck with her tongue. 'There's plenty more like me. Who you think runs this place – ' she made a broad sweep with her hand that took in the entire township ' – but womans? Women,' she corrected herself quickly.

If Sarah had been there, she would have known the answer

from the long-ago conversations round the pine table with Gertrude and Doris, but many of the things Tryphina told her were new to Rose. The husbands who came home drunk or not at all. The jobs that took mothers away for weeks at a time, forcing them to leave young children with feeble old women and child-minders who often drank and siblings barely older than they were. The struggle to fit shopping for a family into the meagre cracks of time left by a full-time job, and hours spent in buses and trains getting to and from it. The chronic exhaustion of coming home late and tired to face housework, cooking, washing, ironing, the supervising of homework and the disciplining of children who roamed the street against orders during the day because no one was there to stop them.

'We are the bones and the blood of our people,' Tryphina said, for once serious. 'We keep everything going. Sometimes I think, what for we need the little things – ' said with immense scorn and a rude gesture ' – of men, when all they do is make more babies for us to look after?'

'You're a feminist, then,' Rose said. 'That's – '

'I know what is a feminist.' Again Rose blushed; she made so many assumptions that were arrogantly wrong. 'Is somebody who thinks she is better than men. Me too, I know I'm better than most men. But I also think, I have three sons. Maybe if I teach them nice like you teach me, they will be good men? Then we can be all the same, good people, nobody better than the other. I think is the job of womans – sorry, Rose, women – to make their kids into good people. Specially the naughty boys.' And she chuckled with such vigour that it turned into a coughing fit that made her clamp her hand over the large breasts joggling under her pinafore.

Rose told Father Basil the following Monday what Tryphina had said. 'She's really thought out what she wants to do with her life, and she's working to make it happen.'

'Is the self-help group helping to fill the Jake-shaped hole in your life?' he smiled.

'I didn't think about him for four whole hours last Saturday,' she said, smiling back. And it was true. But she still listened for the sound of his motorbike coming up the street, and scanned the papers every day. There was nothing about the discovery of an arms cache or the detention of a suspected terrorist. She kept his poems in a file on her bedside table and read them when she could get up the courage. The ache of their last fight and his leaving took months to fade to a dull pain.

She began to go out again with a computer colleague of Boff's called Miles Boardman. Miles was blond and muscled with beach-boy good looks that earned him extra money as a part-time model; he drove a sports car and took Rose to expensive restaurants where it was easy to forget Jake in the wine-drugged ambience of candlelight and *haute cuisine*. She took him home, and was amused to see that he was as impressed by the large Houghton house and Gordon's business standing as Sarah and Gordon were impressed by him.

'He's gorgeous,' Sarah said.

'Presentable, at least.' Rose was cautious with Miles, whose sense of fun did not quite obscure the serious purpose she was beginning to see in his eyes. He's looking for a wife to match him, she thought, and I fit the bill: degreed, well-off, and with distinguished parents. I wonder what he'd think if he knew I'd had a coloured terrorist for a lover? She wondered too what sort of husband Miles would make, and whether she could live with him for the rest of her life. He was bright and had an excellent job as a systems analyst but their conversations were about films they had enjoyed, places to go, things to do and see, not poetry and politics and anguish. He lacked mystery, she decided, puzzling him with her cool acceptance of the good looks and charm that made other girls go weak at the knees over him.

In December Rose read the news of a commando raid on several houses in Maseru with shock, but no tingle of premonition. Forty-two people had been killed by unknown gunmen, including twelve Basotho citizens and thirty 'South African exiles' said to be members of the ANC. She scanned the names of the deceased with dread, but Jake's was not among them. I wonder how long it'll take before I stop loving him, she thought sadly. If ever.

She put on her party smile to spend Christmas day with Miles's family. He was leaving the next day for a fashion shoot in Mauritius, and she would be going with Sarah and a very tired Gordon to spend a week at the Mount Nelson Hotel in Cape Town.

As she wraps the sleeping child up well for the dark walk up to the death hut, Sarah thinks now of that short holiday and the shattering way it ended. If they hadn't gone to Cape Town Rose would not be lying dead. If only they hadn't gone. If only.

29

It is midnight in the hut that serves as a makeshift mortuary, and very still. Rows of trading store candles in tin holders borrowed from all over the village burn at the head and foot of the uncovered wooden coffins in which Rose and Jake are lying. Paraffin lamps set at intervals round the walls cast elliptical haloes of light up the mud plaster, highlighting its rough surface of dried brush strokes. The pale pink everlastings that the child gave Sarah earlier have been put into a small jug, and their stiff shiny petals reflect the light like a jugful of stars.

Jake and Rose lie in their separate satin-lined boxes like a Crusader and his lady, hands folded in front of them, faces calm and washed clean of blood, hair damped and combed. They are dressed in their wedding clothes and she has her wedding flowers in her hair. Sister Quthing has closed her eyes and mouth, and the candlelight gilds her skin, giving it a semblance of warmth and life that made Sarah catch her breath when she came in. Jake's face is more deeply shadowed, his mobile expression replaced by a sombre death mask in which the mouth is twisted downwards. But here again the light plays tricks with the tragic reality, sliding along his slanted cheekbones and sparking deep red glints in his hair as if death were only a sleep from which he will soon wake.

Two armchairs have been brought in and set next to the coffins. Sarah sits in one keeping vigil, her sleeping grand-daughter cradled in the bend of an arm, her head back against a pillow, her eyes gazing up into the geometric shadows of the thatched roof. She is remembering Rose down the years and the joy of having a daughter. Remembering too the times she was less than a good mother to her, the smackings for minor misdeeds, the Buckingham Circle days when she lay on her bed with the curtains drawn and let Rose run wild and alone up on the koppie, the many occasions when she was too busy painting to sit and listen to her growing pains. Regret is not the worst part of mourning, but it is the hardest to subdue.

Gordon sits sleeping in the other armchair, having succumbed at last to exhaustion. He lies sideways with his head on an embroidered cushion; its many colours show rainbow reflections on to his florid cheeks and the bald dome of his head. When he first fell asleep he dreamed of shadow men in balaclavas who kept melting into the dark shapes swimming behind his eyes and reappearing with spitting guns that made him whimper aloud. But Sarah reached out with her free hand to stroke his arm and murmur, 'It's all right, love, it's all right,' and the nightmare subsided. Now he sleeps like the dead, oblivious.

They are not the only ones in the hut. Other mourners have gathered to keep vigil with them: Mrs Mofufi, who was waiting outside the door when they returned, Cordelia, several of the teachers who worked with Rose, and an old woman whom Cordelia has introduced as never missing a death vigil in the village. The younger mourners sit on wooden chairs brought up from the school. The two older women sit blanket-wrapped on the fresh grass mats that have been laid in overlapping rows on the hut's mud floor, legs crooked to one side, weight on one hand, heads bowed. The grass mats smelt sweetly of sunlight and straw.

Didymus sits next to one of the paraffin lamps with his back against the wall and his long thin legs bent up in front, reading the order for the burial of the dead from the small black prayer book that he carries everywhere. He reads it over and over, hoping to find the certainty and the solace that have eluded him all day. 'He that believeth in me, though he were dead, yet shall he live,' he reads, wondering if he still believes. 'I know that my Redeemer liveth,' he reads, and knows only that he is not sure. 'Comfort us again now after the time that thou hast plagued us,' he reads, but is not comforted. Beads of sweat gather along his hairline. Every now and then he sweeps his lank white hair back with his hand until it lies damply plastered against his head, only to flop forward again minutes later. Presently he unzips the front of his track suit and wrestles it off. Underneath, tie-dyed by his indefatigable mother, is a once-purple T-shirt that has now mercifully faded to lavender, out of which his thin neck rises like an asparagus stalk. He does not look like an ordained priest. He looks like a schoolboy who has just lost his position in the first team, and is trying not to cry.

Outside the hut, the village sleeps under a mountain sky so clear and unpolluted that it is spangled with a million glittering stars. The moon has not yet risen. It is very dark. One would need a keen eye to spot the armed men who stand guard at intervals along the dirt track and the valley's rim. Further up towards the training camp, a jackal howls.

On the second day of their visit to Cape Town, Rose was walking down through the old Company Gardens towards Adderley Street when she saw, with a jolting shock, Jake's back. Despite the cropped hair and green paint-spattered overall, she knew it was him by the way he walked down the pathway, looking round at the lawns and the flowerbeds and the morning strollers as if he too were taking his ease, oblivious of the ladder and bucket he was carrying. On the back of the overall in yellow machine embroidery was ACME NATIONAL CONSTRUCTION CO.

Resisting the impulse to run after him calling out his name, she followed him at a distance into the broad oak-shaded walk called Government Avenue, and had a second shock when he turned right towards a gate in the spiked iron railings that surround the Houses of Parliament. She stood under a tree and watched as he walked up to the blue-uniformed policeman at the gate, had the security pass clipped to his overall inspected, and was waved through.

Jake, walking coolly into the Houses of Parliament with a company's name on his back whose initials read ANC? The audacity of it took her breath away. Panicky questions tumbled one after the other in her mind. Is this a one-off trick to get in and plant a bomb, or does he work here? Should I raise the alarm? Tell the policeman on guard? But that's *Jake*. I can't.

Underlying the panic was the warm, still thought that she had seen him again, alive and well.

She decided to sit on a bench further up the pathway and wait to see if he came out. Even if she had to wait for some hours, her parents wouldn't miss her. Gordon had gone off to a meeting with a business colleague. Sarah had been commissioned to paint aspects of the hotel and its garden in return for their stay, and since breakfast had been sitting on a lower terrace making preliminary sketches, rosy with satisfaction at being able to treat her family on her own earnings.

Rose bought a *Cape Times* from a passing vendor and sat down to read and wait. It was one of those hot sunny blue and white days that lures northern visitors to the Cape year after year; the Mount Nelson's chintzy lounges were full of elderly escapees from the British winter. Rose had had a number of doors held open for her by gallant old men in tropical suits and silk cravats whose rheumy eyes tried hard to twinkle.

After she had read the paper, she folded it up and sat watching some children playing on the grass nearby. Three little white girls were holding a dolls' tea party, watched by a benevolent-looking coloured woman in a nanny's apron and white doek who sat on a nearby bench, knitting. A younger child, obviously the woman's, was hovering on the fringes of the feast, longing to partake of the biscuits and sips of cooldrink that were being held to the dolls' mouths and then gobbled with relish by their owners. He crept nearer and nearer to the party, scraping his red shorts along the grass, his eyes fixed on a plate of sweets in the middle of the dolls' tea cloth. When he was close enough, he reached out a tentative hand towards the sweets.

'No, Polla!' A small white hand slapped the little brown one away.

'Asseblief?' the coloured child begged, so close to being part of the fun.

'No, they're for pudding. You can't have one. Dorotheee,' the white child whined. 'Take Polla away. He's trying to steal our sweets.'

The woman put her knitting down in her lap. 'Ag, just give him one, Miss Mary. He's only little.'

'No. Then our dolls will be hungry. They love pudding,' the white child glared.

'Yes, they love pudding,' the second white child said, and reaching for the plate of sweets, began stuffing some down the front of her doll's dress and some into her mouth.

'They love pudding!' the third sang, copying her, and in a few seconds all the sweets were gone and the three white children were rolling round on the grass with their mouths full, giggling.

With growing anger, Rose watched the coloured child retreat from the tea cloth with its array of plastic teacups to stand silently next to his mother, watching the white girls getting hysterical with laughter as they rolled and spat half-chewed sweets all over the grass. His small brown thumb went into his mouth. His mother folded up the knitting and put it into a plastic bag, then picked him up and cuddled him, talking in a low voice.

Rose felt her cheeks burning with shame, and looked away. I'm looking at the source of Jake's rage, she thought, and who can blame him? An incident like this must sear into a child like a branding iron. What would a hundred incidents do? A thousand? Being made to go on separate buses, to stand in separate queues, shoved away from the good things being tightly held by greedy whites, all in the name of some loony notion of superiority. If it were me, I'd want to bomb this whole rotten society out of existence. Yet I condemned him for much less.

'Dorotheee.' The white child was standing in front of the coloured woman, tugging at her hand. 'We want to go home now. Put Polla down and take us home.'

Keeping her face neutral, the woman said, 'Just as soon as you pick up your things and put them in the basket, Miss Mary.'

'You pick them up. It's your job. We've got our dolls to look after,' the child said rudely, turning away.

'Nee wat, my kind!' The woman lassoed the child's arm in a firm grip. 'You pick up your own mess, or I'll tell your mother on you.'

'But Dorotheee,' the child whined, trying to pull away, 'I'm too tired.'

'That's too bad, eh?' It was said from a grim brown face from which all trace of benevolence had vanished. Only when the white child had sullenly complied, calling her friends to help her empty the cups and pack them away, did the woman stand up with her own child on her hip and bend down to pick up the basket. She led the white children away in a small disgruntled flock, dolls dragging, sweet-smeared mouths sulky at not getting their own way for once.

Shaken by the ugly scene, Rose turned back to look at the gate through which Jake had gone. The policeman guarding it was leaning against one of the pillars, looking bored. She could be sitting here for hours, with only the passers-by and the strutting pigeons and the little grey squirrels undulating between the oak trees to watch. She walked across the Gardens to Queen Victoria Street and found a café where she bought several magazines, a packet of sandwiches and a cooldrink.

Back at the bench, she read the magazines and ate the sandwiches. Lunchtime passed. Sarah and Gordon wouldn't worry where she was, as she had told them she'd be shopping for 'teacherly clothes' and might stay on in town for lunch.

'Buy something extravagant and pretty for New Year's Eve instead,' Gordon had urged her, pressing two red fifty rand notes into her hand. 'Something Miles will enjoy seeing you in when we get home.'

'I don't need a new dress,' she had said, trying to give the notes back.

'I insist. What's the use of a daughter if you can't spoil her occasionally?' He had turned away quickly, leaving the notes in her hand.

Typical Dad, she thought. Bored with the magazine in her lap, she sat looking at the serene red-brick Parliament buildings with their white trimmings and tall white columns propping up the classical pediments; beautiful architecture, but rooted in a colonial past that had no relevance today. Parliament was a travesty when only a small section of the citizens it served could choose their representatives. This building was an elegant confidence trick.

The sun was slanting down towards the blue-grey bulk of Table Mountain when the gate opened again for Jake. He walked towards her with the ladder over one shoulder, but no bucket. She dropped her head as though reading the magazine, and watched him covertly. If she stayed like this with her hair falling forward over her face, he would probably go by up the broad pathway without noticing her. What should she do? Did she want to see him again, or should the break be final? She had a chance now to change her mind.

She thought of the wistful coloured child being pushed away from the dolls' tea party while the little white girls stuffed their mouths with more sweets than they could chew, and found that there was no choice. Raising her head, she looked straight at him and smiled.

He was walking with a jaunty stride that she had never seen before, and the cheerful look of a workman who has just knocked off and is thinking only of a drink with his mates. When he saw her, he stopped as though transfixed and dropped the ladder. With horror, she saw the policeman at the gate swing round at the sudden clatter, his hand moving fast towards the leather holster at his belt. As he shouted a command to stop, Jake whirled to face him, dropping to a crouch.

Oh God, what a fool I am, she thought. I'll get him killed!

She stood up quickly, turned her back and walked away up through the Gardens with her heart pounding in her throat. Any minute there'd be a shot, and it would be her fault. Jake lying under the oak trees, dead and still.

She heard a high frightened voice calling in a Cape coloured accent, 'Ag, sorry, my basie. I just dropped it. It's not a criminal offence to drop ladders yet, hey? Don't shoot, my basie. I could get full of holes, and then what?'

Jake, begging for his life with his heart hammering adrenalin. Jake, whose body fitted so well against hers, and whom she had never wanted more than she did now. If he was shot, it would be her fault. If he lived to walk up through the Gardens and the late sunlight after her, she would never send him away again. She walked slower and slower, listening with her whole being for the shots that would end the dream.

There was only the quiet hum of the afternoon traffic, and a squabble of pigeons over a packet of soggy chips abandoned by a lily pond. She turned off the pathway to sit on a bench and slowly, slowly turn her head and look back the way she had come for a figure in a green overall carrying a ladder. When he came into view, whistling to cover the tension she could see in every line of his body, she thought she would never again feel such a rush of relief.

He stopped near her, looked both ways to check that no one was approaching, then said in a furious whisper, 'What the hell are you doing here? You could have got me shot!'

'I just saw you walking in front of me this morning. We're down here on holiday.' Her words were falling over themselves to get out before anyone came along. 'Oh, Jake, I've missed you. I don't care what you're doing. Please come back. I –'

'Can't talk now.' He spoke looking away down the path. 'Where are you staying?'

'The Mount Nelson.'

Even as she said it, she knew what his response would be. 'I should have guessed. Only the best for Daddy, eh?'

'Jake, don't. This is me, Rose, remember?'

He turned his face fully towards her then. 'It's hard to see you, Rose, without Daddy in the background. But hell, I've missed you too.' His swamp water eyes glared at her over the incongruous green overall. 'Dunno why. You're nothing but trouble for me.'

344

'I was nothing but a complication last time.' She tried a quick smile.

There were footsteps coming closer. He said out of the side of his mouth, 'Can't talk. It looks all wrong, you and me, dressed like this. I'll contact you, OK?' and he walked away, whistling *Daar Kom Die Alibama* between his teeth.

It was two days before she heard from him. A folded note handed to her with her room key over the hotel desk said, 'Pipe Track 9 am Saturday. Wait on the first bench.'

'Where is the Pipe Track?' she asked the desk clerk.

'It's the Table Mountain walking trail that runs along from Kloof Nek above Camps Bay, Madam,' he said. 'Quite easy walking. Very pretty.'

'How do I get there?'

'I'm sure something could be arranged, Madam.'

She reached the bench at the top of a long flight of stone steps early, and sat looking down on Camps Bay with its cupped sprawl of houses and calm sapphire sea lapping at a white beach where she and Sarah had gone swimming, and found sand so fine that it squeaked underfoot. Sweeping up behind the houses to the chain of sandstone peaks known as the Twelve Apostles was the mountainside she was sitting on, preserve of hikers and climbers and nature-lovers.

She thought, It's so different to the other side of Cape Town. Here is quietness and sunlight and an extravagance of mountain and sea. The people who live here in their big white homes and abundant gardens are protected even from the sight of the black and coloured townships that have spread like patches of mould across the Cape Flats. On the way in from the airport several days ago, they had passed rows of bleak shoebox houses lining roads where the wind was whipping up dust in billows, and where the yards were crowded with lean-to shacks. If only the contrasts weren't so great, she thought, or so ruthlessly colour-linked. For the really poor a township house must be a blessing, but how would I feel if I had to live in one, even though I could afford something better? I'd be angry all the time. I'd be furious. I'd want to punch every smug white face in sight.

Jake's voice came from behind her, with the touch of his fingers on her neck. 'Why are your hands all bunched up, poppie? Thinking of slugging someone?'

She closed her eyes and leaned her head back against his arm. 'Wish I could. I'd feel better.'

'Better about what?'

'Oh,' she said, 'being white, of course.' She rubbed against him luxuriously, like a cat who has just been let in. 'Being white means feeling guilty all the time, and I'm sick of it. Sick of carrying my conscience around like a hump. Sick of having the contrasts rubbed in every time I turn my head in a different direction. Sick of seeing the envious faces of people trudging along the road while I drive by in my car. I just want to live in a place where I can live like everyone else, and be happy.' She turned her head to kiss him. 'With you,' she murmured as their lips met. Miles could never have existed.

The kiss was brief. Jake pulled back saying, 'We can't stay here. Even in Cape Town people aren't used to mixing coffee and cream yet.'

She opened her eyes to protest and saw first his ferocious grin, then his extraordinary clothes. He was wearing a short-sleeved shirt in loud stripes, maroon trousers, a mock leopard-skin belt and a woollen pull-on cap with a maroon zigzag pattern. The old canvas rucksack he was carrying looked mute by comparison. 'Jake! You look like a – ' she stopped herself just in time from saying 'coolie Christmas' and said, ' – Christmas tree.'

The grin broadened, and she saw that one of his upper teeth had been blacked. 'Local colour, jy weet? I've got to look like a gammat who's working as a painter.'

'What's a – '

'Jeez, you Transvalers are ignorant.' He was using the fast, high, accented voice she had heard yesterday, and once before when the policemen came to the Yeoville house. 'A gammat is a real genuine Cape coloured like in the jokes white comedians tell. You know? The coon carnival clothes, the cheeky backchat, the snoek under one arm, the jug of cheap wine under the other, the – '

'Jake, don't start now, please,' she begged. 'Can't we just make this an ordinary reunion between two people who had a fight but want to make it up – I presume you want to make it up? – instead of a protest meeting?'

'I didn't start, you did.' He spoke in his normal voice, and after checking that the path was empty in both directions, bent to nuzzle her cheek briefly.

As he pulled back again, she said, 'There must be a more private place to talk. We're so exposed here.'

'That's one of the reasons I chose the Pipe Track. So we could meet on neutral ground, out in the open, no more dark secrets.' He was standing in front of her now, his face very serious. 'You know who I am, Rose, and what I'm doing. If we go on together from here, you are putting yourself right outside the white fence.'

She nodded. 'I know. But I made my decision when I looked up at you from the bench outside Parliament. There shouldn't be a fence, Jake.'

'But there is. You must face the facts, not try to wish them away.'

She said, getting up, 'Let's go on then, if we're going to argue.'

The tension went out of his shoulders. 'The other reason I chose the Pipe Track is that we can climb up one of the side paths and get lost. We'll go along past the first few bends, then strike up to our left. This way.'

They walked in silence. The occasional hiker or runner meant that they couldn't hold hands, though her body shivered every time they touched. She thought, Who do these people going past think we are, me in my nice summer dress suitable for the Mount Nelson, him in those dreadful clothes? A madam with her gardener? A botany teacher discussing the finer points of the mountain fynbos with a coloured student? A well-meaning white liberal imparting the bounty of her knowledge to one of the poor blacks? It's so absurd, this subterfuge. She wanted to turn to each one and say, 'Don't get taken in by appearances. He's not a gammat, he's a poet. And a damn good lover too.'

She glanced at him sideways. His face looked browner, as though he had been working in the sun, and the hollows under his high slanted cheekbones had filled out. The swamp water eyes were as warm and deep and green as ever when he turned to her saying, 'We'll go up here. There's a flat rock with some bushes growing round it where I go sometimes when I want to think about you.'

'I wouldn't have thought you'd want to think about me much after what happened.'

His laugh came over his shoulder. 'It wasn't always with regret.'

She followed him up the steep path that climbed the hillside between low tussocky bushes quite different from the highveld grasses she was used to. It was like walking through a sampler of leaf shapes and colours, each giving off an aromatic sigh as they brushed past. The going was hard in her white sandals. Jake was wearing thick-soled running shoes that clung to the rough stones and hardly felt the skidding pebbles. Her sandals slipped and slid and she began to sweat in little trickles, which made her dress cling to her body and legs. She called up, 'You could have told me we'd be going mountaineering.'

'It was your choice, remember?'

'It's easy for you! I've got on completely the wrong shoes.' She was panting now with the effort of climbing, her heart thudding in her chest. 'Let's have a break for a few minutes.'

'Oh ye of little stamina.' He stopped on a rocky ledge waiting for her to catch up, and pulled the zigzag cap off his cropped hair, so different from the full Afro she remembered.

She thought, Nobody could call him a bushy now, and laughed as she climbed up beside him, flapping her dress to cool her body. 'I'm sweating like a pig.'

He reached for her hands. 'Beautiful pig.'

'Can we? Here?'

He looked down at the path they had just climbed, then checked the sections of Pipe Track from which they could still be seen. 'I think we could risk a quick one. You forget that I blend in with the scenery from a distance.'

'Not in that shirt.'

'Shirts don't count.'

The words slowed and stopped as they came together and kissed and walked on and up in a daze of touching and wanting to the hidden rocky place he had found. Here he spread the rug he had brought in the rucksack and they could lie down together again at last, and make the whole mountainside and even the sky disappear with their pent-up loving.

It was the sun burning the side of her body that wasn't burrowed next to his that made her sit up and fan herself with the skirt of her dress. 'I'm going red. We'll have to find some shade.'

'That's the problem with white skins. They're completely wrong for this climate,' he said, lying there like a satisfied python in no mood to move. 'What you need is a permanent all-over tan like mine.'

'Then we wouldn't have any problems, I suppose?'

He smiled up at her. 'Ag, what's problems on a lekker day like this with the sun shining, my girl in my arms, and a place to hide that the Special Branch would never even dream of?'

She felt a chill like a cloud passing over the sun. 'We've got to talk, Jake. I want to know what you're doing here and what sort of future there is for us and when we can – '

'Not so fast, poppie.' He sat up with the sun burnishing the sheen of sweat on his body, and she wanted to reach out for him again, he was so beautiful and smelled so good. Cinnamon Jake. Honey and nutmeg and allspice Jake. But he was pulling on the ugly shirt and trousers saying, 'We should get decent first, just in case.'

'I don't care if anyone sees us.' She stretched her arms above her head and felt the sun burning the soft white skin of her breasts. 'We've got nothing to hide.'

'Speak for yourself.' He was buckling on the mock leopard-skin belt. 'And cut the arm signals, Rose. We don't want people to think you're calling for help or anything. I mean, you know what happens when coloured guys take advantage of white girls.'

'Take advantage!' she laughed, but dropped her arms. 'I don't think I've ever heard that expression outside books.'

He said, 'It's no joke. Even though I don't think anyone could spot us up here, we can't afford to take chances. Here,' he picked up her dress, and the back of his hand brushed across her breasts as he passed it to her, 'put it on before we talk. You're too damn distracting like that.'

While she pulled her dress on and combed her hair with her fingers, he took a bottle of white wine, a corkscrew and two plastic glasses out of the duffle bag, saying, 'I brought these in case we had reason to celebrate. It's an old Cape custom.'

'At this time of the morning?'

'At any time.' He poured her a glass. 'Sorry, it isn't as cold as it should be.'

She held it up to the sun. 'What a lovely colour, palest yellow with a green tinge.'

'Like your hair sometimes.' His voice dropped. 'Hang, I'm glad to see you, Rose. Even in spite of the complications.'

She said, feeling the familiar dread, 'You'd better tell me about them now.'

He had not expected the enormous relief of being able to tell her what he was doing. This was his third mission, he explained, and his brief was to infiltrate the Houses of Parliament and plant listening devices in as many rooms and offices as he could gain access to.

'Not bombs?' She had gone pale.

'Bugs. Communications is what I was trained in, and teach. We've got high-tech stuff that can pick up a cockroach sneezing.'

She shivered. 'I thought you were – '

'Doing a Guy Fox? No chance. Bombing's not my scene. I volunteered in the beginning as a teacher, though I went through the full MK military training like everybody else. When these missions came up, I said I'd come if I didn't have to use weapons.' His full lips firmed at the memory. 'I was so naïve. Soon after I got here, I was ordered to set up an arms cache. "You don't have to sully your dainty academic hands with actually placing the limpet mines if you're squeamish, Van Vuuren," the commander told me, "but we hold you personally responsible for the success of our random bombing strategy in the Transvaal."'

'Does it really make much difference whether you store them or set them off? They're still bombs. They kill people.'

'They're not intended to. Not civilians, anyway. Cops and soldiers and collaborators are another matter. You've got to remember that this is a war we're fighting here, Rose. A war of independence like the Americans fought, and the Israelis and the Algerians and the Kenyans – and the Irish are still fighting.' His cheeks were flushed. 'This Afrikaner government calls us terrorists, but we're freedom fighters exactly like they were during the Boer War. We want to run our country ourselves, just like they did. And we will one day. That's what I'm fighting for.'

'You shouldn't have to! You should be in an ivory tower somewhere, writing your beautiful poetry. I've read it over and over since you left.'

'You have?' He looked pleased. 'I thought you must have torn up the lot.'

'I'd never have done that. But every time I looked at it, I was furious that you'd abandoned it for this.'

'Not abandoned. Left in abeyance, I hope. Poets are notorious for rushing off to wars, remember?'

'And dying in them.' She said desperately, 'Jake, please stop. Can't we go somewhere, to another country, and make a new life together?'

He looked away, steeling himself against her pleading. 'Not yet. I have to finish what I'm doing. MK gave me the job because of Auntie April, because they knew she could get me into Parliament, and I agreed so long as I could work on my own. I can't risk some half-trained mompara wrecking the mission and messing up the life she's built for herself. So I have to finish it.'

'Does she know what you're doing?'

'I'm not sure. When I asked her to get me a job there, she got a funny look on her face and didn't ask me why. I'd like you to meet my Auntie April.'

'Does she know about me?'

Jake looked down at his wine. 'Ja, I told her.'

'And what did she say?'

'She cried for me.' He turned to her, and his eyes were shiny. 'I'd like her to know she needn't have, that you're back and it's OK between us.'

'But we've only got a few days, Jake. I'm going home next week. We've got to make plans, decide, think what to do next.'

'I can't now,' he said, reaching for her hand. 'You've got to understand that I'm under military orders until this mission is over. They've hinted that I might get a post in Lesotho afterwards.'

Hope flared in her face. 'We can go there together, then. Oh Jake, we can get married and live happily ever after. Cheers!' She took a great happy gulp of wine.

'Maybe,' he said, and on the sunny mountainside with the sea spread out below like a sequinned eiderdown and the high blue sky like a fourposter canopy above, neither of them noticed the streak of ugly grey cloud moving in fast from the south, heralding a cold front.

30

Gordon takes off the green felt hat to mop the sweat on his forehead. The cool damp chill of the early morning when Tshabalala came to fetch him has given way to a muggy heat that the earth seems to exhale like marsh gas. Since turning the first sod of the grave, he has been digging side by side with the able-bodied male villagers, Tshabalala, Didymus and a squad of young men from the camp. Now, exhausted, he sits on the dry-stone wall of the small cemetery up the hill from the village, looking out over the valley.

It is quiet at this time of the morning; the children in school, the women hoeing in the fields behind the huts, the cattle and goats and sheep almost invisible on the far hillside. Further down, where the valley widens, a stream runs across a low-level ford into a pool where several women are doing their washing, kneeling on the rocks. The stream comes from the high Malutis, and is fast, clear and bone-chilling cold, even in summer.

The pastoral idyll comes to an abrupt end beyond the ford, where a road-block has been set up: an army truck parked at right-angles across the road, several jeeps, men with rifles, glints of sunlight on metal. As he watches, two cars drive up and are made to park on the side of the road; after questioning, both drivers are told to leave and the cars skid away angrily.

'The human vultures are beginning to gather.' The gravel voice comes from behind him. Gordon turns. Tshabalala is also mopping his forehead, and there are huge patches of sweat on his khaki shirt.

'So I see. Thank you for keeping them off.' Gordon's face and neck feel bloated, too full of clamouring blood, and he fans himself with his hat. 'It seems I misjudged you yesterday.'

The bullet head nods. 'And I you. If nothing else, times like this make us look properly into each other's faces. I'm only sorry I can't keep all the vultures off. We are obliged to admit a quota.'

'Who decides who gets in? Ndlondlo?'

'Of course.'

'So the foreign media will be here in force, TV crews waving microphones, photographers trying to get good angles – God, how I hate that sort of thing! Funerals should be private, not laid out like gutted fish on a slab for the public to pick over.'

'We'll do our best to keep it dignified.' The big man comes closer and a hand like a side of bacon comes down on his shoulder. 'I understand how you feel. But neither of us is a free agent here. Our wishes must be subordinate to the greater need, which is to tell the world of the atrocity that has happened. You want justice, yes?'

'I'll get justice, even if I have to carry it out myself.' Gordon's voice is hard.

'You mustn't even think of it.' The hand lifts from his shoulder and Tshabalala sits down heavily on the wall beside him, dislodging several stones. 'Forgive me, Mr Kimber, but I think you are forgetting your responsibility towards the child. It is she who needs a father and a home, not Rose. Could you not trust us in this matter? Our intelligence unit has extensive contacts. One of the advantages of being black in this country is that we are often completely invisible to whites, so we get to hear a lot of secrets. We should know in a few days where the gunmen came from.'

'And then?'

The big man's face cracks. 'We deal with them.'

They sit looking out over the still valley, letting its peace wash over them for these few shared minutes. Then Gordon says, 'You're right about my responsibility to the child. It's absurd of me to talk about revenge anyway, at my age. If I had those bastards in the sights of my shotgun I wouldn't hesitate to pull the trigger, but I wouldn't know how to go about finding them.'

'We'll do that, don't worry. We're used to dirty fighting.' The huge hands clench together like a giant nutcracker, fingers linked. 'And it's getting very dirty now. You people living in your nice white houses don't know even half of what is going on. You tut tut over every limpet mine explosion and give it massive coverage on TV news, but do you show any great concern over the shootings in the townships? Over the people with wrecked minds coming out of interrogation rooms and solitary confinement, punishments for which they have not even been charged

353

in court, let alone sentenced? The scale of our violence set against your violence is like a drop in the bucket.'

There is another silence between them, then Gordon admits, 'We live like snails with our antennae pulled in.'

'Until something like this happens.'

'Losing a child is a terrible price to pay for enlightenment.' He looks up at the sky in unconscious accusation, and sees with a shock of disgust the bird specks planing in slow circles. 'Look!' he says, pointing. 'Are those what I think they are?'

Tshabalala nods. 'The real McCoy. You always see them when there's a death.'

'Animals out in the veld, yes. But people? In huts?' There is horror in Gordon's voice.

'Any death. It makes no difference to vultures. They know, and they come.'

'It's horrible.'

'It's the law of nature.'

Gordon's voice when it comes again is full of pain. 'The law of nature seems to include the death of its best before they've had time to do much living.'

'Our loss is great.' The big man sighs. 'I don't know how we'll begin to replace the two of them.'

Gordon feels his eyes misting over. 'One thing these two days have taught me is that it's not a matter of my loss and your loss. It's our loss. Will you shake hands on it, Mgwetshana Tshabalala?' He turns and holds out his right hand, which is pink and sore from its punishing contact with the spade handle.

'Ah, the English gentleman's solution. Everything can be put right with a handshake, yes?' For a moment the huge hands don't move, and Gordon thinks, Bloody fool that I am, to think that chasms can be bridged with a puny gesture on a cemetery wall. Then Tshabalala reaches out and almost swallows his hand whole. 'Even though I am not an English gentleman, I shake with you, Gordon Kimber. If it signifies a commitment to a shared future, it is a good beginning.'

They sit there for a good ten seconds, lost in mutual admiration of this big accomplishment, this handshake between two men from different worlds who only yesterday were roaring at each other like lions. Then their hands drop and Gordon says, 'I suppose I'd better get back. I wouldn't like it to be said that Rose's father didn't do his share of the digging.'

Tshabalala starts to get up, and the dry stone wall they are sitting on trembles and shifts. 'No need. I came to tell you that it's nearly finished, and you've done more than your share. Leave the rest to the younger ones. We'll go down and get some breakfast first, then we'll meet with Ndlondlo to discuss final arrangements.'

Rose took a taxi after lunch the next day to Auntie April's large white gabled home in Constantia, telling her parents that she was going to see an old varsity friend. Which was strictly true, though the friend was not able to go in the white taxi with her. He went by train with Auntie Hester and arrived late.

Auntie April greeted Rose at the front door in a flurry of scent and talcum powder and her best blue silk jersey afternoon dress, which turned her eyes the deep blue of the hydrangeas lining the drive, and which swelled over her large bosom like the perfect wave. She held out heavily ringed hands and said, 'Welcome, my dear, so very welcome. Though I'm afraid Jacob and Hester aren't here yet.'

Rose said, feeling awkward, 'Hullo, Auntie April. You don't mind if I call you that?'

'Of course not. Come in, come in. We'll go through to the lounge.'

The plump figure in blue sailed away in front of her through a hallway lined with sombre stinkwood furniture into a large and beautiful room in the Cape Dutch style: high beamed ceiling, elegantly proportioned windows, brass chandeliers, bowls of proteas everywhere. April had worked hard to achieve the correct Old Afrikaner Family ambience, and the fact that she had done it with a team of coloured workers was an irony not lost on any of them. 'Groot-Oupa lived well, nè?' the carpenter had joked as he packed his tools for the last time to go home to his numbered box in the coloured township.

Auntie April waved Rose into a sofa and sat down next to her, Italian shoes side by side on a Persian carpet the colour of spilt wine. She turned and took her hands again and said, 'Let me have a good look at you, my dear. Jacob has told me so little.'

Rose saw inquisitive eyes under brows plucked to a thin arch, and a round pink face that Jake had said reminded him of a powder puff. It had been so well looked after since childhood with sun protection creams that it had hardly wrinkled. Her blonde hair was teased up into an elaborate arrangement of billowing curls that must have come straight from the hairdresser that morning; the curls had the keen chemical gleam of over-enthusiastic lacquering.

She was saying in the sweet high breathy voice of well-nurtured Afrikaans womanhood, 'Such a pretty girl, and clever too, I hear.'

Rose said, 'Not as clever as Jake. I'm just a teacher.'

'But teaching is a very good profession! My Willemien took up teaching. She was at Normal College.' She reached proudly for a photograph in a silver frame on the side table, and Rose was shown a girl with a heavy face under an almost identical arrangement of teased blonde curls. 'She's my first-born. Then come Chris-Jan and Barend; they both went to Stellenbosch. But Jacob has told you this?'

'He's told me a bit about your family, yes.' The blue eyes were anxious. Rose thought, If you're a coloured passing for white, every single encounter you have with strangers must be an egg-dance to find out how much they know. She went on, 'But he talked mostly about you. He's very fond of you, Auntie April.'

'And me of him. He's a good boy, Jacob; a credit to his mother Miriam.' The powder puff darted towards her, followed by a waft of lacquer. 'Do you know what he's doing here in Cape Town?'

Rose thought in panic, What am I supposed to say?

Watching her face, Auntie April nodded. 'So you do know. I know too, though he thinks I don't. My people's struggle is close to my heart, and when I can, I help it along.' She fell silent, her full lips firming together like Jake's did when he dammed up things he wanted to say, and felt he couldn't. Rose felt the formal beauty of the big room closing round her like plastic shrink-wrap that excludes all the air. Is this how Auntie April feels all the time among the white people she chose to join? she wondered. The high breathy voice was saying, 'Did he tell you, or did you find out?'

'I put two and two together. It was a terrible shock. I – we broke up afterwards. It was only coming here to Cape Town and seeing him again that made me realise how much I missed him and needed him.' Rose began to smile. 'We want to get married as soon as this last mission's over.'

'So it's marriage talk, then.' Auntie April dropped her hands and turned away to look out the window, where a broad green lawn sloped down to a swimming pool which a gardener was cleaning with a long brush. 'Have you thought carefully what it means, taking on Jacob?'

'I think so.'

Auntie April swung back to her and said sharply, 'I hope so, because it won't be easy. I know what I'm talking about, though I've had things the other way round. I've had to lie and keep secrets like they're locked up in the bank. I've had to be on guard every minute of the day in case I make a mistake and lose it all – or even worse, lose it for my children.' Her eyes glazed and she reached into her sleeve and took out a lace-edged handkerchief drenched in scent, using it to dab the corners of her eyes. 'But I've had my compensations. I live well. For you, my dear, it will be a lot harder. You'll have people's eyes on you always, marking the differences between the two of you. And looks can hurt, believe me. You'll have to leave your nice home and go to something much smaller, to pinch yourself in and get used to living with people always around you. Then you'll have to try not to care too much, and never to blame Jacob for the things he can't help. Can you do that?'

'I think so. We love each other, and – '

'But love isn't enough.' Auntie April leaned forward. 'You've got to do your book-keeping sums first, put the credit side against the debit side to see if they balance out. Only then can you make a good decision. That's what I did. I weighed the privileged life I would lead and the advantages for my children against the man I would have to live with to get these things.' The blue eyes were tragic. 'For me, I'm still not sure I made the right choice. The man was worse than I thought, and the life has been harder than I thought. You can never relax with these people; never let your hair down and put on slippers and laugh with your mouth wide open like I can at home.'

Rose thought, She still thinks of the township as home. Surely I won't feel the same way about that great pile in Houghton?

'You always feel different, always. It never gets easier. But how could I let Ma down when she'd made such sacrifices for me? And for my children, of course, it's another matter. They have a proper chance in life.' The high breathy voice dies away into the recesses of the room. 'For that only, it was worth it.'

'Are you advising me not to marry Jake?'

'My dear.' The ringed hands clasped hers again. 'All I'm saying is, do your sums first. You're lucky that you can put loving him on the credit side, because that weighs heavy. But don't think that the sums always work out like you think they will.' Auntie April gives her hands a warning shake. 'I'm the only one who can say these things to you. Listen to me good, you hear?'

Rose thought, Now I see why Jake likes her so much, and leaned forward to kiss the powder puff cheek. 'I'm listening, Auntie April. And thank you.'

Into the stillness of understanding between them came the sounds of Jake and Auntie Hester's arrival and Farida's voice as she let them in the kitchen door. Afterwards Rose thought, It was like a midnight feast, that tea party in the heart of wealthy white Cape Town: four coloured people welcomed me into their secret society whose members have infiltrated even the control room of the edifice built to keep them out.

Auntie Hester with her prominent black-haired mole and crimplene dress and dropsical legs ending in misshapen lace-up shoes had been shy of her at first, and cowed by the huge elegance of the voorkamer and the dainty tea Auntie April and Farida had prepared. On a silver tray were ranged porcelain teacups smothered in roses, lace-edged napkins, cake forks, side plates and a selection of home-baked biscuits, iced cakes and a melktert fragrant with cinnamon. But Jake made them all laugh with his jokes about working in Parliament, and when Farida took off her apron and sat down to join them, it became a family party with the feeling of feet being put up and stays loosened. Soon Auntie Hester was telling Rose about her children and Farida was showing photographs, and when Jake moved to the arm of Rose's chair and bent to kiss her, the three older women sighed with pleasure.

'Ag, it's been so nice having you all,' Auntie April said when they stood inside the kitchen door to say goodbye where the neighbours wouldn't see. 'I wish you could come more often. I haven't laughed so much for months.' Tertius Tulbagh De Wet never laughed, and as a strict Dopper, shunned parties other than state banquets and receptions at which he was expected to appear.

'I'm sorry I'm so bad about coming over, April,' Auntie Hester said, 'but it takes a long time to get here, and the walk up from the station is hard on my legs these days.'

Auntie April put her arm through her sister's. 'Shame, I know, dear. I would come to you, but Tertius won't let me move out of the grounds now without the chauffeur, who's also a trained bodyguard. These are dangerous times for Cabinet Ministers and their families, he says. If only he knew – ' She stopped herself, glancing at Jake. 'Well, we must just learn to enjoy the times we do have together. I'll send a taxi for you next month, Hester, if you don't mind walking the last block and coming in the servants' entrance as usual.'

'Why should I mind? I've always done it.' Auntie Hester's bleak acceptance of the indignity wrung Rose's heart, and she kept hearing the words in the days that followed. 'I've always done it.' Gone in and out of servants' entrances, walked up from the station on tired old legs, kissed her sister goodbye behind closed doors because one was born brown and one was born pale-skinned enough to slip through the meshes. I hope Jake is right about the changes that must come, she thought. I'd hate our children to feel second class. Ever.

For the single day left to them before the separate New Year's Eve festivities they would be attending and Rose's return to Johannesburg with her parents, Jake pleaded off work sick and took her up on the mountain he had learned to love. 'The air's clean up there and the views are fantastic, and you don't see other people for an hour at a stretch sometimes,' he said.

Properly dressed for walking this time in thick-soled tackies, shorts, a floppy hat and a sweater tied over her T-shirt, she met him down the road from the Mount Nelson where he stood waiting, discreetly gloved and helmeted, next to the motor bike. In its panniers were a picnic lunch that Auntie Hester had made for them: plastic boxes of cold pickled fish and rice salad, a small pot of atchar relish, four koeksisters wrapped in tinfoil and some fat yellow Jubilee peaches with the pink blush of high summer. They went swooping together along De Waal Drive and past the University to Newlands Forest, where Jake parked the bike and they packed the picnic lunch into his old canvas rucksack, next to a bottle of cold sparkling wine.

They walked up through the tall pines to the contour path which meanders in and out of indigenous bush and kloofs with giant mossy boulders among which lovers can get lost for hours. They climbed the dank crevice of Skeleton Gorge, to emerge almost with their heads in the clouds in a flower-starred valley with views forever over the Cape Flats and the glorious deep blue sweep of False Bay. The valley led on to the irregular Table Mountain plateau with its string of peat-brown dams and its high sunny silence, and here they found a rock ledge to sit on and eat their picnic lunch, and then to lie on unseen and love each other. In the whole long magical day, the few hikers they saw nodded and smiled and said hullo and passed on without the flicker of eyes that notice differences.

'The people who walk up here are special,' Jake said. 'Maybe it's being dwarfed by the landscape. Man seems so insignificant when you're in the mountains.'

'If we go to Lesotho, maybe we can live in the mountains,' Rose said. 'They call it The Roof of Africa, don't they?'

'Don't,' Jake said.

'Don't what?'

'Dream too much. Anything can happen. You haven't spoken to your folks yet, and they'll try to stop us for sure. Or I could get caught,' he shivered, in spite of the hot sunlight, 'and get stuck away on Robben Island. Or worse.'

She threw her arms round him and cried out, 'Jake, you can't get caught! You must stop.'

'Soon, poppie, I promise. Soon, darling,' he soothed, stroking her lovely blonde hair and thinking. She still imagines that you can control what happens to you. She'll learn otherwise if she marries me. I hope it doesn't dim her brightness, or take away this love I never expected, never hoped for.

On the way down, he nearly stood on a snake. It was lying on a rock in the middle of the path, a glossy dark brown with a pale yellow belly, and when his shoe came down near its head it reared up in fright and jack-knifed backwards down the hillside, looping and twisting like a length of live liquorice, more fascinating than frightening.

'Jake, be more careful,' she begged, grabbing his arm.

'It got more of a fright than I did,' he laughed. 'My sister Violet always says that snakes are a bad omen, because she's so scared of them. I don't believe in bad omens.'

This time it was he who did not feel the ghost walking over his grave.

31

Sarah wakes in the armchair to warm wetness in her lap, and a pair of intent round eyes fixed on her face. The hut is dark and quiet, the candles burned down, the other mourners except the old woman silently gone, and the child lies watching her with the tranquil certainty that breakfast will soon be forthcoming. Sarah bends her head to kiss the small honeyed cheek and says, 'We'd better get you changed and fed then, lovey.'

When she lifts her head again she sees Rose lying there, grey and cold as marble, and the dreadful chill of it makes her shudder and tears gush as though they've been turned on and the valve has stuck and won't close again. She uses the child's wrapping blanket to try and stanch them, saying, 'We can't have this now, can we, Hope? We've got things to do.'

The child murmurs in answer to her voice, and when she looks up from the damp blanket, gives her a radiant smile that exposes pink gums and two seed pearl teeth. It is a smile of pure early morning joy and though it doesn't stop the tears, it is a small warm light in a dark place and gets her to her feet and across to the door without looking at the side-by-side coffins again. There will be time to say a proper goodbye later in the day. Now the priorities are to change and feed this little person who has just smiled at her, and to be with Gordon when the funeral arrangements are discussed.

After that, she will have to find something to wear this afternoon. All they have with them in the suitcases in the car are holiday clothes, and she cringes from the thought of the bright shifts and silk caftans she usually loves to wear. Last night she changed into the only sober things she could find, a khaki cotton shirt and skirt, but these are crumpled now and anyway not suitable for a funeral where there will be many prying cameras. She thinks, Oh God, that I should have to think about suitable clothes when all I want to do is tear everything to shreds and cover my head with ashes.

As she leaves the hut Sarah nods to the old woman huddled in her blanket, assured that Rose and Jake will not be left alone. She walks down the track towards the clinic with the baby held snugly against her shoulder and tears running down her cheeks. There are more fowls than people about, scratching and pecking and trampling their busybody arrow-marks into the damp earth. From the hillside comes the long carrying call of a herdboy urging his cattle to walk on, promising sweeter grass ahead. Passing the school, she hears the sound of children chanting in unison, and thinks, As we grow older, we seem to lose the ability to make our many voices speak as one. Why? Why does it become so important to be heard singing our own strident arias, when we could be making beautiful music with the rest of the choir?

A young woman in a print dress comes out of a thatched stockade to greet her, saying shyly, 'Dumela, Ma-Rose.'

'Dumela,' Sarah says, trying to smile at her though it is like a monkeys' wedding, sunshine through rain. The woman begins to walk beside her, one hand resting lightly on her arm, and is soon joined by others who show their sympathy in different ways, with a touch, a sad smile, a soft murmur of Sesotho. Soon she is surrounded by a small phalanx of women whose concern is so comforting that by the time she has reached the clinic, she has managed to stop crying.

Sister Quthing is waiting for her on the top step. She says when she reaches it, 'Could you thank them for me, Sister? They are all so kind.'

'Of course.' The Sister says a few words in Sesotho, and the women nod and smile at Sarah before turning away. 'I was on my way to fetch you when I saw you coming,' she goes on in English. 'I have a surprise for you inside.'

'I don't know that I could cope with any more surprises right now.' Though the walk with the women has cheered her, Sarah's back and neck feel stiff and sore after the night spent in the armchair, and yesterday's bump on the head has begun to throb, threatening a headache.

'You'll like this one, my dear. It's Jake's mother. She arrived a few minutes ago.'

'At last. I was so worried she wouldn't get here. Could you hold Hope for a minute, Sister?' Sarah hurries into the clinic and over to the chair by the desk where a coloured woman in a black dress and hat is sitting hunched over a large handbag, looking dazed. She bends to embrace her, saying, 'Miriam. Oh, Miriam. What a terrible way to meet again.'

'Sarah.' It is all Miriam can choke out. Her throat is almost closed with crying and her green eyes, so like Jake's, peer out through puffy slits. She lifts her arms and clings to Sarah and they rock together, sharing their grief.

'Dis vreeslik,' Miriam sobs. 'Both of them.'

'Cruel and hideous.' Sarah feels the red ball of anger swelling again in her head, searing her eyes dry from the inside. 'But at least we have Hope. I've just brought her down with me from the – from the place where they're lying. Would you like to see her?'

Miriam nods, unable to speak. She has not seen the child of her favourite child yet, her bright flame Jacob who wanted to change everything even as a small boy, and now will never see the changes he worked so hard for. She wants badly to know if this little Hope looks like him. She realises that the other bereaved parents will want to bring her up, will use their money and their white power to make things infinitely easier for the child than they would otherwise be, and in her mind concedes that this is just and proper, since they have nobody else now. But in her heart she worries that whatever the child carries of Jacob will be lost when the white world swallows her up. And that would be unbearable.

'Here she is, Mrs Van Vuuren.' Sister Quthing has changed Hope's wet nappy with the brisk efficiency with which she does everything, and places her now in her other grandmother's arms, moving the handbag to the desk. 'Could you hold her while I go and warm up her bottle?'

Sarah stands watching Miriam make the same inventory she did, touching with a tentative finger the child's soft cheek and her springy dark curls with their reddish gleam, then tracing the tiny well-defined arcs of her eyebrows. Hope gazes up at this new face with a small frown; her ability to cope with new faces is being tested to its limits. 'Jacob's hair,' Miriam whispers, 'and the way he used to look up at me, always trying to understand. She is like him, thanks be to God.'

Sarah bends over them, putting one arm round Miriam's shoulders. 'Yes, she is. There's a definite look about the mouth, though she has Rose's determined chin. She's going to be a handful when she grows up.' She goes on quickly, 'You won't mind if we have her, Miriam? She's all we've got now, and we can give her all the advantages –' She trails off, thinking, Advantages that didn't help our children in the end.

Miriam looks up. 'Ag no, of course I'll not mind. I have my remaining kids and their little ones.' Sarah remembers that she lost a daughter too a year or so ago. So much pain shared between us, she thinks. The halting Afrikaans-accented voice goes on, 'Only I would like to see her sometimes, not to lose my Jacob completely. And I want her to know that I am her Ouma too. This brown face with the so-ugly mark on it,' she fingers the large mole she shares with Hester, 'is also part of her. She must not grow up too proud to know me.'

Sarah kneels down on Sister Quthing's shiny floor and vows, 'She will not, I promise. She will know both her families, and maybe she will be a better South African one day than the rest of us.'

Miriam's slow tired smile is an affirmation of the wish for peace that so many South Africans share, and are increasingly afraid of never being able to achieve. 'I would like that,' she says. 'I would like that very much.'

Jake and Rose came off Table Mountain with blistered feet, aching calves and shaky knees from the long downhill climb, but they were so happy that neither noticed the discomfort until they had parted.

Rose lay soaking her sore muscles in the huge pink bathtub of her suite, thinking, How shall I tell the Aged P's? And when? They're going to have a fit. Their well-nurtured little Rosebud wanting to marry a coloured! She sank under the water and laughed, making a stream of sound bubbles.

But the more she thought about it, the more apprehensive she became. The Mixed Marriages Act prohibited marriages between people of different races*, and Gordon would not give up his daughter without a fight. She turned the tap on with her toes to let in some more hot water. Although I'm twenty-six, well beyond the age of parental control, I wonder if he can do anything to stop me?

She decided to keep the news for New Year's Day, their last day in Cape Town. She and Jake had agreed during their long walk that she would tell them he was an English teacher working

* This Act has since been repealed, on 19 June 1985.

364

in Lesotho, which would fit in with what Sarah knew of their friendship at university, and his poetry. 'By the time we can get married – *if* we can,' he said, not allowing himself to believe yet that it could really happen, 'it'll be mostly true anyway. I'll be teaching communications, which is close enough to English.'

'I don't like deceiving them,' Rose said. 'Mum's always made a big thing about building up trust by being honest with each other.'

'Letting them know what I'm really doing is too dangerous.' His hands began to tremble like they always did now when he thought about being caught. He slid them between his thighs and on to the warm rock they were sitting on so she wouldn't notice, and went on, 'Your folks wouldn't understand anyway. Whites are very quick to condemn what they call terrorism, but the day-to-day, year in, year out violence we suffer is just part of the background.'

'They don't know about it,' Rose said.

'They don't want to know. That's the whole trouble. They close their eyes to what's going on because it would upset their nice comfortable lives to see too much.'

There had been a long silence between them after that, broken by Rose saying, 'I'll open Mum and Dad's eyes. Starting with you as a future son-in-law.'

'But not as a Che Guevara, OK? Revolutionary glamour I don't need, poppie. I'm fighting this fight because I can't do anything else, like those First World War poets in the trenches. When it's finished, I want to get on with my life. Our life, rather,' he corrected himself, and the grin he gave her was a long way from being ferocious.

Now Rose lay in the bath thinking, It's the first time he hasn't qualified the future with a maybe. Now I've got to make sure I make my end work.

She spent the morning of New Year's Eve shopping for the party dress Gordon had wanted her to buy, resisting the urge to go and sit on the bench opposite the Houses of Parliament in Government Avenue, Jake-watching. In the afternoon she went with Sarah to Llandudno beach and lay on a towel tanning and reading next to one of its huge round boulders while she painted. The sturm und drang of her adolescent years, the defiant arguments and door-slammings and flouncings away, had mellowed into a comfortable relationship that they both enjoyed. Now that her reputation as an artist was established,

Sarah had become less manic about her work and would drop her brushes for a chat over a cup of tea or a gin and tonic where before she would have said impatiently, 'I'm much too busy.' They spoke about their work and their concerns as friends do; to Rose's relief her mother had not once whined for a wedding and grandchildren like so many of her friends' mothers did.

'I was married ridiculously early,' Sarah said once. 'I didn't know who I was, and it took me a long time to find out what I was really good at because I missed the experimental years. I hope you're more sensible.'

'It was my fault,' Rose said, vividly remembering the day she had compared her birthday with the date of her parents' marriage. She had written reams about it in her Journal under the heading *I Was A Shotgun Baby!* I wonder where the Journal is now? she thought. I used to be so serious about my writing, scribbling away in laborious detail about everything that happened to me and all the people I met so I'd have plenty of material to draw on to become a famous author, and dreaming about winning the Nobel Prize. Now I teach other people's writing and dream about a poet.

Sarah said, 'Don't ever talk of faults, Rosie. You're one of the best things that ever happened to me.'

'What were the others?'

Her mother looked down at her rough hands that smelled of oil paint no matter how often she scrubbed them. 'David, though there was so much pain. He was a gentle little boy with bones that used to stick out everywhere like a baby bird before its feathers grew. Yet he was so brave.' She stopped for a moment, then went on, 'Painting, of course. And Dad, though it took us a long time to shake down together.'

'What do you mean?'

'We were both spoiled children when we married. I sometimes think it was only your father's determination to do better than everyone else that kept us together. Then we grew up. We actually see each other now, not idealised images of how we wish the other would be. The only thing that bothers me is that he won't look after himself properly. He's much too heavy and takes no exercise at all.'

'I don't know that I want to marry,' Rose had said. It was during the months after she had sent Jake away.

'You will, love,' Sarah said. 'Just take your time about finding the right person. There's no hurry.'

Now she knew she had found him, and her choice would be fought tooth and nail by both her parents. I'll just have to make it very clear that they have to choose between him and me, she thought, or no me.

Strong words. Her resolution ebbed and flowed like the Cape's cold tides. She worried about the coming confrontation all through the New Year's Eve party at an elegant cantilevered mansion high above Clifton Beach. The mansion belonged to Gordon's business colleague, a shipping magnate, and the other people at the party were confident, tanned socialites whose conversation had no relevance at all to Rose's life as a teacher at a black education centre. Sitting on the window seat watching the sun take an age to set in a dramatic red sky that reflected on the sea like blood, a glass of French champagne growing warm in her hand, she thought, People talk about abolishing apartheid as though it could be done overnight. But how can you heal a society where the extremes are so great?

Gordon came to her and said, 'Why so pensive, Rosie? Come and join us.'

'Just thinking.'

'Thinking what?' His face was ruddy with brandy and camaraderie and pride in Sarah, who was the centre of an admiring circle, vivid in peacock blue silk.

'How different we all are,' she said, and that was how she began her explanation the next morning after breakfast as they sat in a corner of the terrace having tea together. At the Mount Nelson, so unabashedly high colonial, it seems more appropriate to have tea than any other beverage. Except perhaps for port.

Sarah looked up reluctantly. She liked lingering over her tea after breakfast with the morning newspaper, and was grumpy about being interrupted. 'What do you mean, dear?'

'It's our differences that make us unique, isn't it? I mean, it'd be very boring if we were all the same.' Rose was sitting forward in her chair with her hands gripping the armrests.

Sarah thought, I smell trouble. She's been like a cricket all week, hopping off on mysterious excursions and hardly able to sit still when she's with us. I hope it's not going to spoil our last morning.

Gordon said in a lazy voice, 'Very boring. I've never liked the idea of clones.'

'You may not like what I'm going to tell you at first either,'

Rose said, 'but once you've got used to it, I know you'll feel differently.'

'Sounds ominous,' he said, smiling at her and thinking how pretty his daughter looked this morning with her flyaway blonde hair catching the sunlight.

'Tell us and get it over with,' Sarah said, putting down the paper. 'You've been building up to this all week, haven't you?'

'Yes. It's – I just don't know how to soften it for you,' Rose said, 'so I'd better come right out with it. I'm going to be married.'

Gordon gave a bellow of pleasure. 'I knew it! As soon as you brought Miles home, I knew he was – '

'It isn't Miles.'

Sarah felt a cold tingle start at the base of her spine and work upwards. 'Who is he?'

'Isn't this a bit sudden if we haven't even met the chap?' Gordon was frowning now.

'Mum's met him. He's been to the house.'

'When? You haven't brought friends round for months.'

'A long time ago, when I was at varsity.' Rose watched her mother trying not to show her alarm, but there was no indication yet that she had realised it was Jake. 'He came for lunch once.'

'So many of them came for lunch, and to swim. They all looked alike: jeans, tackies, T-shirts, beards. You can't expect me to guess who it was unless you put a name to him.' Sarah spoke in a mother's worried staccato. 'Have you been seeing him all this time without telling us?'

'No. He went away for four years and I only met him again a few months ago.' Rose thought, I can't say it was last year, or they'll think I was being sneaky. 'I love him very much. And I know he's right for me.'

'Why don't you tell us who he is, then?' Gordon was still lounging back in his chair, showing none of the alarm signals Sarah was putting out.

'Because I know how you're going to react, and I don't want a knee-jerk reaction.' Rose pulled her chair closer to where they were sitting and leaned forward. 'I wish I could project the kind of man he is into your minds before the shutters go up. He's kind and clever and he writes poetry that people will sit up and listen to one day.'

Sarah was thinking, Shutters going up. All this rigmarole, this secrecy. She knows we'll object to him. But why? Is it Ursula's brother, perhaps? Irritated at being thought a bigot, she said, 'You must know we wouldn't mind if he's Jewish or comes from a family that's hard up, as long as he's right for you.'

'We could even learn to like an Afrikaner in time.' Gordon gave a self-conscious bray, the way all South Africans do after making a racist joke.

Rose said, 'Good guesses. He's both hard up and Afrikaans-speaking. He's also coloured.'

'Oh no.' Sarah remembered him then: the young poet who had taken her painting of Rose with such anger in his green eyes, then sent it back. He hadn't been very dark, but there'd been a broadly flaring nose and fuzzy hair like an African.

'Jesus Christ.' Gordon was bolt upright in his chair now, his face gone bright crimson. 'You can't! It's against the law. You can't. I won't allow it.'

At the sudden loudness, several elderly women who were also having tea on the terrace turned their heads to look. Rose said, 'Keep your voice down, Dad! And you can't stop me. We're going to be married in Lesotho, where it's legal.'

'Why?' Sarah had gone pale. 'Why, with so many suitable young men to choose from at university, did you have to choose someone as – as – ' Her voice faltered.

'As dark-skinned?' Rose shot back. 'As forbidden? Or as lower-class? Specify, Mother.' She had never called Sarah 'Mother'. 'I need to know how deep your racism goes. If it's just skin-deep, we may have a chance. If it's deeper, I can see major problems ahead.'

'As different,' Sarah managed. 'We know how difficult marriage can be, even when you're both from the same background.' She groped sideways for Gordon's hand. 'To marry someone from such a totally different society is asking for trouble, even before you get to the legal complications.'

'I love him,' Rose said. 'We're good together. That's much more important to me than the colour of his skin.'

'Love isn't enough.' Sarah was blinking.

Gordon thrust his jaw forward in the belligerent way Rose had seen him use on employees who were trying to disagree with him, and said, 'No, it bloody isn't enough, take it from me. You've got to have better reasons.'

'Why? It's my life. I don't need to give you reasons for how I choose to live it. Whatever they are.'

Sarah gasped, 'You're not pregnant?'

I knew that'd be the first conclusion they'd jump to, Rose thought. She said coldly, 'No. There are other reasons for getting married, you know.'

'That wasn't necessary.' Sarah's eyes went watery.

'You little cow!' Gordon hated to see Sarah cry. 'Apologise to your mother.'

'For what? Raking up past history? That's a minor offence compared to what you've just been saying to me.' Mindful of the elderly women, who were still watching with interest, Rose spoke in an angry whisper. 'You've made it plain that a: I don't know what I'm doing, and b: the man I love is the wrong colour. Colour! I'm not choosing a car, I'm choosing a husband.'

'It's not his colour,' Sarah moaned, 'it's – '

Gordon broke in, 'The hard truth is that colour matters in this country, whether you like it or not.'

Rose thought, I knew this would happen. I knew they wouldn't listen to what I had to say about Jake the person. All they can think about is Jake the coloured. Why is it that people's minds slam shut when it comes to other races?

She said, 'Let me tell both of you a few hard truths. Jake and I are going to get married whether you or the South African government like it or not, and we will live in Lesotho where he is teaching. If you want to see me, you'll have to accept Jake as my husband. You don't have to like him. I can't make you do that, though if you take your blinkers off you may surprise yourselves, but you do have to accept him. OK? Think about it. When you want me, I'll be in my room.'

She pushed her chair back. Two of the elderly women had got together, and were talking behind their veiny purple hands.

Sarah brushed away the threatening tears with the back of her hand and said, 'Wait a minute. You can't just drop a bomb on us and walk off like that.' She was growing angry now that the initial shock had worn off. 'It needn't have been quite so public, either.'

'I thought you'd both be less likely to get upset if I told you when there were other people around,' Rose said. What she had actually thought was, Dad won't be able to rant and rave.

'How we feel should be a private matter between us, not for general consumption! I think we should go up to our suite to continue this discussion.' Sarah got up from her chair and swept away down the terrace, her striped skirt billowing.

Gordon followed her without a word, his face alarmingly red.

Rose was left to gather their books and the paper and run the gauntlet of elderly spaniel eyes, thinking, Well, that was a failure. But what did I expect?

When she entered the suite a few minutes later, bracing herself, Sarah was sitting in the chintz armchair by the window. Gordon was pacing up and down next to the chair, and burst out, 'What I resent is being told we're racists because of our very natural objections to a man from a different background whom we haven't even been allowed to meet. For Pete's sake, Rose, what did you expect us to say?'

She put the books down on the bedside table and swung round. 'I expect you to trust me! To trust my judgement in choosing this man. I'm not a child any more. I'm twenty bloody six, in case you hadn't noticed, and I know what I want in life. I want a meaningful, lasting relationship with someone I respect as well as love, and I know I'll have it with Jake. I've never felt even remotely like this about anyone else.'

During Sarah's angry march up to her room, the memory of the fight with her mother had lurched vividly into her mind, and she had thought, It mustn't happen to Rose and me! I couldn't bear it. I must keep my temper under control and try to handle this right, or we'll do terrible damage to each other. Now she said, 'It's not a matter of trust. It's just that we don't think you've fully thought out the consequences of marrying a – ' she hesitated, swallowed and went on ' – coloured man. You dismiss all the difficulties as flea-bites, and we know from bitter experience that they won't be.

'When you're young, you see life stretching out before you like some sort of country road bordered with grass and flowers, with grand vistas on either side. Well, it isn't. It's full of pot-holes and dongas and sudden yawning gaps that swallow up the people you love.' Tears trembled in her eyes. 'And you don't go whizzing along by car. You toil every inch of the way along the verge, sweating and sometimes getting sunstroke and sometimes getting mugged and occasionally, if you're lucky, finding a pleasant place to stop and rest. What we're saying is, Don't underestimate the problems ahead.'

Rose had sat down on the bed and was thinking, Do parents ever realise that you've grown up into someone different from them? She said sarcastically, 'Jake would certainly admire your use of the extended metaphor.'

'We're not concerned with him. We're concerned with you.'

'Everything that concerns me concerns him too now,' Rose said. 'That's what I'm trying to tell you.'

Gordon put in, 'Have you thought what it'll mean to have to live far away from your family and friends in a foreign country?'

Rose laughed. 'You could hardly call Lesotho foreign.'

'I'm not joking. Have you thought about the conditions you'll have to live under – I presume he's not earning very much as a teacher?' Rose shook her head. 'Have you really thought about your children? Life won't be easy for them. They'll be classified coloured too.'

'That's what's really bothering you, isn't it?' Rose said angrily. 'Coloured grandchildren.'

Sarah said in a low voice, 'I'd be lying if I said it didn't. But not because I think coloured people are inferior; at least give me credit for that. Some of the nicest women I've known have been black, and they helped me out of some bad pot-holes along my road.' She thought of Gertrude and Doris and neat, respectable Albertina, and wondered suddenly, Was Gordon right all those years ago? Could Rose's early friendship with Mfayedwa have given her a preference for coloured men?

'Why, then?' Rose said, sticking her chin out in the Gordon-gesture Sarah knew so well.

'Because they're just so very different. The facts are that we've been kept apart for so long in this country that we don't know each other at all. We haven't had a chance.'

'That's no reason not to try.'

'But Rosie, the gap is so wide that it's almost unbridgeable now. To try and cross it on your own is madness.'

'Madness,' Gordon repeated, still pacing.

There was a silence in the big room with its draped chintz curtains and ankle-deep carpet. Rose thought, Here we sit in the lap of luxury arguing about gaps and whether they should be crossed or not, when people are starving out there just for recognition as fellow human beings. But all we whites see is a society that runs smoothly, an economy that works, people with better incomes than in the rest of Africa. And the prospect of being swamped if so much as a hairline crack opens up in the dike. Well, I'm going to be a hairline crack, and that's all there is to it.

She said, 'I'm sorry you've both taken it this way. Nothing you say will change my mind, as you probably know. So I asked Jake to come to the hotel this afternoon before we leave for the airport, so you can look him over for yourselves. He didn't want to come because he said the likes of him probably weren't allowed in such a lanie place, but I checked with the desk clerk. Apparently it's all right for him to have tea or even a meal with us, but he can't have a drink in the bar and he's not allowed to dance. God knows why. Maybe the close proximity of brown and white skins is too ghastly to contemplate?'

Sarah said in a bleak voice, 'You're determined, then.'

'Very. So you'll have to accept him or lose me. Which will it be?'

'We'll see him, of course. You leave us, no choice. But it'll take a lot of getting used to.' Sarah got up and came twards her with a long-suffering look on her face, tears still trembling. 'We're going to miss you.'

'For heaven's sake, I'm not going to Timbuktu! I'll be four or five hours away, that's all.' Rose thought, She's trying the old you're-our-only-child routine again.

Gordon burst out. 'He'd better treat you right!' And it was the first thing he said to Jake, after shaking hands under Rose's stern eye at the door of the suite that afternoon. 'You'd better treat her right and make her happy, Van Vuuren. Or I'll have your guts. And I mean that.'

Conscious of the importance of first impressions, Jake was wearing a sports coat and grey flannels with a shirt and tie. He looked down at Gordon's thinning hair and red face and jowly neck and said stiffly, 'I'll do my best, Mr Kimber. More I can't do.'

Gordon went on, 'Rose has twisted our arms in the matter of your marriage, but I want you to know that I'll be tying her money up so tight that you won't be able to get a finger on it.'

Jake had been gearing up all day for the ordeal, telling himself to behave like a gentleman for Rose's sake, and not to take offence at anything her probably appalled parents threw at him. But this was intolerable. Controlling the impulse to hit the fat red face, he said, 'Insults I don't need. Please excuse me,' and turned to leave.

'Jake, please!' Rose put her hand on his arm and blazed at Gordon, 'How can you?'

'Easily.' Even the bald dome of Gordon's head had gone scarlet. 'And I'd say exactly the same to any young upstart without any money who wanted to marry you. Just so that he knows the position from the beginning.'

Jake laughed. It rang out like the iron bar farmers beat to summon their labourers, through the gracious room and out over the elegant terrace where the elderly women had gathered again to take afternoon tea. 'Phew, what a relief,' he gasped. 'For a moment there, I thought it was my colour you were objecting to. Being a penniless upstart I can handle.'

Sarah, who had sat down at the low table by the window to pour tea with a hand that shook, put the teapot down with a bang and began to laugh too. Soon they were all laughing, even Gordon, who had been quite surprised at how well the man spoke and how presentable he looked. At least he's educated, he thought sourly; small mercies.

Later when the tea had been poured and they were sitting politely drinking it and watching each other over the rims of their cups, Jake started to talk to Sarah about township art and Gordon thought, He's also a very shrewd bugger. And I wonder what else?

32

Sarah is outraged by the rifles that bar the way into the government offices. 'Let us through!' she demands. Even in crumpled khaki, her large body and pale silver hair swept up into a heavy bun give her an imperious presence.

'You must stop,' the soldier in the camouflage cap repeats. 'Everybody must stop.'

'But we are here by invitation.'

Miriam tugs at her arm and says, 'Better we wait outside until somebody comes, eh?'

But Sarah the white woman is not used to waiting patiently in queues for officialdom's mills to grind, as Miriam the diffident coloured woman has had to all her life. She says to the spokesman with the rifle, 'Send a message at once that we are here, please.'

'We cannot leave this place.' Is there a hint of satisfaction on the impassive face?

'Then I will have to shout.' Sarah opens her mouth wider and calls out, 'Will somebody let us in?'

A third soldier appears from the direction of the corridor, so quickly that he must already have been standing there, and says something in Sesotho.

The rifles snap back, and Sarah and Miriam walk into the public area with its slowly revolving fan and wooden counter and flyblown calendar of King Moshoeshoe. The third soldier says, 'Come with me,' and they follow him down the corridor where more armed men are standing guard, into the large office at the end. Gordon and Tshabalala are already there, seated on one side of a desk. Across from them, leaning forward with his hands splayed on a sheaf of papers, is a black man with knobbed eyebrows whose angry voice they have been hearing from the other end of the corridor. As the women walk in, he looks up

375

and snaps, 'Good morning. You're late, Mrs Kimber. May I remind you that time is short today?'

Sarah remembers Gordon's warning. 'The man's very bitter and twisted, but he's calling the shots. Try not to put his back up when you speak to him.'

She says in an even voice, 'I'm sorry, I had to see to the child. But I have brought along Jake's mother, Miriam Van Vuuren.'

Gordon and Tshabalala stand up, offering their chairs. Ndlondlo comes round the desk to take Miriam's hand between both of his. 'I'm pleased to meet you, Mrs Van Vuuren, though this is a very unhappy occasion. Jake was a good comrade. We'll miss him.' Turning to Sarah, he says, 'Rose too, of course, though she was not one of our members.'

'She did enough for your cause to merit a little more enthusiasm, don't you think?' Sarah says sharply.

Ndlondlo's face closes up like a fist. 'We are burying her with full military honours. I'd call that enthusiastic, Mrs Kimber.'

'*We* are burying her,' Sarah says. 'That is what this meeting is about, I understand.'

Ndlondlo looks at her for a long moment, then gestures at the two chairs. 'We'd better sit down before we go into the details. I'll get one of the men to bring more chairs from next door.' As Sarah and Miriam sit down, he goes to the door and speaks to the armed guard outside.

Sarah says under her breath to Gordon, who is standing behind her, 'I see what you mean.'

Gordon mutters, 'He has arranged for a military escort, pallbearers in ANC uniform and a choir. Won't listen to my objections.'

'No!' she says out loud, and turns to confront Ndlondlo as he sits down in the swivel chair across the desk. 'I will not have my daughter buried like a tin soldier!'

The thin mouth purses into a hard ridge. 'As I said to your husband last night, you have no choice. We are making the arrangements. We decide.'

'Not for my daughter, you don't.'

Ndlondlo shrugs. 'Suit yourself. Maybe you'd rather take her home and bury her in a fancy white cemetery where there are flowers and grass and expensive tombstones to keep her company?'

'Need you be so bloody offensive?' Gordon says on a rising note.

The cold voice comes across the desk in a slither of dislike. 'It seems I learned my lessons from you whites well.'

The guard comes in with two more chairs and Gordon and Tshabalala sit down. Forcing herself to speak in a more conciliatory voice, Sarah says, 'Our daughter's marriage was to Jake, not to your organisation, and she deplored all forms of violence. We would not like her to be carried by soldiers to her grave, or for rifles to be fired over it.'

Ndlondlo says, 'Since I understand there is only one grave, this will be difficult to avoid.'

'But you've got to see our point,' Gordon insists.

'I haven't got to do anything, my dear sir.' In England they have polite verbal insult down to a fine art, and 'my dear sir' which Ndlondlo learned there is one of his favourites. By varying the intonation, he can use it to maddening effect.

Gordon rises at once to the bait. 'Goddammit, I demand – '

Sarah interrupts, 'I thought we were asked here to discuss the arrangements, not to be presented with a *fait accompli*. Our wishes must surely be respected?'

'Bloody right!' Gordon's face is taking on a brick red flush.

'Your wishes are a small drop in the ocean of tears that is Africa!' Ndlondlo shouts. 'Why must they prevail?'

'Please.' Tshabalala, who has been silent until now, hunches his great khaki bulk forward in his chair and says, 'I'm sure we can work out a compromise here. Disagreements could spoil this funeral that so many will be watching. How about if Rose's colleagues from the school carry her in the procession? And maybe we could have the rifle salute to honour Jake when he is lowered first into the grave, so it is clear who it is intended for. The choir and the singing of the anthem *Nkosi Sikelel' iAfrika* would, I am sure, be acceptable to you, Mrs Kimber?'

'Of course.'

'Mrs Van Vuuren? Mr Kimber?'

Miriam nods, too sad and too tired and too conditioned by years of acceptance to join in this angry discussion. All she wants now is to go to her Jacob.

Gordon says, 'That sounds reasonable. I trust it will not be a choir in camouflage uniform?'

'We are too busy fighting for our rights to be able to take time off for singing practice, Mr Kimber.' The cold voice is scornful. 'We have engaged the Maseru Marvellous Singers, a professional group. They wear traditional dress and sing genuine

African music, not the pop rubbish that passes for music in the townships these days. They also sang at the wedding, I'm told.'

'Oh yes, we had photographs.' Sarah is relieved. Tshabalala's solution seems a fair one. She looks at him, remembering the sad smoky wail of his saxophone at her teenage parties, so long ago. On an impulse, she says, 'I don't suppose you would play your saxophone for them, Mr Tshabalala?'

'Out of the question.' The big man's hands chop a denial. 'I gave all that up in 1976, after Soweto. It didn't seem right to go on playing music when there were so many bad things happening.'

'Do you still have your saxophone?'

'Yes.' For a moment Tshabalala's face reveals the magnitude of his sacrifice. 'I take it out and look at it sometimes, but I haven't blown a note for nine years.'

Sarah leans towards him, putting her hand on his arm. 'Maybe this would be a good opportunity to start again? A sort of – reconciliation, if you like. Your world and ours. A fitting way to say goodbye to two young people who brought them together.' Her eyes are full of tears.

Tshabalala gives a reluctant nod. 'That is an idea. 'I'll think about it, Mrs Kimber. More I can't promise.'

'You have the gall to talk of reconciliation while our country is in flames?' Ndlondlo's bitterness licks across the desk like a petrol-fed flame. 'While your army's soldiers shoot our people with impunity?'

Sarah says angrily, 'It's not my army! I'm sick of being damned for a government I never voted for, as though all whites in this country are automatically racist oppressors. You know it's not true.'

The smile across the desk is like a knife slash. 'What I know is what that great British statesman, Edmund Burke, said. "In order for evil to succeed, it is only necessary that good men do nothing." Apartheid must be one of the most successful evils the world has ever known.'

'Oh no, you don't!' The accusation makes Sarah furious. 'I may be guilty of thoughtless behaviour sometimes, but I know I'm not evil. Your deliberate, calculated violence is evil. There is no possible justification for terrorism.'

'The right of my people, of any people, to live like human beings is justification enough.'

'Never!' Sarah's rage explodes in her head like a grenade. 'To kill in the name of human rights is the worst hypocrisy. But you don't care, because men love violence. All men, I think, though some are better at controlling their lust to fight and hit and hurt than others. You can see it in their eyes at sports matches and motor races, in the way they swing along on army parades cradling their weapons of war, and in pubs when they've had too much to drink. They love it! The worst mistake women ever made was to let men assume the role of decision makers, because their instinctively violent response to any threat or crisis always clouds the real issue, which is to find a solution. If more women were in power, I guarantee there would be fewer wars. A woman who has nurtured life does not easily destroy it.'

The knife-slash broadens. 'I suppose the Falklands war was just a figment of Mrs Thatcher's imagination?'

'She's a politician, and they're exceptions to the rule.' Sarah would like to hit the smug face across the desk. 'All politicians care about is getting power and keeping it, along with all the perks that go with it: money, status, free travel, and at the end, inflated pensions. The white man may have raped Africa, but her own political gangsters will finish her off. Do you know that the supposedly dirt poor Third World accounts for one fifth – one fifth! – of the world's spending on arms and ammunition? This can only mean that people's sufferings, the hunger and shanty homes and preventable diseases that sap their health, aren't as important to their politicians as grabbing power and staying there.'

'How dare you question our good faith!' Ndlondlo's eyes are a molten, malevolent black. 'We have been working for years for the liberation of our people.'

'But what good is liberation to a starving person who can only choose from one party anyway, and then only if an election actually happens? Africa has a very poor record in this respect. We whites down here at the tip aren't the only culprits.'

'Tell that to the world's press.'

'They wouldn't listen. They're only interested in the bad things we do, not the good.'

'The bad things being in the vast majority.'

'You can talk! What about necklacing?' Sarah demands, trembling now. 'It's barbarism pure and simple, yet you've encouraged it rather than condemning it. Rose wrote to us, horrified, only a few weeks ago because she had heard on a *Voice of Freedom* broadcast someone saying "The strategy of burning

379

sell-outs seems to have paid out well in the ultimate end." Don't you think that putting a petrol-soaked tyre round someone's neck and setting fire to it could conceivably be an evil act, Mr Ndlondlo?'

'It's not "Mr", just Ndlondlo. It means the horned adder, a very poisonous snake, and it was not given to me lightly.' The venom in his voice would paralyse anyone but a furiously angry mother. 'I say, how much less evil is necklacing than shooting children in the back when they're running away, as your people do?'

'Not my people, that's what I'm trying to say!' Sarah cries. 'But yes, that is equally evil, and I condemn it equally. I condemn all violence, and most specially when children are involved.'

Gordon and Tshabalala have been sitting watching the exchange, having gone over much the same ground yesterday. But Gordon sees the familiar mottling on Sarah's cheeks and mindful of her blood pressure says, 'Babe, there's no point in this. Let's just leave it there. We've got the rest of the day to get through.'

'No! I want to ask this man something I've been wondering for a long time. Why doesn't the ANC call our government's bluff by publicly renouncing violence – for six months or a year if you can't give it up altogether as a bargaining point? You already have world-wide sympathy, but you're squandering a lot of it because no civilised society can condone terrorism. Just think what a strong case you'd have if you dropped the bombings and the killings and said to our government, "OK, we've stopped. Now what are you going to do?" You'd have them in a corner. They'd be forced to start bargaining.'

'Never. You know as well as I do that the Boers will never give up their power. It must be taken away by force.' Ndlondlo's fist pounds the desk. 'And we will do it. The revolution is already beginning.'

'Bullshit!' Sarah doesn't normally swear, but she is so angry now that it explodes from her. 'You people take no account of reality. You're deluding yourself and everybody else who listens to those old communist fairy tales if you think a revolution is about to happen here. It can't! The people are nowhere near strong enough to take on a government backed by a very well-trained army and police force packed with its own tribesmen, so there isn't the faintest chance of a mutiny. And the superpowers aren't interested in getting embroiled in a dirty little southern hemisphere fight, however much they may huff and puff. The only way is negotiation.'

'It is you who take no account of reality. Our strategy was proved to work in Algeria.'

Sarah blazes, 'But we aren't Algeria! We're not colonists who can run home to a mother country. All that your strategy can promise is more bloodshed and more suffering, specially if sanctions are applied and people begin to lose their jobs. How do you think they'll feel then about all you comrades riding on the exile bandwagon, trailing clouds of self-righteous glory, secure in the knowledge that you won't have to suffer? Answer me, please. I am a mother who has lost a child in this conflict, and there are many angry women like me. We have had enough of your solutions.'

Ndlondlo says, with a return of the knife-slash smile, 'This is exactly why women cannot be trusted to run governments. They get too emotional. Rose was just like you: full of wonderful ideals, but ultimately white and therefore privileged. Not us. Not even like us.'

Sarah says, 'My God, you're more of a racist than I'm supposed to be.'

'Pardon me, that is not racism, my good lady. I am talking about the survival of my people.'

'That's just what the Afrikaners say.'

'Precisely. That is why we understand each other so well, and why we are fighting this war to the death for our country. You English are irrelevant – '

'Don't call me English!'

Ndlondlo ignores her. ' – and so is all this hot-air talk. I have things to do, people to see, interviews to give. You must please leave me to get on with them. I will see you later at the funeral. Now, please?' They are dismissed by an impatient gesture, and he bends his head to read one of the papers on the desk.

Sarah gets up first, seething, 'If you are a parent, I hope you suffer one day like we have.'

Without looking up, he says, 'A family would have distracted me from my main purpose. Goodbye.'

Gordon hustles her out before she can open her mouth again. Halfway down the corridor, as they pass the armed soldiers in angry silence, Tshabalala puts one huge hand on her shoulder and another on Miriam's and says, 'Please, we are not all of the same belief as Ndlondlo. Many of us think that the way of negotiation is better, even if we don't get exactly what we want straight away.'

'It's the only way,' Gordon says. 'We have to settle things between ourselves, not make them worse.'

'Easy for you to say, my friend. Not so easy for those with few bargaining chips.'

Gordon nods. 'I accept that. But we've got to start somewhere.'

They have reached the public area. The two guards on either side of the door salute Tshabalala, who grunts an acknowledgement. Sarah says, still angry, 'Men like Ndlondlo really frighten me. I wonder whether we will ever achieve peace.'

Tshabalala opens the door for her. 'He has good reasons for being the way he is, I assure you.'

'I know a killer when I see one.'

The big man follows her down the steps. 'He is mild compared to some. In this crazy African chess game the opposing pieces may be black and white, but they are shaped the same.'

She turns to shake his hand. 'And it's the pawns who get pushed around. That's exactly it. You restore my faith, Mr Tshabalala.'

'And you and your husband, mine.' He retains her hand for a moment and says, 'About your request. I will take out my saxophone before this afternoon and see if I can still squeeze out a note or two. What would you like me to play?'

'One of your own pieces, please.' She smiles up at him in the bright sunlight, showing her age in a mesh of fine wrinkles and the crease lines on her neck.

Gordon says behind her, 'Play *Sweet Sibusise*.' He has been introducing Miriam to Cordelia, who has come to take her up to the hut where Jake and Rose lie.

Tshabalala's bullet head jerks a nod. 'I will try. Where are you going now?'

'To Maseru. We have to get Sarah something to wear. How long will it take?'

'Two hours plus shopping time. Make sure you tell them up at the road block that you'll be coming back, OK? I'm going now to see to the roasting of the oxen.'

'Thank you for being there this morning,' Sarah says.

'Eh, it was nothing.'

With a farewell jab in the air he turns to go. Gordon and

Sarah walk round the corner to their car, and try not to look at the pram and the presents for Rose on the back seat as they get in and drive away down the gravel road.

Gordon and Sarah had been home a month when he suffered his heart attack. After a long, fraught day at the office which started with an early business breakfast and ended with too many drinks after a tense board meeting, he had stopped the driver of his new 380 SE Mercedes at the gate so he could walk up to the house through the garden. From the studio Sarah saw him sitting on the bench near the swimming pool with his suit jacket over his knees and his head bowed. Worrying about Rose, she supposed.

They had talked of little else since their return. 'I don't know what's got into her,' Gordon kept saying. 'She had the pick of Wits University, and she has to go and fall in love with a coloured who never even finished his degree. What does she see in him, do you think?'

'Intelligence and ability, that's clear. And he's not bad looking.'

'If you leave out the hair and the thick lips and the nose.'

Sarah felt herself blushing. That had been her thought exactly, though she would not have said it out loud. She said, 'Of course, it's the thing for her student generation to show off how terribly open-minded they are about such mundane matters as race, so they can moan about what bigots we are. They don't realise how grim the reality of racial laws can be. She talks about her radical friends in detention as though they're on some sort of high-minded holiday, rather than in jail.'

'I suppose we ought to be grateful that she's going to marry and not to jail,' Gordon said, unable to shake off the feeling of impending doom that he had brought back from Cape Town.

As South Africa's reputation plummeted, so the shipping business had begun to falter. Only the day before, dockers in Australia and Texas had refused to unload two freighters carrying what were beginning to be called 'apartheid-contaminated goods'. We're becoming a skunk in the eyes of the world, he was thinking, sitting by the pool. We who were respected Allies in two world wars are now a black and white country that stinks. How could we let it come to this?

He felt a sudden wave of dizziness and then a bolt of pain that slammed into his chest like a pile-driver, leaving him breathless and stunned. His first thought was, Is this it . . . ? Heart attacks are common in the South African business community; a deadly combination of over-indulgent eating and drinking, too much fatty meat, stress and a faulty gene from a Dutch founding family sometimes fells even young, fit men.

His second thought was, Sarah. He struggled against the terrible weight pressing down on his chest, trying to get to his feet. From the studio window, Sarah saw him lurch away from the bench, staggering like a drunk and trying to wrench his collar open. As she saw him fall, she screamed, 'Agnes! Joseph!' and began to run.

For the next few weeks they lived through a Technicolor nightmare. The purple-blue colour of his lips as the ambulance howled its way through the evening traffic. The pale greens of the intensive care unit with its winking red eyes and black rubber intestines snaking everywhere. The exhausted khaki of Gordon's eyes as he lay listening to the specialist's verdict: he would need a triple coronary bypass as soon as the immediate danger was over. The pinks and mauves and yellows of the stiffly formal flower arrangements people send to those who are sick, because it is easier and less upsetting than going to visit. The starched white of long hospital days and restless nights when nurses prowled the perimeters of light, murmuring to each other just below the level of hearing. The comforting blonde glow of Rose's hair as she sat by the bed whenever she could find time away from school, heavy with guilt at perhaps being the cause.

'Of course it wasn't you,' Sarah said when she broached the subject as they were driving to the private clinic where Gordon was being prepared for the operation. 'Dad's arteries were already badly clogged. It was only a matter of time.' Her face had aged with tiredness and worry.

'Maybe the suddenness of Jake and me pushed him into it sooner. I should have prepared you both, worked up to it somehow. It seems so selfish in retrospect.' Rose gnawed at a hangnail.

'That's nonsense.' Sarah could not say that Rose's problems had faded against the dark terror of death.

Rose said, pink-cheeked, 'I know you'll feel better about Jake when you get to know him better. He can be terribly cutting and defensive, but when he's comfortable with you, it all seems to roll away like barbed wire.'

Sarah said, 'Rose, I know this may come as a shock to you, but I haven't the energy to worry about you and Jake right now. You're twenty-six, quite old enough to decide for yourself how you want to live. If you're determined to go ahead with this marriage, knowing what could be in store, so be it. You have seen a genetic counsellor about the cystic fibrosis problem, I presume?'

Rose nodded.

'What you must realise is that Dad and I have to concentrate on our own problems now. They want to operate as soon as possible. After that, we'll have to take some hard decisions about our future.'

'What do you mean?'

'The specialist says Dad will be off work for at least two months after the op, and will have to take it easy for a while after that. When he heard that, Dad said, "I don't know that I want to go on battling to keep my head above all the ambitious little shits who're after my job. Maybe I'll take early retirement." '

'I can't believe it. What will he do instead?'

'Nothing for a while, he says. Just mosey around and learn to enjoy life again.' Seeing Rose's sceptical look, Sarah said, 'No, I can't imagine it either.'

'He won't know what to do with himself.'

'He says he may look at farming. He's had this secret dream, apparently, of sitting on a veranda gazing out over acres of pasture dotted with pedigree cattle. It's strange. You think you know a person after living with him for twenty-five odd years, and suddenly you discover that he has a dream he's never told you about.'

'I like that,' Rose said. 'The unexpected. It puts Dad in a new light, thinking of him hankering in the middle of a city for a field of cows. How would you like living on a farm, Mum?'

Sarah shrugged. 'I wouldn't look forward to moving, but as long as I can go on painting I don't mind where we live. Apart from the business entertaining, we've never been great socialisers.'

Rose hesitated before she said, 'Jake and I were planning to get married at the end of April, or early May. Will Dad be well enough to come to the wedding then? If not, we could put it off.'

'Don't do that, love.' Sarah pulled up in the clinic parking lot and turned to take Rose's hands. 'I've thought about it, and feel we should use this operation as a reason not to come.'

'Why?' Rose was aghast. 'I thought you quite liked Jake. You were smiling when he left the hotel.'

Sarah thought, How can I put this so she understands our reservations without holding them against us? She said, 'You have to give us time to adjust to a situation we find difficult, our only daughter marrying a man we hardly know, in defiance of a law that may be unjust but can't be ignored. We did like what little we were able to see of Jake; he's got a good sense of humour, anyway. But we feel awkward with him. You're forgetting that you presented him to us as an ultimatum.'

'I had to, or you'd have done or said something unforgivable and ruined everything. Admit it.'

Sarah thought back to the first time Rose had brought Jake home to lunch in her studio, and saying to him, 'I'll make a deal. One of my paintings for a read of your poetry. Fair exchange.' Only she hadn't intended a fair exchange. Pretending to speak as one artist to another, she had tried to barter a picture for her daughter in the spirit of the first white settlers conning the natives into accepting handfuls of glass beads for huge tracts of their land. She remembered her surprise at the passionate brilliance of his poems, and the bitter message he had sent when he returned the painting: 'Tell your mother she can keep her thirty pieces of silver.' The memory had been in his eyes when he had come to their hotel room.

She said, 'Did Jake ever tell you why I offered him the painting?'

'I was mad when he did. And ashamed of you.'

'I thought it was the right thing to do at the time. Mothers will do anything to protect their young.'

'From what, for God's sake? Contamination by association with an inferior? That's disgusting!'

Sarah thought, I wonder if she realises quite how far she's putting herself beyond the pale by marrying out of the white tribe? She said, 'It's not going to be easy for you, Rosie. Or for us. Or for Jake, with your background to contend with. One of the reasons I think it would be best for us not to come to the wedding is that I wouldn't want to hurt his feelings again.'

'You're hurting mine, just by talking like this.' Rose had a lump in her throat.

'I'm trying to be honest.'

'Does this mean you definitely won't come?' Rose could hardly believe that her parents were refusing her something she had always taken for granted.

'I think better not. It'll be easier on all of us. Though we'll pay for everything, of course.'

Rose flared, pulling her hands away, 'We wouldn't take your racist money! Or Grandpa's damn trust fund.'

'Don't burn all your boats at once, Rosie,' Sarah said. 'You may need them one day. Look, I understand how you feel. Couldn't you try to understand our position too?'

'Oh, I understand all right. Jake's not good enough for me because his skin's the wrong colour, and you're terrified to come to our wedding in case you have to sit next to any of his relatives. If that's how you feel, we wouldn't want you there anyway.'

Rose got out of the car and slammed the door and marched across the parking lot towards the clinic, while Sarah sat staring through the windscreen, wondering where awkwardness stopped and racism began.

While Gordon had his bypass surgery, recovered, suffered a setback after a staphylococcal infection, and gradually gained strength again, Rose lived in an unhappy limbo, punishing her parents by seldom visiting and unable to communicate with Jake except through occasional letters sent via Auntie April. The job was proving longer than he had expected, and wouldn't be over until the middle of May. She had been offered a teaching post in a village school near the camp to which he was being sent; there was a small house available ('very small,' he stressed). They would meet in a Maseru hotel as soon as he was free, and could she see to the wedding details?

Didymus, recently ordained, offered at once to marry them. 'I'd be honoured to do the magistrate out of a job,' he said, his spotty face pink with pleasure. 'I haven't had a chance to marry anyone yet, and I'm dying to have a go.'

Rose laughed for the first time in weeks. 'Are you sure you'll do it properly?'

'With my usual suave aplomb,' he assured her. 'I'll lay on a lovely service wherever you choose.' When she cried on his bony shoulder about her parents' decision not to come to the wedding, he said, 'Give them time to get to know Jake better. They'll come round.'

'They've always talked as though they're so open-minded, so

scornful of the racial laws, would *never* vote Nationalist, heaven forbid! But when you scratch them, they're just the same as all the other whites. Terrified of actually having to put their beliefs into practice.'

Didymus said, 'Don't be too hard on them. You're all they've got, remember?'

'Don't you start. They've been harping on that theme ever since my little brother died.' Rose tried to remember what David had looked like, and failed. 'It's a heavy load, being an only child. Jake and I are going to have lots.'

'God willing.' Didymus said a quiet prayer for his friends. He hoped with all his loving heart that their brave relationship would succeed, and did not imagine for one moment that it would kill them.

33

Maseru. Sesotho for 'red sandstone'. Once a sprawling village of civil service bungalows, one of the furthest outposts of the British Empire, now a bustle of independent government, new buildings, new industries and a thriving community of earnest foreign aid experts.

It is already hot when Gordon and Sarah drive down the main street. They pass the thatched building shaped like a Basotho hat that houses the tourist shop run by the village industries co-operative, then a gaggle of small hotels, shops and office buildings. Higher up the hill they can see the stone fortress that is the Lesotho Hilton Hotel, with its casino and porn movie theatre to which deprived South Africans flock at weekends; it will change owners soon and become the Lesotho Sun. A little further down the street, a patrol of red-jacketed Lesotho Mounted Police clop sedately towards morning practice in a nearby stadium, their pennants and pith helmets reminders of the British past.

Gordon parks outside the dress shop Cordelia has recommended. As he leans forward to set the car alarm, an automatic gesture now for owners of expensive cars, he says, 'Shall I come in with you, babe?'

'No, don't.' Sarah has to drag herself out of the dream she has been creating since they left the village, in which Rose will be waiting for them outside her cottage when they return, sitting on the step with Hope. She sighs. 'You said you had things to do?'

'They can wait if you'd like me to stay.' He reaches to tuck a drooping strand of silver hair into her bun, and drops his hand to caress the back of her neck. 'I don't want it to be another ordeal for you.'

She leans her head briefly against his arm before turning to open the door. 'I'll manage. You get your things done and we'll meet back here in half an hour or so. Will that be long enough?'

'Ample.' The things he has to do are pay for the coffins, and phone home from the post office to his farm manager to warn him about possible intrusions by press people investigating Rose's background. 'Just send them away and say "No comment" to everything,' he intends to tell him. 'I'm not having our private life pawed over. Call Sergeant Bezuidenhout if there's any trouble.'

Gordon is not one of those English-speaking South Africans who heap scorn on the police, but don't hesitate to demand their protection. He is on first-name terms with the local station commander, invites him to guinea fowl shoots, and respects the way he keeps a careful eye on activities in the district. He wonders how Sergeant Bezuidenhout will react to Hope when he meets her, and decides that he will probably demand a kiss from her as he does from every white girl child he meets, blandly ignoring her permanent tan. Afrikaners are a strange people, he thinks. So kind and hospitable on a personal level. So arrogant as a group.

'I'll see you in a while, then,' Sarah says as they part on the pavement.

Inside the shop she explains what she needs and a sympathetic assistant, with a practised sweep of the eyes over Sarah's waist and hips, leads her to a rack labelled 38–40 and selects several black dresses and a loose-waisted grey linen of which she says, 'Try this one first, Madam. It will be cool, and won't crush.'

Sarah had intended to buy black, a non-colour she normally shuns. But the grey linen is so flattering that she stands indecisive in front of the mirror, turning to look first at her front view and then her back, thinking, It makes my bottom look much smaller.

'Madam should wear this style more often,' the assistant says. 'It suits you.'

Oh God. She feels the tears welling again. How can I even consider how I look when we're burying Rose? Rose, my baby. She begins to cry with her head bent. The falling tears make darker grey blobs down the front of the dress and she thinks, Now I'll have to take it.

'Never mind, Madam.' The assistant helps her to the chair in the corner of the dressing room. 'Sit there, and I'll bring you a cup of tea.'

'But – ' Sarah tries to struggle to her feet. 'I have to meet – '

'Just sit, Madam. I saw your husband when he left you at the door.' In a small town people notice strangers. 'We'll keep a look-out for when he comes back. Please, I know how it is with funerals. I lost my mother not so long ago.'

Sarah looks up through glittering wetness to see answering wetness on the assistant's face. 'Here I am worrying how I'll look when – when – ' She is overwhelmed by the subterranean force of the tears that won't stop.

'You should look your best for the one who has died,' the assistant says. 'Goodbyes are for remembering, nè?' And she puts her arms round Sarah until the crying subsides, when she goes to get her tea and tissues and to watch out for Gordon's return.

He has settled the funeral parlour bill and is standing in a queue at the post office waiting his turn at one of the public call boxes when a man's voice behind him says, 'Don't turn around. I just want to ask you a few questions.' As Gordon begins to swing his head automatically, he feels a hard jab in his back and the voice repeats, 'Don't turn around, I said!'

'What do you want?' Gordon has caught an impression out of the side of his eye of a man not much taller than he is, a white shirt and sunglasses.

'Answers. Is Ndlondlo there?' The guttural accent is pronounced.

Gordon thinks, South African Intelligence. They want the bastard, of course. Resisting a strong impulse to lead them to him personally, he looks straight ahead and says, 'I don't know what you're talking about.'

'Ag, don't give me that,' the voice says impatiently. 'We reckon he was in the group that flew in yesterday, so you must have seen him.'

This could be one of the men who killed Rose and Jake. Gordon's heart gives a heavy double thump and begins to pound in his chest. He clears his throat and says, 'I know nothing.'

There is a cluck of annoyance behind him. 'You better tell us, Kimber, or we can make big trouble for you. Pick you up at the border when you come through. Send people around to your farm.'

Gordon clenches his teeth in rage. 'Fuck off!'

There is another jab in his back. 'I wouldn't use that type of language if I was you. Tell us.'

'Do you think for one moment that I would tell anything to the people who butchered my daughter?' Gordon speaks in a hard whisper that makes several people turn their heads to look at him.

'It wasn't us. Keep your voice down.'

'I don't believe you.'

'I'm telling you. We've got better fish to fry than white girls who go and get involved with coloureds. Like Ndlondlo. He's a danger to the State, man!'

Gordon has believed that Rose was shot because she was standing near Jake when South African commandos on a cross-border raid opened fire. Now this man, obviously in security, is denying it. Could he be speaking the truth? Did some other, more sinister, group kill them? Why?

He says, 'Get it straight. I'm not going to tell you buggers anything. Leave me alone.'

'We can force you.'

'Not here.' Gordon turns his head just far enough so the man behind can see him grinning. 'The blacks are running the show, in case you hadn't noticed. Quite successfully too.'

'Kaffirboeties like you should stay here and see how you like it!' The voice is furious. 'I'll be reporting your attitude to my people, I'm warning you.'

'Be my guest.' Gordon is beginning to enjoy himself.

The pressure from the hard thing jabbing into his back begins to ease off. The guttural voice says, 'Just for the record, we don't go around killing innocent people like the ANC does. But Ndlondlo is something else. Communist scum.'

'One step worse than a kaffirboetie,' Gordon taunts.

'You'll be sorry for this, Kimber!'

And then the man is no longer there. Gordon turns quickly to see if he can spot him, but there is no white shirt in sight. He feels a tap on the shoulder and swings round, but it is only a man saying, 'Your turn, sir. The telephone is free.'

'Oh. Thank you.' He wishes black people wouldn't call him sir but they often do, with the same reflex flattery that he once used towards his schoolmasters. How does one break the habits of servility? he wonders as he steps into the phone box.

When he leaves the post office, he does not notice the owl-faced black man who falls into step behind him; there is no particular reason to, since he has never seen him before.

Back at the dress shop, he is taken to the dressing room where Sarah is sitting with an assistant on each side of her, telling them about Rose. The story is pouring out of her like a river in spate, and though her eyes look damp and pink, the tears have stopped. He stands in the doorway watching her, and thinks that he has never loved her more than now. Her back is bowed and her voice heavy with sorrow, but she is like a well-engineered bridge, strong and enduring with the beauty that comes naturally with good design. Maybe that's what women really are, he thinks. Bridges that span the past and the future. She looks up and sees him, and smiles.

He spends the long drive back to the village trying to puzzle out who could have wanted Jake and Rose dead if it wasn't South African Intelligence. The conclusion he reaches, that it could be a group of people who don't want peace and reconciliation to happen in Southern Africa, is so chilling that even in the midday heat of the car he shivers.

With 1983 came the first woman astronaut and, to demonstrate just how mindful people have become of minorities as well as women's rights, the first black man in space. A Korean airliner was shot down by an over-zealous Russian pilot, killing 269 civilian passengers, the publishing world got into a tizzy over Hitler's alleged diaries, the US invaded Grenada, making a lot of noise but few friends, and people in Australia began to call the developing drought 'The Great Dry'. In South Africa there was growing protest in black schools, and new black political movements were springing up everywhere. Drive-in movie theatres which had been declining since the advent of TV were opened to all after a lot of whining from their owners, and the dawning realisation that parking next to a carful of people belonging to another race was not the same as sitting next to them. Zola Budd set off for Britain with her inherited passport and her eyes fixed on the Olympics.

In May, when Rose was making the final preparations for her wedding in a Basotho mountain village she had never seen, a massive car bomb exploded outside a Defence Force building in Pretoria during the evening rush hour, brutally killing nineteen people and wounding 200. Sickened by the TV newsreels and newspaper photographs, and at the same time dreading what the resultant police crackdown could do to Jake, Rose phoned Auntie April in Cape Town.

'It's Rose. Can I talk?'

Auntie April's high breathy voice said, 'Coast's clear, my dear.'

'I have to talk to Jake. This bomb – '

'I know. Puts what he's doing in another light, nè?'

Rose said, 'He can't go on justifying it to me after this. I won't listen.'

'That boy was always clever with an argument.' Auntie April sighed. 'He could make you believe black was white if you listened long enough. He should have been a politician.'

'He's experienced enough at deceiving people.'

Auntie April murmured, 'Shame, my dear, don't be too hard on him. But I know how you feel. I always get maddest with people when I'm afraid for them.'

'I am afraid,' Rose admitted. 'We're so close now. Are you coming to the wedding, Auntie April?'

'Ag, I wish I could.' The sadness of her isolation from her own people could be heard in her voice fourteen hundred kilometres away in Cape Town. 'But Tertius has house meetings all this month in the constituency, and he likes me to go with him.'

'I'm sorry.' Rose was apologising as much as expressing regrets.

Auntie April said, 'Never mind. I can see the photos after.'

'I mean, I'm sorry for – '

'I know just what you mean, my dear. But don't forget I chose this life of my own free will, like you're choosing Jake. Once you've made your choice there's no turning back. Be good to him, you hear?'

'If we ever get as far as Lesotho together, I will. But I want a promise from him first. No more missions.'

'I'll ask him to phone you.'

'Please, Auntie April.'

But the phone call, when it came a week later, was not from Cape Town. It was from the home of a friend who was living in exile in Maseru. 'I'm out!' Jake was almost sobbing with relief. 'I promise, no more! Can we get married now?'

34

It is late afternoon in the makeshift mortuary. Having been used as a death hut, it will have its roof caved in tomorrow by the village boys, who will salvage the door and window and any sound timber, but leave its brittle grey thatch and mud walls to melt back into the earth they came from.

As Jake and Rose will. Their families are with them now, saying their last goodbyes.

Miriam stands in her black dress and hat looking down at her son with her head bowed and her hands clasped, thinking how remote he looks. The bright flame has gone, though some of it lingers in the child. His mouth droops in a downward twist and his face is scored with deep lines that make him older, grimmer, stern as a judge passing the death sentence. The only time she has ever seen him like this was the day before he disappeared across the border, when he was so angry about the shootings in Soweto that he could not speak, just clung to her squeezing what seemed like all the breath from her body.

She stoops to touch his hair, and with a sob bends lower to kiss his forehead. 'Jacob,' she whispers into the cold ear that can no longer hear, 'sleep good, my boy. We'll never forget.' The words keen with her loss and sadness.

Sarah has pulled her hair back into a severe knot. She looks like a Puritan in the new grey linen dress as she kneels on the grass mat next to Rose's coffin with Hope in her arms. She murmurs against the small round cheek, 'Say goodbye to your Mummy, darling. She loved you very much. I hope I can make up for her.'

For a moment the child gazes down at her mother. Then the still-burning candles catch her eye and she turns her head away. Sarah holds the warm little body closer to ward off the marble chill of Rose. Even the faint semblance of life that the candlelight gave her during the night is gone now, obliterated by the glare of daylight from the small square window. Sarah looks and looks but can't touch her, can't kiss that calm cold grey face with Rose no longer inside.

It is Gordon, standing next to her, who bends to touch each of his daughter's closed eyes and to say, 'Goodbye, Rosie. We'll look after her. And oh God, we'll miss you.'

The hut door swings open and Didymus comes in, unfamiliar in a long black cassock over which he wears a white surplice and a purple satin stole. With him comes the sound of subdued voices and a blast of afternoon heat. He says, 'They want to know if you're ready.'

Gordon stands up, tears on his cheeks. 'Not ready. Resigned.'

Didymus is not quite sure how to phrase what he has to say. He blurts, 'Could – could the undertaker come in, then? He needs to – '

Gordon rescues him. 'We'll wait outside. Sarah.' He helps her up, then turns to Miriam. 'Miriam?'

'I will rather stay.' She is no stranger to the closing of coffins.

'We'll see you in a minute, then.' With his hand on Sarah's shoulder, they follow Didymus through the door.

Rose and Ursula drove down from Johannesburg to the village the day before the wedding, having been invited by Cordelia to spend the night in her home. 'It would be nice for us colleagues to get to know each other,' her voice had said over the phone, 'and I could take you and your friend up to see your new house.' Jake was away in southern Lesotho until the next morning, having spent several days painting out the house and bringing the basics they would need from Maseru.

The three women had talked late into the evening over cup after cup of strong tea about the school and the people in the village, then Cordelia had shown them into a white-washed room with just enough space for two narrow iron beds covered in patchwork quilts. On the windowsill was a jug of pale pink flowers. By the dim, warm, shifting light of the candles they were holding, it looked like a room out of a fairy-tale cottage – Hansel and Gretel's, perhaps. Rose had a vivid memory of reading the story to David and Albertina; David hunched over his thin little knees in bed, wheezing, and Albertina muttering her disapproval of parents who abandon children in the woods. Both of them would have recognised this room instantly.

To block the thought of the brother who would have been here to give her away, Rose said, 'What pretty flowers.'

'We call them – ' Cordelia used a Sesotho word. 'They grow in the grass up the hill. I think you call them everlastings? The children like to weave them together in a circle to wear in their hair.'

'That's it, Rosie,' Ursula said.

'What?'

'Your headdress for tomorrow. A circle of pink everlastings.'

'Oh, yes. Do you think they'd make me one?' Rose asked Cordelia. 'I thought a veil would look wrong with a caftan, so I didn't bring anything for my hair. Pink flowers would look just right.'

'Of course,' Cordelia beamed. 'It's a lovely idea. The children will be so happy to do something for their new teacher.' And next morning there was a group of shy girls at the door holding out a coronet of pink everlastings so beautifully made that Rose hung it afterwards on the wall of her new home to remind her of one of the happiest days of her life.

Didymus arrived soon afterwards with a large tin in one hand and a bulging sports bag in the other. 'Your travelling Reverend reporting for duty,' he announced, his pale spotty face almost transparent with pleasure. 'I also thought you may forget in the heat of the moment to provide the essential cake, so I asked my mother to oblige. She makes the best cakes in Kuruman.'

Rose hugged him. 'How thoughtful of you. Come in.'

Cordelia's house had begun to fill with plates of food and gifts: woven grass baskets, clay bowls, gourds with carved decorations, crocheted doileys, pot-holders and a blanket of knitted squares in bright colours made by the children. 'Each child made one square, even the boys,' Cordelia said with pride. 'We are trying to teach them from a young age that men's work and women's work need not be mutually exclusive.'

'It's not easy to do this in Lesotho,' one of the younger teachers said. 'Some of the fathers were mad with us for teaching their boys how to knit. But the kids loved it.'

Rose looked round the small room where she and Ursula and Didymus were sitting surrounded by village women, everyone buzzing with the excitement of the wedding. They've made us feel so welcome, she thought, and wondered whether her white friends would have been as warm towards black strangers.

Didymus was saying, with a nervous swallow that sent his Adam's apple bobbing up and down, 'Shouldn't I be getting things ready? Where are we going to hold the wedding? I'll need a table.'

Cordelia said, 'Jake and I thought that seeing as it's not too cold, the wedding should be under the tree in the school yard, with chairs brought out from the classrooms. The ox and the two sheep Rose's father sent money for are already cooking over fires nearby.'

'Dad sent money?' Rose had been able to say only a brief goodbye to Gordon, who was still convalescing in the clinic.

Cordelia looked surprised. 'Your mother telephoned me last week already to ask what they should provide for the wedding feast. I told her the meat, and we would do the rest. Your father signed the cheque.'

'I didn't know.' Rose felt an ache in her throat, and was not sure if it was anger or sadness at their not being with her.

After a diplomatic moment Cordelia went on, 'Jake will be here at eleven. Because he doesn't have to pay bohali, that is cows, for you, which he would have to bring to your family's house in the morning, we thought the wedding should start in the middle of the day. Then we can have the leeto ceremony in the afternoon, and the older ones can go home in daylight before it gets too cold. The young ones will not, of course, go home until long after dark.' All the women laughed merrily.

'Leeto? What is that?' Rose asked in alarm. She had expected a short service conducted by Didymus and something to eat afterwards, not a complete ceremony.

'Probably skinning the ox or something,' Ursula teased. 'Don't you remember studying African wedding customs in anthropology? Brides have to impress their new mothers-in-law with their housewifely skills before they're accepted into the family. You should have put in some practice with a sharp knife, kiddo.'

Rose thought, I hope she's not offending anyone. But Cordelia was saying, 'Jake said he didn't think you'd want to skin the ox. Normally both families would do it together, with the bride's people on the left and the groom's on the right. The family who finishes first is supposed to be the one that will dominate. But that is not leeto. You'll just have to wait and see what leeto is.' She chuckled. 'Don't worry, Jake has organised everything, my dear. He wants this day to be extra special for you, because your mother and father can't be here.'

'It's special already because I'm marrying him.'

398

Cordelia nodded. 'He's a very nice man. Already he has made many friends here. But we don't have time to sit talking now, nè? There's the food to get ready, and you, Didymus, must tell the people up at the school what you need. Ursula and I will dress the bride. See, I keep the best part for myself.'

The village people are gathered in the yard outside the makeshift mortuary, dressed in their best: ethnic print skirts and head-scarves, clean shirts, venerable suits. A collective sigh goes up as Gordon and Sarah, who carries Hope in the crook of her arm, are seen coming out the door. The crowd begins to surge forward, eager to see, to touch, to show sympathy. Their faces are like a field of sunflowers turned to the sun; Sarah can almost feel the heat of their concentrated attention. Several women begin ululating, the high thrilling cry reserved for moments of deep emotion.

Hope is startled by the blare of light and voices after the hut's dimness. Her little starfish hands clutch at the lacy white dress her mother bought a week ago in Maseru for showing her off to her grandparents, and will never see her wear. Her chin begins to tremble.

Sarah swings back towards the door with her hand protectively cupping the child's curly head, saying, 'Can't you keep them back, Gordon?'

But Tshabalala materialises out of the rising cloud of dust, followed by a group of young men in khaki who wear black berets and scarves in the ANC colours, green, yellow and black. He holds up an arm like a gum-tree trunk and calls out an order in Sesotho. The booming authority of his voice quietens the crowd at once, stilling the clamour to a simmering murmur. The young men in khaki begin to urge people back, forming a corridor down which the funeral procession will move. Tshabalala calls out to Gordon and Sarah, 'Don't worry. Everything's in order.'

'It's just the baby,' Sarah calls back. 'Maybe we should have left her with someone in the clinic. I didn't realise there'd be such a crowd.'

Tshabalala pushes his way towards them, his clean khaki shirt already showing damp patches of sweat. 'This is nothing yet. Only the villagers have been allowed down here. Up at the cemetery, people are swarming like wild bees.'

'Who are they?'

'Besides the press? Chiefs and mourners from other villages. Officials from Maseru.'

'I thought numbers were to be limited?' Gordon is sweltering in his jacket and tie and grey flannels, and pulls out a handkerchief to mop his red face. 'This is bedlam already.'

'We turned a lot of journalists away, but we could not do so with friends and neighbours. They have come to pay their respects.' Tshabalala bends down to see how Hope is, the grizzle of hair on his bullet head glinting like steel filings, his huge hand shielding her back. She looks up at him, quivering on the verge of a wail. 'Meisietjie, don't cry, please,' he says, using Jake's pet name for her. 'My men will keep you from any harm.'

Gordon feels a stab of fear. 'Are you expecting trouble?'

'We are always prepared.' He is stroking the child's cheek with a gentle forefinger, calming her fright. When the little mouth falters into a tremulous smile, he says, 'That's my girl.'

'What if the gunmen come back? Hope is an obvious target.' Gordon is in a sudden panic, afraid of who may be hiding in this muttering crowd. 'We'd better do as Sarah says, leave her with someone in the clinic.'

'We shouldn't have brought her.' Sarah has gone pale. 'I'll take her back inside.'

'She must come. I assure you both there will be no trouble.' Tshabalala speaks in a grim undertone so as not to alarm the child. 'Men have been brought in from all the other camps. They are covering every single inch of the valley. We are not taking any chances today.'

'But they're mostly boys! What chance would they have against a commando raid – say, by helicopter?' Gordon can see it in his mind's eye already: a nightmare of swooping gunships, bullets, blood and death.

Tshabalala's hand clamps down hard on his arm, his eyes turned to black pebbles again. 'You underestimate us, my friend. These what you call boys are well trained, and they fight with fire burning in their bellies. Not even a mosquito will get in here today without my permission.'

Gordon thinks, Maybe that's the basic problem between black and white. We continually underestimate each other. He says by way of apology, 'I would hate to be that mosquito.'

Tshabalala nods, releasing his arm. 'Just so.'

The door opens behind them and a man in a black suit comes out. 'We are ready,' he says. 'Are the pallbearers here?'

'I'll call them.' Tshabalala gives another order. Eight of the young men in black berets and ANC scarves step forward, followed by the group of teachers and villagers who have volunteered to carry Rose. As they file into the death hut, they duck their heads at Sarah and Gordon; several of the teachers greet Hope with a touch and a smile. The crowd falls silent, watching.

Sarah thinks, I can't believe it. Here we are in this hot dusty alien place about to bury our daughter. For a moment her head swims with the unreality of it. The mud hut. The silent people with their watching sunflower faces. The two priests waiting to lead the funeral procession, Didymus looking strained and nervous, the Reverend Monaheng from the nearby mission absently massaging his hands. She looks up and sees the dark bird specks planing in wide circles, lower now, sure in their instinct for death. With a prickle of horror, she thinks, I wonder how many more are waiting for us up at the cemetery?

Cordelia took great delight in helping Rose to dress for the wedding while Ursula sat on the bed cross-legged, reminiscing about their school days. She was a senior lecturer now, her effervescence channelled into a fierce passion for sociology that gained her as much fear as respect from her students. She wore clothes that were as bold, bright and eccentric as she could find, with knobbly African necklaces made of bone and chunks of copper and stone that looked as though they could double duty as offensive weapons if necessary.

She was saying, 'Do you remember the Louse Club? And the day Miss Ramsden tried to put a stop to our mini rebellion by inveigling us into becoming prefects? We must have been hell on teachers. Sometimes when I get a really bolshy student, I blush at the memory.'

'I'll never forget what she said to us that day. I've thought of it often since I met Jake.' Keeping her head still for Cordelia, who was pinning on the circle of pink flowers, Rose looked sideways at Ursula. 'She said, "It's not enough to protest against and undermine a system you find inadequate or unjust. You have to have a better system to offer in its place before you destroy it, or you will leave a vacuum." '

'Wise words,' Cordelia said through the hairclips in her mouth.

'Prescient for the early 1970s. We're still looking for that better system,' Ursula said.

'Jake thought he had found it, but I don't think he's so sure now.' Rose was fiddling with her hairbrush. 'He's got an ulcer, did you know? Worry and stress, the doctor says. Trying to be an Action Man was the worst possible thing for him. He should really be in a university like you are, teaching and writing poetry.'

'Why does he not apply to Roma?' Cordelia said. 'There's always a need for good teachers.'

'He never got his degree, like so many others of his generation. The struggle has a lot to answer for.' Rose's laugh was strained.

'Hey, this is no talk for a wedding day.' Ursula swung her legs over the edge of the bed. 'I can see I shall have to get you in the mood by doing my impression of a hysterical bridesmaid getting dressed.'

And then the singing started.

Rose looked towards the window. 'What's that?'

Cordelia said, 'Keep still, I'm nearly finished. That is Jake's surprise for you.'

Unaccompanied, men's and women's voices were filling the room with joyful song. Ursula, who had gone to the window, said, 'Rose, you've got to come and look. This is fantastic.'

'Can I?' Rose turned pleading blue eyes upwards at Cordelia. 'Have you finished?'

Looking down at her, so flushed and happy and eager, the older woman thought, How could her mother not be here? If Phalise had lived, maybe this could have been her wedding day too. To banish the thought, she gave Rose's shoulder a little push and said, 'I can finish just now. Go and see your surprise, my dear.'

She watched the two friends standing side by side at the window, one dark, the other blonde, these two surprising white women with whom she had felt such an instant bond. Is it because we're all teachers, she wondered, or because I still grieve for Phalise and see little bits of her in them?

'Oh.' Rose stood entranced by the window. Ten men and ten

women stood in a beaming semicircle, the women in vivid Java print dresses and head-scarves, the men in matching shirts, swaying in unison as they sang. To one side two little girls in matching dresses stood holding an embroidered banner that read MASERU MARVELLOUS SINGERS. Standing behind them, wearing his most ferocious grin, was Jake.

'I must go and thank him.' Rose turned towards the door. 'It's the most wonderful surprise.'

'Are you crazy?' Ursula shrieked. 'It's bad luck for the groom to see the bride before the wedding.'

Rose laughed. 'You don't really believe that?'

'I do! My grandmother was always most specific about it. "Ursula, liebchen," she'd say, "make sure of one thing, that your bridegroom does not see you until the synagogue." ' Ursula's face was unexpectedly serious.

'But he's seen me already, through the window.'

'Then don't tempt fate any further. Come and sit down and let Delia finish doing the veil.'

Ursula's hand on her arm was clammy. Rose thought, How strange. I've known her all these years, and never had any idea she was superstitious. I suppose it was that sad old granny.

'Yes, come and sit, Rose, so I can finish. You'll have plenty of time to thank him later.' Cordelia bent over the blonde head again. 'Just close your eyes and listen meantime. This is a song of wishing for future prosperity and happiness. They are singing, "May the kraal be filled, even to the uttermost corners." '

Rose closed her eyes. The men's voices, deep and resonant, were a subtle warp through which the women's voices wove their rich high harmonies, creating a fabric of sound that seemed to wrap her in joy. This is when I know I'm African to the core, she thought. Oh Jake, I'm glad I'm marrying you.

Miriam appears in the doorway of the hut, looking dazed. Gordon reaches out and takes her hand. 'Come and stand with us. We'll walk together.'

She nods, too close to tears to speak.

Behind her, feet shuffling, the young men in khaki bring Jake's coffin through the door, feet first as tradition demands. The crowd gasps as it moves into the sunlight, a splendour of polished mahogany and silver handles seldom seen in the village, where pine is all most people can afford. Gordon has ordered the best for his daughter and son-in-law's last journey; if they must lie in a small mountain cemetery, they will at least lie in state.

Tshabalala comes forward unfolding an ANC flag, broad bands of yellow, green and black, which he drapes over the coffin, smoothing the top and fussing with both sides until it is hanging straight. He gives a command and the young men hoist the coffin up on to their shoulders, four on each side. When it is settled Tshabalala gives another command and they punch the air with their free hands, fists clenched, shouting in unison, 'Amandla!'

There is a deep surging roar from the crowd. 'Ngawethu!' Fists shoot up everywhere, even those of the smallest children; many of the women begin to applaud.

'Amandla!'

'Ngawethu!'

The single sound from so many throats vibrates through the body like a low cello note, tugging at cords and sinews and buried fears. 'Power is ours,' Gordon mutters, feeling the sparse hair prickle on the back of his neck. To his surprise, Hope is not frightened by the roar. She lies in her safe place in the crook of Sarah's arm watching the shouting, stamping, gesticulating people with calm interest.

Jake's pallbearers stop halfway down the corridor of people, and the shouting dies down. The priests file past it to take up their position at the head of the procession. The Reverend Monaheng is carrying a tall brass cross that glints whenever it catches the sun. Didymus looks paler than ever; his stomach is churning, and he is having to concentrate very hard on not being sick. God has still not answered him and, stricken with doubt, he is not sure whether he should even take part in this funeral of the dear friends he married.

There is another gasp from the crowd as Rose's coffin is carried out through the door by eight friends and colleagues. Cordelia is one of the pallbearers. 'I will miss her like I miss my own daughter,' she has told Sarah with tears in her muddy eyes. There is no flag this time, and no hoisting on to shoulders, just the small bunch of pink everlastings from the jug lying on the coffin, tied with a twist of ribbon. The coffin moves slowly past the waiting parents and into the sunlight, silver handles sparkling, wood gleaming, almost festive in its beautifully crafted severity. It stops near Jake's. Like a proper African wife, Sarah thinks. At a lower level and two steps behind.

Having overseen the moving and disposition of the coffins, Tshabalala comes back to where they are standing and says, 'Are you ready to go now?'

'Yes.' Still holding Miriam's hand, Gordon puts his other hand on Sarah's arm so the three of them are linked together. 'Tell us where to walk.'

'Just after the people who carry Rose, please. The choir is waiting outside the gate, and will fall in behind you. I will be at the back with the rest of my men and the firing party.' He pauses, expecting Gordon and Sarah to object. When they don't, he says, 'You understand that it is necessary?'

Gordon nods. 'We know. Thanks.'

'Just – ' Sarah stops.

'What?'

'Please, Maxwell – please find us a place to stand out of the way of the cameras up there, if possible. I couldn't bear to have all those eyes watching us every minute, *dwelling* on us.'

'I'll do my best. Maybe ask some of the taller men to stand round you.' His head hunches further down between his huge shoulders, a sign his men dread because it means trouble. 'But it won't be easy. Photographers will do crazy things to get a good picture. So if you want to leave at any time, just make me a signal, OK?'

Sarah nods. 'You've been so kind.'

'It's nothing. We'll go now.'

The crowd in the yard hushes as he turns and motions towards the head of the procession. The two priests move towards the gate, cassocks swaying. Behind them, Jake's coffin jerks forward, his khaki pallbearers walking in perfect step, heads up, eyes forward, the sun gleaming on the black leather binding of their berets. The people carrying Rose move awkwardly, shuffling and changing feet, unable to find a comfortable rhythm on the stony ground.

Gordon walks between the two women, holding himself as tall and straight as he can, keeping the paunch in and his shoulders squared. He has left the green hat in the car; it is his farm hat, not dignified enough for the burial of his daughter.

On his left Miriam walks with tears running down her cheeks, seeing nothing but a blur of faces, following the pressure of his

405

hand. On his right, Sarah walks with her blue eyes looking straight ahead, her head up, her grandchild in her arms. Hope in her white lace dress draws murmurs of 'Shame!' and soft cluckings of sympathy from the village women they pass. Hands reach out to touch her and the white grandmother who carries her with such loving pride. In the long day's sadness, they are a symbol of the better future that could be.

As the coffins reach the gate, the choir standing outside begins to sing. It is *Abide With Me* in Sesotho, the hymn of those going into darkness. There are no Java print dresses today, no banner, no joyful smiles. The men wear white shirts and sombre navy trousers; the women are in navy robes with black, grey and bronze beadwork at the neck. They clasp their hands and sing of faith and sorrow with their eyes cast down. When Gordon and the two women have passed, they file into place behind them, still singing. The village people follow, the men walking in front, the women behind with their hands crossed over their breasts, the children looking round with big solemn eyes.

The procession moves up the dirt track through the village, past the huts with their pecking hens, past the kraals where the animals, penned early, are milling restlessly. No work is done in the fields during a funeral. Over the richly interwoven harmonies of the choir, now singing a Zulu lament for the fallen in battle, and the low murmuring of the crowd, Gordon hears the regular tramp of boots and the clink of rifles against belt buckles.

Ndlondlo will be waiting up at the cemetery for his big moment in the world spotlight.

After Ursula had shooed Jake away, Cordelia called in the Maseru photographer who had been waiting outside, a wizened little man like a garden gnome made in bitter chocolate, carrying an old-fashioned camera on a wooden tripod.

'Oh, I hate formal photographs,' Rose said. 'Didymus promised to take a few snaps, isn't that enough?'

'No. Your mother was most insistent,' Cordelia said, posing Rose by a window and fussing over her caftan, twitching the cream wool into becoming folds and patting the neckline to make it lie smoothly. She stood back to check the effect, then said, 'More lipstick, I think,' and hurried off to get it. To Ursula, who disliked wearing make-up, she said sternly, 'You must make yourself look nice for Rose, nè?' and went on nagging until she capitulated.

'You're almost as bad as the headmistress we've been talking about, Miss Ramsden,' Ursula moaned. Cordelia's lipstick tasted of wax cherries.

'I'm sure she also got good results.' Cordelia was pleased with herself. The two young women standing by the window looked radiant, each holding a small posy of creamy roses from the Houghton garden that Sarah had insisted they bring down in a coolbag. As the photographer clicked and flashed, Cordelia thought, I don't know why the mother has not come, even if the father can't because of his operation; she sounded so nice on the telephone. But if I can possibly help it, she will have a complete record of this day.

The photographer took more pictures in front of Cordelia's house, with Rose and Ursula surrounded by the jubilantly singing choir. It was a fine clear winter day, sunny but crisp at the edges, promising an overnight frost that would freeze water troughs and frost the conical thatch roofs. At ten to twelve, bossy as a mother hen, Cordelia formed them into a procession with Rose and Ursula in front and the choir behind, and led them up the track towards the school. People and children ran out of the huts as they passed to wave and cheer, and then to join in; weddings were feast days for everyone in the village. Many of the children were carrying wild flowers picked up on the hillside and they ran laughing next to Rose, their bare feet kicking up the dust, their grubby little hands reaching out to touch her for good luck.

Looking down at them, Rose thought, What does it matter if I get a bit dusty too? This is the most joyous way of going to a wedding. It's as though Ursula and I are being carried along by smiles and songs. Why can't it always be like that?

As the funeral procession passes the last of the huts, several horsemen fall in behind the stragglers at the back, a mounted guard in bright ceremonial blankets and straw hats with intricate topknots. Gordon will always associate the sound of stumbling hooves and the sharp crack of rifles with the funeral of his daughter. Sarah will remember the faces of the villagers who stand by the track watching them pass, many with tears running down their cheeks, and the weight of Hope in her arms, and the snuff-coloured dust. Miriam will remember only pain.

Up in front, walking a few deferent steps behind the Reverend Monaheng, Didymus raises his eyes to the brass cross moving against the sandstone cliff with its base layer of weeping stones. Beyond and above it are the Malutis, range upon range of peaks that rise indigo on purple on mauve on palest lilac behind it. The sun is low in the western sky, throwing a wash of orange on to the sandstone and turning the lengthening shadows to slate. On the green-gold swell of the hill ahead of them, knots of people stand round the deep red gash in the earth, east-facing as custom demands, that will soon swallow his friends. He thinks, The colours today are too bright. They should be black and white, or sepia, or grey. Mildew. Rust. Ashes. He feels the satin stole round his neck burning like purple fire; he is beginning to sweat under the hot robes. He thinks, How can I bury them pretending piety if I don't believe a word I'm saying? His thin-soled black leather shoes, more used to church tiles than mountain paths eroded down to the bare knuckles, flinch from the stones underfoot as though from a bed of nails.

Cordelia feels the weight of her dead friend growing heavier with every step, as her heart does. She is apprehensive about the coming ceremony at the graveside. She thinks, Will Ndlondlo temper what he has to say out of consideration for the bereaved parents and friends, or will it be just another public relations exercise where our true feelings are smothered under a lot of high-sounding words? How can I go on believing in a struggle that indiscriminately kills people I love? She reels off the conventional answers: Because I am black. Because I have suffered. Because I too want my place in the sun. But is that place going to be worth what we pay for it? The sun is low and hot. She can smell, faintly, the drifting smoke from the fire in the school yard over which the two young black bulls slaughtered early that morning are being turned on spits.

The people round the graveside draw closer together as the procession approaches, to make room. Among them is an elegant woman in emerald green silk with a matching turban that emphasises the grace of her long neck. It is Pinky Benghu, now the wife of a Soweto liquor magnate, who has come in her imported Ferrari to lay the memory of Isidore and his meetings to rest along with her friends. The owl-faced man is there too, inconspicuous as ever; unknown to his comrades in the underground protest movements, he has recently received an award for long service in the South African Police.

Ndlondlo is resplendent in starched, pressed, knife-edged khaki. He stands apart, surrounded by a phalanx of men in camouflage uniforms among whom Aubrey Stimson is the odd man out with his untidy grey hair and rumpled tweed jacket. A bunched group of journalists and photographers explodes like a hand grenade as each scrambles for a good vantage point; the whirr-click of motor drives and the intrusive buzzing of TV cameras will punctuate the next hour.

Conscious of the winking lenses, Jake's pallbearers stamp their feet in unison as they reach the grave and come to a halt; their leader mutters something and the fists shoot up into the air again. 'Amandla!'

'Ngawethu!' the answering cry is thinner up here on the hillside, snatched up into the air and sent echoing against the cliffs.

'Amandla!'

'Ngawethu!'

The coffin is lowered on to the flattened mound of soil, the ANC flag fluttering and slipping sideways. One of the young men reaches down and twitches it straight, then snaps up to attention again. Rose's pallbearers approach the other side of the grave and put her coffin down in silence; no 'Amandla!' here. Tshabalala is keeping scrupulously to his agreement with Gordon and Sarah.

The Reverend Monaheng steps forward and the short, sad service begins. He and Didymus share the Bible and psalm readings, and the prayers.

Didymus hears, 'Man that is born of a woman hath but a short time to live, and is full of misery.' He thinks, Why full of misery? It's always bothered me. That, and the terrible assumption that we are all born sinners. How can the beautiful child over there possibly be a sinner?

Sarah hears, 'He cometh up, and is cut down like a flower,' and thinks, That's the cruel truth. They were cut down like flowers before they reached full bloom.

Miriam hears, 'He fleeth as it were a shadow,' and thinks, He didn't run far enough, my Jacob.

Gordon hears, 'In the midst of life we are in death,' and thinks, looking at the stern faces of the young men in khaki, We are in the midst of death here. Where will it stop?

Cordelia hears, 'Thou knowest, Lord, the secrets of our hearts,' and thinks, The secret of my heart is a wish for peace. Are you listening, Lord?

Ndlondlo hears, 'O God most mighty, O holy and merciful Saviour, thou most worthy Judge eternal,' and thinks, This is what I can't stand about religion, this fawning reliance on some mythical boss up in the sky who is supposed to run the show. It's imperialist propaganda designed to sap people's initiative so they stop believing in themselves.

'Forasmuch as it hath pleased Almighty God . . . we therefore commit their bodies to the ground . . .' The hallowed English words of the funeral service rise into the blood heat of a late African afternoon, mixed with muffled bursts of sobbing. One of the young men in khaki takes the flag from Jake's coffin, folds it, and gives it to Miriam; he is crying. Only two days ago Jake read out a poem he had written in front of the whole class, and he was so proud.

As the coffin is slowly lowered on ropes by the pallbearers, Tshabalala gives an order. Six men with rifles step forward, and there is the harsh crack-crack-crack of rifle fire whose diminishing echoes can be heard ricocheting off the cliff all the way down the valley. Two village men climb down into the grave and lift the coffin partly into the niche on one side. They stay there while Rose's coffin is lowered. The dreadful noise of small stones dislodged by the ropes rattling down on to the polished wood is partly alleviated by the choir's hushed singing of a Negro spiritual.

When Rose too has been lifted into her niche, Didymus picks up a handful of red earth and says in a voice that squeaks painfully, 'Earth to earth, ashes to ashes, dust to dust.' He lets it fall, and it thuds on to the bunch of pink flowers, half covering them. 'Lord, have mercy upon us.'

The Reverend Monaheng gestures towards an elderly woman, who hands a basket down to one of the men still in the grave. He places it between the two coffins. In it are the symbolic offerings that will accompany the dead on their last journey: sorghum, pumpkin seeds, bread, wisps of plaited grass and water in a small clay pot.

Ndlondlo steps forward now, facing the cameras, to begin his funeral oration. 'This is more than an outrage, my friends. This is murder most foul, committed by a government most foul, the racist regime whose name stinks all over the world, and rightly

410

so. For Jacob Van Vuuren, poet and patriot, we mourn today. For Rose Van Vuuren – '

He is eloquent and personable, and his image will flash round the world by satellite tonight to appear on tomorrow's TV screens and in tomorrow's newspapers, pleading for stronger sanctions, military and moral assistance, punishment of the oppressors. His arguments are unassailable, his demand that justice be done to a people who for decades have been denied the liberation granted to others, passionate and convincing. No judge in the world could fail to award him his case, with costs.

But it's not the whole story! Gordon fumes, frustrated at not being able to state his argument in this world-wide TV forum with its magnificent backdrop of mountains. The reality is being glossed over. And the reality is that might is right, and in Southern Africa might is white. Meekly to hand over a country one has fought and suffered for is unthinkable to an Afrikaner. He would rather die, but before he does he will scorch the earth as the British soldiers did to his lands in the Boer War, laying waste to the beloved country rather than letting someone else have it. We are going to have to negotiate our way out of this desperate impasse, not make demands the other side can't possibly meet. Gordon looks down into the grave. Rose faced reality. So must we all, or we're lost.

Didymus had no doubts as he conducted the wedding under the tree in the school yard, using a teacher's desk as an altar. Rose and Jake took their vows, the choir sang, the village audience beamed and clapped and danced their happiness, and afterwards there was feasting. Plenty of meat for everyone, a rare treat. Beer brewed in traditional gourds, bread freshly baked by Cordelia, phuthu in three-legged iron pots, bowls of vegetables picked that morning and tasting like vegetables never taste in the city. Peanuts and chips and sweets and cooldrinks for the children, and a large cool-box full of ice-creams that made everyone sticky and the children even dustier.

Rose would not let go of Jake's hand. 'I can't imagine a happier celebration,' she said, and turning to Ursula, 'You know what it would have been like in Houghton. Speeches and formality and champagne flutes and petits fours.'

'Nice expensive presents too,' Ursula reminded her.

'Who needs presents when we've got each other?' She lifted Jake's hand and kissed it, sending a group of elderly women who were sitting watching them into titters of approving laughter.

After they had eaten, the choir went on singing: hymns, Zulu and Sotho songs, Bach, English rounds, even the Beatles. African choirs don't just stand and sing, hands soulfully clasped. They sway from side to side, they clap their hands, they stamp their feet and dance, expressing with their bodies as well as their voices their delight in singing. Rose was enchanted with Jake's surprise.

He in turn was vastly amused by the leeto ceremony, which took place late in the afternoon when the shadow of the sandstone cliff lay across the school yard. They were made to stand together while they were instructed in the roles they would be expected to play in marriage. A woman she had met at Cordelia's earlier that morning danced up to Rose with a pumpkin and a broom to symbolise cooking and keeping house, while a man leapt about in front of Jake making stabbing gestures with an assegai, 'To give you the virtue of courage,' Cordelia explained.

'You'll need it, marrying Rose,' Ursula said. 'Did she tell you that her father eats bridegrooms for breakfast?'

'Don't worry, I'm tough meat.' Jake sounded more confident than he was, and for good reason. It would take several visits to the Natal farm (driving there separately and sleeping in separate bedrooms in case of police raids) before he and Gordon began to feel comfortable with each other, a feat only achieved after they had gone on a long bumpy drive in the farm truck looking for a stray cow. Jake discovered in Gordon a sharp sense of the absurd and a surprising facility with words that he had not expected from a man who had spent more than half his life in the dull grey business world. Gordon discovered, to his astonishment, that by the third visit he had forgotten Jake was coloured. When his first book of poetry was published, Gordon proudly bought twenty copies and lined them up in the bookshelf to give to anyone who showed the slightest interest in his son-in-law's achievements. There were few takers. The neighbouring farmers and their wives stopped visiting when they learned that Gordon and Sarah had had a coloured man staying in their house, which was considered to verge on the dangerously liberal even if he was a poet who had been favourably mentioned

412

in the Sunday papers. The fact that he was Rose's husband was not generally known.

'Talking of meat,' Cordelia was saying, 'it's a pity your mother couldn't be here either, Jake. The correct thing for Rose to do now would be to give her a present of meat from the ox; if she accepts it, it means she accepts Rose into the family.'

'I already have been,' Rose said. She had gone to see Jake's family in Bosmont several times. It had not been easy without him there. His sisters had treated her with reserve, and his mother with an almost paralysing shyness. His nieces and nephews had whispered and peeped round the doors, ducking away when she turned to smile at them. She had felt awkward, remembering Jake's long-ago remark about white girls slumming, but she had persisted. On the last visit before the wedding, Miriam, ill in bed with pleurisy, had whispered, 'I know you'll be good to my Jacob. I'm happy for you, Rose,' and she knew she had been accepted.

Bosmont had seemed like the other side of the moon from Houghton. Jake's home had been identical to all the others on the street: peach trees in the yard, brick walls laid in a hurry, corrugated asbestos roofs, steel windows that soon began to rust, leaving beard-shaped stains down the walls. The furniture had been cheap veneer, programmed to self-destruct after a few years of hard use so its owners could be kept in perpetual hire purchase bondage.

But what had shaken her most was the difference between Miriam and Auntie April. April had been confident, worldly, a woman who walked with her tinted blonde head up, ready to tackle anything. Miriam had been timid and worn down by hardship and anxiety, ill at ease with anyone except her own family. They both came from the same background, yet one had been educated in whiteness where all doors are open, and one in brownness where doors are open a grudging chink or permanently locked. If we have children, Rose vowed, we will not live where doors can slam in their faces.

'There is another custom we should maybe observe,' Cordelia was saying, light-headed by now with beer and laughing and the enjoyment of playing mother to the bride. 'In the olden days, the gall bladder of the ox would be taken out and the gall poured over Jake's hands. Then the bladder would be tied round his right wrist, symbolising the ring which binds the couple together.'

413

'Yuk,' Ursula said.

'On second thoughts, maybe we'll spare you. But that's nothing compared with after a funeral. The stomach of the bull or cow, whichever, is taken out and the unchewed cud – '

'Double yuk!' Ursula shivered.

But Jake and Rose weren't listening. They were looking at each other with eyes that said. Let's go now. Let's go home.

And as the red winter sun was setting, they did, accompanied by the choir and the guests, who danced and sang them up the path to the small whitewashed cottage whose windowpanes gleamed gold in the last of the light.

The sun is close to setting when Ndlondlo's oration comes to an end, the last prayer is said and the two coffins are slid deeper into their niches. Large stones brought from the foot of the cliff that morning by the young men are handed down to seal the openings, and the interstices are plugged with grass sods. The two men are helped out of the grave.

Tshabalala comes to Gordon and says, 'It is time to say the final goodbye now. I ask you to give a sign, as head of the family.'

Gordon nods. 'Is that all right?'

'Yes.' Tshabalala turns to the other mourners and says something in Sesotho. Everyone bends down and picks up a small stone or pebble. He says to Gordon, Sarah and Miriam, 'We each spit on a stone and drop it into the grave, saying something like, "Sleep peacefully" or "Go in peace". It is the same principle as the luck-heaps of small stones called vivane that you find hereabouts where mountain paths cross territorial borders. They are built up over the years by travellers asking the ancestral spirits for protection. We feel our ancestors to be very close during a funeral. Would you like to be the first?'

Miriam shakes her head, but reaches out to take the child so Sarah can do what is necessary.

Gordon picks up a stone, spits on it and says as he lets it fall, 'Rest in peace, my darling. And Jake.'

As Sarah's stone falls, she is able to whisper only, 'Goodbye, both of you,' before turning to Miriam and Hope and clinging to them. The sight of the empty red hole is too much. They are really gone now, is the thought howling in her head. Unobtrusively, Tshabalala motions to several of his men to surround

414

the two women so the cameramen with their prowling zoom lenses are unable to pry into their grief. He sends others to spread the message that as soon as the funeral is over, the press will be required to leave.

One by one the mourners approach the edge of the grave, spit on their stones and pebbles and throw them down, murmuring, 'U re roballe boroko,' and 'Tsamaea ka khotso.' The children are fascinated by the falling stones and stand watching at the edge of the grave until they are pulled away by their parents. Several of the young men in khaki and many of the villagers are crying. Pinky Bhengu does not cry. After she has thrown her stone down, she lifts her head swathed in its silk turban and glares at the sky as if to say, 'Just try this again, if you dare.'

Ndlondlo stands to one side with Aubrey Stimson, his arms folded across his chest. He has the look of a man who has accomplished something worthwhile; it was a good speech, and he knows it. ANC offices around the world will be taping it off this evening's TV news reports, and tomorrow there will be another spate of critical editorials about the horrors of apartheid in South Africa.

Didymus turns away from the inching queue of people and the thud of stones to see how much further the sun has to go before it sets, when the funeral must be completed. It is perhaps fifteen minutes above the horizon, a great reddish-orange ball sinking into a bank of grey thunderheads, its warmth fading by the second. As he watches, the cloud edges begin to glow like a halo and several thick rays of sunlight radiate up into the deepening blue of the sky. Is this the sign? he thinks, and then, Do I really need a sign? Is my faith so weak that it needs omens and portents to prop it up? He closes his eyes and tries to pray, but all he can think is, You shouldn't have let this happen. You know they didn't deserve it. They were too young, too vital, too necessary to dispense with. The repercussions –

To his surprise, Didymus realises that he is arguing with a friend who is as palpably there as the people casting their stones into the grave, as the bereaved mothers sobbing together and the child's dark curly head between them. He feels a great wash of relief and opens his eyes on the sunset again, thinking, I don't understand, Lord, but I'll try.

Didymus will become the youngest bishop in South Africa, and the first to be jailed for civil disobedience. His white rabbit hair and Adam's apple will inspire a generation of cartoonists, and he will win a posthumous literary prize for Jake by editing a second book of his poetry, dedicated to 'Hope – our future'.

The last stone is cast down. Gordon and Tshabalala and several village men pick up spades to fill in the grave, but after a few minutes one of the young men in khaki comes to him and says, 'Please let me help, sir. Jake was my teacher.'

'Was he a good one?' Gordon stands upright slowly, easing the stiffness in his back. 'And don't call me sir. My name's Gordon.'

The young man ducks his head in acknowledgement of the courtesy, but is too shy to use his name. 'He was a good teacher, yes. So was Rose. They said things you could hear with your heart. You understand what I mean?'

'I understand. But you,' Gordon looks at him with the unnerving white man's eyes that you can see so deep into, 'if you can hear things with your heart, what are you doing learning the arts of death?'

'Because I have no choice,' the young man says, taking the spade from him and driving it into the soft soil with a vigour that makes the muscles under his shirt bunch into knots. 'Because I have no choice at all.'

The sun dips below the horizon as the last few shovelfuls of earth are thrown on to the mound where Jake and Rose lie. In the morning, Tshabalala will come with the parents and the village elders to pay their last respects according to custom. At sunrise each person will take a small handful of the unchewed cud from the stomach of one of the bulls slaughtered for the funeral feast, will sing the praises of the dead, spit on it and throw it on to the mound. 'It is to make the grave firm,' Cordelia explains to Gordon and Sarah now. 'In the meantime, you will sleep at my house, of course.'

'Oh, we couldn't – ' Sarah begins.

'Please. I would be honoured, even though the room I can offer you is very small,' Cordelia says. 'Rose stayed with me the night before her wedding, with her friend Ursula. She almost – in many ways, she took the place of my daughter who died. You would comfort me by staying, as I hope I could comfort you.'

Sarah thought, Such kindness. Such pain we share. She said, 'Thank you. But there's Miriam too.'

'She and Hope will be staying with Sister Quthing so they can have a little time together. It is already arranged.' Cordelia takes Sarah's hand. 'Come, we will sing with the choir now.'

The choir leader hums the first phrase of the beautiful anthem, *Nkosi Sikelel' iAfrika*, God Bless Africa. Silence falls with the gathering darkness over the people standing round the grave. High above in a sky that is rapidly deepening to indigo, the bird specks are spiralling up and away.

'Nkosi sikelel' iAfrika . . .'

He'd better hurry, Gordon thinks. We can't afford to go on bleeding our best young people like this.

'Maluphakamis'u phondo lwayo . . .'

Tshabalala, singing in a deep voice that seems to come from the core of his massive body, thinks, I wonder how much this white man will take away with him. Will he open his eyes now and see what is really happening in our land, or will he pull his pleasant, easy life around him like a blanket to shut out the cold? And the mother, this big woman with the pale angry eyes and the hands of a worker, will she go on hiding behind her paintings and her love for the child? I will hope for the best. We must have hope, or we will be lost, all of us.

'Sechaba sahesu, Sechaba sa Afrika . . .'

Soothed by the beautiful singing, Sarah lifts her head and looks across the raw mound of earth to a group of four women who stand close together, their blankets pulled round them and across their mouths, their faces already in darkness. It is easy to imagine that these are Lindiwe and Doris, Albertina and Agnes come to say goodbye to the little white girl they once looked after, ever kind, ever patient and gentle with her even when the contrast with the lives of their own children must have stuck in the throat like a fish bone. Thank you, Sarah says in her head, thank you all. And for what you did for me too. I would have accomplished so little without you. The thanks are honestly meant. Her next exhibition will explore the relationship between white women and their domestic workers, and the sell-out profits will go into a trust fund for the education of domestic workers' children. It is only a small repayment of what she owes, but she will make others.

The anthem comes to an end, dying with the day. Tshabalala makes a sign to one of the young men in khaki, who has been carrying a black leather case. He steps forward and opens it to expose a glitter of complicated brass, the famous saxophone that until this morning has lain silent for a decade.

Gordon says, 'You are doing them great honour, Mgwetshana Tshabalala.'

The cameras begin to whirr and click, zooming in on this unexpected visual bonus, their black irises widening to take advantage of the last light. Ndlondlo frowns; he has not been told about this unscheduled display, which will cut into the TV news time allocated to his speech. He has never understood why people make idols out of musicians, who have mere mechanical skills; his passion is only for politics now. He has dedicated his life and his talents singlemindedly to the destruction of the apartheid regime, and if he succeeds (*when* he succeeds, he corrects himself) he will make reparations his first priority. Reparations for three hundred years of oppression and deprivation. I will make smug white bastards like that pay until it hurts, he thinks, watching Gordon with hard black eyes.

Tshabalala raises the saxophone to his lips and begins to blow the first phrase of *Sweet Sibusise*, and the notes soar up into the deepening blue that is already blurring the edges of the mountains against the coming night. Bats swinging down from the cliff face after flying ants seem to loop and swoop with the music, atoms whirling round the still nucleus of mourning people.

Rose and Jake lie at peace, unaware of the terrible revenge for their brutal killing that is being planned at this moment by a young man in a rage of grief: the bombing of a white suburban shopping centre in which many will die, and many more be injured.

And thus the violent debate rages in Southern Africa. You hurt us, we hurt you back. An eye for an eye, a tooth for a tooth. Both extremes digging ever deeper into their trenches while the people in the middle have to live with shells whistling over their heads, in constant fear, and the arms dealers grow richer and richer.

Who will dare, who will have the courage, to raise the first white flag?

Epilogue

THE SONG OF THE PEACEFUL MAN

I am a peaceful man.

In the evening when cooking fires smudge the setting sun
And I come home tired from work,
I would like to sit in a cool place
My wife by my side
A cup of tea in my hand
And watch my children running on green grass.

But my children run dusty-legged
On broken glass
And my wife toils
Over someone else's stove;
My front door is inadequately barred
Against the violent street where I must live.

I am a peaceful man.
I do not believe in the raised fist
The swift cold sentence of the knife
The whispered threat
The barking voice of the gun.

Yet my wife's empty place in our bed
Mocks me in the restless night,
My children scorn my quiet words
— All I have to give them —
My friends laugh at my simplicity
And the man in the zoot suit calls me a coward,
A puppet dancing to the pull of alien strings.

When I hear these things
I feel a savage drumbeat in my blood;

I do not know how long I can remain
A peaceful man.

And because I value peace
Before I cease to value peace
I ask:

In our vast and beautiful land
Surely there is room for all our children
To run on green grass
To choose where they may live
To learn the ways of work and friendship,
That they may grow straight up to the sun
Unmaimed by hatred
Unmarred by fear
Unmildewed by creeping distrust of one another?

We need tall strong trees, timber to build a nation
Not brittle firewood
That briefly burns, and turns to ashes.

Jacob Van Vuuren

Glossary

Afrikaner: South African of Afrikaans descent.
ag: oh (similar to the German 'Ach').
ai!: a cry of anguish or disbelief.
aikona: never! (an emphatic negative).
allewêreld: an exclamation, usually of surprise.
amagundane: rats or mice.
Amandla . . . Ngawethu!: Power . . . is ours! (a liberation cry).
amatungulu: Carissa Grandiflora, an indigenous shrub with glossy green leaves and red fruit.
ANC: African National Congress.
asseblief: please.
assegai: spear.
atchar: hot pickle or relish.
Bantu: from the Zulu word 'abantu', meaning people; it is the former official designation by the SA government of black Africans, and much disliked.
berg wind: hot dry wind.
bioscope: cinema, movie theatre.
bleddy: corruption of 'bloody'.
Boer: an Afrikaans word meaning 'farmer', used offensively by blacks to denote an Afrikaner.
bra: brother.
braai: barbecue.
broeks: knickers, pants.
check you: see you again.
clapped: exhausted.
coolie: offensive word for an Indian person.
coolie Christmas: offensive term for a garish occasion or appearance.
coon: offensive word for a black person.
dagga: marijuana, cannabis.
dankie: thanks.
devil thorn: type of many-pointed sharp thorn.
dhobi: Indian laundryman.
dis die einde vir ons: it's the end for us.
dis vreeslik: it is frightful.

421

doek: head scarf tied round the head in various ways.

dominee: minister of the Dutch Reformed Church.

donga: dry eroded gully.

dopper: Member of the strictly Calvinist Gereformeerde Church in SA.

dorpie: small country town or village.

dreck: excrement, meaning bad or worthless.

ek weet goed: I know very well.

finish and klaar: that's the end of that, or that's that.

fowl hok: fowl run.

fynbos: Mediterranean-type vegetation found in the Cape, equivalent of the French maquis.

gammat: Cape Malay person, or coloured.

gemors: a hash or mess-up.

Groot-oupa: great-grandfather.

hakea: alien plant formerly much used in hedges.

hawu!:   an exclamation of surprise or dismay.

highveld: the high grassy central plateau central plateau of Southern Africa.

indaba: a word that has come to mean concern or problem, as in, 'It's not my indaba'.

ja: yes.

jislaaik: an exclamation, usually of surprise.

John Vorster Square: police headquarters in Johannesburg.

jou: your.

jy weet?:   you know?

kaffir: offensive word for a black African.

kaffirboetie: offensive term for white person thought to be too friendly with blacks, equivalent of US niggerlover.

kak: excrement, equivalent of shit.

kappie: a starched cotton sunbonnet worn by pioneer women in SA (and America).

kaya: an African hut or house.

khaki weeds: alien weeds said to have been introduced during the Boer War by the forage imported for the British troops' horses.

klim af: climb down.

klonkie: a young 'coloured' boy.

kloof: a deep craggy-sided ravine or gorge.

koeksister: a plaited doughnut, dipped in syrup after frying.

koppie: a small rocky hillock, feature of the veld.

kraal: an enclosure for farm animals, or a cluster of huts.

krantz: cliff-face or crag.

krissy: crinkled; when applied to hair, insinuates that the person is of coloured descent.

kwaai: bad-tempered.

kwela: pennywhistle music; also a dance to the music.

lanie: white person; also posh.

legevaan: monitor lizard, usually the water monitor (also spelt 'likkewaan' or 'leguaan').

lekker: a term of general approval: nice, good, tasty, etc.

liewe God: dear God.

lobola: bride price, usually paid in cattle.

long-drop: pit latrine.

maak gou, skepsel: hurry up, creature (an offensive term when used of an African).

maak julle oop!: open up!

magtig: exclamation of surprise.

Malutis: mountain range that covers most of Lesotho.

man: used in South African English for emphasis at the end of a sentence, even when the person being spoken to is a woman.

mandrax: an addictive drug much used in South Africa (originally a trade name).

mealie meal: maize or corn meal.

meisietjie: little girl.

melktert: traditional Cape custard tart.

metsi: water.

middelmannetjie: hump between the double wheel ruts of a bush or dirt road.

miesies: missus.

MK: abbreviation for Umkhonto we Sizwe, q.v.

moenie panic nie: a somewhat droll expression meaning 'don't worry', 'don't panic'.

mompara: idiot, fool.

monkeys' wedding: simultaneous rain and sunshine.

morena: Sotho title of respect for a man.

muti: medicine.

my basie: 'my little boss' (usually obsequious).

my kind: my child.

naartjie: mandarin orange; 'to feel a naartjie' is to feel awkward or embarrassed.

nè?: isn't that so?

nee wat!: emphatic no, as in 'Oh no!'

nkosazaan: respectful address to an unmarried woman of the upper class, once much used by nannies and domestic workers when addressing their employers' daughters.

Nkosi: mode of address to a male superior, similar to the English 'sir'; it means 'Chief' or 'Lord'.

nooit!: never!

ntate wa . . .: father of . . .

nyaniso: it's true, or I speak truly.

ons sal jou nooit vergeet: we'll never forget you.

ouma, oupa: grandmother, grandfather.

423

poes: pussy, meaning the female genitals.

poppie: mode of address to a young girl or woman.

phuthu: mealie meal cooked to a stiff of crumbly porridge.

Robben Island: island in Table Bay off Cape Town, used in recent times as a place of detention for political prisoners.

samp: stamped maize kernels.

sangoma: witchdoctor, usually a woman.

schlep: a drag or a bore or an effort; used as a verb, meaning to make a boring, wearying journey.

sersant: sergeant.

se voet!: equivalent of 'my foot!'

shame: exclamation of sympathy or warmth towards something endearing or moving.

shebeen: establishment where home-brewed or illicit liquor is sold.

sis, sies: an exclamation of disgust.

sjambok: a tapered whip, once made of hide but now usually of plastic.

snoek: edible fish common in Cape waters.

sorghum: millet used for porridge or sprouted for brewing beer.

Special Branch: police department for the investigation of political as opposed to criminal or civil matters.

spook-a-spooks: rascals.

stinkblaar: rank weed, literally 'stink-leaf'.

stoep: veranda, porch, stoop.

s'true's bob: as true as god.

suka!: go away!

surfie: surfboard.

tackies: rubber-soled canvas shoes, sneakers.

thakathi: bewitched.

thula wena!: be quiet, you!

tickey box: public call box, pay telephone.

tokolosh: an evil earth spirit.

township: area set aside for non-white occupation.

totsiens: goodbye.

tsotsi: black street thug.

Umkhonto we Sizwe: Spear of the Nation, the armed wing of the African National Congress.

Vaal Triangle: area which includes Johannesburg, Pretoria and Vereeniging.

velskoen: rough suede ankle boot; literally 'skin shoe'.

vetkoek: fatcakes made of deep-fried yeast dough.

voorkamer: the formal front room of a Cape Dutch house.

Vroue Federasie: Women's Federation, an Afrikaans women's organisation.

wat dink jy?: what do you think?